A *New York Times* bestseller many times over, **Eloisa James** lives in New York City, where she is a Shakespeare professor (with an M.Phil. from Oxford). She is also the mother of two children and, in a particularly delicious irony for a romance writer, is married to a genuine Italian knight.

Visit Eloisa James online:
www.eloisajames.com
www.facebook.com/EloisaJamesFans
www.twitter.com/EloisaJames

Praise for Eloisa James:

'Sexual tension, upper-class etiquette and a dollop of wit make this another hit from *New York Times* bestseller Eloisa James'
Image Magazine Ireland

'Romance writing does not get better than this'
People Magazine

'[This] delightful tale is as smart, sassy and sexy as any of her other novels, but here James displays her deliciously wicked sense of humour'
Romantic Times Book Club

'An enchanting fairy-tale plot provides the perfect setting for James' latest elegantly written romance, and readers will quickly find themselves falling under the spell of the book's deliciously original charact

ne

C333380646

Your Wicked Ways

Eloisa James

piatkus

PIATKUS

First published in the US in 2004 by Avon Books,
An imprint of HarperCollins Publishers, New York
First published in Great Britain in 2013 by Piatkus
by arrangement with Avon

A CIP catalogue record for this book
is available from the British Library.

ISBN 978-0-7499-5952-4

Typeset in Bembo by Hewer Text UK Ltd, Edinburgh
Printed and bound in Great Britain by Clays Ltd, St Ives plc

Papers used by Piatkus are from well-managed forests
and other responsible sources.

MIX
Paper from
responsible sources
FSC® C104740

Piatkus
An imprint of
Little, Brown Book Group
100 Victoria Embankment
London EC4Y 0DY

An Hachette UK Company
www.hachette.co.uk

www.piatkus.co.uk

Your Wicked Ways

Chapter One

In Strictest Confidence . . .

The Countess Pandross to Lady Patricia Hamilton

. . . my dearest, as to what you tell me of the exploits of Earl Godwin, I can only say that nothing will ever surprise me. The former Countess Godwin (who was, as you know, one of my very dearest friends) would turn in her grave if she knew that her son was entertaining opera singers in her house! And I shudder to think that one of these infamous women may actually be living with him. How his poor wife is able to hold her head high, I shall never know. Helene has always showed edifying composure, although I did hear a whisper—just a whisper—suggesting that she may request a divorce. I can't imagine how much that would cost, but Godwin must have at least fifteen thousand pounds a year and can probably afford it. At any rate, my dear, what I am truly longing to hear about are your plans for sweet Patricia's debut. Didn't you tell me that you were planning a ball for the weekend of the fifth? Mrs. Elizabeth Fremable tells me . . .

Helene Godwin, Countess Godwin, to her mother,
currently residing in Bath

Dear Mother,

    I am most sympathetic to your distress over the continuing debacle of my marriage. I fully recognize that my decision to elope with Rees brought scandal into the family, but I would remind you that the elopement was years ago. I am equally aware that a divorce would be far more grievous. But I beg of you, please accept my decision. I simply cannot continue in this fashion. I am heartsick when I think of my life.

Your loving daughter,
Helene, Countess Godwin

22 April 1816

Rees Holland, Earl Godwin, to his brother, a vicar in the
North Country

Dear Tom,

    Things are all right here. Yes, I know that you are fretting over my infamous reputation, but you will simply have to overlook my slurs on the family name. I assure you that my sins are even more plenteous than your pious correspondents have told you. Women dance on top of the table in the dining room daily.

Yours with all proper sentiment,
Rees

Miss Patricia Hamilton to Miss Prunella
Forbes-Shacklett

Dear Prunes,

It is too bad of your mama to bury you in the country!
When is she planning to bring you to town? I assure you that
it is already very crowded here, and if one does not make an
appointment, it is impossible to find a mantua maker who will
even discuss a court gown. But Prunes, I met the most absolutely fascinating man yesterday. He is apparently quite,
quite notorious—a veritable rake! I am not going to put his
name here, in case my abominable little brother obtains this
letter before I mail it, but he is an earl and his initials are
RH. You can look him up in Debrett's. Apparently he threw
his wife out of the house some years ago, and now lives with an
opera singer! My mother (as you can imagine) was in a flurry
of anxiety and told me later not to even think of dancing with
him, as there is talk of a divorce. Imagine: me dancing with a
divorced man! Naturally I shall do it if the opportunity ever
presents itself . . .

Rees Holland, Earl Godwin, to Helene Holland,
Countess Godwin

Helene,

If you'd like to see me, you'll have to come to the house, as
I'm trying to finish a score that's needed in rehearsal directly.
To what do I owe this charming, if unexpected, pleasure? I
trust you are not going to request a divorce again, as my
answer will be the same as the last. I'll tell Sims to wait for
a reply as I think it doubtful that you will find the backbone
to enter this den of iniquity.

Rees (should I say, Your Darling Husband?)

23 May 1816

Mr. Ned Suffle, Manager of the Royal Italian Opera
House, to Rees Holland, Earl Godwin

Without putting undue pressure on you, my lord, I must have
the score of The Quaker Girl by the end of this month latest.

23 May 1816

Helene Holland, Countess Godwin to Rees Holland,
Earl Godwin

I shall visit you this afternoon at two of the clock. I trust
you will be alone.

Chapter Two

The Key to Marital Harmony

Number 15, Rothsfeld Square
London

The Godwin carriage pulled up before her former residence, but the countess did not emerge. The footman was holding open the carriage door, and the steps were down. But Helene was unable to force her limbs to move her forward, along the walk, into the house. She hadn't even looked at the house in years. She'd gotten in the habit of glancing the other direction should she visit a friend in Rothsfeld Square. It was easy enough to let her eyes drift away, or examine the lining of the carriage as if she'd never seen it before. Because if she did peer at the house, *her* house, what if she glimpsed what her former neighbors saw daily?

What if she saw the woman who by all accounts was living in Helene's own bed chamber, sleeping in Helene's bed, in the room next to Helene's own husband? A bitter taste of metal rose into her mouth. What then, indeed? She could only hope that Rees had abided by her request; it would be just like him to include his doxy in the conversation she had requested this morning.

Her footman was standing perfectly still. She could see him out of the corner of her eye, as curious as the rest of the servants about her unexpected excursion to this side of town.

They knew she and her husband never met. Servants always knew everything. She rose, descended the steps, and walked up the path to the house. She held her head high, as always. It is not my fault that my husband is a reprobate, she told herself. It is not my fault. I will *not* accept the shame. Helene had spent a great deal of her time in the past few years refusing to accept shame. She was tired of that particular mental exercise.

The great house looked just the same, from the outside at least. One might have expected literal signs of the moral dissipation within: shutters askew or missing railings. But other than the need for a good polish on the brass, her house looked just as she had left it ten years ago. It towered above them, the highest in the square, home of the Godwins before Rees's father was born, before his grand-father became an earl, since the days when King James reportedly stopped by for a cup of the new extravagant beverage, tea, by which Rees's great grandfather had made his fortune. Even then, the Godwins were no merchants; that early Lord Godwin was an extravagant madcap courtier, who threw his entire inheritance into shares in the East India Company. His stroke of genius had turned a minor Stuart lord into the forefather of one of the most powerful families in England. Successive Godwins had augmented their fortune by shrewd marriages, and their reputations by political acumen . . . until the birth of Rees Holland.

Far from showing a flare for political life, Rees had occupied himself since reaching majority by attempting to shock polite society, and by writing comic operas of dubious artistic value. In both endeavors, he succeeded with flamboyant success. The very thought of it steeled Helene's back. It was no more her fault that Rees was the way he was, than it was his mother's for giving birth to him. A carriage clattered by and still no one had answered the door. Her footman banged the knocker again. She could hear it echoing away in the vast reserves of the house, but a butler did not appear. "Try the door, Bindle," she ordered.

Bindle pushed on the door and, of course, it opened. Helene marched up the steps and into the hallway and then turned: "Take the carriage around the Park, and return for me in one hour, if you please." The last thing she wanted was her carriage to be recognized.

So she entered the house alone. It was utterly silent. Rees must have forgotten their appointment. Not a servant was to be seen. Helene had to admit to a spark of satisfaction at that. A month or so after she left the house, most of the staff had decamped, informing all London of their displeasure at being witness to a troupe of Russian dancers practicing their art on the dining room table. Naked, or so they said. At the time Helene had been glad both to be vindicated in the eyes of her peers, and at the thought that Rees might be uncomfortable without adequate staff.

But naturally he wasn't. She wandered into the sitting room and it was abundantly clear that Rees was anything other than uncomfortable. True, there was some dust about. But the ornate and vastly uncomfortable sofa given them on their wedding by Helene's Aunt Margaret had disappeared altogether, likely banished to the attics. Instead the room was home to three pianos—three! Where a Hepplewhite secretary used to stand, there was a harpsichord. A grand piano blocked any view of the street. And a pianoforte stood at an awkward relation to the door, clearly plunked down wherever the movers happened to put it. Surrounding the feet of all three pianos were piles of paper: half-written scores, scribbled notes, crumpled drafts.

Helene's mouth twisted. Rees wrote music anywhere, and on anything. One couldn't discard a single sheet of paper due to his overwhelming fear that a brilliant phrase or a snatch of melody might have been scratched down and forgotten. From the looks of things, not a single sheet of foolscap had left the house since she did, and many reams had entered the door.

She sighed and glanced in the mirror over the mantelpiece. It was rather dusty and cracked in one corner but it showed her precisely what she wanted to know: all the trouble she had taken dressing was worth it. Her walking costume was made of a pale primrose fabric that made her hair look even lighter, almost white blond. Rees loved her hair. She remembered that. Her lips tightened. She remembered that, and a great deal more.

Helene walked briskly over to the nearest piano. She might as well see what frivolities Rees was concocting while she waited for her carriage to return. Unlike everything else in the room, the piano at least appeared to have been dusted. But Helene grabbed a handful of the haphazard compositions that were floating around her feet and used it to dust the stool, just in case. Then she threw the sheets back down on the ground, where they floated into a drift of foolscap. The layer of paper looked like a snowbank; her sheets floated down like fresh flakes atop an older accumulation.

The music on the piano was rather more than scrawled notes. It looked as if Rees's partner, Fen, had given him the text of an aria, a young girl's song about spring amidst the cherry blossoms. Helene snorted. Richard Fenbridgeton wrote all the librettos for Rees's operas, and he tended toward flowery exuberance. How Rees could spend his time with this twaddle, she didn't know.

Without removing her gloves Helene picked out the melody with her right hand. The melody was rather enchanting, tripping up and down until—*plunk*.

That had to be a mistake. It was utterly clear that he needed an ascending scale to an E-flat. He was making the girl sound like a dowager. She tried it again. Hum-di-de-lala-*plunk*. Luckily Rees had ink wells positioned all over the top of the piano, so she stood up, pulled off her gloves, stuck the score atop the piano, and began rewriting. After a while, she started singing as she rewrote, taking huge pleasure in jotting sarcastic comments in the margins. The idiot kept pushing the poor girl into the lower register when she *had* to stay high or the whole pleasure of springtime would be lost.

Rees Holland was as appreciative as the next man of a curved female derrier, particularly when the possessor was clearly trying out his aria, just as he'd requested. It was hard enough to coerce Lina into singing for him; it was a true pleasure to find her engaged in the exercise on her own. He crossed the room in a few strides and clapped an appreciative hand onto Lina's sweet little bottom. "For this I'll buy you—"

But his promise turned into a strangled exclamation. The woman who jumped and spun away from his hand was no Lina.

"God above, I forgot you were coming!" Now she was facing him, Rees could hardly believe he'd made such a mistake. Lina was a plump little partridge, and his wife was a gaunt stick of a woman, with cheekbones that could cut you, if her eyes didn't first. They were narrowed at him in that way he detested.

"Helene," he said resignedly.

"I gather that charming greeting was meant for someone else?" If her eyebrow went any higher, it would dance right off her face.

"I apologize." As always, he felt a mantle of awkward, heavy resentment settle about him. Helene had a way of looking at him that made him feel like a great hog. A huge wallowing beast of some sort.

He turned away and sat down, ignoring the fact that she was still standing. To his mind, after a woman has poured the contents of a chamberpot over your head, one needn't stand on occasion anymore. Not that the chamberpot-throwing happened recently, but it wasn't the sort of thing one forgot.

She raised her chin in that way she had and sat down opposite him, as dainty and precise as a bloody little sparrow. He eyed her for no good reason other than because he knew it made her nervous.

"Lost more weight?" he finally said when the silence grew oppressive. He liked a ripe armful of flesh, and she knew it. Her lack of curves always used to be good for an outburst. But she ignored him, just twisted those thin hands of hers in her lap.

"I've come to ask you for a divorce, Rees."

He settled back into the corner of his settee. "Didn't my letter say not to bother? I haven't changed my mind on the matter."

When she didn't answer immediately, he added a sardonic comment that surely would drive her into a fury. "I find your request all the more surprising, since it appears that your future bridegroom has already changed *his* mind. The last time you asked me—April a year ago, wasn't it?—you wished to marry Fairfax-Lacy. But from what I've heard, he's up and married another, as the old ballad goes. So who are you wishing to marry now, Helene?"

"That is irrelevant to my desire to divorce you," she said, her voice disappointingly steady.

"I disagree. As I told you at the time, if you find a man brave enough to stand at your side during the proceedings, brave enough to allow himself to be sued as your consort, I will go through with it. For your sake. But if you haven't found such a man . . ." He paused. Her jaw was set in a manner he still dreamed about sometimes.

"Why not? Why can't you simply divorce me without knowing who I would marry?"

"Divorce would cost us thousands of pounds," he said, folding his arms over his chest. "I may look like a lackluster estate manager, Helene, but I'm not. Why in God's name would I put that drain on the estate when there's no point to it? Besides, remarrying would take an Act of Parliament. Fairfax-Lacy might have been able to obtain it, but there's few others with the same power. If you want to take a lover, take one. God knows, it will do you good."

He watched with satisfaction as color crept into his wife's porcelain cheeks. Damned if he knew why one of his primary pleasures in life was to get Helene to show some signs of life.

"I don't wish to take a lover," she said. "I merely want to rid myself of you, Rees."

"By means other than murder, I suppose you mean?"

"I'm willing to consider all options," she said coolly.

Rees laughed, more like a bark than a laugh. "You'll have to take a lover. *You* cannot petition on the grounds of adultery, only I can. Has someone already replaced Fairfax-Lacy, then?"

Her cheeks flared and she swallowed. "I could hire a man to stand as my consort," she said in a low voice.

"I see no reason for wasting substance on lawyers and bribes and the rest of it."

"I can pay that sum out of my dowry. And I'm quite certain that my mother would contribute a substantial amount as well."

"I don't give a hang whose money it is. There's no point to it, Helene! We married, and married we stay. I don't think it's such an uncomfortable life. After all, it's not as if I'm a dog in the manger, am I? Surely you can find someone in London to warm your toes!"

Helene barely heard him, barely listened as insult after calculated insult broke over her head. She just stared at him instead. Every time they were apart for a length of time, she managed to school herself into remembering only her husband's disgusting habits and his slovenly dress. But then, when she saw him again, she couldn't help noticing the way his eyelashes cast shadows on his cheeks, and the fact that his lower lip was so full. The better to sneer at her, obviously. But then he had dimples in both cheeks and they offset how deep-set his eyes were. Oh, Rees wasn't beautiful. He had a broad nose, after all, and a shambling way of walking, and he was far too big for beauty. Simon Darby, now there was a beautiful man. Simon and Rees together were like Beauty and the Beast, except that God help her, she couldn't help but think the Beast was—was—

"Damn it all, Helene, I'm doing my best to drive you into a frenzy and you're not even listening," Rees said now, with obvious frustration. "I must be losing my touch."

"I don't care if you don't want to spend the money," she snapped, looking away from his face with a tinge of self-disgust. "I ceased to take your wishes into account quite a few years ago."

"There's my Helene," Rees said, leaning back again. "It throws me into a fidget if you don't snap back with a rejoinder. It's as if the sun didn't rise."

"Don't you see how much better it would be for both of us if we divorced and didn't have to snap at each other anymore?" she said. "We're at our worst around each other.

12

I know I am. I turn into a veritable shrew and you—you—"

"My wife a shrew?" he said mockingly. "Never say so!"

Helene swallowed. Somehow she had to break through the barrage of mocking remarks he always threw at her. He had to listen. "We would both be better off if we were no longer married to each other."

"Can't see that it would make any difference. I'm quite comfortable as I am. I rather like having a wife around."

"You can hardly say that I'm *around*!"

"Your presence, ephemeral or otherwise, keeps the fortune-hunters away," he pointed out. "Were we to divorce, I'd have carriages breaking down before my railings every other day, with debutantes waltzing in here to play me their scales."

"But Rees," Helene said desperately, "I wish to marry someone else."

"Who?"

She was silent.

"Are you telling me," Rees demanded, "that you don't care who you marry, as long as you rid yourself of me?"

She nodded, a trifle jerkily. "Precisely."

He opened his mouth and shut it. "I can't imagine why we're having this conversation," he said finally. "I refuse to grant you a divorce." Rees stared at his wife in frustration. In general, he had no trouble understanding women. For the most part, he found them bland, foolish, and greedy in a petty sort of way for things like bonnet strings and silk stockings. But he had never made the mistake of underestimating his wife's intelligence.

"I should have left that house party the very moment I met you, back in '07," he said suddenly. "Young fool that I was."

"I wish you had," Helene said.

"But I didn't." Rees's voice had a harsh edge that surprised himself. "I still remember walking into the drawing room and seeing you playing the piano—"

She shook her head. "It was a harpsichord."

"Anyway, there you were, wearing a yellow sort of gown and playing Purcell's *Fairest Isle*."

"I had no idea you were so sentimental, Rees," she said with perfect indifference.

"I would hardly call it sentimental. I try to keep the image in mind because it encapsules the most crack-brained impulse of my life: asking you to elope with me."

He couldn't tell whether he was annoying her or not. Lord, but she had gained control since they were married! In those days, the merest comment would drive her to burst into tears and throw something at his head. He eyed her rigid, dried up posture and wondered if he didn't prefer the old Helene.

"It was hardly an impulse, Rees, given as we had known each other for some months by the time you asked me to marry you. But believe me, if I could take back my acceptance of your drivellingly insulting request, I would. It has ruined my life."

There was a heartfelt truth to her statement that silenced the witticism Rees was contemplating. He looked harder at his wife. She had dark shadows under her eyes and her hair was pulled up as tightly as it could be in those infernal braids she fancied.

"Is something the matter, Helene?" he asked. "I mean, something more than the usual?"

"You are." She raised her eyes, and the despair in them struck him in the chest. "You are, Rees."

"But why?" he asked, in honest bewilderment. "I'm far less scandalous than I was a few years ago, when I . . ." he paused and decided to skip over the Russian dancers, "when I was younger. I have never interfered with your doings. What could possibly be so awful about being married to me? I think it's a position that many women must envy. If you're lucky, I'll fall dead to the ground like Esme Rawlings's first husband, and you can become a rich widow."

That was a fairly lame joke, but surely it deserved a twitch of a smile.

"Honest to God, Helene, I simply don't see what's so objectionable about my being your husband. If I were requiring you to fulfill your wifely duties, I could understand." He stopped and the sentence hung on the air. He wished he hadn't brought up that old painful subject.

"I want a child," she said quietly. "I—I feel quite strongly about it."

"Still?" he said, without thinking. Helene was perched on the very edge of the couch, her delicate fingers clenched in her lap. There wasn't much that he liked about his wife's body, not really, but he always loved her hands. More fool he, he thought, remembering that he had been stupid enough to think that she would caress him with the same tenderness with which she caressed the piano keys.

A slight frown creased her forehead. "Yes, still. As I told you last spring. Why wouldn't I still wish for a child?"

When Rees was surprised, he generally spoke what he was thinking and regretted it later. "Because you're not exactly . . ." he eyed her.

"What?"

"Well, motherly," he said, feeling, belatedly, a distinct sensation of danger.

"Do explain precisely what you mean, Rees." She seemed to be speaking from between clenched teeth.

15

Rees resisted an impulse to check for breakable objects in her vicinity. He waved vaguely in the air. "Motherly . . . ah, fertile, fecund, you know what I mean!"

"Fertile?" He could hear her teeth grinding. "You venture to say to me that you think I am lacking in *fertility*? You have assessed my abilities, as if I were a sow you thought to buy at market?"

"Wrong word," he said, floundering deeper. "I only meant—"

"Yes?"

But Rees had woken to his own foolishness. "Why in God's name would you want a child, Helene?" Then he narrowed his eyes. "What am I thinking? Naturally you want a child because all your friends have children, don't they?"

"That has nothing to do with it."

"Esme Bonnington dropped that brat last spring," he said with deliberate crudeness, "Carola Pinkerton has a daughter, and there's Darby with a son. That pretty much covers your intimate circle, doesn't it? Oh, wait . . . I forgot the Duchess of Girton. She too has produced an heir, has she not?"

There was no color whatsoever in Helene's face now. He almost felt a gleam of pity.

"Gina's son was born last December. But I assure you, Rees, that my desire for children has little, if anything, to do with the good fortune of my friends."

Rees made a rude sound and stood up, wandering toward the piano. "That's garbage, Helene. Women are all the same. You want what everyone else has, and you'll go to any means to get it. Well, don't count on me. I refuse to petition for divorce. I see no reason to put myself through an experience so expensive and ruinous to my reputation"— he threw it over his shoulder—"aren't you pleased, Helene? I am finally gaining an aversion to scandal."

Just then something caught his eye. "What the hell!" He bent over the sheets of paper on top of the piano. His vicious little wife had clearly enjoyed herself by destroying his score. "What in the hell did you do here? That line must dip. You've turned it to a bloody orange seller's tune!" He spun around but the room was empty.

Chapter Three

In Which Tempers Are Lost

Number Forty, Berkeley Square
London

After women have been friends for ten years, or even one year, they can generally judge each other's state of mind from five yards. Esme Bonnington, sometimes known as Countess Bonnington and sometimes as Infamous Esme, counted herself a near scientist when it came to the nice art of reading emotion. When her friend Helene's braids were elegantly nestled on her head, without even a stray strand of hair to be seen, all was well. But today Lady Godwin's backbone was as rigid as if it had been welded in place, her eyes were narrowed to chips of ice, and—most telling of all—wisps of hair were framing her face.

"What on earth is the matter?" Esme asked, trying to remember whether she, Esme, had done anything to outrage Helene's sense of propriety. No. Since her second marriage, Esme quite prided herself on being about as scandalous as a cow. That meant Helene had encountered her husband.

With one chilly glance, Helene sent Esme's butler, Slope, from the room. "I was going to ask Slope to bring us some tea," Esme said with some disappointment.

"You can live without a lemon tart for at least another hour or so," Helene snapped.

Helene lived on the air, from the look of her. But Esme was used to solid nourishment, and having asked Helene for tea, she would like to partake. She rang the bell to summon Slope. "I would guess that you have asked Rees for a divorce again?"

"He won't even listen to me, Esme." Despair and anger battled in her voice. "He doesn't care a bean that I want a child."

"Oh, Helene," Esme said. "I'm so—"

"He laughed it off as a matter of competition," Helene interrupted. "He won't even try to understand what it feels like to watch other women have children and know that you are unable." Her voice caught on the last word.

"Men are insensitive brutes," Esme said sympathetically. "And your husband is among the worst of the species."

"Anyone's husband is better than mine! Do you remember when I told you after Miles died that I envied you your rapprochement, even if it was brief?"

"Of course."

"I meant it. I would give anything to have married someone like your first husband."

"Miles and I were far from an enviable couple," Esme pointed out. "When he died, we hadn't lived together in ten years. How can you envy a marriage like ours?"

"I don't envy your marriage. I envy your *husband*. When you told Miles that you wished to have a child, what did he do?"

Esme's eyes filled with understanding. "He agreed."

"And if you had asked him for a divorce?"

"He would have agreed to that as well," Esme said, swallowing a lump in her throat. "Miles was a truly amiable person."

"He was better than amiable," Helene said fiercely. "He was a kind person. He would have done anything for you, Esme, you know he would have."

19

"You wouldn't have liked being married to Miles, Helene. He was so placid, truly."

"*I* am placid!" The only argument one might have with that statement came from Helene's voice, a near shriek. "I would have—would have—oh, this is absurd! I don't want to argue over who has the worst husband. It's just that I want a child so much. I have for *years*! And now Carola has a perfect little daughter, and you only had to ask Miles in order to have a baby, and now Henrietta Darby, who didn't even think it possible to carry a child, has a son—" her words were lost in a torrent of sobs.

Esme stroked her arm. "I'm sorry, Helene. I'm so sorry."

"It's just not fair!" It burst from her like rain from a drain-pipe. "I don't ever complain about my husband; you know I don't, Esme. But why did I ever, ever have to meet Rees Holland and marry him! Why didn't my mother stop me? Why didn't someone come after me when we eloped? Why did I have to end up married to an utter degenerate when the rest of you—you and Carola and Gina—all of you have taken your husbands back and they have been utterly decent about it?"

"Actually, my first husband is dead," Esme felt it necessary to add.

"That's irrelevant! Sebastian will probably give you five more children if you wish."

Esme had never seen her friend Helene show a stronger emotion than annoyance and once, when Esme had behaved appallingly, a sharp disgust. Helene's every motion and thought was effected with a maximum of grace and control. But now the intricate braids that graced the top of her head were tilting slightly to the side. Her pale blue eyes were blazing and her normally pale complexion was pink with rage and grief.

20

Still, Esme thought she ought to point out that her first husband Miles's death was hardly *irrelevant*. "That seems a bit harsh," she said cautiously. "After all, Miles would far rather be alive than—"

Helene cast her a look that stopped that proper sentiment in its tracks. "Save it for the Sewing Circle," she snapped. "Miles's death means that you didn't have to live with the man."

The reference to the Sewing Circle stung; Esme had had a brief-lived foray into respectable widowhood before making a scandalous second marriage, whereupon the righteous woman leading the Circle repudiated Esme's skills with the needle. "Miles and I may not have suited each other, but it isn't as if I disliked marriage itself. After all, I did marry Sebastian, and I live with him, very happily too."

"Cut bait," Helene said impatiently. "Can't we speak the truth in private? Men are a dreadful aberration of humanity: selfish, disgusting and forever rooting about looking for their own pleasures. Carola may well be besotted with Tuppy's dubious skills at fishing or whatever skills he claims to have, but will it last? There'll come a day when she'll realize that he's just like all the rest."

"Why, Helene, I had no idea that you felt this way!" Esme cried. "What on earth did you like about Miles, if you find all men to be selfish beasts?"

"Miles would have given you anything you asked for. He honored the vows of marriage. You wanted a child; he gave you one. You wanted him to leave the house; he did so. And he never bothered you again, did he?"

"No," Esme said, "yet—"

But Helene had risen and was pacing back and forth. "Rees and Miles are like night and day! Rees threw me out of our house years ago; he hasn't said a civil word to me since;

and all of London knows the depths of depravity to which *he* has sunk!"

Esme had to admit the truth of that. "Miles did have a mistress," she put in.

"A quiet, respectable liaison," Helene said. "No hysterics on either side. Lady Childe is an indubitably respectable woman, and while I can hardly sanction such a liaison outside marriage, it's infinitely better than taking a woman of the streets and putting her into your wife's bedchamber. If one more person tells me how much they sympathize with me due to my husband's proclivities, I shall—I shall scream!"

Somewhat to Esme's relief, Slope appeared with a tea tray. He didn't seem to notice Helene's disheveled appearance, but then he was highly paid to overlook any sort of irregularity. Esme had hired him in the days when she was the toast of all London and doing her best to live up to a reputation as Infamous Esme.

"We'll think of something," she said consolingly, as she poured tea. "For one thing, Rees is far more likely to agree to divorce if you actually had a lover, Helene. How can he possibly sue you for adultery? You have one of the most irreproachable reputations in London. We have to change that before divorce is possible."

"It won't work," Helene said dully. "I know that you like creating these little scenarios, Esme. But I could hardly trick a man into my bed. The only person who has shown interest in years was Fairfax-Lacy. That came to nothing, and now he's married and probably Bea is in a delicate condition already!" She stood at the window, with her back to the room, but Esme didn't think she was admiring the view.

"You have to trust me," Esme said, trying to sound confident. "Didn't I arrange for Carola to bed her husband? Not to mention Henrietta and Darby!"

"You sound like some sort of vulgar matchmaker," Helene said, not turning around.

"I do not!"

"Yes, you do."

Esme pressed her lips together. She had a policy of courtesy toward sobbing women, although she was willing to bend the rule if needed.

Helene wheeled about and walked aimlessly to the other side of the room. "I will not be party to one of your absurd schemes. You think that you can manage everyone and everything, just because you're beautiful and you've always had your way and got whatever you wanted—"

"*I*? I have got whatever I wanted?" Esme threw policy to the wind. "You're the one who married for love, Helene, remember? So you made a bad bargain. At least you chose the man! I was married off to a man I'd danced with once and with whom I had exchanged exactly five words. A plump, balding man who may have been sweet but he certainly wasn't the answer to a young girl's romantic dream. You thought yourself in love with Rees when you eloped, if you remember!"

"Who cares how we got into our marriages?" Helene said, just as hotly. "If I was idiotic enough to elope with Rees, I've paid for that mistake in humiliation! Whereas you simply went your own way, and took whatever lovers you wished, and Miles never caused you a moment's worry. And then when you decided on a whim to have a child, he accommodated you immediately—not to mention Sebastian Bonnington's contribution!"

Esme could hardly remember being as enraged as she was at this moment. She jumped up and pointed a finger at her friend. "Don't you *dare* say that I decided to have my child on a whim! Don't you dare say that! I desperately wanted

William. Otherwise I would never, ever have stooped to ask Miles to visit my bed, not when he was telling all and sundry that Lady Childe was the love of his life. I would never have done it!"

Helene narrowed her eyes. "I would undergo *any* humiliation to have a child—*any*! And you dare to complain because Miles loved Lady Childe more than you? Why the devil should he have loved you? You were unfaithful to him the very night before you reconciled! There was a whole nine months when you didn't even know whose child you carried, if you remember!"

Esme took a deep breath. She and Helene were friends; they had been friends for years. But all friendships end at some point. "I see no reason to discuss your views of my behavior further," she said. "I fully understand your opinion of me." She had gone from being burningly angry to icy cold. "Please do not hesitate to finish your tea. I am afraid that I have a headache and shall retire to my chamber."

"I didn't mean—" Helene said.

Esme cut her off. "Yes, you did mean it. And you clearly have been thinking it for a long time. I'm glad that you expressed yourself so clearly. Now we both know where we stand."

"No," Helene said flatly. She walked around Esme and sat down again. "I won't leave."

"In that case, I will." Esme walked toward the door.

"I apologize if I offended you."

Esme paused for a moment and then turned. "I am sorry as well, but forgiveness is hardly the issue, is it?"

"What did I say that was so terrible?" Helene said, looking her straight in the eyes. "One of the things I have always loved about you, Esme, is that you don't lie to yourself. You have never hidden from me the fact that you bedded Sebastian Bonnington the night before you reconciled with your husband, and therefore you initially had no idea who fathered William. Why would it wound you to hear that fact repeated by me?"

"You called my wish to have children a whim," Esme said, feeling as if Helene were stealing the ground out from under her feet. Just a moment ago she had been righteously furious and now—

"I shouldn't have said that," Helene said, her voice wavering a bit. "I only said it because I have so desperately wanted a child for years. I am sure that no one has ever wanted a child as much as I. I spoke out of jealousy. I'm sorry. You're my closest friend, and if you throw me over, I might as well jump in the river because—because—"

"Oh, for goodness' sake!" Esme said, walking back and plumping down next to her. "All right, I forgive you, you sharp-tongued viper!" She wrapped an arm around her.

"Rees always said I had the temper of a devil," Helene said with a wobbly smile.

"What temper? We've been friends for years, and you have always been calm, to my memory," Esme said in honest bewilderment.

"I have to be in control because I'm a true witch otherwise. Rees couldn't live with me. I threw a chamberpot at his head."

"You *what*?"

"I emptied a chamberpot over his head."

"My goodness," Esme said with some fascination. "I presume it was . . . in use?"

"He keeps a chamberpot in the sitting room so that if he has the urge to use it, he doesn't have to waste time visiting the water closet," Helene said wearily.

Esme shuddered. "That is truly revolting. Rees got what he deserved."

"So I try to remain collected. Otherwise I might throw plates at people's heads regularly."

"Thank you for the warning," Esme said with some amusement, moving the lemon tarts to the far side of the table.

"Not at you. But I doubt that I could live with a man at this stage in my life. I'm all of twenty-seven years old. I don't think I could put up with their disgusting habits."

"Sebastian hasn't any disgusting habits. And what does that make me, an old woman? I have twenty-eight years myself. Are you telling me that I'm too old to live with a man? Or that men aren't attracted to me due to my advanced years?"

"Don't be silly! You will always be enticing. I expect that men are even more attracted to your figure now that you've had a child."

"You've bats in your belfry," Esme replied. "I'm plump, and I know it."

"I'm like a board, all flat and dried up, whereas you are even more curvy than before."

"As you said earlier, cut bait. If my body curves, it only curves *out!*"

Helene stood up again and walked over to the window, wrapping her arms tightly around her chest. Finally she said, "I have to do something. I cannot go on like this."

The raw misery in her voice caught at Esme's heart. Sunlight was falling on Helene's hair, making it look like spun sugar, gleaming white-blond.

"I can't bear this life anymore," she said. "I'm warning you, Esme, I am about to create a far bigger scandal than Rees ever did with his tawdry little singer and his Russian dancing troupe. And it will all be his fault, the utter unmitigated bastard."

Esme blinked. "What are you thinking of?" she asked cautiously. "Do sit down, Helene."

"I'm going to have a child," Helene said, setting her jaw so that she looked as bullish as a Norse goddess. "I'm going to have a child, with *or* without a divorce. I've been thinking of nothing else for months."

"Are you certain that Rees won't—"

"Absolutely," Helene said, cutting her off. "I've spoken to him about divorce repeatedly. And why would he ever change his mind? He's cosily tucked up with that singer of his. Rees was never one to consult a book of etiquette on any matter, let alone in questions of marriage."

"I suspect you're right, but—"

"I have two choices, Esme: I can wither on the vine asking my husband for a divorce that he won't give me, or I can simply have the baby I desire, and let the devil take the consequences."

"It will be a terrible scandal," Esme warned her.

"I don't care. I literally don't care."

Esme took a deep breath and nodded. "In that case, we'll forget the whole idea of divorce and simply select an available man to father your child." Her imagination was already jumping to the task. "Neville Charlton has lovely hair. Or there's Lord Brooks. He has that gorgeous Roman nose."

"I wouldn't wish my child to have a father whose first name is Busick," Helene put in wryly.

"Excellent point," Esme agreed. "We'll just pick exactly the facial features and names that you would appreciate, and there we are."

Helene shook her head but didn't say anything, so Esme rattled on.

"Lord Bellamy has very broad shoulders, Helene. What do you think of him? And he has black hair as well. I'll make a list. For goodness' sake, it's not so hard to have a child. It only took me one night. Rees won't repudiate you once you're with child. He's a decent sort."

Helene snorted. "Decent? *Rees?*"

"Well, at any rate, he's far too lazy to repudiate you," Esme amended.

"He wants to make my life a misery for some reason," Helene said flatly. "It's the only explanation for his continued behavior toward me."

"Well, Rees is not a skinflint," Esme said. "He's one of the richest men in England, and he would hardly leave you and the babe to starve."

"The greater problem is that someone has to father the babe," Helene said. "With *me*." Helene's eyes were swollen and red; her skin was patchy from crying.

"This isn't your finest hour," Esme said consolingly, "but—"

Helene plucked at the front of her gown. "Esme, there's *nothing here*!" She waved her hand in front of Esme's chest. "Just compare you and me."

There was no question that Esme won that sweepstakes. Helene was wearing a very tightly buttoned walking costume that emphasized the fact that she had only the faintest, faintest curve in the front.

"Admit it," Helene demanded. "You haven't looked like me since you were fourteen years old!"

"More like twelve," Esme admitted. "But gentlemen are not only attracted to large bosoms, you know."

"They like curves. I don't want to get excited about impossibilities. I don't have curves. I can't flirt in that way you have, as if you were—"

"As if I were what?" Esme asked, bristling a little.

"Oh, you know, Esme. Promising them *things*. I can't do that. I loathed being in bed with Rees, what I remember of it. I can hardly look at a man as if I would want to do such a thing voluntarily!"

Esme bit her lip. Helene's marital relations had obviously been unpleasant. "You'll have to feign desire," she said bluntly. "Because it matters far more to a man that you desire him, than that you have a large chest."

"I'm not sure I even know how to do that. Stephen Fairfax-Lacy wasn't fooled for more than a few moments, to be honest. He could tell that I didn't really want to go forward with it."

"We'll work on that part later," Esme promised. "It's not hard to fool a man into thinking that you think he's Adonis himself, if you go about it the right way." She looked over Helene again. "First we have to order some new clothing."

Helene smiled, a tiny curl of her lips. "You can turn me into a blaze of fashion and it won't make any man wish to bed me."

"Nonsense! You are ravishing, darling. There's many a woman who would be more than grateful for that lovely hair of yours, not to mention your cheekbones. What we're going to do is advertise the fact that you are available for bedding. I'm afraid that men are rather slow and foolish when it comes to these things, and they rely on obvious signals, such as clothing."

Helene sighed and began wrapping her braids back into a stack on her head. "I'll have to just cover up my chest with a sign, then. *Available tonight. Please inquire within.*"

Chapter Four
Of Song Birds and Strumpets

Number 15, Rothsfeld Square

Alina McKenna was bored. Lord, who would have thought that the life of a courtesan was so tedious? There were more and more days when she would give anything for the frantic hither-and-yon of the opera house, to be back there, knowing that a line of gentlemen were at the stage door, just hoping for a glimpse of her. Of course, she hadn't been a prima donna, and she'd had less attention than the leads, but even so . . . Her eyes softened, remembering a certain Hervey Bittle who gave her a pair of blush-colored gloves and took her for a ride around Hyde Park. It was rather sad to think that these days she would never wear such poorly made garments.

Which reminded her precisely of her own situation. Naturally Hervey Bittle couldn't compete with a genuine earl, once Godwin had made it clear he was interested. All the other girls were mortified with jealousy, properly mortified. Especially when Rees whisked her off to his grand house on Rothsfeld Square and said she could have whatever she wanted in the way of new gowns, just as long as she'd sing for him when he wished. And bed him, naturally.

She brooded over that for a moment. He wasn't the first gentleman in her life, although it was hard to know if Hugh

Sutherland, back in Scotland, really counted as a gentleman. Probably not. He was the son of a butcher, and people had called him Cow when he was a boy. But Hugh grew up well enough to catch the eye of a bored vicar's daughter longing to take her fine voice and flee to the city.

Ah well, Hugh was far in the past now. There was no need to wonder what her father would think of her now. He was surely praying every night for the safety of her soul, even without knowing she'd become a fancy woman. Lina pressed her lips together hard. She didn't like to think of her mama crying, but life was what it was. She wasn't made to live in that dreary old vicarage.

She glanced around her bedchamber. The only relief she had from the tedium of it all was when she summoned decorators. Perhaps she should change the appointments again. At the moment her bedchamber was hung entirely in blush silks, the color of the faintest damask rose. No, she'd leave it for at least a month or so.

She sat down at the dressing table, virtually the only piece of furniture left in the room from when Rees's wife lived in the house, and dragged a brush through her already shining hair. She felt dreary, properly dreary. Rees did most of his writing at night, and so he refused to go anywhere, not to a concert, not to a ball, not even to Vauxhall. It must have been months since he had taken her out of an evening. She couldn't go back and talk to the girls at the opera because she ended up feeling embarrassed by her circumstances, for all they envied her. And she missed it, oh, she did. All those cosy conversations about who had a pair of stockings without a run, and who had lost a garter on a dark night, and who might be chosen to sing . . .

Lina's eyes darkened. *He* had taken her away from there. He could bloody well accompany her out the door.

Rees was in the sitting room, naturally. Lina walked in, distastefully aware of the papers brushing her ankles. It reminded her of walking down a street filled with rubbish. But Rees would no more allow one of those sheets of papers to be discarded than he would dress in a gown. The thought of burly Rees in a petticoat made her giggle and he looked up.

"Lina!" he said in that abrupt fashion he had. "Sing this phrase for me, will you?"

"Are these the words?" she asked ungraciously. "*I trip through the green woods, all covered with dew*. What is Fen thinking? That *trip through* is going to be very difficult, if not impossible, to sing."

"I don't give a damn about the words, or what you think of them," he said impatiently. "Just sing until you get to the end of the second page."

"I don't like the melody either," she said with some satisfaction, a few moments later. "The way that line drops to a lower register is a disgrace. It makes me sound like a hymn-singer."

Rees's lips set. "I particularly like that section of the line."

She was about to poke fun at the melody when she remembered that she wanted to go shopping. So she leaned against his shoulder instead. "Perhaps I sang it too quickly. Here, let me have another go."

This time she gave it her best effort. And since Lina had a voice that rivaled that of Francesca Cuzzoni, the best operatic voice of the last century, her best was very good indeed. In fact, Lina pretty much thought that she could make any plunking old tune sound better than it really was.

He looked happier now, which was all to the good. "It's lovely. I was wrong," she cooed into his ear. "Rees, I should like you to accompany me to Madame Rocque's French Trimming shop on Bond Street."

He twitched away from her kiss and was scribbling on paper again.

"I'll do whatever you wish . . . tonight," she whispered throatily, leaning against him again.

This time he gave her a little shove. "I'm busy, for God's sake, Lina. Go practice your tricks on someone else, will you?"

She narrowed her eyes. Madame Rocque made the most ravishing creations in all London but to Lina's fury, she had discovered that if Earl Godwin did not accompany her to the modiste, she was treated like ditch water.

"I'll sing the entire aria for you after we return," she said, not bothering to add a throaty intonation. He hardly ever visited her bed anyway. In fact, it had been months since he darkened her bedroom door, now she thought of it. Rees's skills in that area weren't of a sort to keep a girl awake at night wondering where he was.

He didn't say anything, just kept scribbling on his sheet.

"Three times," she said. "I'll sing that"—she swallowed the word stupid—"I'll sing your lovely new aria *three* times, Rees."

He shoved back from the piano and stood up with a sardonic look on his face. "Since I'm obviously not going to be allowed to work until you've gotten your way, we might as well go. Did you call the carriage?"

"How could I? Leke is nowhere to be seen," she pointed out. Rees had a great deal of difficulty keeping servants. The butler, Leke, was the only servant who never left, but he kept his own hours and couldn't always be found.

"Damn it," Rees said elegantly, heading for the door.

Lina paused for a moment and very delicately, with just the tip of her rosy finger, pushed his score off the piano so that it drifted into the scads of trash wafting around her feet.

"Coming, dearest!" she thrilled, adding a little tremolo to give him a frisson. Because it hadn't taken her long to realize that her personal accoutrements did nothing for Rees Godwin. The luscious body and suggestive glances that had reduced Hervey Bittle to a stammering fool hardly interested the earl at all. Witness the fact that she was living in his wife's bedchamber as if she were a nun.

It was her voice that he had wooed from the opera house, and her voice was the only thing that he really wanted in his house. More fool she, to have been so blinded by infatuation that she didn't notice.

Oh well. Native Scottish practicality forced her to recognize that singing a few lines of music was infinitely preferable to being at a man's beck and call in the bedroom. It wasn't as if the earl had been any great shakes in the bed anyway. Mind you, he had a lovely body. But it was a matter of here, there, see you later.

Lina shrugged and headed out to the hall to join the earl. But first she nudged the libretto once more with her boot to make sure it was completely buried in paper.

Madame Rocque maintained an establishment at 112 Bond Street, an enclave that whispered money and screamed elegance, to Lina's mind. She took a deep breath the moment they walked through the door. There was nothing she loved more than the elusive fragrance that wafted through silk-draped rooms like this one. It was the smell of rich satin, of French perfume, of ladies who changed their clothing four or five times a day and thought nothing of ordering three bonnets to match a gown, or two gowns to match a favorite bonnet, for that matter.

The antechamber was made up to look like a lady's boudoir, complete with a dressing table lined with ruffle after ruffle of crocus-colored silk. The walls were hung with silk of the same dulcet yellow. To one side, an exquisite evening gown was hanging over the back of a chair, as if a distinguished beauty might waltz into her chamber at any moment and put it on. One of Madame Rocque's innovations had been her habit of making up each of her new models so that one could actually see a gown before ordering it.

Rees stuck out in the midst of this exuberant femininity like a sore thumb. He looked like the very worst kind of degenerate today, with his hair falling out of its ribbon, and too long to begin with. Not to mention that sulky lower lip of his. Yet his title was the only thing that truly mattered to Madame Rocque. Sure enough, with the earl stomping along at Lina's side they were ushered into an inner room the moment they entered the establishment, and by Madame herself. In the past Lina had been relinquished to a minion after being asked to wait in the antechamber for upwards of a half hour.

Madame fluttered about Rees like a rather weedy sparrow courting a hawk. If she wasn't such a fool, she'd realize that twittering like that would simply make his temper grow, Lina thought. He was like a child being told to wait for dinner. Madame had yet to greet Lina herself; she was obviously walking a delicate balance between desire for Rees's patronage and a lavish desire to make it clear to her, Lina, that she wasn't welcome.

All right, Lina could accept that. There were other modistes who would be ecstatic to gown the chosen mistress of Earl Godwin, given his thousands of pounds. But she wanted the best. To her mind, if she had to live with Rees, she deserved the very best, and that meant patronizing the establishment where ladies went.

So she sat down on a spindly chair upholstered in green silk and disregarded the way Madame Rocque was cooing over Rees. Perhaps she should refurnish her chambers in this green color. It would look like the first breath of spring in the woods behind her father's vicarage. Lina crossed her legs and swung her ankle gently. She was willing to wait.

As soon as Madame Rocque left the dressing room, Rees took out a piece of paper and began jotting down notes without saying another word to her. Madame Rocque's establishment was rather flimsily constructed, Lina decided. Even draperies of green silk couldn't hide the fact that the inner rooms were perfectly audible to each other. Two ladies in the next room were having a most interesting conversation.

"Men like to see an expanse of bosom," one lady said. She had a sort of honeyed, husky voice that Lina associated with stage actresses. She was an alto, a seductive, opulent contralto. Men must adore her voice: she could have made a fortune on the stage.

The other woman had a higher voice that was rather bell-like. In fact, it was rather like Lina's own, so she was probably a soprano. The soprano didn't agree with her friend, which was utterly foolish. Lina firmly agreed with the alto. Show a man a bit of bosom, and he'll blather himself into a frenzy. She cast a glance at Rees. He was the exception to the rule. She could have dropped her gown to her waist and he wouldn't notice, Lina thought rather bitterly. He had never shown much interest in her breasts, even in the first few weeks when he was so gratifyingly attentive.

And when they were in bed, well, she could have been in a dead faint, for all he caressed her. Lina was practiced at turning her mind away from depressing subjects, so she went back to the conversation next door.

The alto sounded a little exasperated. "How in the world do you think to catch a man's attention if you dress like a

Puritan?" The soprano presumably was in need of a husband. She must be coming out of mourning, since her voice had far too much maturity for a debutante. At that moment Madame Rocque came burbling into the ladies' room—so that's where she was!—and Lina could hear the swishing of silks being held up.

The alto was obviously in charge. "We'll try that one," she said, sounding coolly approving. Lina memorized her tone. It was hard not to allow a note of pleading to enter her own voice when she spoke to Madame Rocque.

There was some rustling as the gown was cast over the soprano's shoulders, or so Lina assumed, and then the alto and Madame Rocque started cooing.

But the soprano cut through it decisively. "I look like an orange without its rind," she said firmly. "More so because this silk is quite an odd shade of yellow, Madame, if you'll forgive me saying so."

No doubt Madame Rocque had put her in one of her newest gowns, the ones cut low in the back and even lower in the front. They were being worn with bared shoulders. Lina, naturally, wanted one of those herself, ever since she'd read a description in *La Belle Assemblée*.

The alto was doing her best to convince her friend. "You look splendid—"

But the soprano seemed to have a practical turn of mind. "No, I don't. I look like a plucked chicken. There's no point to wearing a gown designed precisely to expose one's bosom when one hasn't that bosom to expose!"

She had a sound argument, to Lina's mind. There is nothing worse than a stringy set of shoulders. She looked rather proudly at her own plump figure. Mind you, boredom had made her rather plumper than she'd like to be, but it was in all the right places.

More to the point, Madame Rocque appeared to have chosen sides with the soprano. "I have another idea," she said in her heavily French accent. Lina was absolutely certain that accent was contrived. She'd had to study in order to rid herself of her Scots accent, and she knew how easily an accent could be faked. Likely Madame Rocque was really Mrs. Riddle from Lower Putney, Lina thought to herself sourly.

There was a moment's pause and she heard Madame say something curt to one of her assistants. A moment later there was a light knock at their door and a girl entered holding a gown, obviously the *same* gown, since it was orange. Lina's eyes narrowed. How many orange gowns could there be in this establishment? She expected to be served by Madame Rocque herself, not by a stammering girl clutching a gown that had just been rejected by another client. She had a mind to refuse to try the gown at all.

"Put on the damn thing," Rees growled at her. "I have work to do."

Lina took a closer look and changed her mind. The gown was lovely. The assistant began nimbly unbuttoning her walking costume.

Next door, Madame had returned with another costume. "This gown is a concoction that I offer only to my most daring clients," she said in her strident, Frenchified voice.

There was a moment of absolute silence in the room next door. Lina strained her ears. Was the soprano being offered something more daring than the creation she herself had just slipped on? Because if so, Lina wanted it as well. Not that the gown she wore wasn't lovely. It was precisely as described in *La Belle Assemblée*, and Lina fully intended to order one in primrose, and perhaps another in lilac. But—

"I couldn't!" That was the soprano. But she had the awed voice of a woman who clearly *could*.

"My lady, if you will just remove your chemise, and corset, I will put the gown over your head. I think you will be most pleased."

"Remove my corset? I would feel quite uncomfortable without a light corset," said the soprano. "I'm afraid that's out of the question."

Lina almost giggled. She had given up wearing corsets the moment she left Scotland. She heard some rustling, presumably the gown going over the soprano's corset.

The alto cleared her throat. "Glory be, Helene, you look—you look—"

"Exquisite, is it not?" Madame Rocque sounded extremely pleased with herself. "You see, when a lady has not quite the endowments that one would like—" she caught herself.

The soprano must be flat as a chessboard, Lina thought with some amusement.

"This style of dressing compliments the grace and delicacy of your form, my lady. It is sensual, enticing, and yet, as you see, there is nothing uncovered."

The alto laughed. She had a dark chocolate laugh, and Lina thought again that men must love that laugh. Proving her point, Rees raised his head to listen.

"It's utterly glorious," she said. "I think you'll have it in amber, Helene? Amber will suit your hair, and it's quite the rage these days. And perhaps in a shot silk as well, Madame?"

Madame Rocque's voice had all the satisfaction of a cat encountering a bowl of cream. "I would suggest just a delicate pearl border, Lady Bonnington, if you agree."

Rees had snapped to attention like a terrier confronting a mastiff. Lina cast him a curious glance.

"Do you like this gown, Rees?" she asked, twirling in front of him. A man would have to be a limp lily not to appreciate the way her breasts swelled from the crimped satin riband that wound its way over her shoulders.

He didn't even notice, just said, "That's my wife next door, for God's sake. My *wife*. With Esme Rawlings—Esme Bonnington now. Christ."

"What?" Lina said, hardly listening. Perhaps she would order the gown she was wearing in white, with black trim. That way men would instinctively look to the black ribbons outlining her breasts. She smiled and turned before the mirror again.

"That's my wife next door!" Rees hissed at her. "Take your pelisse. We're getting out of here."

This time Lina caught what he said. It was too delicious! She had been dying of curiosity about Rees's wife. The papers ignored the countess, never even reporting on her gowns. Had she, Lina, been Countess Godwin, she would have ensured that every costume she wore was reported in detail.

She deliberately raised her voice, knowing full well that her voice rang as clear as a bell and had the power to carry to the back of a theater. "Why Rees, darling, why such a hurry? Surely you can't wish to return home already?"

Rees narrowed his eyes at her and if she didn't have the fortitude of an elephant—and she did—she might have been almost afraid. But she'd learned long ago that Rees's bark was worse than his bite.

There was absolute silence next door, not even a whisper.

"I'm not ready to return to the house," Lina said. "Why this gown, even if it is a quite *odd shade of yellow*, is positively enticing, isn't it darling? Or . . ."—she let a teasing hint of delicious pleasure enter her voice—"is it the very delightful nature of the bodice that has inspired your wish to return home, Rees? And in the midst of the afternoon!" She giggled naughtily.

Rees had turned an ugly shade of dark red and Lina thought he was probably at the boiling point. Still not a sound next door. "Your manly enthusiasm is *so* gratifying," she cooed.

"Shut up!" he growled at her in a low voice.

"Of course, you may suffer from some competition once men see my figure in this gown!" Lina continued blithely.

He rose and was coming toward her. It was probably time to go but oh, what fun that had been! She hadn't had an audience in over two years. She pranced toward the door, pausing for one last second. "I hardly think, Rees dar—" But a large hand clamped over her mouth and Rees carried her straight through the anteroom and almost threw her into the carriage.

Alina McKenna hadn't gotten free of a dark and draughty vicarage, the cold fields of Scotland, and the windy corridors of the King's Theatre in the Haymarket without regular use of her not inconsiderable intelligence. That same intelligence suggested that she sit quietly in the corner of the carriage and not say a word about her walking costume, left behind at Madame Rocque's. Instead she spent the ride home examining the exquisite workmanship that made up the deep yellow gown she was wearing. The stitches were so small they could hardly be seen against the silk. She would send a message immediately requesting another of these gowns in a deeper color. She changed her mind about white and black. That was a bit garish. Perhaps amber.

Since amber was a fashionable color these days, or so she'd heard it said.

Quite the rage, really.

Chapter Five

Hair Today, Gone Tomorrow

Esme had often thought that the only thing lacking to make Helene into a devastatingly beautiful woman was a little animation. Helene was always calm, always exquisitely polite, always . . . evasive.

Not at the moment.

"I cannot believe that I patronize the same shop as that doxy!" Helene snapped, eyes flashing with rage.

Madame Rocque rushed into a frothy waterfall of apologies, but Esme cut her off. "If you would be so kind as to bring a cup of tea to soothe Lady Godwin's nerves."

As Madame gratefully closed the door behind her, Esme observed, "I'm afraid the coincidence is not unusual. After all, Rees's mistress must be flush with money, and there is no more fashionable modiste in London than Madame Rocque."

Helene narrowed her eyes. "For the demi-mondaine, perhaps!"

"I have bought all my gowns from her for the past two years."

"She should maintain higher standards in her clientele." Helene shuddered. "That woman is wearing the yellow gown that I had on my body a mere moment ago. And Rees likely overheard everything we said!"

"Good," Esme said uncompromisingly.

"Good?" Helene's voice rose to a shriek. "What's good about it?"

"Perhaps Rees will wish to join the competition for your favors." Esme pointed to the mirror before which Helene still stood. "Look at yourself."

Helene swivelled. "The last thing I would want is for that reprobate to approach me." But she looked, obediently.

"You must remove your corset. The fabric is so fine that I can see the trim on your chemise in the back. But the gown is vastly becoming to you."

"Likely all the courtesans are wearing the same piece!" she said rather shrilly.

Esme shrugged. "You're getting a little priggish in your old age, darling."

Helene turned on her like a viper. "Don't you dare call me priggish simply because I am overwrought at being made fun of—humiliated!—by my husband's mistress. Lady Childe was never less than gracious to you, when you were married to Miles and she was his mistress." She collapsed into a chair. "The woman was making a game of me. Did you hear that comment about her bosom? Clearly, Rees has told her every-thing about our marriage."

Esme busied herself with looking into her reticule. She didn't want to make Helene embarrassed, but naturally she was longing for more details about her marriage. "What might he have told?" she said, trying to look utterly uninterested.

"Oh, that he—we—"

"Yes?"

"Bedroom details!" Helene snapped. "He has told his mistress of private events."

"I gather your marital intimacies were not all they could have been," Esme said delicately.

43

Helene stared at her. "How would I know? Listening to your jokes about bedding men, I have always felt as if we lived in two different worlds. No sane woman could possibly wish to repeat that experience. And yet you have *willingly* engaged in—"

"Bedding," Esme put in cheerfully, powdering her nose.

"How you do it, I shall never know," Helene said with stark conviction in her voice. "I found the experience repulsive. It's some defect in myself, no doubt. Rees said I was incapable of women's pleasure, if there truly is such a thing."

"But did it never occur to you, Helene, that perhaps the fault was with him? In my experience, men often try to cover up their own failures by blaming the woman in question."

"I fail to see what skill has to do with it." Helene seemed to have thrown her customary reticence to the wind. "It hurt. It hurt initially and then it continued to hurt, and I do think Rees was right in thinking that I simply am not suited to the act. And I have to say, Esme, I am much happier *not* having to perform those duties. It's very hard to countenance a man pawing me about in that manner. Last year, for example, I could not bring myself to allow Stephen Fairfax-Lacy any intimacies. I am not accustomed to it."

Obviously whatever happened between the bedsheets in the Godwin bedchamber was beyond repair at this point, so Esme reverted to practicality. "When do you think to wear your new gown?"

"If Madame Rocque can have one made up so quickly, I might wear it to Lady Hamilton's ball," Helene said.

"That's not for two weeks! Believe me, Madame Rocque will make you a gown with two days' notice at most, given what just occurred in her own establishment."

"But I'm working on a new waltz and it's going well. I don't want to lose my direction with this sort of foolishness."

Helene rose and stood before the mirror again. "Do you truly think that I must discard my corset?"

"Absolutely."

"What will I do with my hair?"

"Why don't you wear it down?"

"It's dreadfully unfashionable," Helene said dubiously. She pulled a number of pins from her hair and undid her braids. When she was finished, she was surrounded by a shimmering curtain of hair falling, waterfall-like, to the top of her legs.

"Goodness," Esme said faintly. "It certainly is long, isn't it?"

"Braids make it a manageable length."

"It's exquisite."

"Rees loved it," Helene said, narrowing her eyes. "I do believe it was the only thing he liked about me. He—" She stopped. "I'll cut it off."

"Cut it off?" Esme was astounded. Helene's great woven mound of braids was an integral part of her regal, calm character.

Helene nodded. "All of it." She drew her hands through sleek masses that fell like cornsilk. "*Now.*"

"What?"

"Madame Rocque must have a pair of scissors," Helene said. She flung the door open. Madame had left a girl in the hallway. "Fetch a pair of scissors!" she commanded, and the girl fled.

"No!" Esme gasped. "You cannot do such a thing without forethought. We'll send a footman to request that Monsieur Olivier attend you this afternoon. Helene!"

Helene grabbed the shears from the girl.

"You!" Esme said, waving at the maid, who was standing, mouth agape, staring at the beautiful woman about to chop off her hair. "Send about to Monsieur Olivier, Number

Twelve, Bond Street. Beg him to come here immediately, with kindest compliments of Lady Bonnington. Tell him we have a challenge for him. Did you get that?"

The young girl fled.

Even as Esme turned back to Helene, the first great sheaf of hair fell to the ground. And Helene was already hacking off another chunk.

"Oh lord," Esme moaned. "You never do anything by half measures, do you?"

"Why should I?" Helene said. She didn't look like a Danish queen now, remote and icy cold, but more like a belligerent English dairymaid. "Why should I keep all this hair? Do you know, it just occurred to me that I haven't cut it in the past because of some misguided sentiment leading back to Rees's fondness for my hair? Rees, who dragged his inamorata home so that he could have his way with her in the middle of the day? *Rees? The hell with Rees!*"

"Helene!" Esme gasped. She was quite certain that she had just heard the very first profanity ever to leave Helene's mouth.

"And the same to all of them!" Helene said gleefully, wielding her shears. "I don't care what men think of my hair, do I? All I want is their participation. Their cooperation!" She sliced off the last hank of hair and threw it to the ground. "There! What do you think?"

Helene's hair stuck out around her shoulders like the stubble from cornstalks left on a harvest field. She was shaking her head and grinning like a fool. "Oh, Esme, it's wonderful not to feel all that weight on my head. I had no idea! I would have done this years ago." A moment later she pulled Madame Rocque's gown over her head and began unlacing her corset. The corset hit the floor, followed by her chemise, and the gown went back over her head.

A mere ten minutes later, a sharp knock sounded on the door and Monsieur Olivier trotted into the room. He was small and round and very French. His own hair was pomaded and brushed in such a fashion that it rose straight from his forehead like the curl of a wave.

"Where is zee challenge?" he said, but his voice died as he caught sight of Helene.

To Esme's mind, if anyone could repair what Helene had just done to her hair, it would be Maurice Olivier.

He moved toward Helene, delicately kicking a sheaf of hair away with the toe of his boot. "I gather you committed this outrage yourself, my lady?"

Helene tossed her head and the chopped ends of her hair flew about her shoulders. "If you're going to be impudent about my hair, Monsieur Olivier, I shall summon another stylist."

"That would be your downfall," Olivier remarked, prowling about her for all the world like a stout tiger, who has cornered a pullet. "I am the only man in London who may— *may*—be able to recapture your natural beauty, my lady."

"What do you think of your gown now, Madame?" Helene demanded.

Everyone looked. Madame Rocque's creation was made of rose-colored silk, so delicate that it fell to the ground like a stream of water. It was formed of two layers, drawn tight under the breasts with silver ribbons. Halfway to Helene's knee the upper layer of silk was caught back by small clusters of embroidered roses. It had a fairly high neck, trim around the neck of a slightly darker color and short sleeves. In all . . . unexceptionable. Appropriate for a debutante, really. Except . . . except . . .

Except it was almost transparent.

Where two layers clung together, one could see nothing other than the outline of Helene's body, which was revealed to be slender but not angular. She had curves: her waist curved in, and her breasts curved out. The thin silk of Madame Rocque's gown hugged each of those curves in a way that revealed them to be deliciously rounded.

And then where only the underskirt was revealed, below her knees, one could see everything: Helene's delicate ankles, the garter holding up her stockings, the delicate shape of her knees.

Esme blinked. She suddenly felt fleshy and over-plump.

"I gather zat we are considering something of a major reconstruction, are we, Madame?" Olivier asked.

Helene laughed. "Something along those lines."

"Never fear," he said, clashing his scissors. "I am the only man in London who is up to zis challenge! Now, if you would have a seat."

Helene sat down. She was feeling a little bit daunted. She had spent so many hours—nay, years!—of her life tending to her hair: washing it, combing it, drying it endlessly before the fire. And in two seconds, it was gone. Truly, Rees was right when he said that she had a monstrous temper. More and more hair was flying to the floor. Helene tried not to look. She concentrated on the gloriously weightless feeling of her head.

"What are you thinking of doing, Monsieur Olivier?" Esme asked.

"We must be daring," he announced. "It is zee only way. Courage!"

"How daring?" Helene asked, feeling a qualm.

"Very daring! It is zee only way to recover your beauty. More audacious than Lady Caroline Lamb ever dared to be."

Esme giggled. "Really, Monsieur Olivier! Didn't that young woman chop off hair from . . . another place and send it to Byron?"

Helene looked at her, scandalized, but Monsieur Olivier just chuckled. "An indiscreet young woman, but she did have acceptable hair. It's been all of five years since I gave her that short hair, and now I'm tired of making frizzled ringlets, day in and day out. With luck you will start a rage, Lady Godwin, and I can shear off hundreds of tired curls in the next few weeks."

Helene tried not to look at the mirror. More and more of her hair flew from the scissors. An hour later, Helene didn't know whether to faint or applaud. Her hair was short now. Truly short. It clung sleekly to her head until her jawbone, where little wispy curls softened the angles of her cheekbones and emphasized her eyes.

"Oh, Helene," Esme said in an awed voice.

"Zhee looks spectacular!" Monsieur Olivier said in a smug voice. "Only I could have done this for you, Madame! You see, I have given you zee appeal."

"Appeal?" Helene said, still staring at herself.

"You look utterly delicious," Esme put in. "You are going to turn heads with a vengeance!"

"As long as I can turn one head, that's enough," Helene said, staring at herself. In truth, she looked like another woman: a bold, impudent, sensual sprite of a person.

"He will be yours!" Monsieur Olivier kissed the tips of his fingers. "Believe me, Madame, zere is no man in London who will not be at your knees!"

"Good," Helene whispered. "I hope they *all* are."

"Rees as well?" Esme said with an eyebrow raised.

"Only so that I can spurn him," Helene said firmly. "But yes, Rees as well!"

Chapter Six

With the Wave of a Wand

Hyde Park

"And then she said *what*?" Rees's friend Darby was utterly fascinated by the debacle of the dressing room.

"Lina announced, loudly, that I must wish to return home because I was overcome with desire at the sight of her in that gown, and had to have my way with her," Rees said gloomily. "Which is rubbish. I haven't been to her room in weeks. Months perhaps." Come to think of it, he couldn't remember the last time.

"Why on earth not?" Darby asked, startled.

They were walking in the woody part of Hyde Park, where one never saw the fashionable sort of gentlemen. Rees kicked a trailing strand of faded wild roses to the side but didn't answer.

Darby stopped and chose a coral bud to put in his button-hole. He was wearing a morning costume of bronze broad-cloth. The rosebud looked strawberry-pink against his chest, perhaps just a shade pinker than he would have desired.

"I don't know," Rees said. Darby wasn't looking at him, just shaking back his deep lace cuffs and examining all the rosebuds on the bush, so Rees knew he was burning with curiosity. You couldn't be friends since you were both in short coats without being able to read each other's minds.

"The prospect simply isn't appealing anymore. I'd move her out, but I need her voice to help me with this opera."

"Appealing? Just when does making love to a woman with a body like Lina's lose appeal?"

"I must be getting old," Rees said, kicking a stick off the path. It hit a mulberry tree that dropped a glossy spray of water over them.

"For Christ's sake, Rees," Darby said, examining his shoulders to see whether the water had left stains. "Why we can't take a civilized promenade around the duck pond, I'll never know."

"I like it here. At least we don't meet any simpering matrons." They walked on.

"How's Henrietta?" Rees asked, after a bit. He liked Darby's wife immensely. In fact, now that he thought about it, his disinclination to knock on Lina's door had started around the time that Darby found Henrietta. Not that he desired Henrietta for himself, not that. He just wanted . . . he wanted the fire that burned between Henrietta and Darby.

Sure enough, a smile curled on his friend's lips. "She is being very cool to me at the moment."

"Why?"

"Because I'm a dandified fool," Darby said, without any sign of regret. "I wouldn't pick up Johnney after he'd been sick all over his crib and was wailing."

Rees gave an involuntary shudder. "Why on earth would she wish you to do such a thing?"

"The nursemaid had her half-day," Darby explained. "You know Henrietta dislikes allowing the servants to care for the children. So she was bathing the girls and we heard Johnney being sick. So I went to have a look, but of course I didn't pick him up, not while I was wearing velvet. I was just taking

51

off my coat when she came running in, acting as if a few screams from the lad would be mortal."

Rees couldn't think what to say to that. He'd rather slay himself than pick up a child covered with vomit. "Doesn't Johnney seem to cast up his accounts rather frequently?" he inquired, more to be polite than anything else.

"Too much," Darby said. "He's seven months now. He'll never get married at this rate."

"Fortunate for him."

"So have you seen your wife since your near encounter in Madame Rocque's establishment?"

"No. But I gather I'll see her tonight."

"Don't tell me that you are venturing into polite society?" Darby asked, greatly entertained.

"Lady Hamilton's ball."

"Why are you going there? Debutante sort of affair, isn't it? We've declined."

"Because that wretched friend of Helene's, the one who married Sebastian Bonnington, wrote me a note and said that my wife intends to go to the ball specifically in order to acquire an heir, and that if I wish to join in the competition, I should make an appearance."

There was a moment of stunned silence. A chestnut tree dropped cream-colored petals on their hair and Darby didn't even notice. "*What?*"

"You heard me. Helene told me she wanted a child, but I had no idea that she would go to such lengths."

"She told you that she wanted a child? What did you say?"

"I told her that she ought to resign herself to the truth of the matter, which is that our marriage is not going to produce offspring," Rees said irritably. "It never occurred to me that Helene would decide I had given her carte blanche to put a cuckoo in my nest! This is *Helene* we're talking about here.

52

From the way she's harped at me over the years, you'd think reputation was the most important thing in the world."

"My God," Darby said slowly. "She must have a crack in the upper story."

"She had that years ago."

"But she'll be ruined!"

"I can only think that she doesn't care about her reputation anymore." Rees kicked a rock across the path. "Perhaps I should have shown her more consideration. I would have divorced her, if she had made a convincing case for it."

"So you're going to Lady Hamilton's ball . . ." Darby said, clearly still in shock.

"Have to, don't I? I've been thinking about it for two days, ever since I got the note from Esme Bonnington."

"And that's an odd thing," Darby put in. "Why on earth did Esme let you know of Helene's plans?"

Rees shrugged. "She didn't explain herself. But I can't let Helene bed just anyone and make the child into my heir. Tom is my heir, obviously, and while he seems to be rather slow in the marital department, presumably he'll get around to producing a child at some point."

"Yes, but—"

"I can't allow her to give me a cuckoo. But if she's that determined, I can"—he paused and considered his words for a moment—"be of assistance."

"So you'll—what *are* you going to do?"

"I'll tell her that if she wants a child that much, she'll have to take me. It's unfortunate that the process is going to be about as much fun as going to a tooth-drawer."

Darby blinked. "I didn't know it was that bad between you."

"In the bedchamber it was."

It was Darby's turn to stay silent. He couldn't imagine being married to someone under those circumstances. They walked along, and Darby decided that he would go home and lure Henrietta into their chamber for a little dalliance. They were in danger of forgetting how fortunate they were.

"I must be cracked myself," Rees suddenly said. "I'm actually thinking of trying to get her back in the house."

Darby gaped. "Going respectable in your old age?"

"Hell, no. I need help with the opera," Rees said grimly. "It's garbage. I was thinking of trading my assistance in creating offspring for Helene's help with the scores."

"Are things that bad with the current piece?"

"Worse. It's overdue by months, and I have nothing worth hearing. Nothing."

"Helene will murder you if you put it so bluntly," Darby said after a moment. "You'll have to emphasize the fact you want your children under your own roof. But what will you do about Lina?"

"She's bored to death with me. I'll give her an allowance so she needn't take another lover. She has a quite prudish streak, and I dislike the idea that she might have to take on a curmudgeon like myself."

One thing Rees hadn't told Darby was that he was going to the ball as much for Helene's sake as for his own. Who the hell would want to sleep with Helene? Likely she would be humiliated by discovering that gentlemen wanted a ripe little body and a come-hither manner when it came to dalliance. They didn't want a stiff scarecrow with a pile of braids bigger than a halo, and a reputation to match. True, Helene somehow inveigled Fairfax-Lacy to follow her about last summer, but then he'd up and married another woman within a few weeks. That can't have been easy for Helene.

It was almost amusing to realize that he was feeling both guilty and protective. Perhaps his wife's reckless wish to destroy her own reputation *was* his fault. If they were still living in the same house, this child business likely would have worked itself out in the normal way, years ago. And estranged though they might be, Rees couldn't stand the idea that his wife would be rebuffed at the ball. She was no Cinderella, after all, with a fairy godmother waiting in the wings.

He would just have to wave his own magic wand. He found himself grinning at that, and decided not to share the joke with Darby. They'd never been the kind of friends who sat around trading bawdy jokes and hawing with laughter. And it didn't seem polite, not in reference to his own wife.

Chapter Seven

Undergarments Are Vastly Overrated

Helene wasn't sure she could do it. It was one thing to stand half-naked in a small dressing room, with Esme, Monsieur Olivier, and Madame Rocque enthusiastically applauding. But it was quite another story to appear in public wearing a costume not much heavier than a nightrail. Although the bottom layer of rose silk was just slightly darker than the top, individually, each layer was transparent. Helene's entire body was on display. The silk was so fine that it clung and then swirled, just barely concealing her most private areas.

The only saving grace of the whole situation was that her mother was paying a visit to friends in Bath. Helene could just imagine her reaction to Madame Rocque's gown. She would have locked Helene in the wine cellar rather than let her be seen in such a state. This gown didn't hide her lack of breasts; it put that lack on display for all to see. Color rose in Helene's cheeks at the memory of the only person who had seen her unclothed, in her adult life. Her husband had laughed out loud the first time he saw her breasts.

Rees's laughter had been the beginning of a disastrous night. They were on their way to Gretna Green but had stopped at an inn, as Rees had pointed out that her father would never bother to chase them. Of course, he was correct. It wasn't every day that the heir to an earldom elopes with one's daughter, and Helene's father was likely swilling champagne at home while his daughter waited in a bedchamber, fairly trembling with adoration for her almost-husband.

She had waited, and waited, and waited. But Rees had apparently decided to loiter in the tavern, and when he finally appeared in her doorway, he had to catch himself against the door frame so as not to fall down. She had giggled, thinking it all romantic. There was nothing Rees could do wrong: not this big, beautiful man who thought about music as much as she did. When he kissed her, Handel's arias exploded in her mind, aching, arching waves of sound stretching to the very tips of her fingertips.

Well, if their kisses were Handel, then the actual bedding was naught more than a Beggar's Opera. Because Rees pulled off her gown and then fell about laughing, finally asking whether her breasts had evaporated in the last rain. By an hour later, it was clear to her that the rest of her body was as unsuited to matrimony as was her chest. Helene dismissed the memory with a little shudder.

Saunders, Helene's personal maid, obviously didn't know what to make of her mistress's transformation. At the moment she was bustling about folding clothing, but she kept stealing glances over her shoulder. "Would you like me to make some nice curls in your hair, my lady?" she said now, waving a curling iron. "We could wrap a bandeau around your head and with just a few curls, it would look quite, quite—" Saunders couldn't bring herself to say *fashionable*. The fashion was for ringlets bobbing around one's ears, and Lady Godwin didn't have enough hair for even one ringlet.

Helene smiled and seated herself at her dressing table. "I like my hair as it is, thank you. Saunders, do we have any rouge?"

"No, my lady."

Helene bit her lower lip. Her cheeks were the color of a frightened ghost.

57

"Mrs. Crewe has a large collection," Saunders added. "Would you like me to fetch it?"

"Mrs. Crewe?" Helene said, picturing her mother's starchy housekeeper. "I don't believe I've ever seen Mrs. Crewe wearing face paints!"

"She confiscates them from the maids," Saunders explained. "No one is allowed to use paints in the house, of course. Once in a blue moon, when she's in a good mood, Mrs. Crewe takes out the basket and allows the downstairs maids to play about in the evening. Not that I've done so for years." Saunders had developed a strong sense of her dignity when she was promoted to personal maid five years ago.

A few moments later Saunders plumped a large wicker basket on the floor. "Oh my," Helene said, fascinated. She picked up a small tin box.

"Chinese colors," Saunders said importantly. "Too dark for you, my lady." She burrowed in the basket. "If I remember correctly, there's a box of red sandalwood in here. That Lucy, who only lasted a few weeks before she was let go for stealing Mrs. Crewe's own brooch, she had it. Likely nimmed it from her previous mistress, unless I'm much mistaken." Saunders held out a round box, enameled all over with pansies.

"The box is very pretty," Helene said uncertainly.

"I'll use a little on your cheeks," Saunders said. "We'll use the darker one, the Chinese colors, for your lips. And here's black frankincense. We can darken your lashes with this, and your eyebrows as well."

"My goodness, Saunders," Helene said, smiling at her maid. "I had no idea that you had so much facility with face paints."

Saunders was standing back and looking at her work. "I'm that used to seeing braids atop your head," she said slowly.

"But shorter hair does make you look years younger. Everyone said so, below stairs."

"That's good," Helene said, cheered.

Saunders was expertly sweeping frankincense onto a brush. "Tomorrow you might wish to go to that perfumer, Henry and Daniel Rotely Harris, where all the ladies go. They'll make up colors just for you."

"Goodness," Helene said rather faintly, "I had no idea that was a possibility."

Saunders began wielding the tiny brush around Helene's eyebrows. Helene had to admit that the change was very dramatic. Her brows suddenly appeared as high arches, emphasizing her eyes.

"Now your lashes, my lady," Saunders said. "If you would just close your eyes, please."

Helene obediently did just as she said, and then almost gasped when she opened them again. Her ordinary gray eyes had been transformed into jewels: they looked green and seductive, like mermaid's eyes. And instead of her cheekbones sticking out like those of a hungry beggar, a delicate wash of color emphasized the heart-shaped triangle of her face.

"Oh, Madam," Saunders said, sounding awed by her own work. "You look ravishing!"

"Thanks to you," Helene said, smiling. She *could* do this. The face paints helped. The timid, skinny woman who wrote waltzes and was never asked to dance them was hidden behind the colors on her face. The pale, timid Helene who had cried when her young husband laughed at her breasts was behind a mask. *This* Helene had impudent, seductive eyes. This Helene wouldn't care a bit that her husband preferred women with udders rather than breasts. She walked across the room and the delicious feeling of thin silk made her feel like dancing. There was something about the way the silk caught between

59

her legs as she walked and then swirled away that made her feel far more naked than when she rose from her bath.

It remained for her to take herself, her gown, and her determination to have a child . . . and let events take their natural course. Because Esme had promised, nay had sworn up and down, that the gown would do all the work and Helene could simply choose a father for her child from a bevy of suitors. And for the first time, Helene began to believe her. Courage rose in her. Men would like the way she looked.

"Will you wear the diamonds tonight?" Saunders enquired.

"I believe my rubies would suit this gown." Helene never wore the rubies set because they had belonged to her late mother-in-law, and she herself had never really felt like Countess Godwin . . . but the color would be perfect. The rubies settled around her neck with a delicious rosy glow. Saunders put ruby drops in her ears. Helene almost laughed with the surprise of seeing her own reflection, even as Saunders fastened rubies around her wrist. Could this glowing, beautiful woman be *her*, Helene?

At that moment there was a knock and Esme tumbled into the room. "Hello, darling! I've just come to—" she said and stopped.

There was a moment of extremely gratifying silence. Then:

"You are not to come within two feet of my Sebastian, do you hear? Not within *two feet*!" Esme squealed.

Helene made a little pout. It was the most delicious thing in the world to pout with cherry red lips, rather than her own pale pink mouth. "But Sebastian *must* dance with me at least once. We are attending the ball together, after all, and he's so handsome."

Esme was laughing. "I think not, my girl. I'm not letting him anywhere near you. However," she took a list from her reticule, "here are a few men with whom you *may* dance."

Helene dismissed Saunders. The last thing she wanted was the entire servants' quarters enjoying the contents of Esme's list, let alone discovering the reason for its existence.

Esme, meanwhile, had thrown herself into a chair and taken off her slippers. "It is so distressing," she said, revolving her slender foot in the air. "These slippers are deliriously beautiful but they already hurt, and I've only been in them for an hour or so. I shall have to dance barefoot, and that will offend Sebastian's sensibilities."

"I thought your husband was a reformed man, and no longer had any sense of proprieties," Helene said rather absentmindedly. And then, without waiting for an answer: "Esme, are you out of your mind? I can't lure Lord Guilpin into my bedchamber. The man is obviously searching for a wife. I myself saw him in Almack's the other week. The last thing he wants to do is dally with an aging, married woman!"

"*You* are no aging, married woman," Esme said. "You are about to be revealed as the most desirable woman in all London. And I like Guilpin's looks. Those gray eyes are very taking, don't you think?"

"I never gave his eyes the slightest thought."

"Well, you'll have to do so now," Esme said. "To my mind, Guilpin is tired of looking for a wife. We're well into the season, so he's seen all the young women being presented. More to the point, he's not dancing attendance on any of them, which means that he's quite likely to dance attendance on you instead. All three men on that list are debauched enough to lure you into a chamber at the ball and do what comes naturally to them. And each of them is both intelligent and reasonably good-looking. That way, your child won't be born hunchbacked or hare-brained."

"I don't care very much about looks," Helene noted. "More important is that he know something of music.

Just imagine if my child wasn't musical!" She looked horrified.

"Any child lucky enough to have you as a mother will undoubtedly end up horse-mad and unable to sing a note," Esme said, laughing.

Helene was still looking at the list, and she had begun to laugh as well. "Garret Langham? You mean the Earl of Mayne? The very idea of Mayne trying to tempt me into a side chamber is ludicrous. Half the women in London would like to bed him!"

"And the other half already have," Esme said smugly. "I being one of them. So I can tell you that Mayne's aristocratic nose is echoed with becoming size in other parts of his body, *and* he knows what he's doing."

"He's predatory," Helene moaned. "I couldn't allow such a thing!"

"Why on earth not? Mayne may be a wee bit rapacious, but I have only the most ravishing memories of our night together. And darling," she said, slipping her foot back into her slipper, "obviously poor Rees is a bungler in the bedroom. A night or two with Mayne and you'll feel entirely different about the whole experience of bedding. I'm quite certain he's very red-blooded. My mother-in-law informed me that red blood is the trick to conception, and she seems to know that sort of thing."

"Everyone is red-blooded," Helene told her, wondering if she should slip the little box of sandalwood into her reticule. If there was even a chance that Mayne would approach her, she would need ruby-colored lips for courage.

"There are matters of degree, I suppose," Esme told her vaguely. "Well, at any rate, Mayne may be a libertine, but he's not overly dissipated, and he happens to be between attachments. The very moment he sees you in that gown, he'll be dragging you into the library." She smiled fondly. "If I remember correctly, it was a library."

"Esme, you're married to Sebastian. You oughtn't to be sighing romantically over Mayne!"

"Of course I'm married to my darling Sebastian," Esme said with a wicked grin. "And I have every intention of dragging my libertine husband into a library if the opportunity presents itself. But marriage hasn't damaged my memory." She stood up and readjusted her bodice before the mirror.

"Mayne would never consider me." He was like a bird of prey—beautiful, untamable, and far above her head. Helene shook off the thought. She wouldn't want such an uncomfortably sensual companion. "You look absolutely lovely!" she said, looking at Esme in the mirror. "If only I looked like you, this whole escapade would be simple."

"This is the gown that you discarded," Esme said rather smugly. "I had it made up in violet. It only arrived this afternoon, but Sebastian was quite gratifyingly dumbstruck when I tried it on."

"I have no doubt," Helene said. Esme's black curls tumbled down in such a way that they promised to cover the lush expanses of breast barely confined by her gown, although they didn't quite do it. She looked back at the list. "Why on earth is Rees on your list?"

Esme wound her arm around Helene's waist and met her eyes in the mirror. "For practicality's sake. It would be considerably easier if you had a child with your own husband. I know Rees is an uncomfortable companion, and even worse, he's inept between the sheets. But should Rees show the inclination to drag you into a side room, you might want to give it some thought."

"You're out of your mind!" Helene said, shaking her head. "He would never consider such a thing, even if he were at the ball. Lady Patricia Hamilton is giving this ball for her daughter's debut, if you remember. Persons such as Rees and his inamorata won't be welcome!"

"The opera singer certainly is not," Esme said, "but Rees is. I asked Lady Hamilton to send him a card." She decided not to mention that she had also sent Rees a separate note.

Helene was frowning at her. "I may have jested about wishing to attract Rees, but truly, I was just funning. He's likely to burst with laughter when he sees me in this gown!"

"Now that," Esme said with satisfaction, "I truly doubt. He might puff up, of course, but it won't be a matter of humor."

Helene rolled her eyes. "Your puns grow worse and worse, Esme. Rees and I are *married*. Rees has never shown the faintest interest in what I wear, and the idea that he might drag me off to a side chamber in a surfeit of passion is laughable! In fact, I haven't heard of many husbands who have inclinations in that direction."

"My husband does," Esme said. "And we'd better return downstairs, Helene. I'm not sure that Sebastian and your Major Kersting have much to talk about, since Sebastian is not fond of opera."

Helene let Esme walk down the stairs before her. Only a deranged woman would stroll through a door arm in arm with Esme. She lingered for a moment and looked at herself in the hallway mirror. A fire of determination went up her spine. She *could* do this.

She heard the low rumble of Esme's husband, Sebastian, asking a question, and the quieter voice of her escort, Major Kersting, answering. If she didn't walk through the door, she was betraying all her dreams of having a child. She was dooming herself to living with her mother for years to come. More years. They had already lived together for eight years of her married life.

Helene straightened her back (which caused her breasts to point forward, she couldn't help noticing), and marched through the door.

Chapter Eight

Of Cravats

Number 15, Rothsfeld Square

"He's at it again," Rosy shrieked, bursting into the butler's pantry. "Uncle John, the master called me a bad name!"

John Leke, butler to Earl Godwin and uncle to Rosy, looked up from the silver he was polishing. "There's names and names," he said. "The master may be one screw short of a dozen, but he's not ill-tempered. What did he call you?"

"Hell-begotten brat," Rosy said rather triumphantly. "And Mum said that I wasn't to stay in this position if I heard anything low. So I think I would do best to leave the house immediately."

"Why'd the earl call you such a thing?"

Rosy pursed her lips. "I needn't give any notice, Uncle John, not after such an objectionable thing was said to me. It's bad enough that I'm working in a house of *sin*, but to take abuse is more than a person such as myself need endure!"

Leke had known his niece since she was a mere bantling, and he took her dramatics with a grain of salt. Moreover, he and Rosy's mum had agreed that Rosy was a headstrong girl, and the better for working under her uncle's eye. "Now what did you do? I'm guessing that you earned the phrase the earl called you. What was it again?"

"Hell-begotten brat!"

"Nothing that I haven't thought myself," Leke said, eyeing her. Rosy was just fifteen, but her bouncing ringlets and saucy manners had started to bring entirely too much attention for her own good. The sooner they found her a solid husband, the better. "Rosy?"

Her pout turned sulky. "It's the master's own fault for not hiring enough staff."

"I'm in charge of hiring the staff," her uncle pointed out. "If we don't have many, it's because I won't hire the ones who aren't straight, and the others don't want to work in this house."

"Well, I burned his neck cloth, ironing it," Rosy said in a rush. "But if he had a proper valet, I wouldn't have had to go near an iron!"

"Bring him another cloth, girl. Step to it."

"There aren't any more!" Rosy moaned.

"What do you mean, there aren't any more? The man has at least five cravats. Mind you, in a proper household, he'd have upwards of two dozen."

"I ruined them," Rosy admitted.

"You ruined them *all*?"

"Honestly, Uncle John, I didn't know I was doing it! You know how untidy he always looks. I thought I'd better starch them. I did it just as mama does, with a cloth over them. Course the iron was sizzling hot, but I was thinking about not burning myself, and there was a terrible amount of steam, and then I don't like the smell of starch, so I just rattled through them as fast as I could—"

"You burned them *ALL*?" her uncle roared.

"They aren't exactly burned," Rosy protested. "The starch just put yellow streaks . . ."

But Leke was already bounding up the servants' stairs. He found the earl seated on a chair by the fire, scribbling on a piece of paper. He was tapping his finger against the armrest, looking as balmy as a breadbasket.

Leke gave a silent sigh of relief. Godwin didn't show signs of being driven mad by Rosy's ironing. "I am distressed to hear that your neck cloths have suffered an injury due to my niece's inept ironing, my lord," he said, bowing.

Godwin looked up, pulling his hand through his hair. He must have been dressing for the evening when he discovered the loss of his cravats; at any rate, he was wearing pantaloons. "Never mind about that," he said with his sudden smile. "My fault for not wanting a valet around the place, fussing with my clothes. Likely my neck cloths should go out of the house for laundering along with Lina's clothing. Could you send Sims out to buy a few more?"

"I'm afraid that the Christian & Sons have closed their doors for the night," Leke observed. It was at moments like these that he remembered why he hadn't yet deserted Earl Godwin, even when the rest of the household staff had fled like fleas from a dying dog. The man lived an irregular life, and one could not approve of the fancy piece living in the countess's quarters. But there was something disarming about Godwin, and he was far more reasonable when it came to household crises than many a gentleman Leke could bring to mind.

Rees grunted. "Well, if they're all closed, perhaps you could just pick out the least singed of those cloths, Leke. I can't say it really matters much to me."

Hell-born brat, indeed, Leke thought, turning over the cravats. Had Rosy confessed her ironing failures immediately, he could have bought more cravats, and no one the wiser. Instead, here was the master going out for the evening, and nothing to wear but yellowed cravats.

"I believe, sir, that if you tie a Mathematical with this pale pink cravat, the discolored starch will be inconspicuous.

And may I offer my deepest apologies for this deplorable event?"

"Don't give it a second thought," Godwin said. "Does it have to be the pink one? I feel like a man-milliner in it."

"The white cloths are beyond use," Leke admitted. "I shall obtain new cravats at first light tomorrow."

"Right." Godwin bounded up from his chair and threw the cravat around his neck. Far from tying a Mathematical, he merely pulled it into a rough knot.

Leke restrained himself. He was no gentleman's gentleman; he was a butler. "Will Miss McKenna join you this evening?" he asked, backing toward the door as Godwin wrenched on a tailcoat in a russet color that clashed abominably with his pink cravat.

"No," Godwin said, folding up the paper he was working on and sticking it into the pocket of his waistcoat. "I'm off to Lady Hamilton's ball for her daughter."

No more needed to be said. The strumpet (as Alina McKenna was known to the staff) obviously wouldn't be welcomed by Lady Hamilton. Leke bowed and retreated back to the butler's quarters. But he was burning with curiosity.

Why was Rees Godwin attending a ball being given for a debutante? Could it be that he was the girl's godfather? Surely they would have heard something of that in the past.

"You *are* a hell-born brat," he told his niece severely. "I'm docking your wages to pay for those cravats, girl, and you're lucky to be a family member or I'd have you out the door in a twinkling!"

Rosy scowled but kept her silence. Neither the earl nor her uncle had noticed the little brown tinges around the cuffs of Lord Godwin's shirts, and she didn't want to push her luck.

Chapter Nine

Of Great Acts of Courage

Lady Hamilton's Ball
Given in Honor of Her Daughter Patricia
Number 41, Grosvenor Square

There are moments of great bravery in every woman's life. Helene had gathered from her friends that childbirth was one of those. She herself had exhibited a remarkably stupid form of bravery at age seventeen, when she agreed to elope with the heir to the Godwin earldom. But other than that one foolish act, there had been little cause for courage in her life. Until tonight.

Helene was fairly sure that there was no moment more terrifying in her entire life than when she removed her pelisse and handed it to one of Lady Hamilton's footmen. There she was: practically undressed in the antechamber of the house. The door behind her swung open and a crisp breeze went straight through two layers of silk. She could feel the chill all over her body, even parts which normally never felt a draft, such as her bottom. There was only one thing to be done, and that was to brazen it out.

Sebastian Bonnington put a hand under her elbow and said "Courage!" in his deep voice. Then he gave her a look of such deep appreciation that Esme elbowed him and said laughingly, "Isn't it lucky that I already warned Helene to stay away from you?"

But then Sebastian turned from Helene to Esme, and the look in his eyes when he looked at his beautiful wife was far more potent than mere appreciation. He dropped a kiss on her lips that was so indicative of passion that Helene turned pink. Just seeing it stirred envy in her heart and an odd winkling feeling in her stomach.

They were announced by Lady Hamilton's butler. Helene had the distinct feeling that she was an imposter, and as such, she should have a new name. Was she really still Lady Godwin, the prim, contained Lady Godwin who was just announced? But at first, no one seemed to notice any difference. Lady Hamilton was frazzled by the stress of her daughter's first ball; she smiled at Helene's hair and whispered a compliment, but didn't notice her gown.

But little by little, the news spread. It was almost as if she could see it rippling through the ballroom. Helene solemnly paced through a country dance with Major Kersting. He and she, who had always been so comfortable with each other in the past, were quite the opposite now. He kept fingering his narrow mustache, and when they were greeted by three gentlemen at the close of the music, he fled with a look of extreme relief.

Helene had never had more than one aspirant for a dance at the same time. The thrill of seeing three gentlemen before her went to her head like midsummer wine. None of the three were on Esme's list, alas. Moreover, Lord Peckham was out of the question. The man was married, although he preferred to ignore the fact, and she would never be party to causing Lady Peckham the distress that she herself had suffered due to her husband's infidelities. She raised a cool eyebrow at him and accepted the hand of Lord Ussher. He was a bit younger than she would have liked, but perhaps that meant his blood was redder.

But by the end of their dance, she had quite decided against Lord Ussher. For one thing, he had sweated through his gloves, and his touch was unpleasantly damp. For another, he appeared to be quite overcome by her gown; he kept glancing down and then wrenching his eyes back to her face as if he were a starving man faced by an apricot tart. *Tart* being the appropriate word, Helene thought with some amusement. But the truly crucial thing was that he was unable to follow the music, and trod on her toes several times.

When the music stopped, instead of three gentlemen asking for her hand, there were *seven*. They crowded around her, brown-eyed, blue-eyed, young and old: surely Mr. Cutwell was far too old? Helene smiled at them all, trying desperately to remember what she had heard about each. Did anyone here have an affinity for music? How would she know if they did? Presumably the only way to tell was to dance with each, and assess his ability to keep from stepping on her toes.

She put out her hand more or less at random. Some minutes later, she returned from dancing with the Honorable Gerard Bunge to find that the crowd that surrounded her now rivaled any that had ever surrounded Esme, even at the very height of her popularity as Infamous Esme. But this time it wasn't so difficult to choose a partner. For as she smiled at the circle, acknowledging their bows with the smallest inclination of her head, Garret Langham, the Earl of Mayne, effortlessly brushed the other men aside without even seeming to notice them.

Mayne had never paid Helene the least attention. Yet now he walked toward her as if they'd known each other their entire life. He looked the epitome of a London buck: his hair brushed into a perfect tumble of curls, his pantaloons sleekly following the line of muscled thighs, his eyes alive with a wicked combination of laughter and desire. "Lady Godwin," he said easily, holding out his hand. "I believe this is our dance."

To Helene's utter surprise, rather than babbling agreement, she found herself raising an eyebrow and looking him over from his hair to his glossy boots. It was a look that she had seen Esme give various gentlemen, and never thought to use herself. But it seemed to come naturally to a woman surrounded by men, all of whom were clambering, nay panting, for the same thing. A dance. Or (insisted Helene's common sense), a chance to lure her into a side chamber.

Mayne seemed unbothered by her survey, just waited with a little smile playing around his mouth, as if he had always known that they would be partnered, and he had merely waited for her to discard her corsets before telling her.

The thought hardened Helene's heart. He thought he could just *have* her, did he? Well, he could. But on her terms.

She stepped forward, and silk embraced her legs. The other men seemed to melt away. "Lady Hamilton has an exquisite Broadwood piano," she said, giving him a provocative smile from Esme's repertoire. Goodness knows, she'd spent enough of her time in the past six or seven years watching Esme seduce gentlemen. "Would you accompany me to the music room? I should like to play . . . *a tune.*" She lowered her eyes and watched him through her eyelashes.

He didn't show even a flicker of surprise. "That would be my pleasure," he said, holding out his arm.

Really, men were absurdly easy to seduce, if that was the right word. Last spring, she had invited Mr. Fairfax-Lacy into her bedchamber merely by reading a poem. Of course, the whole event hadn't turned out exactly as she planned, but the invitation itself was effortless.

Mayne was just as amenable as Mr. Fairfax-Lacy. They strolled into the music room; he closed the door behind them; she leaned against the polished wood of the Broadwood piano.

Surely he would lunge at her directly? But no, he strolled over to the sideboard and poured them each a glass of wine.

As he handed it to her, he said, "Lady Godwin, you are quite ravishing in that gown."

She said, "Thank you."

And he began kissing her. It was all quite effortless, really.

Five minutes later, he drew a teasing finger down her neck and stopped just at the edge of her bodice. It felt white-hot, as if his very finger blazed a trail on her skin. Helene drained her glass of wine, and Mayne promptly poured her another. Then he put his finger in the glass and put it back on her throat. Helene could feel her eyes growing wider as his wet finger slid across her skin, inside the frail silk of her bodice.

"I should very much like to escort you home," he said, his eyes blazing down into hers.

"Home?" Helene repeated. She was having trouble paying attention. One part of her was absolutely enthralled by his games with the wine. The other side of her (alas for her practicality!) was hoping that he wouldn't stain the silk. She wanted to wear this gown again.

"Yes, home," Mayne said, smiling down at her. "Your home or mine."

Helene gulped. She didn't want to take the man home, for goodness' sake! Didn't he realize that he was supposed to get the job done here and now? "Absolutely not," she snapped, and then realized she didn't sound very agreeable. So she put her hands on her hips and gave him one of Esme's curling, seductive smiles. "Why don't you just kiss me again instead?"

His eyebrow went up. "Why, Lady Godwin, you are growing more surprising by the moment," he murmured, bending to her lips.

74

Of course, he immediately started plunging about with his tongue. Helene had never liked that sort of kiss. To be honest, it reminded her of the marital act, and both things were just far too intimate for her. But she had to admit that Mayne seemed to be better at it than Rees ever was. His tongue felt rather delicate and enquiring, rather than bullishly trampling. Naturally, he wished to continue kissing long past when she, Helene, would have closed her mouth and moved on to other things. Her mind started wandering. What was it that Esme said she must do? *Be encouraging, show enthusiasm, and be intimate.* Intimate must mean use of his Christian name. Helene ran her hand up Mayne's shoulder and gasped, "You're so marvelous, Gerard!"

"Garret," he murmured. "And you, Lady Godwin, are a very interesting bundle of womanhood indeed." His hand was running down her back to her—to her bottom! Helene almost jumped out of her skin.

"No corset," he murmured against her cheek.

She shook her head.

"No chemise?" he suggested.

She shook her head again.

"A package wrapped just as I most like them," he murmured, and captured her mouth again. Helene stifled an inward moan. Wasn't he ever going to be done with the kissing? And, "Do call me Helene," she said, once she managed to get some air in her lungs. "Shouldn't you lock the door?"

"In a moment," he said. His hands were stroking her back. It felt rather as if he believed her to be a cat: up and down, his hand sliding against the sleek silk. Helene had to admit that it felt quite nice. Although he did end up touching her bottom quite a few times. The caress made her feel rather wiggly and pleasant, rather than outraged. She took advantage of a moment's pause to gulp her second glass of wine.

Really, she was quite getting into the spirit of the thing now, she thought rather dazedly. He kept kissing her ear. Well, nibbling it really. And although the thought of such an action wasn't very enticing, Helene felt it was something she could definitely live with. If only ear-nibbling gave one a child!

Time to give him some more encouragement. If he were as slow with the rest of it as he was with the kissing, she wouldn't get home until the wee hours of the morning. That was one thing she could say about her husband: he never wasted any time in the bed. "Gareth," she whispered into his ear, running a finger down the side of his cheek. He really did have a lovely lean cheek, and he smelled good too.

"Helene," he whispered back. "My name is Garret." There was something about the slightly husky tone of his voice that gave her the oddest feeling between her legs.

She was about to suggest that he hurry along, but she gasped instead. Because he scooped her up in his arms and carried her over to the couch in one long stride. A moment after that, she had almost forgotten that she wanted him to hurry. Because Garret, as it turned out, liked her breasts. Adored them, in fact. He said so, several times.

"They're perfect," he said, in his faintly husky accent. His hand ran over her bodice, again and again, shaping the silk against her nipple and running his thumb over it. Helene had to admit that it all made her feel most peculiar.

"Where is your accent from?" she said, and was surprised to hear her voice was slightly breathy.

"My mother was French," he replied. And then: "Helene, I believe it might be time to lock that door. Would you be agreeable if I were to do so?"

And Helene stared at him, knowing that her eyes were as big as saucers, and feeling that odd sparking queasiness between her legs, and whispered, "I would—yes, please, Garret."

He stopped for one second to kiss her again. Helene was thinking that perhaps kissing wasn't all *that* terrible, when there was a noise at the door and someone walked in.

"*Merde*," he said under his breath and pulled back. But he didn't seem terribly perturbed. "One moment, Cherie, and I will—" Mayne turned to look over the back of the sofa and his body stiffened.

"Who is it?" Helene said, wondering if she should stand up. She would be ruined anyway, once she had a child, so she couldn't bring herself to care overmuch about being caught kissing. Besides, as Esme said, half the women in the *ton* had kissed Mayne.

"Your husband," he said briskly, putting her on her feet. "Good evening, Lord Godwin," he said pleasantly. "Perhaps you were looking for your wife?"

And there was Rees, looking like an olive-skinned, brawling prizefighter in comparison to Mayne's sleek elegance.

"Yes, I was looking for her," Rees snarled. "I'd be grateful, if you'd give us a moment to speak before you add my wife to the list you keep nailed to your bedside table."

For a moment, Helene thought there would be a fight. The air in the room seemed to have vanished, and the menace on Rees's snarling face was matched by the potent fury on Mayne's. Then she blinked. She had almost forgotten that Rees had relinquished any claim to being her husband, that in fact he had virtually ordered her to find a consort. *It'll do you good*, wasn't that what he said?

She put a hand on Mayne's arm. "Will you give me a moment to speak to my husband?" she said, giving him a significant glance. "I will rejoin you in a moment."

Mayne had gone white with fury and looked even more amazingly beautiful. Rees's ancestry was just as ancient, but his face looked as if all his ancestors were farmers rather than courtiers. "I dislike the idea of leaving you with a man who may not be able to control his temper," Mayne said.

She gave him Esme's liquorish smile, and this time it didn't even feel like Esme's—it felt like *hers*. There was something in the smile that thanked him for the tingling feeling she had all over her body. Thanked him and welcomed it again. "My husband is of little concern to me," she said softly, but not so softly that Rees couldn't hear it. "Although I thank you for your concern."

Rees moved backwards with mocking gallantry as Mayne started for the door. But Mayne stopped just beside him. They were of a height, and oddly enough, although Mayne's rippling muscles were so much more in evidence because of his well-fitting clothing, they seemed to be of similar body weights as well. But the comparison ended there. The Earl of Mayne was dressed with a Gallic flare; his neck cloth, for example, was an exquisite snowy white, tied in a complicated fashion. Earl Godwin seemed to have knotted an old kitchen cloth around his neck; the outline of an overly hot iron was face out, for all the world to see.

"I suggest that you not exercise your temper overmuch," Mayne said, and the French tinge to his voice sounded truly dangerous now.

"The day I take orders from a dissolute frog like yourself is the day I go to my grave," Rees stated.

"I will excuse your passion on the grounds that you appear to have suddenly recognized that Lady Godwin is your wife," Mayne said with precision. "Although you have given very little sign of that in the past few years, and I believe you discovered it too late." Then he walked out.

Helene had to admit that it was a magnificent exit line. "What on earth are you doing?" she demanded of her husband. "You told me—"

"I know I told you to take a consort," Rees bellowed back at her. "I didn't tell you to spawn a child with one!"

"You know that I'm—*how do you know that?*" she cried.

"Your friend Esme was kind enough to inform me."

Helene felt a red-hot blaze of fury go up her body. Esme—Esme—had betrayed her? Esme, her closest friend in the world?

"I came to tell you that I won't allow it," Rees stated.

"You won't allow it," she said slowly.

"No. I won't allow it. You can't have thought clearly about the fact that any child you carry would become my heir. I can't allow that. Tom, or Tom's son, once he has one, will become the earl when I kick up my heels. I couldn't let a cuckoo take over the estate before Tom's child. It wouldn't be right."

"You're got nothing to say about it," Helene managed. Alarmingly, the fact that Esme had betrayed her was making her feel rather teary.

"I certainly do." Rees strolled over and locked the door. "I'd rather that people don't walk in on us at this moment, if you don't mind."

"I can't see that it matters," Helene said. Why had Esme done such a thing? She had been so close to having her baby, so close to success!

Rees was sitting down. "What are you doing?" she asked with patent scorn.

"Taking my shoes off," he said.

Helene's mouth fell open. "You cannot possibly think—"

"I certainly do. If I understood Lady Bonnington's message appropriately, you came to this ball precisely to find a man to act as stud for you. I'm as available as any other man in London, and a hell of a lot more in your style than the Earl of Mayne."

He pulled down his pantaloons and threw them to the side.

Chapter Ten

In Which Salome Begins Her Dance

The Yard at the Pewter Inn
Stepney, London

Reverend Thomas Holland, known as Tom to friends and parishioners alike, hadn't been in London for years, but it looked just the same: dirty, crowded, and wretchedly poor. It was early afternoon, but it might as well be stark night for all the sunlight that made it through the sooty air. He got off the mail-coach and stretched his limbs, ignoring the ground-shaking thumps near him as stableboys pulled pieces of luggage from the top of the coach and tossed them to the ground. Shrieks echoed off the wooden walls of the Pewter Inn as passengers protested the ramshackle treatment of their belongings. Tom didn't care. He was mostly carrying books, and they wouldn't break.

Someone tugged on his coat and he turned.

"Would you like to buy an apple, mister?"

She couldn't be more than five years old. She had on a grimy pinafore but her face was clean, and the little collection of apples she carried in a basket seemed to be clean, too. "Where's your mum?" he asked, squatting down before her.

She blinked. "Would you like to buy an apple?" she repeated.

"Yes, I would. Shall I give the money to your mother?" He took the apple. "How much is it?"

"Tuppence," she said, holding out a small hand for the payment. There was a bruise on her wrist.

This is why he didn't come to London. He simply couldn't bear it. "Damnation," Tom muttered to himself. "Where's your mother, Sweetheart?"

She looked away again. But Tom had some practice talking to children in the village; he took her hand and said, "Take me home, please."

She didn't move. "I don't go places with men."

"And you're absolutely right," he said, dropping her hand. "Going home is not the same as going *places*, though, is it?"

She thought about this for a moment. She had a sweet, rosy little face, although her eyes were terribly serious. Tom had a familiar feeling, as if his chest-bone were pressing into his stomach.

"I don't go home until I sells all my apples."

Tom got out four pence, for which he received two more apples. There was almost a smile in her eyes: almost. Then she started walking away, so he tossed all three apples to a stable-boy and asked him to keep an eye on his luggage. She didn't head out into the series of twisting little streets that surrounded the Pewter Inn, but straight around to the back and into the kitchen.

"I've told you not to come back in here until you've sold them all!" he heard someone say, as he pushed open the door.

A red-faced, middle-aged woman was standing in the middle of the kitchen floor, scowling down at the apple-seller.

"I did sell them all," the little girl said, giving the woman her money. "To him." She pointed at Tom.

The woman swung around and her face changed instantly from irritated to menacing. Tom almost took a step back, as she reached behind her and palmed an enormous rolling pin, as long and wide as his arm. "You get out of here," she ordered. "I've had your kind around here before, and we don't hold with them." She grabbed the girl and pulled her behind her apron. "Meggin is not going anywhere with you, no matter the money you offer!"

"I'm a vicar," Tom said, loosening his traveling cloak so that his collar showed. "I was merely worried about little Meggin being by herself in the posting yard."

"She's not by herself. The posting yard is safe enough. And I never heard that being a vicar stopped nobody from being wicked." Mrs. Fishpole had heard enough stories about the roguery of men in black to distrust the very sight of a collar.

"I'm not one of them, Madam. I'm from the North Country, though, and not used to seeing children as small as this earning their living. But obviously you are taking excellent care of Meggin, and I apologize for disturbing you."

Mrs. Fishpole narrowed her eyes. He was a good-looking man, for a vicar. Nice eyes, he had. "Whereabouts in the North Country?"

"Beverley, East Riding," Tom said cheerfully. The odd tightness in his chest was easing. "I've a small parish there. I'm only in London to visit my brother."

A huge smile spread across the woman's face. "Beverley, eh? I'm Mrs. Fishpole, Reverend, originally from Driffield meself, though I haven't seen it in years. So you must be in the Minster, isn't that what it's called? My dad took me to Beverley once when I was a youngster and we delivered a load of sand to the Minster. It's a beautiful church. I've never forgotten it. I do think that it rivals Paul's."

"Perhaps the sand was used when they were refurbishing the west transect," Tom said. "I'm actually not the reverend of the Minster, but of an adjoining parish, St. Mary's. Reverend Rumwald is the vicar of the Beverley Minster."

"Lord Almighty, is old Rumwald still alive, then?" Mrs. Fishpole's whole face had softened. "He taught me my catechism, he did. He used to come over to Driffield once a month, seeing as we didn't have a parish priest. Too small, we were."

"I'll give him your best," Tom said. "I'll tell him of your happy situation here, as cook in this excellent establishment. And about your lovely daughter as well." He smiled at Meggin but she looked away.

Mrs. Fishpole pursed her lips. "Meggin isn't my daughter. And she doesn't earn her living with these apples, either. I have to feed her from the servants' scraps."

"Meggin isn't your daughter?"

"No," Mrs. Fishpole said, pushing Meggin out from behind her skirts now that she seemed to be in no imminent danger. "Her mum was no better than she should be, I've no doubt. We found her here one night, all but set to have the child on me own kitchen doorstep. The poor woman didn't survive the birth, God bless her soul."

"In that case, Meggin is doubly lucky to have you," Tom said. "I shall have to congratulate Reverend Rumwald on how well he taught you the catechism."

But Mrs. Fishpole was looking at him like a dog that's found a string of sausages on a street corner. "And what if you had found Meggin in a bad situation, Reverend? What was you planning to do next?"

Tom hesitated. "I'm not certain."

"I expect you know of them charities, though, don't you?" she demanded.

"Something of them," Tom admitted, thinking that most of what he knew about London charities wasn't very cheerful.

"You take her!" Mrs. Fishpole said, giving Meggin a little push. The girl gasped and tried to dart behind her skirts again.

"What?"

"You'd better take her. She'll be better off in East Riding than here in London. We looked after our little ones, back home. Here, it's all I can do to keep her out of the way. And she's getting bigger, don't you see?"

"Yes, but—"

"You'll have to do it," Mrs. Fishpole said decisively. "I can't keep her safe anymore. She sleeps there, you see—" she nodded toward a heap of rags in the corner. "But she's getting on towards five now. I don't know how much longer they'll let her stay in the corner, and the older she gets, the more worry I have, to be honest."

Tom could see the truth of that.

"I've done my best with her. I've taught her thank you, and she's learned to say please as well. She knows the difference between right or wrong. I didn't want her turning out like her mum. So you can tell Rumwald that I did my charitable duty with her."

Meggin made another concerted effort to get behind Mrs. Fishpole's skirts and hide from Tom.

"It's not that I won't miss you," Mrs. Fishpole said, putting the rolling pin down on the counter and pulling Meggin around before her. "Because I will, Meggie. You know I will. You're a willing little girl, and you've always been cheerful."

Meggin was blinking very hard. "I don't want to go nowhere."

"You've never carried on and screamed the way some of them children do. But I can't keep you here, Meggie. It's not safe. And you know I can't take you home." She looked up at

Tom. "Meggin used to live with me, but Mr. Fishpole died three years ago, and I went to live with my sister-in-law. Her husband doesn't want to take in an orphan, not given the circumstances of her birth and all."

Tom nodded and held out his hand. "Meggin, would you like to come with me to visit my brother? And then after a visit, we'll go home to my village, and I'll find you a family of your own to live with." And between now and then, he swore to himself, I will not even *glance* at the children sweeping the streets.

"No!" Meggin wailed, big fat tears rolling down her cheeks. "I don't go home with no men, I don't! I belong with you, Mrs. Fishpole." She ran at the cook, butting her head against her legs and wrapping her arms around her skirts, just as a hosteller burst into the kitchen shouting something about a sausage and fish pie.

Mrs. Fishpole ignored him, kneeling down on the none-too-clean floor. "I'll come see my old da in East Riding, and I'll see you as well. But I can't let you sleep in the kitchen anymore, Meggie."

"No one will see me," Meggin wailed. "I'll stay so small. And I didn't talk to *him*, I didn't! I'll sell all my apples to ladies after this."

"We needs more sausage pies," the hosteller broke in. "You don't want as Mr. Sigglet to have to come here. You know he doesn't like the brat."

Mrs. Fishpole picked up Meggin and held her against her chest for a moment. Her jaw was set very firmly, and Tom had the impression she would never recover from the mortification if she let a single tear fall. "If I'd had a daughter, Meggie, I'd want her to be just like you," she said. "Now you go with the Reverend here because he'll keep you safe. I can see it in his face. I want you to grow up to be a good girl."

"I won't!" Meggin cried. "I wants to stay here!"

Mrs. Fishpole handed Meggin to Tom. "You'd best go," she said roughly. "She's the most biddable girl usually." For a moment her face crumpled and then she spun around and screamed at the hosteller: "Go on then! Fetch me a sausage pie from the pantry. What are you, crippled?"

Tom held the struggling little body close and walked out of the door to the accompliment of a howl of despair from Meggin, who was holding out her hands and struggling to get free.

"I don't want to go!" she cried. "I don't want to be a good girl. I want to be a cook, just like you, Mrs. Fishpole!"

And then, heartbreakingly, "*Please?*"

After listening to the pounding on the front door for a good ten minutes, Lina decided that Leke must have given the servants the evening off. Finally she traipsed downstairs dressed only in a French negligee, hoping that it would be one of Rees's more prudish acquaintances so that she could watch him dither with embarrassment.

She carefully arranged her negligee so that the lace bits showed off all her best assets and pulled open the door with a flourish.

But it wasn't anyone she'd seen before. A man dressed in a dusty black cloak was standing on the doorstep, clutching a sobbing child and accompanied by a sulky ostler with two boxes on his shoulder.

"Who the devil are you?" she demanded, knowing exactly who he must be. Rees only had one relative in the world, after all, and the man had Rees's nose and mouth. But Rees never said that his oh-so-proper brother was married, nor that he was encumbered with a child. And he certainly never mentioned that the man was paying them a visit.

87

"Thomas Holland," he said with a bow. "This is Meggin, and these are my boxes, as I've come to stay with my brother. More to the point, Madam, who are you?"

At that moment, the child, who had been eying Lina's negligee with her swollen eyes, said in a choking wail, "I knows who she is! She's the Whore of Babylon, she is! Mrs. Fishpole told me all about her. You's lied to Mrs. Fishpole, and taken me to a house of sin!" She started screaming as loud as she could and kicking Rees's brother in the leg.

Lina raised an eyebrow. This looked as if it might be a most complicated situation. She opened the door further and stepped back. "I gather the vicar is returning home," she said sweetly. "If I'm the Whore of Babylon, wouldn't I be dressed in scarlet and purple? Let me see . . . if I'm the Whore of Babylon, wouldn't that make *you* John the Baptist?" She giggled and turned to go upstairs. "I suppose you can choose whatever bedchamber you wish, although I have to tell you that they are not as clean as one might wish. And I haven't any idea about the condition of the nursery."

She kept walking as she climbed the stairs, raising her voice above Meggin's howls. "Rees will return sometime this evening, and until then you shall have to entertain yourself."

"Where are the servants?" Rees's brother asked, sounding desperate.

Lina ignored the question, pausing on her way up the stairs. "I may not be dressed for the part, but I just realized that I *do* know what the Whore of Babylon would sing. Popish hymns, wouldn't it be? That's what my father would have said. Alas, I don't know any, so this will have to do." And she burst into a magnificent rendition of *O God Our Help in Ages Past*.

Tom stared up at her, stupefied. Even Meggin stopped crying. The music rolled off the walls. She had the largest voice that Tom had ever heard, a gloriously rich, velvety, dangerous voice. At the very top of the stairs she paused and grinned down at him, looking the picture of a godless wench, her body softly gleaming through peach-colored silk, hair rippling past her shoulders, ruby lips laughing. "This is my favorite verse," she announced. "Do pay attention. *A thousand ages in thy sight are like an evening gone. Short as the watch that ends the night, before the rising sun.*" She turned and kept singing, the words falling to them like silken rain as she walked away down a corridor.

"Blimey!" the ostler muttered. "There's a cracked-brained one, for you. Bedlam, this is."

Tom stood absolutely still, staring up the stairs. He felt as if he'd been poleaxed. He could feel Meggin pulling at his hand, and he was aware that the ostler wanted to be paid for tossing his boxes to the ground. But the only thing he could think of was that girl's rosy mouth, and the way she laughed, and the way her voice flew all the way to the rafters of the dusty antechamber, and (God forgive him) the way her hips swayed in that peach-colored negligee.

Chapter Eleven
Marital Consummation

"Well, for God's sake, Helene, it's not as if you'd be doing it for pleasure. At least I won't give you a disease which, let me point out, is entirely possible if you dally with a Frenchman. Everyone knows that Frenchmen have the pox."

"Not Mayne," Helene said weakly. But in truth, she wasn't entirely sure what the pox was. It didn't sound pleasant.

Rees was down to his smalls now. "You get the pox from sleeping with the wrong sort of women," he said, quite as if he weren't unbuttoning his most intimate undergarments in Lady Hamilton's music room.

"I will *not* do this with you!" Helene hissed.

"Why not?"

"Because I don't wish to!"

"You can't tell me that you were looking forward to doing the deed with Garret Langham," Rees said reasonably. "He may be a very pretty man, but you and I both know that your body isn't really suited to this sort of thing, is it?"

To her utter fury, there was no way to interpret his look but as honest sympathy.

"I'm sorry that Fairfax-Lacy went off and married Beatrix Lennox," he continued. "But can you honestly tell me that you two were happy in bed?"

Helene swallowed. There was something even worse about

being comforted by one's husband than there had been in failing as a lover to Mr. Fairfax-Lacy.

"It's the devil and truly unfair," he was saying. "But don't you see, Helene? If you're that eager for a child, we might as well do the deed now and get it over with. At least it will be my child that inherits my estate. I couldn't make Mayne's child into an earl ahead of Tom's son."

Helene saw what he meant. She hadn't even remembered the existence of Rees's brother Tom. It wasn't fair to him.

"I'm not a very good earl," Rees said, "but damn it, I suppose you and I could make a child without too much trouble, and at least I would have done my duty."

Helene bit her lip. "Esme says it only takes one time," she heard herself say.

Rees put his hands on her shoulders. "Right. So would you mind giving up Mayne and allowing me to father the child instead?"

"All right," she said, swallowing. It was rather disappointing, but she knew perfectly well that once Mayne had reached a certain point, she wouldn't have liked it any more than she did with Rees, years ago. So what was the difference, really?

Then she realized that Rees was staring at her. "Your hair's gone," he said.

Helene tossed her head, and felt the pure glory of weightlessness again. "I cut it all off."

"And where did you get that gown? No wonder I found Mayne in here with you. That gown is a siren call to rakehells."

Helene resisted the impulse to cover her breasts with her hands. Mayne had said they were beautiful. "If you're going to laugh at my chest, why don't you get it out of the way immediately," she said coolly.

"I'm not," he said, his voice rather strangled with surprise.

91

Helene looked down at her gown. It was already crumpled by the exertions of the evening, so she needn't worry about taking it off and further exposing her inadequacies. "I suppose we might as well simply get it over with," she said, turning and walking back to the couch. "Are you going to remove your shirt?"

He followed her and stood looking at her as she lay down. "Are you certain that you wish to do this, Helene?"

She actually smiled. "Yes. I think you're right. It's such a relief not to have to pretend with you. I'm not going to enjoy this much, but I would be very, very grateful if we could make a child."

"I wish that wasn't the case for you," Rees said.

But Helene's eye had been caught by something else. "I'd forgotten that it was quite so large," she said faintly.

He blinked and looked down.

"Could we get this over as quickly as possible?" she said, feeling rather dizzy. She never liked pain.

Rees carefully lowered himself onto the couch. He didn't wear any kind of scent, unlike Mayne, who smelled faintly of some male fragrance. Rees was horribly careless about his style of dress, but he did bathe every day, and so there was always a combination of soap and, well, Rees.

He was just as heavy as she remembered. She wriggled a little in protest, and then gasped when she felt his hand between her legs. "What are you *doing*?"

"I just have to make sure—" his voice sounded very husky now. And his fingers—Helene gasped again. Little lightning strokes went down her legs. But then his fingers were gone and then he presented himself in their place.

He was braced on his hands, looking down at her. A lock of hair had fallen over his forehead. "I'll make this as fast as I possibly can, Helene. I'm sorry for the pain of it. I always was, you know."

"I know that," she whispered, tucking the hair back behind his ear. Rees wasn't all bad.

He started to push inside and Helene almost stopped him. But she bit her lip instead. Really, the fear was worse than the pain.

In fact . . .

In fact, the pain didn't really seem to be there. There was a feeling of stretching that wasn't entirely pleasant. But it wasn't really unpleasant either. He managed to push his way right to the back of her, and Helene couldn't help it; she wriggled again.

There was a scrabbling noise at the door and the door handle turned. Helene went rigid. She could hear a female voice raised in fury. "I'm certain that I left my reticule next to the harpsichord."

"I'm sorry, Madam"—that was surely the voice of Lady Hamilton's butler—"if you will just come this way for a moment, I will look for the spare key."

"Hurry up," she hissed at Rees.

"Does it hurt very much?" he asked, not moving.

"Not so very much," she said, riddled with anxiety. "Rees, do make haste! The butler will return in a moment with another key."

"No, he won't," Rees said, and there was a thread of amusement in his voice now. "He said that to warn us to leave."

"Well, let's comply shall we?" Helene snapped. There was something about having Rees *there*, between her legs, that gave her the oddest feeling. It wasn't anything she had ever experienced before. She felt edgy, as if she wanted to move against him, though what an odd thing that would be! Everyone knows that gentlemen do all the necessary moving.

"All right," Rees said, and he seemed to be talking between clenched teeth. "I hope this doesn't pain you too much, Helene."

"It's quite all right," she said. "Just—just . . ."

But she lost track of that thought. For he'd withdrawn and then pushed his way slowly back against her, and it did the oddest things to her stomach. It felt quite—well—it wasn't good exactly. Helene clutched his shoulders and felt a huge bulge of muscle as he braced himself and lunged forward again. It seemed to be going fairly easily now, as well as she could judge it.

The only problem was a slight burning sensation—probably friction, as when two ropes are pulled together. It must be because he was going so quickly. That must be it.

"Almost there, Helene," Rees said, "sorry," and the guttural sound of his voice did it again, gave her that odd liquid feeling in her legs, a feeling that made her want to buck up against him.

At that moment Rees positively lunged toward her and Helene couldn't help it, a little cry flew from her throat. It wasn't due to pain. Then she braced herself because she remembered quite well that he would flop on top of her like a beached whale and she would lose all the air in her lungs, but he didn't.

"Oh God, Helene, did it hurt that much?" he said a moment later, putting his lips on her forehead for a moment. "I heard you cry out."

"No," she said, feeling queerly as if she were going to weep. "It didn't."

"You needn't pretend. That's the one thing that makes me a better choice than Mayne, remember?"

But Helene didn't say anything. It hadn't hurt. She couldn't say what it did feel like. He seemed to have shrunk, though, which was good. Rees withdrew and then sat on the edge of the couch to draw his smalls back on. He ran a hand up her slender thigh. "You have beautiful legs, Helene," he said, almost absentmindedly.

Helene raised an eyebrow. He *liked* something about her? Probably that was because she had made the right decision to keep her gown on and her bosom covered so that he wasn't faced with those laughably small breasts of hers.

"Thank you very much for the compliment." It was all a bit embarrassing. "I think I would like to go home," she finally said.

He yanked her gown down over her legs. "Wait here, and I'll tell the butler to summon my coach."

He unlocked the door and walked into the hallway. Helene could hear him brusquely telling the butler to fetch his carriage, as his wife wasn't feeling well. His wife! How odd it felt to hear him use that word. But, to tell the truth, she'd never felt more of a wife.

Wives were taken home in fits of exhaustion by their husbands; wives knew the deep pleasure of thinking that they might be carrying a child . . . That night, Helene fell into bed with an ecstasy of happiness and anticipation.

Chapter Twelve

The Saint and the Sinner

"What in the devil's name are you doing here, Tom?"

Tom opened his eyes sleepily. He'd fallen asleep in the library, waiting for Rees to return home. "Came to visit you," he said, his words almost strangled by an enormous yawn.

"Well, you can take yourself home again tomorrow morning," Rees said with a ferocious scowl.

Tom had woken up by now and he watched his brother's back as Rees poured himself a glass of brandy.

"Do you want something to drink?" Rees tossed over his shoulder.

"No, thanks."

"How could I forget," Rees said, obviously between gritted teeth, "men of God don't drink or fornicate, do they?"

Tom bit back a rejoinder. It had taken him the five years since their father's death to decide that Rees wasn't going to visit him, so he would have to make the trip to London. But he'd forgotten what an utter bastard Rees could be when he wanted to. Which was generally when he was unhappy, as Tom remembered it.

"How's Helene?" he asked.

"Fine." Rees tossed off the brandy.

"Have you seen her recently?"

"Saw her tonight," Rees said, putting down the glass with a thump. "Actually, you'll like this, Tom, with all your sanctimonious views of matrimony. Helene's moving back to the house."

"I'm glad to hear it."

"I don't know if she will be," Rees said, turning around and giving Tom a wolfish grin. "I haven't told her yet. But I've decided to get myself an heir."

"An excellent provision."

"Since you look to be just as hen-hearted as you ever were," Rees said with brutal precision, eyeing Tom's collar. "I suppose you haven't done a thing about getting an heir for the estate. Unless you're planning to introduce me to a pious hymn-singing wife?"

Tom's muscles tensed and then he counted to ten. Just because their father delighted in pitting them against each other didn't mean that he had to play the game any longer. He couldn't tell from Rees's face whether he expected him to lose control, or not.

Instead, he rose. "I've taken the Yellow Bedchamber."

"How long are you planning to stay?" Rees asked, pouring himself another drink.

"As long as I wish to," Tom said with a flash of the old anger.

"Why did you come in the first place?"

"I'm staying until I find my brother again," Tom said evenly. "That would be the brother I had until I was ten years old. The brother I miss."

"I am your brother," Rees said, with a twist of his lips. "I can't say exactly when you turned into such a Holy Willie, but if you would put the transformation at ten years old, so be it."

Tom shook his head. "I became a priest at twenty-two, Rees. Ten years old is when our father first noticed me."

"Well, I'd prefer that you left," Rees said flatly. "Touching though I find your concern, it's going to be very tricky with

Helene back in the house. I'd rather do the straight and narrow without my moralistic little brother poking his nose into everything."

Tom felt a slow burn in his chest and managed to count to seven. "I have never questioned your life. If you hear reprimands in your ears, they come from Father, not from me. And he *is* dead, Rees. You could stop trying to get his attention any day now. He hasn't the faintest idea that you have an opera singer living in Mother's bedchamber."

There was a chilly moment of silence and then Rees laughed, except it sounded more like a bark than a laugh. "It must be enviable to understand the world in such a clear fashion, Tom. I never think about the old man anymore. Lina lives with me because I want her to. And she lives in Mother's bedchamber because it's convenient to mine."

Tom snorted. "She lives here because you're still trying to make Father spit fire and actually look at you. But the man is dead."

"I like Lina," Rees said softly, rolling her name off his tongue like a delectable sweet. "I gather you met her. And what did *you* think of her, little brother? Isn't she a luscious bit of goods?"

"Are you planning to toss her out the door tomorrow to make room for Helene?" Tom asked, not trying very hard to keep censure from his voice.

"That's the way of the world." Rees shrugged.

"Where will she go?"

"A dissolute man like myself doesn't worry himself with trifles, does he? Probably to the streets, brother. That way, if you were very lucky, you could whisk her off to some charitable home for wayward ladies."

"Your attempts to bait me are a poignant reminder of how much Father meant to you," Tom observed.

Rees narrowed his eyes. "So do give me the churchman's views. What *does* one do with a discarded mistress? Wait! I wasn't supposed to commit adultery, was I? How could I forget that little detail?"

Tom turned toward the door. "I imagine you know precisely where your Lina will go after you turn her out. I can't think why we need to discuss it." He paused and grappled with his temper for a moment. And lost. "I don't know how you can live with yourself, debauching a girl like that."

"I continue to do my best to live up to my family reputation. As do you. Couldn't you take that infernal dog collar off even when you were making a trip to the big bad city?"

"I *am* a vicar," Tom said, shrugging.

"I suppose if you removed the collar, you'd lose the authority to hand out moralities like sweets at Christmas, would you? I wouldn't want all that talent of yours to be wasted." Rees's eyes would have set the room on fire, were it physically possible. "I've just changed my mind, and it's all due to you, brother. I'll keep that poor debauched girl here even when Helene returns. She can stay in Mother's bedroom, where she belongs. I need Lina close enough so that I can tup her at a moment's notice, wouldn't you say?"

Tom paused, hand on the doorknob. He could hardly speak, he was so angry. "And Helene?" he managed. "Your wife? I thought you planned to *get an heir*, brother."

"I shall," Rees said casually. "I'll put Helene on the third floor, up where the nursery is. That will nicely symbolize her role in the household."

Tom yanked open the door and stalked out. He doesn't mean it, he thought. He can't mean it. He's just unable to be himself. Damn Father. And when the Reverend Holland brought himself to use a word like damn, he really meant it.

Tom managed to make it into the hall and start up the stairs without going back and throwing himself at Rees until they hit the ground in a rolling pile of fisticuffs, which was exactly what his brother wanted him to do. Rees was never any good at talking out grievances; he preferred to rush into action. It was Tom who had given Rees his broken nose; Rees who had blackened Tom's eye not once but three times.

And it was their father who applauded from the sidelines, feeding the fire with judiciously placed little barbs that pitted his godly and his ungodly son against each other. Except they weren't that, they were never that.

I never wanted to be the godly one, Tom told himself. Not if it was at the expense of my big brother, who had to become my opposite.

He stuck his head into the nursery and looked in on Meggin. He hadn't been able to get her onto a bed. Finally he had given her a sheet and she had arranged it into a nest in the corner. She seemed to be sleeping peacefully, so Tom returned to his own room with a sigh. If things were different, he could have been the one nestled up to a songbird like Lina.

He couldn't quite imagine it. Dog collar or no dog collar, a woman like that would never want him.

Chapter Thirteen

An Odd Household, Indeed

Rees stamped his way down to breakfast in a fit of irritation. Tom had to be booted from the house directly. The maddening comments he had made the previous evening stuck in Rees's mind like a burr. Rees actually found himself up in the middle of the night, wondering whether Lina's presence in his house had anything to do with their dead father, until he decided that Tom, as usual, was being overdramatic. Reading had addled his brother's brain, or so their father always— Father! What on earth was he doing even thinking of the man?

He pushed open the door to the breakfast room with a snap and then stopped short. Lina was sitting at the head of the table. Thank goodness, she appeared to have decided to dress herself this morning, instead of appearing in negligee, as was her custom. Even more startling, next to Tom was a small girl who looked to be his image.

"You didn't tell me that you had a child!" he said, staring at the girl and then at his brother. She had precisely the same sweet expression as had Tom when he was a boy. They were two of a kind; Tom had obviously sprouted a hymn-singing four-year-old, if there was such a thing. His mind spun: Tom, father of an illegitimate child?

"This is Meggin," Tom said, his hand touching the child's head for a moment. "She's not my daughter."

Meggin looked up at Rees. "I belongs to Mrs. Fishpole."

"Belong," Tom corrected her.

Of course. Meggin must be one of Tom's strays. It was always animals when he was young; one might have guessed that he'd move past livestock once he became a vicar. Rees walked into the room, nodding at Leke to give him a plate of coddled eggs.

"You have an excellent cook," Tom said cheerfully.

"I gather you have met my brother?" Rees asked Lina, dropping into a chair to her right. She nodded around a piece of dry toast. She must have decided to go on a thinning plan again, a move he usually deplored because it turned her into a shrew. Truthfully, though, if you compared Lina's and Helene's bodies, Lina did look a bit overly round. Not lumpish, exactly, but her waist must be twice the size of Helene's.

Rees had always thought that it was best to get over rough ground as lightly as possible. Brutal honesty had generally worked for him in the past, although not, he had to admit, with any consistency during his marriage. "I'll be bringing Helene back to the house later," he announced, without fanfare. Then he forked up some eggs.

"You can't have really meant what you said last night?" Tom said slowly.

Lina had dropped her toast. "Helene, your wife?" she gasped.

Rees would have felt a pulse of guilt, but he saw a fugitive gleam of excitement in her eyes. If he had been tired of Lina, she seemed to be positively blue-deviled with boredom. She would likely adore the idea of returning to the opera house with a large settlement in hand. He was perfectly well aware that he had been just as disappointing from Lina's point of view as he was from Helene's.

102

"I'm not putting you out," he said, taking another bite of eggs. When he was finished, he looked at Lina. "You won't even have to move rooms. Helene will stay on the third floor, in the room next to the nursery."

"I was planning to put Meggin in the nursery," Tom said. He shook his head. "What am I saying? Helene will never agree to this absurd plan!"

The memory of his wife's anguished face saying that she wanted a child—and a similar memory from over a year ago—flashed through Rees's mind. "Yes, she will," he stated.

"You're dreaming."

"I threw her out of the house. Now I'm taking her back."

Lina started to laugh. "You want me to stay in your wife's bedchamber? While she moves to the third floor? You don't know much about women, do you?"

"No. But I do know Helene."

"Why?" Tom demanded. "Why in God's name would she humiliate herself in front of all London society in such a way? I doubt very much that she's been pining for your presence."

He didn't say it with scorn, but Rees felt the pinprick all the same. "She wants a child," he said shortly, forking the eggs in his mouth as quickly as he could. He wanted this conversation over. The sooner he could go to Helene's house and take care of arrangements there, the sooner he could get back to work.

"I never heard of a woman wanting a child that much," Lina said. She had put down her toast. "The scandal will be tremendous."

"If Father was going to turn in his grave, this would do it," Tom put in. "Do you suppose if I showed you disturbed earth, you would stop trying to wake him?"

Rees just looked at him. "I need Lina in the house."

A flash of distaste crossed Tom's face.

"To sing what I compose," Rees finished calmly. He took the last bite of his eggs. "Where, might I ask, did Miss Meggin come from, Tom? And what are you planning to do with her?"

Meggin looked across the table at him. Now that he'd had a moment, he could see that she didn't really resemble Tom. Her eyes were light blue and utterly bewildered. She didn't seem to know what to do with her fork and kept putting it down and trying to eat eggs with her fingers.

"She sold me three apples," Tom said. "I shall take her back to East Riding and find a family to care for her."

Rees looked at the little girl. Her pinafore was stained and crumpled, and she didn't look terribly clean. "Have we any maids at the moment, Leke?" he asked the butler.

Leke was obviously listening with all his attention. This must be the most exciting morning of his life. "My niece Rosy, my lord."

"Of course, I'd forgotten Rosy. I hope she's better with children than she is with an iron. You'd better ask her to help us out with Meggin until my brother decides to return to his parish, which I dearly hope will be very soon." Rees shot Tom a look. "And Leke, send a message to Madame Rocque and ask her to send one of her assistants to measure the child."

"Lovely!" Lina said, "I should like Madame Rocque's current pattern book as well, Leke. Just think of the cosy times Lady Godwin and I shall have, pouring over *La Belle Assemblée* together." She laughed. "You're a fool, Rees."

"We need sturdy, serviceable clothing, not the kind of thing that—" Tom's eyes skittered over Lina's elegant morning gown.

"I'm sure they can provide whatever Meggin needs," Rees said with perfect indifference. He rose and bowed to the room at large. "I'm sure you'll all excuse me. I have to collect

Helene. You should expect your mistress in the house by supper time, Leke."

But he was followed by a light swish of silk. "Surely you were wishing to speak to me, Rees?" The sarcasm in her voice pricked his shoulder blades.

Rees pushed open the door of the sitting room. "Right. We can speak, and then work on that aria."

Lina strolled before him. "I think not." She walked over to a couch graced by three towering stacks of paper and plumped herself on top of one of them.

"What are you doing?" Rees bellowed. "Get up at once! You're sitting on Act One."

"Mmm, what a pity," Lina said sweetly. "Don't worry, Rees. I shall restrain myself from the obvious joke about having had the trots."

Once again, he had underestimated a female's anger. Rees ground his teeth for a moment. He should just give Lina a payment and send her on her way. Boot out the mistress, get back into good odor with his saintly brother, bring his wife back into the house, spawn an heir . . . It felt as if the prison gates were closing about him.

"How much do you want?" he asked abruptly.

Her eyes narrowed but she said nothing.

"You know I'll give you a large settlement when you leave," he said impatiently. "But how much extra do you want to stay in the house for a few more weeks, at least until Tom goes home?"

She still said nothing.

He had the uneasy feeling he was missing something, but that was nothing new. He ran a hand through his hair. He didn't know why other men seemed perfectly capable of understanding women. He found Helene and Lina equally incomprehensible.

105

"You're tired of me," he pointed out.

She nodded at that.

"So the problem is staying in the house with my wife, then?" He turned away and the score waiting on his piano caught his eye. It was hogwash, no question about it. The awful feeling of failure dragging at his ankles just made him feel more stubborn, and more obstinate. If he wasn't writing comic opera, what was he? Nothing. Nothing more than every other self-satisfied pisser of an earl in this country. At least he made people laugh with his music. But the scores he'd written in the last year wouldn't do more than send people to sleep.

"What do you want, Lina?"

"Nothing you can give me," she said.

"I can—"

"This is not about money."

Rees ran his hand through his hair again. He knew that Lina had left the opera house for love of him. But Christ, that was two, almost three years ago. Surely she had time to get over her infatuation? It only took Helene ten days. "I'm sorry," he said, turning around and leaning against the piano.

To his relief, she didn't look broken-hearted. "Why are you taking your wife back?"

"She wants a child. I need an heir."

"*You* are thinking about heirs?" Lina hooted.

Rees scowled at her. "I'm not getting any younger," he said coldly.

"Are you trying to tell me that you're suffering an old man's complaint, and that's why you avoid my bed?"

"No! No," he said more calmly. "We're finished, Lina. You know that."

She shrugged. "So why am I still here?" There was a faint bitterness in her voice that found its way straight to his conscience. "Why haven't you already set me up with a little house of my own and a snug allowance, to assuage your conscience until I find another protector? Or am I incorrect about the fate of a high-flung courtesan?"

"You're not a courtesan," Rees said.

Her eyes blazed scorn. "Only courtesans can be paid to humiliate themselves. I truly am curious, Rees. Why *do* you want a courtesan in your wife's bedroom, and a wife in the nursery?"

At the moment he wanted nothing more than for her to be gone. He shrugged. "An impulse. Obviously a stupid one."

"Afraid of your wife?"

She knew him far too well. "Absolutely not!" he snapped.

"Afraid of your brother, then."

"Bored at the idea of domestic bliss," he drawled. "After all, given the little scene you created at Madame Rocque's, I can always count on you to enliven the atmosphere."

"I won't do it," she said flatly. "You must be cracked to think I would. The woman will likely kill me, and she would have every reason to do so. I may have lost my virtue, Rees, but I haven't lost every crumb of common decency. I'm not staying in your wife's bedroom while she sleeps upstairs. I wouldn't enter the door while she's here."

"Don't make a Cheltenham tragedy about it," he snarled. "Go if you want to go."

But she just stayed there, her eyes glinting at him. "You told your brother that you wanted me in the house to sing your compositions. I think it would have been easier for both of us if you had clarified that particular aspect of our relationship some time ago."

"I know. I've been a bastard." He said it impatiently: he'd had this sort of conversation with women before and it didn't interest him.

"Well, if I'm to be here to sing for my supper," Lina persisted, "do tell me: just what do you have in mind for your wife?"

"She'll help with—" he stopped. Too late, he saw the trap.

"Help with the opera?" Lina enquired in a particularly sweet voice. "Ah, yes, we all know that the Countess Godwin is a brilliant musician, do we not? I thought there was something fishy about your sudden wish to beget an heir. But if we take your recent musical compositions into account . . . well, now I understand. So the countess will write the score, and I will sing the score, and you merely do your bedtime duty, is that it?" She laughed. "Your wife must be desperate indeed."

Rees was at her side with a snarl of rage that startled them both. "Don't you *dare* speak of Helene in that tone!"

She shook his hand from her arm. "I'll pack my bags."

Rees gritted his teeth. "If you stay and sing when I ask you to, I'll make Shuffle give you the part of the Quaker girl."

She paused, hand on the door.

"You are no courtesan, Lina. We both know it. What are you going to do with the rest of your life? There'll be no second protector for you."

Lina laughed briefly. "Not after what I've learned of men from you."

"You'll go back to the opera house, won't you? So how would it feel to go back with a lead part under your arm, *and* the part already learned? Six weeks at most," he said. "You can learn the Quaker's part by then. Hell, I'll even toss in a little of that coloratura that you do so well. And I'll clear it with Shuffle and the rest of the management."

There was a moment of silence.

"I'd rather have the role of Princess Mathilde," she said. "Not the Quaker girl. I'm no Quaker."

"You'd make an excellent Quaker. For all your beauty, there's a deep down Puritan side to you."

She pulled open the door. "Must be pretty far down. I haven't seen a twitch of it in years. I want the Princess."

He touched her arm. "It wasn't that bad, was it, Lina?"

She looked up at him, remembering how deeply she fell in love with the big, shaggy earl, his dimples and his abruptness, his burly body and his secret kindness. He was the one with a secret Puritan soul, if anyone. She shook her head. "It's been lovely," she said flippantly. "Nothing more than constant gaiety."

Rees had to let her go. What more could he say? What could either of them say?

Chapter Fourteen
An Outrageous Proposal

Helene had a shrewd feeling that she would be besieged with morning callers. No staid matron could chop off all her hair, put on a flagrantly outrageous gown, and disappear from a ballroom with the Earl of Mayne, without every single female acquaintance she had in the world—and several whom she did not—developing a burning ambition to partake of tea at her house.

So she instructed Mrs. Crewe to prepare for callers and then put on a recklessly daring morning gown sent by Madame Rocque, so that she could entertain all those who might have missed her appearance the previous night. The morning gown was of a style with the gown she had worn to the ball: the cut of the bodice was almost prudish, but the fabric was so fine that it floated around her body, allowing every curve to speak for itself.

But she felt no pleasure in shocking her visitors. In the morning she had discovered that she had her monthly, and only the fact that she had already darkened her lashes prevented her from bursting into tears. It wasn't until she read the very first card brought in by her mother's butler that Helene shed her listlessness like a snake sheds its skin.

Her heart started beating quickly and her cheeks suddenly turned a pink that had nothing to do with cosmetics. "How could you?" she cried, the moment the door opened. She had been thinking about blistering Esme's ears ever since waking up.

Except Esme was followed by William, a plump, cheerful one-year-old. William didn't see the point of solitary walking; he trusted his nursemaid, Ivy, to keep him upright while he tugged on her finger and pointed. And now he wanted to go to Helene, so Ivy walked him across the room. William had his father's golden hair and blue eyes, but that mischievous twinkle in his eyes was all Esme's.

"Hello, sweet William!" Helene said, holding out her arms. He let go of his nurse's hand and walked one step alone, toppling toward her like a falling star. She scooped him up and tickled him for a moment, and then kissed him all over his curly little head. He smelled wonderful, like bread-and-milk pudding and baby.

"This was very clever of you," Helene observed, giving William's mother a narrow-eyed glance.

"I know," said Esme happily. "I expect you've consigned me to the dungeon, darling, and Lord knows I deserve to be." She turned to Ivy. "I think William will be just fine with us for a short while, Ivy, if you'd like to greet Mrs. Crewe."

William's nursemaid curtsied and took herself out of the sitting room with dispatch. "Ivy is in love with one of my grooms," Esme said. "Now she'll peek out the door and drive the poor lad to distraction."

"How could you do such a thing?" Helene scolded, although it was difficult to sound severe when William's giggles filled the air. "How *dare* you tell Rees that I was intending to get myself with child?"

"It was the most practical solution," Esme said, looking not at all repentant. "I gave a lot of thought to illegitimate children two years ago. Miles and I hadn't lived together for ten years, and there he was in love with Lady Childe. But I decided finally that it made far more sense to approach my own husband than to bear an illegitimate child, and the same is true for you."

"You should have simply told me," Helene scolded. "As it was, I was positively mortified. You should have seen Mayne's face when—"

"No, wait!" Esme cried. "You mustn't describe what happened last night until Gina arrives. She said she'd be here early, and she threatened me with murder if I allowed you to begin the tale without her. We are both quite moribund with curiosity. And Helene, we must instruct your butler that you're not receiving for *at least* an hour. You do realize that all of London will be here this morning, don't you?"

"Of course I do," Helene said irritably. "Why would I be wearing this drafty garment if I didn't know that? Every scandal-mongering matron from here to York will be on my doorstep."

"Matrons!" Esme cried. "Who cares for such trifles? All the men in London will be here, which is why it matters that you look exquisite. Do you know, I think that lip color is more suited to you than anyone I have ever known? It makes your mouth look as ripe as a berry."

"You sound like the worst kind of flatterer. The foolish things were said to me last night! I danced with Gerard Bunge and he kept sighing, and saying that I looked like a tree-nymph in springtime."

"What a coincidence," Esme said acidly. "So did he."

At that moment, Harries announced the Duchess of Girton, Esme announced she was positively starved, and William fell over and bumped his head against a table, so the conversation proper didn't start again until Ivy had borne William downstairs for a consolatory pudding, and Harries had been instructed to bring sustenance, and deny entrance to anyone for one hour.

"Now tell me *all*!" Gina said gaily. The Duchess of Girton had beautiful green eyes and pale red hair. She could turn in a heartbeat from being the most composed, regal woman in London, to being doubled over with fits of wicked laughter. "Helene, darling, you look so elegant! I sent a message to Madame Rocque this morning for an appointment. After hearing about your gown from at least four different women last night, I want precisely the same. Although I promise to order it in a different color," she added.

Helene couldn't help smiling. "How is Max?"

Gina wrinkled her nose. "A despot. I do believe he's the only child in all England who doesn't sleep at night. Now he's teething, and he must have his mama at night or he screams so loudly that even the staff can't sleep. Cam says I must just leave him, and then he'll get used to Nurse, but I can't bear his cries."

"William howls his head off during the night sometimes," Esme said cheerfully. "I must be a very unnatural mother, because I leave him to Ivy."

"I wish I could do that," Gina said.

"Much more important," Esme told Gina, "is the fact that just before you arrived last night, Mayne swept Helene into the music room, and Rees came pounding after her, and the next thing I heard, Mayne had come out with a brow like thunder, as they say."

They both turned and looked expectantly at Helene.

"I got my monthly this morning," she blurted out.

"Oh, what a shame," Esme said softly, winding an arm around her shoulder.

"I'm a little worried that I may be barren," she said, and her voice shook.

"You are *not* barren," Gina said. "I was married for several months before I found myself in a delicate condition

113

and"—she colored—"there was no lack of the necessary activity."

"The idea is absurd!" Esme said. "But I would suggest that you choose a more private setting for your next encounter with Rees."

"I live in anticipation," Helene said with a curl of her lip.

"I don't know why you're so preoccupied with the idea that Helene must reconcile with her husband," Gina said to Esme. "It's almost as if you wish Helene to return to her husband simply because you reconciled with Miles."

"Nonsense," Esme said tartly. "But Helene wants to have a child, and Rees is the obvious choice. If she finds herself in an interesting condition due to the efforts of some other man, who could say how Rees will react?"

"I don't even care," Helene said. "I would retire to the country and raise my baby."

"But I would miss you," Esme pointed out. "We would both miss you, and you would miss us. You would miss London."

"No, I wouldn't miss London," Helene said stubbornly. "I agree with Rees as far as that goes: the season is a dreadful waste of time. As long as I had both my pianos in the country, I would be completely happy."

"She's right," Gina said. "*You* were bored in the country, Esme. But the fact that you happily abandoned your Sewing Circle doesn't mean that Helene would feel the same. For one, I enjoy living on our estate."

"Be that as it may," Esme said stubbornly, "it's always better if a child's father *is* his father."

"Of course that's true," Gina admitted.

"And I'm the only one of us who has actually committed adultery," Esme said. "So I can tell you with some authority that it makes a person feel rather loathsome, after the fact."

"That may be true," Helene said, "but bedding Rees makes me feel just as loathsome, I'm sure."

Gina bit her lip. "You'll have to give us some details, Helene." And, when Helene said nothing, "You must, you absolutely must. Otherwise we'll never be able to decide whether you should return to Rees or look farther afield."

"Perhaps *I* should be the one to decide that!" Helene said tartly. But then she gave in. "Bedding simply didn't work for us," she said with a faint shrug. "I was disgusted, and he disliked the fact I am so thin. The pain didn't go away after the first time, the way it is supposed to. In fact, it only really started to fade after several months, and by then it was clear that our marriage was an utter disaster."

"Oh, poor you," Gina said, giving her a hug.

"It was very distressing at the time, naturally. But I have come to the conclusion that the bedding process is not for me, and I can't say that the fact causes me much grief."

"I'd be inclined to ascribe that to your husband's ineptitude," Esme said.

"I agree," Gina said, nodding.

Helene shrugged again. "It isn't worth discussion."

"Poor you," Gina repeated. "Well, I vote for the Earl of Mayne. Why should Helene be forced to petition her husband for a child? Rees is living with an opera singer, after all. I say that Rees deserves what he gets. And I also think that Helene should not be forced back into a situation that causes her pain and humiliation!"

"That's all very well," Esme said stubbornly, "but I still think that Rees, unpleasant though he is in bed—and out, for that matter—is the better option. I simply believe that Helene will feel a good deal more comfortable if her son actually *is* Earl Godwin, rather than being illegitimate. And if we think ahead, what of your son, Helene? How would he feel if he knew that he was really an illegitimate offspring of the Earl of Mayne, all the time he was carrying the title of Earl Godwin?"

"Perhaps I'll have a daughter," Helene pointed out.

"The fact is," Esme went on, "my little William has inherited the title of Lord Rawlings from Miles although he's really Sebastian's child. I don't feel right about that although I am persuaded that Miles would forgive me, under the circumstances. But it also means that Sebastian's eldest son won't inherit his title . . . it's all very complicated."

"I forgot that you were entangled in something of an inheritance mess yourself, Esme," Gina said.

"Luckily Simon Darby, who would have been Miles's heir, is so hopelessly rich that he says he doesn't give a pea about the inheritance or title. I actually think it's hardest on Sebastian."

"Miles was a decent, good man," Gina said. "And so is Sebastian. But Rees isn't. Oh, I know he's not a murderer or anything. But I don't think that he deserves very much consideration, given the way he has treated Helene. He threw her out of her house!"

"Let's change the subject, shall we?" Helene said, rather wearily. "The question is moot, for the moment anyway."

"Have I told you how much I adore your hair?" Gina asked. "Are you using lampblack to darken your eyelashes? Because I am an expert on the subject. The best product is resin. It's rather hard to find, but you can buy it in Haymarket."

"I have been using black frankincense," Helene said, perking up. "How does that compare to resin?"

There was a knock at the door. "An hour has passed, my lady," Harries announced. He was holding a salver strewn with cards. "Twenty-four persons have called and left their cards; one person just arrived. Shall I announce him?"

"Who is it?" Helene asked.

"The Earl of Mayne."

"Of course!" Gina said, clapping her hands.

When Harries had closed the door and gone to fetch their caller, Esme added quickly: "I do think that you should continue a flirtation with Mayne, for the moment anyway. Rees obviously responds to competition. Look at last night!"

"What about last night?" Helene said, wondering whether she should put on more lip color.

Gina answered her unspoken question by handing her a small pot of the color she had just put on her own lips. "Why are you beautifying yourself?" Helene said, taking the color. "You *are* married."

"I could say the same to you," Gina replied, grinning. "I would never even think of being unfaithful to Cam. But that doesn't mean that I have to look like a corpse in the presence of a man as delicious as Mayne."

"Thank goodness for that," Mayne himself said, strolling into the room. "I have a peculiar dislike of corpses in a lady's sitting room." He bowed elegantly. "Well, this is a true pleasure. Three of the most ravishing women in all London in one room!"

Helene couldn't help thinking that the earl had shown no sign of considering her ravishing a month ago. But it was hard not to appreciate his compliment. When he looked at her with those deep-set eyes, marked by straight black brows, Helene felt a thrill straight down her spine. He himself was, quite simply, ravishing.

"If you'll forgive me, ladies, I will play Prince Paris. Surely you three are Hera, Athena, and Aphrodite." He grinned down at them, and even Gina, who was starting to think that she'd left Max for rather longer than she wished to, felt a spark of pleasure. But then Mayne turned to Helene and gave her his madcap, suggestive grin. "As Paris, I award the golden apple to Aphrodite. Because she has been hiding her radiance for so long that it's burst forth with particular brilliance."

Helene raised an eyebrow, but Esme nipped in before her. "A tediously overwrought compliment," she said reprovingly. "Surely you can do better than that! Besides, I was labeled the Aphrodite when I debuted, and I would take it very amiss to find that I've been demoted to Hera."

"Every Aphrodite has her day," he said, twinkling at Esme. "If you ladies would allow me a private visit with Lady Godwin, I assure that I could wax far more eloquent."

"Well, I expect we shall have to give you free rein for your eloquence, Mayne," Esme said, rising.

He bowed and kissed the very tips of her fingers. "It's a pleasure to see you so radiant, Lady Bonnington."

Esme laughed.

"Good-bye, Helene," Gina said, pulling Esme toward the door. "No, don't worry, Mayne. You can kiss my hand next time." Giving him a conspiratorial smile, she closed the door behind them.

Mayne turned around and looked down at Lady Godwin. She was faintly pink, and seemed to be examining her skirts with great curiosity. He sat down next to her on the couch, stretching out his legs before him. "I am enchanted to see you so unscathed by last evening's debacle," he said.

Helene could feel herself blushing so hard that her ears were going red. If only she didn't blush so much! "My husband and I are—are friends, Lord Mayne. Truly, there is little disagreement between us."

"That sounds remarkably refreshing," Mayne said, picking up one of her hands and running his thumb delicately down each finger. His grin really was irresistible. Helene smiled at him a little shyly. She wasn't used to the heady pleasures of flirtation.

"Won't you call me Garret?" he said softly. "You did so last night."

Helene just knew that she looked unattractively pink in the face. "I apologize for leaving the ball after I informed you that we would meet directly."

He turned her hand over and began brushing kisses onto the rounded part of each finger. "The occasion lost all interest after you left." He spread her hand against his. "How slender your fingers are, compared to mine. Musician's hands."

"Yes," Helene said rather uncertainly. Her heart was thumping quickly.

Suddenly his fingers curled in between hers. "May I kiss you?"

Helene hesitated. He took that for a yes, and she caught one last glimpse of his dark eyes before his head bent and he brushed a kiss on her lips. And another. Another. His kisses were very sweet. Delicate. Helene relaxed. He had very large hands: without question he would be able to span one-and-a-half octaves.

"Do you play?" she said, against his mouth.

"All the time," he answered. He went back to his brushing kisses, without seeming to be in any hurry.

Helene found that she was quite enjoying it. Then she realized that perhaps he hadn't understood her question. "I mean, do you play music?" she asked.

"That too." He moved closer and put a finger under her chin to tip it up. "May I play with you?"

Helene could feel her heart pounding so hard it was likely visible through the thin fabric of her gown. That was the important question, wasn't it. And yet—she *couldn't* do anything of that sort. "It isn't the right time," she managed.

He bent his head again and his lips drifted across hers. She wouldn't mind if he tried to kiss her a bit more . . . intently.

But he didn't. Instead his mouth drifted off to the corner of her lips. "Curiosity is my besetting sin," he said silky. "Also a ruthless wish to have things absolutely clear between play-fellows. Is it not the right time because you are, alas, attached to that shaggy husband of yours, or is the issue a rather more ephemeral one?"

Helene opened her mouth to answer but he took advantage of it and slid inside. She found her arms around his neck without conscious volition. I don't like this kind of kissing, she thought to herself, rather wonderingly. But she liked Mayne's kiss. He was so debonair and restrained.

Finally Mayne himself drew back, and Helene was startled to see that he was looking at her with distinct hunger. No man had ever looked at her with that expression, although she'd often seen them looking at Esme that way.

"I want you, Helene Godwin," he said, and there was a dark throb in his voice that made Helene's legs feel weak.

"I couldn't—I've never—" she stumbled, and then pulled herself together. "I've never done such a thing before."

His hands were holding her face lightly. "You are so exquisite," he whispered. "Was I blind before last night?" His fingers ran over her cheekbones. "I must have been blind not to see your beauty."

"Thank you," Helene said awkwardly.

Then his mouth came to hers again, and this time it was easier; this time she sank more naturally into the circle of his arms, and her mouth opened up to his with a little gasp. And when he let her go, Helene found that her hands were trembling.

"I hope that you will give me a place in your life," Mayne said, and Helene registered the hoarse note in his voice with a feeling of pure triumph. "I generally do not think myself a fool," he continued, with a rueful tilt of his eyebrows. "But

I've been a fool. In the last few years, I've ranged far and wide amongst the ladies of the *ton*, Helene. Frankly, I've stopped caring very much if a particular lady refused my attentions. And yet I find myself caring a great deal about your answer. And that is a truth."

Helene knew that he was, indeed, telling the truth.

Chapter Fifteen

In Which Helene Finds Herself Unaccountably Desirable

Helene was having one of the most thrilling mornings of her life. The Earl of Mayne had left her with her heart beating quickly, stooping over her for one second before he left and kissing her cheek. "You are utterly enchanting," he whispered.

Helene had grinned like a fool. No one had ever called her *enchanting*. Mayne had left only when the butler announced that there were fifteen ladies crowded into the library, and then he strolled out so slowly that everyone knew exactly why she was pink and slightly breathless. All of which gave her a sense of power that went to her head like fizzy wine.

She didn't even blink when he kissed Lady Winifred's hand, and complimented Mrs. Gower on her reticule. He was *hers*. He turned back, for just a moment, before he took his cloak from Harries, and she saw it in his eyes.

Thus Helene greeted her guests with the smile of an utterly confident woman. "How lovely to see you, Lady Hamilton!" she said. "Your ball last night was a remarkable success."

"Due to you," Lady Hamilton replied cheerfully. "There's nothing like a sensation to give one's ball polish. I came to thank you, my dear . . ."

And so it went. The whole morning was a series of delightful conversations. Even Mrs. Austerleigh's waspish comment that the Earl of Mayne was nothing more than a rakehell didn't disturb Helene. She knew as well as anyone that Mrs. Austerleigh was lucky to have gained the earl's attentions for one evening. She should have been happy with that, instead of lamenting his supposedly wandering eye.

"I find him a pleasant companion," Helene assured her. "Nothing more."

"But your husband!" Mrs. Austerleigh tittered. "Do you find *him* a pleasant companion as well? You could have knocked me to the ground with a feather when I saw Lord Godwin stride into the ballroom last night. I had to ask dear Patricia whether she actually invited him. An odd decision on her part, to be sure."

"Rees and I are comfortable together," Helene said cautiously.

"You must be!" Mrs. Austerleigh laughed shrilly. But her laugh broke off in midair as Rees himself strode into the room.

He ignored all her guests and walked straight over to her, with his usual lack of common courtesy. To Helene's mind, his behavior presented an eye-opening contrast to that of the Earl of Mayne.

"Rees," she said, holding out her hand for a kiss. It was a bit odd knowing that his legs were as muscled under those breeches as she had discovered last night. The very thought made her want to giggle.

"Helene," he said, "I must—"

But then he seemed to realize that fifteen pairs of eyes were watching him with keen curiosity. "Perhaps we could speak in private for a moment?"

"Alas, this is not a convenient moment," she said, her smile not slipping an inch. "If you send me a note, we could fix on a mutually agreeable time . . . next week, perhaps?" He frowned, probably thinking that she was acting like a recalcitrant servant.

123

Actually, Rees was making a rather unpleasant discovery that had little to do with servitude. He had forgotten, again, that this Helene wasn't the girl he married. He seemed to have to make that discovery over and over: he had married a hysterical, high-strung young girl, easily driven to tears by a few strong words. But in the last few years, she had utterly changed.

"I would prefer to speak to you now," he said. He turned and gave a hard-eyed stare to the madams twittering with each other, their teacups halfway up to their mouths, fairly trembling with curiosity. Finally Lady Hamilton put down her cup, hopped to her feet, and made a quick apology to Helene. The others followed suit like a flock of chickens running from a rainstorm.

"There," he said with satisfaction, when the room was empty. He strode over and sat down on a comfortable-looking couch. There was a cup of tea in front of him likely not even tasted, so he drank it.

"You are revolting," Helene said, sitting opposite him. "I'll pour you your own cup of tea if you'd like some."

"I loathe tea," he said. But he was interested to hear from her voice that she wasn't really that angry with him. Perhaps tupping on a couch was the key to wifely good temper. He wouldn't mind a few more sessions, if they resulted in a peaceful household. She was wearing another one of those gowns like the one she wore last night. He could see the long line of her thigh. Suddenly his breeches felt a bit tight.

"Why are you here, Rees?" Helene asked him.

"I've come to bring you back to the house," he said bluntly. There were two cucumber sandwiches left, so he ate them. He'd been up since five in the morning, working on those damn orchestrations, and he was famished, even given the coddled eggs he ate for breakfast.

There was silence, so finally he looked up. Helene was looking rather amused.

"Don't tell me you actually think I'm taking you seriously?" she asked.

"You're my wife. I want you back. Tell your maids that I'll send over a couple of footmen to carry your boxes."

"You must be cracked!"

"No. Unless I'm much mistaken, we have decided to have an heir, and we may already have begun the process. Under those circumstances, obviously you have to move back into the house."

She shook her head. "I wouldn't move into that house for a million pounds. And you cannot have really expected that I would do so!"

"I know you, Helene. You'll want what's best for the child. And living in his family home with a father on the premises is by far the best." Darby had been absolutely right. He could see in her eyes that fatherhood was a potent argument.

"I see no reason why we should live under the same roof," she said.

"Because the child will be my son or daughter."

"Mine as well!" Helene snapped.

"Of course. I may be a rakehell," he said, unconsciously echoing Mrs. Austerleigh's condemnation of his rival, the Earl of Mayne, "but I'm growing old. I seem to be gaining some measure of responsibility towards my name."

"That's the first I've heard of it!" Helene scoffed. Then she asked the question Rees was rather dreading: "Is one to suppose, then, that you are planning to reorder your household to accommodate my presence? Won't that be a sacrifice?"

The delicate irony in her voice made his stomach churn. He picked up a half-eaten cucumber sandwich.

125

"Don't eat that!" Helene screeched. "It belonged to Lady Sladdington, and she has very bad teeth."

Rees shrugged. "Do you think they're catching?" But he put the sandwich down. "At any rate, no, I haven't."

"You haven't what?"

"Told Lina to leave the house." This was harder than he thought, now he was looking right at Helene. "I told Leke to clean out the bedchamber—the *large* bedchamber—next to the nursery for you."

"You must be joking," she said, staring at him with what appeared to be fascination.

"I'm not." This was the tricky part. "You want a child, Helene, am I right?"

She laughed. "Not under those circumstances."

"I want an heir as well. I hadn't really thought about it until you brought up the question, but now I realize that I do. Tom shows no sign of marriage; he's about as wet as a water-lily, and he's never shown any interest in women that I know of. If neither of us has issue, the title and the estate would revert to the crown, you know. My father was an only child and as far as I know, there aren't any far-flung cousins waiting for my obituary in the *Times*."

"Why would you care?" she asked. "You've never shown any interest in the honor of your name. The very suggestion is laughable."

"Well, now I do," Rees said, picking up the sandwich and eating it. Who cared if all his teeth fell out? Not his wife.

"This is all very well," Helene said impatiently, "but I fail to see that it has any relevance to the presence of a strumpet in my bedchamber, not to mention your absurd suggestion that I take over the nursemaid's quarters."

"You want a baby," he said shrewdly, meeting her eyes. "Don't you, Helene? All these"— he waved his hand at her

—"these changes in your hair and dress, they're because you want a baby."

"Yes, although," she said with a little smirk, "they have compensations of their own."

"Mayne, I would gather."

"Precisely," Helene replied, noticing with appreciation that the idea seemed to irritate him. Esme had said that Rees was jealous and while Helene thought it was unlikely, the idea of causing her husband any sort of annoyance was too pleasurable to ignore. "Mayne was here this morning, and his attentions are most marked."

"If you have a child with Mayne," Rees said deliberately, "I'll make its life a misery. I will divorce you, of course. Did you know that I keep your dowry in the event that we divorce on grounds of adultery? How will you raise the child, Helene?"

Her heart was sinking, but she kept her chin high. "My mother and I shall live together, just as we do now."

"Now you have an extremely generous allowance from me," he snapped. "As a divorced woman, you will have to live in the country, of course, but I believe your mother's dower estate includes only this house in town. So you'll rent some small house somewhere. Your child will go to the parish school, if there is one, *and* if they allow bastards to attend these days. I'm not sure about that. I am certain that he will be ostracized, though. And what if you have a daughter, Helene? Who will she marry? What will her life be like?"

She stared at him, lips pressed together.

"She'll live a life like yours, I suppose," he continued ruthlessly. "She'll grow old living with her mother—*you*. Except there won't be very much money, especially after your mother dies and the dower estate reverts to your father's cousin." He didn't feel good about what he was doing. She still hadn't said

127

a word, but he remembered something else that had to be said.

"And don't think that Mayne will obtain an Act of Parliament to marry you," he added. "Even if he stayed with you through the divorce proceedings. The man may be rich, but he's slept with most of the wives of the men sitting in the House of Lords. They're just waiting for some miserable cuckold to up and shoot the man, and believe me, they'll pardon the offence as justifiable."

"Why?" she asked between white lips. "Why would you do such a cruel thing, Rees?"

"Because I want you in the house," he said coolly. "You're my wife."

"I'm not your property!"

"You're my wife," he repeated. "It's that simple. You merely need to decide how much you want that child. We made a dog's breakfast of our marriage, but we can surely pull ourselves together long enough to get this taken care of."

"You just want me to be wretched," she said flatly. "You must be out of your mind to even come up with this plan. Never mind my feelings about the matter: my reputation would be ruined!"

A great surge of resentment rose in his chest at the very mention of reputation. "Of course, your name is all important to you. It remains to be seen whether it's more important than having a child. And may I point out, Helene, that your reputation will also be ruined if you have a bastard with Mayne? All the *ton* will watch the two of you like hawks on a pair of frolicking mice."

She seemed to be huddling in her chair, and Rees had a terrible feeling, as if he'd wounded a bird in flight. He stood up to go, but he couldn't quite make himself leave. She looked like a wounded sparrow, all shorn of its feathers now that she'd cut her hair.

"This bombast on your part doesn't explain why you want me in the house alongside that woman," she said, looking up at him. "If indeed you want an heir, get rid of her."

"No." Rees knew he was being stubborn, but he didn't care.

"Then you wish it merely to force me to live in a house of sin due to some perversion in your character. You're a devil, Rees."

"It's no house of sin," he said brusquely. But he could feel a wave of guilt coming. "Tom arrived yesterday. We have our own resident vicar."

"Your brother Tom? What does he think of your domestic arrangements? And did you even dare to tell him of this scheme?"

Rees's lips twisted. "He's worked up some sort of idea that blames my father for all my excesses. He didn't seem to mind Lina too much, but he said you wouldn't come to the house."

"He's right!"

"And I told him," he continued, staring down at her with that fierce look he had, that seemed to look into her very soul, "that he had no idea how desperately you want that baby. Or am I underestimating you, Helene?"

"You're mad," she said, standing up. "You were always odd, and now you've gone stark, raving mad. I'm actually glad that we didn't manage to create a child yesterday, because I wouldn't want to pass on any sort of dementia."

"We didn't?" he asked, staring at her. "You already know?"

"Yes," Helene said, glaring back. She had gone from shock, to rage, to despair, and she was back to rage again. But threads of rational thought were stealing back into her mind. He was bluffing. He had to be bluffing. It wasn't truly in Rees's nature to act in such a cruel—nay, almost wicked—fashion.

129

He took her arm, stopping her from leaving the room. "How much *do* you want a child, Helene?"

"Enough so that I accepted the fact that it may look like you," she said coolly. "And enough to know that you're not the only man capable of making one."

"You would condemn your own unborn child to bastardy. She will hate you someday, when she has no one to marry except the local cowherd. Let's face it, it's not as if you and I would particularly enjoy being next door to each other anyway. Did you really want me able to enter your room at any hour of the day or night and slip between your sheets?"

She spat it at him. "Absolutely not!"

"Right. The chamber on the third floor is easily larger than my mother's room. You can fit a piano in there."

"That's not the point! I do not wish to spend even a moment under the same roof as your doxy, a fact which should be clear, even to a person with your *perceptive* nature."

"All right," he said. "We'll compromise. You live in the house until we conceive the child. You can come in secret, so there won't be any scandal. And then you can take the child and raise it elsewhere. Here, with your mother, if you wish. But I refuse to continue trailing around after you and stripping off my pantaloons in public."

"You could come here on occasion."

"I'm not going to waste my time flitting around to balls, and to my mother-in-law's house, trying to find my own wife. I have work to do."

"I don't spend my time flitting around to balls!" she retorted. "You know as well as I do that I spend most of each day here working on my piano. You could come here."

"I noticed an advertisement for Arrangements of Beethoven Piano Sonatas for Four Hands, by a Mr. H. G.," Rees said, distracted for a moment. "Are those the pieces you were working on last summer?"

She nodded. "I'm writing a waltz at the moment," she said. "Well, this has been an utterly enthralling conversation, Rees, but I really must—"

"I need you, Helene."

"*What?*"

"I need help." He said it jerkily, in the tone of a man who hasn't asked for help since he was eleven years old. "I have to put an opera on the stage next season, and I've only written a few songs that are even decent. I shouldn't have left the house this morning."

"That's not like you. I thought you poured out all that comic stuff as if it were dishwater."

There was a muscle working in his jaw. "Believe me, Helene, the stuff I'm writing now is worse than dishwater."

He met her eyes with the old flare of obstinacy and anger, but there was something else too. A plea? She frowned. "You need my help? How could I possibly help you?"

"I thought perhaps we could make an exchange. You've gotten better and better over the years. Whereas I've become pedestrian." He couldn't think how to frame it in proper terms. "If you can help me turn my score into something playable, I'd be grateful." It was clear how his gratitude would be expressed.

Helene felt her cheeks going pink. "That's—That's—" she spluttered. "Absolutely not."

He turned away, raking his hand through his hair. "All right."

Helene watched him suspiciously. He was giving up, just like that? He must not have wanted her help very much. And did he really think that she was a better composer than he?

"If you can wait nine months or so, until the opera is rehearsed and opens, I'll start coming over here whenever you want me to," he said, sounding extremely tired.

"Couldn't you possibly do so now?"

"I really couldn't." He was looking out the window, back to her. "I've dried up, Helene. I slave over the damn melodies, and they get worse every time I touch them. I lost most of last night due to the Hamilton ball. I can't afford to do that again."

"What part is *she* taking?" Helene said sharply, suddenly realizing something.

He looked at her. "The lead."

"So you need her in the house to sing the parts," Helene said, working it out.

"Yes."

"And for other reasons," she pointed out with a little edge to her voice.

He'd got his satirical gleam back now. "It's not as if you would like to do any recreational bedding, is it, Helene?"

"No!" It was madness. Utter madness. And yet, she couldn't bear the idea of waiting months. She'd already waited half her lifetime, or so it felt. If she were honest, there was also a small part of her reveling in the idea that he wanted her help. That he admired her music. Fool that she was.

"I'll do it for one month, and on one condition."

"What?" Rees was rather startled to find how much he wanted her to agree.

"You can't even *enter* that woman's bedchamber while I'm in the house. Not under any circumstances, Rees. Do I make myself absolutely clear? You are not going to parade from one bed to another. She can stay and sing, but that is all."

He looked at her, and for a moment she thought he was going to refuse. Bile rose in her throat.

But then he said, "I see no problem with that request."

"And no one can know that I've returned to your house," Helene commanded. "I'll inform my household that I'm traveling in the country. It's not as if anyone from polite society would think of paying you a call."

"No one ever comes to visit. But you would have to be a virtual recluse, Helene. And servants talk."

"Do you still have Leke?"

Rees nodded.

"Leke won't talk," Helene said. "You'll have to let anyone go whom you think might gossip."

He shrugged. "We haven't hardly any staff at the moment. There's Rosy, Leke's niece, a couple of footmen, and Cook."

"How you can live in such a pigsty, I don't know," she said.

"I'll tell Leke to expect you this evening then," Rees said, controlling his voice so that not even a trickle of pleasure came through.

"No. I'll arrive in a few days. What did you tell your singer?"

"The same thing I told you." He pulled open the door and told the butler to fetch his greatcoat. "Her name is Lina McKenna, by the way."

"What did Miss McKenna say of this scheme?" Helene demanded, dumbfounded to find that she was even considering such an action.

Rees shrugged. "Something about the two of you pouring over fashion plates together." He left Helene staring at the door.

Chapter Sixteen

The Nature of My Sex

"What do you wish to do this morning?" Tom asked Meggin as they left the breakfast table. She didn't seem to have eaten much, although who knew what a child this age should eat? And why didn't he think to ask Mrs. Fishpole when her birthday was? He wasn't even quite certain how old she was. He'd have to return to the inn. How did children amuse themselves?

Meggin just looked up at him and didn't say anything.

"Would you like to have a bath?" he asked.

She didn't reply. It was rather irritating. Or it *would* be irritating, he quickly corrected himself, if she wasn't such a little girl. One couldn't be annoyed by an innocent orphan. Could one?

"What would you like to do today?" he said, rather more loudly. They were climbing the stairs. Meggin wasn't even pretending to pay attention. She was caressing the satiny finish of the stair rail as if it were a cat. What was needed here, obviously, was a female.

He paused. "Wait here," he instructed her and then turned around. Meggin was nothing if not obedient. She sat down on the stair and began stroking the stair railings.

Tom clumped down the stairs feeling extremely irritable. He'd been thinking about this trip for over two years now. He had planned to arrive at Rees's house, and—and there's

134

the rub. Talk to him. Tell him he missed him? Their father's taunts rang in his ears just as loudly as they obviously still did in Rees's: expressing such an emotion would be girlish. How could he tell Rees that he missed his big brother, that he missed talking to him, that he wished they were friends? From what he could see, the only friend Rees had was Simon Darby, and that all went back to the days when Rees would flee the house and disappear to the Darby household for days.

Tom sighed. "Leke!" he shouted.

"Here, sir." The butler trotted through the green door, drying cloth in hand. "I'm just on my way to the employment agency, sir. I think we could use a few maids."

"Undoubtedly," Tom said, allowing faint irony to enter his tone. The corners of his room were festooned with cobwebs.

"Had I known of your arrival, sir," Leke said majestically, "I would have had your room prepared."

"Never mind that, where's your niece? The one and only maid? I need someone to care for the child."

"I'm afraid she has let us down," Leke admitted. "She's run back to her mum this morning. I'm sure my sister will send her back with a good ear-warming, but meanwhile, there isn't a woman in the house barring Cook. And Cook is not the sort to do any child-minding. Takes her position very seriously. After all she cooked for the Prince of Wales once; his lordship pays her one hundred guineas a year just to stay in the household."

"Bejesus," Tom muttered. One hundred guineas was nearly what he made as vicar, and more than most of his parishioners made put together.

He started back up the stairs. Cook wasn't the only woman in the house. Lina was a woman. Anyone except a blind man could see that. Halfway up the stairs, he passed Meggin and she got up without a word and started following him, for all the world like a curious kitten. At the top of the stairs he turned left and marched down to his mother's room.

The door opened immediately. "Well hello, Reverend," Lina said, smiling as wicked a smile as any self-respecting Whore of Babylon would give a bishop.

Tom felt that smile all the way down to his groin. No wonder his brother had thrown his wife out and moved Lina into the bedchamber next to his. God help him, he probably would have done the same. He gave himself a mental shake. She's a fallen woman. Someone to pity and succor, not lust after as if he were a common ruffian.

She had changed into a tight costume made of green velvet that buttoned down the front and made a man's hands itch to stroke it. A green velvet hat nestled on her glossy brown curls. All in all, she looked like an enchantingly naughty wood elf.

"I gather you like my walking costume?" she said, as he remained silent.

"It's delightful," Tom barked, embarrassed. Meggin had inched forward and was stretching one dirty finger toward the white fuzzy stuff that edged Lina's jacket. "I came to request your assistance."

Lina raised an eyebrow. "You'd better come in, then. These shoes are the very devil to stand in, and 'tis against the nature of my sex to stand, anyway."

Tom followed her, trying to sort that out. Why not stand? Could she possibly have meant a joke on a man *standing*? Or rather, parts of a man, standing? Surely not. He must have misheard. Perhaps she was simply referring to her shoes.

Meggin followed Lina into the room as closely as she could, still touching her jacket. "It's swansdown," Lina told her briskly. "You may touch it as long as you don't soil it."

136

"May I borrow your lady's maid until Leke hires a temporary nursemaid?"

"I don't have a maid," she said, slipping into a seat next to the fireplace.

"You don't?" His mother had employed two personal maids.

"I had one when I first arrived, but I decided I could do without her. She didn't really approve of my situation." She wrinkled her nose. Her eyes were merry, and not at all bitter. "I always managed to dress myself at home, after all."

"Where is home?" Tom asked. "Do you mind if I seat myself as well?"

"A long way away, alas," she said, and it was as if a curtain fell over her face. "Now how can I possibly help you, Mr. Holland?"

"Meggin needs a wash, and I don't think she'll feel comfortable with me."

"Probably not," Lina murmured. She looked down at the little girl. "I suppose I could supervise a bath."

Tom was looking around the chamber. If he hadn't known it was his mother's bedchamber, he'd have never recognized it, hung with rosy silk as if it were the inside of a sea shell. It didn't look like a strumpet's boudoir, not that he had personal acquaintance with such a room. There weren't any portraits of naked gods and goddesses, or anything else to signal that Lina was a kept woman. Damn his brother, anyway.

Lina stood up, unbuttoning her jacket and tossing it on the bed. She wore a shirt of thin muslin, which made it obvious that she was graced with one of the most glorious bosoms Tom had ever seen, with a sweet little waist that curved in and then out. He had to take a deep breath. He hadn't had a woman since he became a vicar. It wasn't for want of desire, either, for all his father used to call him a molly. But a vicar who happened to be the younger son of an earl, and possessor of a large private income inherited from his mother, learns very quickly to avoid conversation with unmarried women unless he can countenance marrying them. He had a deep-down, abiding respect for the vows of marriage, and the vows he had made when he entered the churchhood, which prevented him from frivolous flirtations—or worse. I'm not in tune with the age, he thought ruefully. Lina's breasts strained in the thin muslin of her shirt as she bent toward Meggin and said something into the little girl's ear.

"Perhaps I will leave," he suggested. He had to get out of the room. One glance at his breeches and the oh-so-experienced Lina would know exactly how he was reacting to her presence. "I'll send a footman with a tub of hot water," he said, hand on the door.

He turned to watch, just for a second.

Lina had managed to coax Meggin's dirty pinafore over her head by giving her a swansdown tippet to hold. Meggin was stroking the tippet with an expression of utter bliss, and rubbing it against her face. Lina didn't seem to mind. She had got out a brush and was making a determined assault on Meggin's tangled curls. And all the time she talked, a low stream of chattering, joking conversation that continued even though Meggin didn't reply.

Her accent was unmistakable. Rees's little songbird, as he called her, was indeed from a long way away: Scotland. Tom stored away that scrap of information, and went to order a tub and buckets of hot water.

It was to be a council of war, if held in Helene's mother's elegant drawing room. Something along the lines of the

Council of Vienna, Helene thought to herself, and Rees was their renegade Napoleon. If only Rees would go live on an island somewhere . . . Elba would be perfect.

She moved a plate of gingerbread cakes away from the edge of the table and fussed with the linens for a moment. At least she didn't have to tell her mother. Of course, she didn't *have* to tell anyone. She could change her mind.

Too late. Esme rustled into the room. She was supremely elegant, wearing a morning frock of Italian crepe with a painted border of shells. An exquisite little reticule decorated with the same shells dangled from her wrist.

"Darling, you just caught me!" she said. "I am on my way to Madame Rocque's establishment. And I mustn't miss my appointment; I have nothing to wear, and from what I hear, Madame Rocque is being barraged with requests, entirely due to *your* successes! I have no doubt but that half the women in London are hopeful that a gown fashioned by Madame Rocque will ensure them attention from the Earl of Mayne."

"That's a lovely gown," Helene said.

"I had to dress to impress," Esme explained. "I'm afraid that if I don't appear a veritable blaze of fashion, Madame Rocque will fulfill other requests before mine."

At that moment Gina rushed in. She looked the opposite of Esme; her hair was rather more disarranged than fashionable, and she was wearing a Pomeranian mantle that was supposed to be worn over a ballgown, rather than a walking costume. "I'm here!" she called. Then she collapsed into a chair. "Barely. I'm afraid that I find child-rearing a detriment to the normal business of paying morning calls."

Helene poured her a cup of tea. "I do apologize for summoning you both to my house at short notice," she said apologetically.

"Never mind that," Esme said. "Tell us *all*!"

"Rees arrived after you left yesterday morning. He frightened away all my callers—"

Esme's deep chuckle punctuated the sentence.

"And told me that he wants me to move back into the house."

Esme's laughter stopped. "Really?"

"He wants me to move back into the house," Helene repeated, well aware that she hadn't exactly told the whole truth . . . yet.

"Oh, my goodness," Gina said with fascination. "What has happened to the rakehell husband himself?"

"He must be feeling his age," Esme said. "Perhaps he was infected by that odd malady called respectability."

"Not exactly," Helene said.

"What do you mean?" Esme raised an eyebrow. "I should tell you that Miles's reaction was just the same. When I asked him for a child, he said that he would move back into the house, and he would bid Lady Childe farewell. Which he did do," she added conscientiously, "although he and I never had the chance to live together again."

"Well, once again Miles and Rees are shown to be not precisely of the same caliber," Helene said, twiddling with the delicate handle of her teacup rather than meet her friends' eyes.

"How do you mean?" Gina asked. "I don't follow. How does Rees's request differ from Miles's?"

"Rees wants me to return to the house," Helene said, raising her chin. "But his mistress, Lina McKenna, will remain in the house as well. And those are the only circumstances under which he will father a child." She had decided to keep Rees's offer to engage in the business nine months in the future to herself. Her friends would undoubtedly argue for waiting, and if there was one thing Helene knew for certain, it was that she could not wait months.

A second later she took a deep breath and hoped that Harries was a good distance from the front hall so that he wasn't shocked out of the few strands of hair he had left by the shrieks issuing from the drawing room.

On the surface of it, Gina was the more furious. She literally turned red and spluttered, unable to put a complete sentence together.

Yet Esme was, in her own way, more dangerous-looking. There was something positively terrifying about her expression. Helene wouldn't have been at all surprised if her black curls suddenly turned into snakes and she transformed into Medusa herself.

"The dissipated fiend!" Esme said between clenched teeth. "How dare he even suggest such a revolting thing to you. How dare he even say such a thing in a lady's—in his wife's—presence!"

"He dared," Helene said calmly. Having thought of nothing else all night long, she no longer felt any surprise over the occurrence. "Actually, it's quite like Rees, if you consider the proposition at length."

"There's no word to describe him!" Gina screeched.

But Esme was looking at Helene, and something in her eyes made Helene shift uneasily in her seat. "And just what did you tell him in reply, Helene?"

"That's hardly the question, is it?" Gina said. "The question is—The question is—" But she stopped and blinked at Helene. "Of course you said no."

Helene stirred her tea with a small silver spoon and then put it precisely to the side. "Not exactly."

"You cannot enter that house under those circumstances!" Esme said, her voice low and fierce. "I will not allow it."

141

"While your concern is endearing," Helene replied, "I am a grown woman."

"You wouldn't!" Gina gasped. "You'll be ruined. Absolutely ruined! And that's not to mention that the very idea is revolting."

"I agreed to his proposition, with certain conditions."

"Let's hear them," Esme said grimly.

"I shall enter the house for one month only, and no one is to know of my presence."

"Unlikely," Esme said. "It's bound to get out."

"Rees has few servants, and no callers. I shall take a hackney to the house and live as a recluse."

"This is all irrelevant," Gina said. "You can hide in the attics if you want to, Helene, but you're still entering the house—living in your own house—with a nightwalker!"

"She's not quite so repellent. I did meet Miss McKenna, if you remember. I judged her remarkably young, and certainly not practiced in her profession, if you can call it that. I do believe that she was, in fact, merely an opera singer before Rees debauched her."

"Yet a brief encounter with the woman was enough to send you fleeing into the country," Esme reminded her. "And now you are considering sharing a house with her? With your husband's *mistress*? Have you gone raving mad, Helene?"

"Perhaps. Sometimes I think so." Helene bit her lip hard. "I want that child. I will go to any lengths to have a child. Any lengths."

"Every sensibility must revolt against the notion!" Gina said, shuddering.

"True. I know it's a horrifying proposition. I would not have told either of you, except I could not imagine how I was to explain my ensuing delicate condition."

142

"Of course you had to tell us!" Esme said, crossly. "Lord knows, I certainly engaged in some deranged behavior myself in the past."

"Nothing like this," Helene said.

"True." Esme gazed at her in wonderment. "How you've changed, Helene! Just consider your customary severe attitude towards my wicked ways. Why, I've never had to develop much of a barometer of societal opinion because I could count on you to know precisely how little the *ton* would approve of an action. But now—"

Helene smiled. "Perhaps I'm doing this for the sake of our friendship. Now you need no longer feel like the wicked one between us."

"I think you're both missing the point," Gina broke in. "How are you going to get rid of her, Helene?"

"What do you mean?"

"I mean the strumpet, of course. How are you going to get rid of her?"

"Why should I?" Helene said, shrugging. "I did force Rees to promise that he wouldn't frequent her bed—"

"Ug!" Gina wailed. "I don't even want to *think* about that!"

"I apologize," Helene said calmly. "I am rather used to considering the whereabouts of my husband's mistress. For all I know, she's sitting at my dressing table as we speak."

"Gina's right," Esme said. "You'll have to get rid of the woman. It's the only way to protect your reputation. The moment she's out of the house, your presence there is acceptable. The gossips will, no doubt, be fascinated to learn that you've returned to the house, given the very public state of your separation from Rees, but reconciliation is certainly acceptable."

"And how on earth am I to dispense with Rees's mistress?"

"Perhaps she'll just leave," Gina said hopefully. "After she meets you, I mean."

"Nonsense," Esme said. "You'll have to buy her off, of course. How long has she been in the house?"

Helene put down her cup with a little clink. "Two years and three months."

"Oh," Esme said, clearly taken aback by Helene's precision. "Well, you will make her a persuasive offer. Monetary, of course."

"I suppose I could do that," Helene said, biting her lip. "I could use my allowance. I rather like the idea of using the money Rees gives me, as a matter of fact."

"And she will accept it," Gina put in. "No woman in her right mind would choose to live with Rees." She broke off. "That was inexcusably rude, Helene, please forgive me."

"True, none the less," Helene said with a smile.

"If you give her a goodly sum," Gina continued, "she'll likely return to whatever village she was from, and you need never think of her again."

"That would be . . . pleasant," Helene said. "Very pleasant. I will try to find an occasion to make such an offer."

Esme shuddered. "How you will survive in that house, I don't know. I think I would succumb to the vapors, and I don't have a sensitive constitution."

"I will not succumb to the vapors," Helene said, and the clear determination in her voice rang like a bell. "But I will return to this house in a delicate condition. I have made up my mind."

Esme shook her head. "I just can't get over how much you've changed, Helene. I feel like a character in that Shakespeare play, the one where the Bottom appears out of the woods with a donkey's head instead of his own: 'Oh Helene, thou art changed! Bless thee, thou art translated!'"

144

Helene smiled at her. "You're lucky that we are old friends, otherwise I should take exception to being likened to an ass."

"Well, if the head fits!" Esme said, laughing as she dodged a small cushion thrown in her direction.

Chapter Seventeen

Trouble Comes in Many Guises

It wasn't until evening of the next day that Tom truly understood just how much trouble he was in. The butler's errant niece had returned, thank goodness, and Meggin was tucked away in the nursery, still clutching Lina's tippet.

"She seemed to like it so much," Lina told him, "that I gave it to her. I remember quite well the joy I felt on first feeling silk next to my skin." The smile that curled her lips sent a stab of pure fire down Tom's legs.

He was indeed in trouble.

Rees had appeared only briefly at supper, laconically announcing that Helene would return to the house in three to four days. He bolted his food and went back into the salon, from which they could hear discordant fragments of piano music emerging.

That left Tom and Lina together. It was, literally, the first time he'd been alone with a woman in six years, since the night before he took his vows when he'd said good-bye to a certain Betsy Prowd. He looked up from his almond custard to find Lina's brown eyes fixed on him. She bewildered him. One moment she was a little brandy-breasted songbird that looked as if it would nestle sweetly in one's hand; the next she was like a scarlet redbreast, shaking her feathers with all the insouciance of a *très-coquette*.

"What made you decide to become a priest?" she asked. Her voice was as clear and fluting as a bell. It made him wonder how it would sound calling his name, if they were in bed together.

Tom dragged his attention back to her face. "There was never really any question but that I would," he explained. "My profession was established long before I can remember. The church is a common occupation for the younger son of a nobleman."

"You wouldn't have chosen to go into the church on your own?"

"I don't know that I would have," he said slowly. "But that doesn't mean that I'm not happy now."

She wrinkled her nose. "Drafty old vicarage?"

"There are a few drafts, but—"

"Leaky roof in the springtime?"

"There is—"

"Far too many rooms to keep clean, and just one little maid, trundling about with blue fingers, and not enough money to buy coal!"

"No," he said startled. "It's not at all like that."

Her mouth curled into a teasing smile. "Have you heard the jest about the vicar who wandered into a bawdy house, Reverend?"

"I wish you wouldn't call me by my title."

"I apologize. In that case, Mr. Holland, have you heard the jest about the misinformed vicar?"

"No," he said in a measured voice. "Would I like it?"

Lina looked at the man before her. He was like a younger version of Rees, without the barbed tongue. He had the same tousled hair, and the same broad shoulders, but without the sharp edges. "Don't you like jests?" she asked, picking up a slice of hothouse peach and slipping it slowly between her lips. He was watching. This was more fun than she'd had since she left the stage.

"Yes, but not those that you're wishing to tell me," he said, calmly selecting an apple from the dish before them.

"And what kind are those?" she asked saucily.

"I suspect your plan is to tell me jokes not suitable for a vicar's ears," he replied. "But I know those jokes, and I don't find most of them funny. They're all to do with men making themselves like sailing ships and spending their main masts, and I can't say the subject interests me."

Lina burst out laughing. "I don't know any shipping jests, Mr. Holland."

"But undoubtedly your jokes are of the same caliber, Miss McKenna."

She tossed a grape into her mouth. "It's too late to save me, as they say, Reverend, so best leave the chastisement to your congregation. Why don't you think of your time in London as an education in improper pursuits?"

Tom felt a wave of black rage. She was so beautiful, so witty, so utterly charming: how dare his brother have taken her to his house and made her into a concubine?

She seemed to guess his thoughts. "I expect you'd like a full confession," she said with a little pout, "but you shan't have it. I will tell you, though, in case you plan to lambaste your brother, that Rees effected no corruption. To be frank, Reverend, I lost my maidenly virtue back in my own home village." Her eyes twinkled mischievously. "There are some of us who never agree with societal strictures. Haven't you noticed that yourself? I listened to my mama's dictates, but I couldn't picture myself marrying one of the boys I grew up around. And I couldn't see any good reason why I shouldn't bed Hugh Sutherland, if I wished to. So I did bed him, and then I turned down his request for my hand, and then I left. And I haven't any desire to return. I simply didn't fit in."

"I suppose you couldn't return now," Tom said, hardening his heart against her tempting gaiety. "'Tis base to be a whore, after all. It would cause your mother some grief."

Her fingers froze for a moment. Then: "Am I that name, John?"

"I see you know *Othello*. But why are you calling me John?" he asked, irritated beyond all control. He drained his glass of wine and poured another.

"You *are* John the Baptist, are you not?" she said. In the candlelight, the skin of her throat glowed a creamy delicate white. And her throat led down to sweet mounds of breast, looking like snow against the dull gold of her gown. "I rather think that young Meggin called it right," she said, and the husky amusement in her voice had deepened. "If I am the Whore of Babylon, perhaps I should serve as your temptation. Or have I got it wrong? It *was* John who was tempted in the desert was it not?"

"No," he said, "it wasn't. And I believe you know that as well as I do, given the rather surprising extent of biblical knowledge you've already demonstrated."

"Ah, it must have been John who lived in the desert for years. Now how long did you say that you'd been a priest, John?"

He met her eyes. Hers were deep pools of chocolate-brown mischief, and yet with a hint of vulnerability. That label *whore* had stung.

"I shouldn't have called you that word," he said. "I wished to hurt you. I'm sorry."

"It was very difficult to make my way to London on my own," she said casually, peeling herself an apple, her hands absolutely steady. "Do you know, I actually contemplated, one night, whether it was better to live poor or die in sin? But I chose to live poor, Reverend. Believe it or not, when

I chose to move to this house, it was because I thought myself in love with your brother." Her smile was self-mocking now.

"I'm sure that he feels the same," Tom said, cursing Rees.

"No. He never did, although he might have experienced some sort of temporary infatuation with my voice." There wasn't a trace of self-pity in her voice.

"I—I'm sorry," Tom said finally.

She shrugged. "He's kind enough. He's a gentleman, your brother, for all that most of the nobility think he's a degenerate. He has rather wished I wasn't living in the house any time in the last two years, but he's caught by his own integrity, you see. He can't put me out because he's honorable, and he doesn't really want me in, because he's honorable."

"And do you wish to leave?" One of the candles was guttering, casting her half of the table into a shadow that hid the sparkle in her eyes and made her look as if . . . but he couldn't stand the idea that his cursed brother had broken her heart.

"I believe I shall return to the opera house in the very near future, and yes, I will welcome that."

"But do you like London? Has it been as enthralling as you hoped to find it, back when you were a girl in Scotland?"

"No," she said. "London is disappointing, like so many things in life. Don't you find it so, John?"

"On occasion."

"I find it so virtually all the time," she said almost dreamily. "Your brother is a prime case in point. Disappointing."

"I'm sorry," Tom said, feeling a surge of gratitude for his brother's shortcomings.

She stood up. "I am worn quite ragged with all this confession, John. I believe I shall retire."

He came to his feet, and walked to her side in order to escort her from the room. He stopped her with a touch on her arm, just as she was about to open the door. "Please don't call me John."

She looked up at him, and there wasn't a hint of sadness in her eyes; he must have imagined it. Instead, she came up on the tips of her toes and brushed her mouth across his. Tom froze.

"Don't do that," he said, and he was shocked by the roughness of his own voice.

She didn't seem to realize her own danger. She thought it was all a game. "Tempting the vicar?" she said pertly. "A crime, I'm sure. But I never could tempt *you* into sin, Mr. Holland. From everything Rees told me about you, back a few years ago when we used to converse, you are the perfect son."

Tom tightened his jaw and kept his hands at his sides.

"Always kind, always forgiving, always Christian. I suspect Meggin is not the first waif you've rescued. If I remember the stories correctly, you've never put a foot wrong, isn't that right?" She smiled up at him, as seductive a woman as he'd ever seen in his life. In fact, he had never seen anyone like her.

And just like that, he snapped. He put out his hands and drew her into his arms. His blood was pounding so that all he could hear was the roar of seawater in his ears. And all he could see was the tempting sweetness of her mouth.

It was the kind of kiss that brings drowning men back from the edge of death. He pulled her against him hard, relishing every inch of silky satin flesh, so giving to his hardness, so very unlike his own body. He even pulled her off her feet because he had to have her closer, all that soft, warm flesh. And she didn't protest; instead she melted against him, curling her arms around his neck, letting him ravish her mouth.

151

After a bit, she started teasing him with her tongue until he growled and sucked her tongue into his mouth. She made a little noise, a funny little hoarse noise but it didn't sound like a giggle.

Still, that tiny noise reminded him of where he was. Of who he was. He put her back on her feet and tried to think of an apology. If there was an apology for that sort of behavior.

But she cut him off. "Am I to suppose that the Baptist has succumbed to temptation?" There was a trace of wonder in her voice, and the words seemed to hang on the air. For a moment, she stood there, staring up at him with her beautiful lips stung by his kiss and her eyes all lazy with pleasure.

Then she turned and was gone.

Chapter Eighteen

Dancing in the Desert

Two days later, Tom was fairly well convinced he might as well be John the Baptist. Lina made an excellent Salome: everywhere he turned, she seemed to be dancing, just like Salome before the King, and he had the feeling he was about to see his head on a platter. She left the room before him, and the only thing he could think about for an hour afterwards was the curve of her waist. She bent to pick up Meggin, giving him a view of the deep hollow between her breasts, and Tom could scarcely breathe for the hunger that swept over him. She smiled at him over the table, and her skin gleamed bronze in the candlelight. He wanted to lick it, all of it. And when she touched him lightly on the arm, and said cheekily that she had been practicing the dance of the seven veils, his whole body went rigid with the effort not to pull her into his arms and kiss her silliness into silence.

So he did the only thing he could think of: retreated to his bedchamber and prayed for help. At first, he prayed for guidance. Then he gave that up and started just praying for self-control. For help.

On Tom's third evening in London, Rees announced that he would begin to train Lina in some aria or other. Tom trailed into the sitting room after them even though he was conscious that an ice water bath was a better proposition. When Lina started to sing, his heart almost stopped from the pure beauty of it. Her voice fluted higher and higher, dancing in the rafters of the room.

"Her voice is incredible," he breathed to Rees, sitting next to him.

But Rees was frowning at his score. "Lina!" he said, cutting her off. "Try that last bar with the count as written. It's a dotted quarter and an eighth note, not two quarter notes."

Lina nodded, but her eyes slid to Tom's, holding him prisoner. She took a deep breath and began to sing again. For a moment it looked as if her breasts would surely topple from her bodice. Tom found himself tensing, as if to jump forward and protect her, shield her beauty—and from whom?

There was no one in the room but himself and her protector. His own brother. Tom felt a surge of primitive hatred, one that went back more than twenty years, a gift from their father. The old earl had reveled in creating divisions between his two sons. He whipped them with his taunts from the moment they were out of the nursery. Who knew why? From the distance of the five years since the earl's death, Tom rather thought that their father was afraid that they might present a unified front and rebel against him. Not that they ever had. Obedient as hunting dogs, they turned out exactly as he had prophesied. The earl had told Tom that he was too wet to marry, and that he would end up in a minor parish, unable to get his spineless self into a sufficiently political position to achieve a large parish. That was true enough. Tom couldn't seem to bring himself to flatter the right people, to grease the right palm, to take those steps that would have him rising toward being a bishop. The fact that he loved his small parish and his wayward parishioners wouldn't have mattered to their father.

"I suppose you'll marry one of those prim do-gooders who flock in churchyards," their father had sneered the day

Tom fastened on his collar. "Thank God one of my sons has red blood in his veins."

Something died in Tom's heart every time Rees snapped at Lina, every time she took a deep breath and started singing again. If he was the man his father had prophesied, Rees was exactly the rakehell that their father had wanted him to be: a man of vicious habits, a man who would bring a young girl into his house and make her his mistress, a man who would force his wife to return to the same house.

Lina was singing the same bar for the tenth time. Her voice was not soaring quite as easily now. There was a little line between her brows, and she'd stopped throwing Tom teasing glances. Surely she was getting over-tired.

"Damn it all," Rees bellowed, "don't you listen to anything I say, Lina? Read your score. That trill begins on E-flat, not G-natural. I shouldn't have to be your *répéteteur*, teaching you each aria note by note!"

She glared at him and her soft mouth trembled. Tom longed to spring to his feet and take her in his arms, but he stayed where he was. Lina was Rees's mistress. Not his to protect.

With very little emotion, she picked up her glass of wine and tossed it in their direction, stalking out the door.

"For Christ's sake," Rees muttered, shaking the papers he was holding, and paying no attention to the red splotches marring his shirt.

Tom wiped the wine from his face. "You drove her too hard. Do you have to be so brutal?"

"Stay out of what you don't understand," Rees growled.

"I understand that Lina has the voice of an angel," Tom said hotly. "Yet you keep shouting at her. I don't know why she puts up with it."

"She has to. I'm trying to prepare her to sing a lead role." Rees tossed the papers on a stool. "Lina has a gorgeous voice but she doesn't have the drive to be a great singer. If I don't prod her, she won't practice. You saw her. She pays no attention to the score, even when I'm standing before her, shouting the notes."

"You made her sing one phrase over and over!"

"She should be doing that on her own: over and over until she could sing it correctly in her sleep. But she doesn't want it enough." He rubbed some drops of wine from his forehead wearily. "I know you'd like to make me out to be some sort of miscreant, Tom. But in this case, I'm actually doing my best."

"I fail to see how shouting is doing your best."

"I've promised her the lead in my next opera. She's not ready, and she doesn't deserve it. But if I can somehow whip her into shape before the management realizes that she's inadequate, and perhaps even make her smooth enough so that she's a success—and that's doubtful—the victory might just carry her into another lead role. After that, it's out of my hands."

"Oh."

"You always see things in black and white." Rees was leaning his head back against the couch, staring up at the ceiling. "If I'm shouting at Lina, I must be evil."

"What about you?" Tom asked boldly. "Did you always know you were a rakehell, or did you have to be instructed in your wicked ways by Father?"

"I suppose I received instruction," Rees said, sounding rather bored. He was still staring up at the ceiling.

"How well we both understood our orders."

Rees turned his head so that his eyes flicked over Tom's face. "Is that why you're here, then?" he drawled. "Are you sick of being the godly vicar, and you've come to the house of sin for lessons in titillation?"

"No!" Tom said, horrified to find that some part of his soul leapt at the idea. Could that be the truth?

"Good," Rees said, turning his head and staring back up at the ceiling. "Because for all Lina looks like a little strumpet, she's not."

"I would *never* treat her so," Tom said, and the memory of the way he had kissed Lina, the way he had pulled her body against him, lent urgency to his tone.

"I didn't mean to imply such a thing," Rees said, sounding utterly exhausted. "I'd better take a nap. I have to work all night."

"Is there anything I can do to help?"

Rees was already off the couch and heading for the door. "If you could keep Lina out of my hair tomorrow, I'd be grateful," he said over his shoulder. "She has an annoying habit of wishing to leave the house, and she expects to have an escort."

Tom sat there by himself for a while, staring at the washes of paper surrounding his boots and thinking about temptation.

But thinking about temptation, let alone praying for help, never seemed to help much when he was faced with the living, breathing woman herself.

He was walking down the corridor toward his bedchamber when she opened her door and slammed right into him. He drew in a deep breath. Her curvy, fragrant body seemed to leave an imprint on his skin.

"God's bodkins!" she said, pulling back. "How you startled me!"

He stared at her, and the desire in his heart must have been written on his face, because she turned a delicate rose pink.

"Lina," he said and his voice came out with a harshness that not one of his parishioners had ever heard. "If you don't want to be kissed, you should run back into that room of yours."

Instead, Lina raised her fingers to his cheek. "Kiss me, then," she said in a voice like velvet.

But he didn't, holding back due to a grain of wisdom, some shred of sanity.

"*Tom*," she added, using his Christian name rather than the bevy of labels she gave him. Not John the Baptist, not Reverend, not Mr. Holland.

Tom.

His lips came to hers with the hot, insistent hunger of a starving man. And she succumbed to him with the same fervor, the silky touch of an arm around his neck setting his skin on fire. Even that fugitive touch made him understand for the first time in his life what a blessing it is for a man and a woman to be unclothed together. But he didn't—couldn't—think of that or he might sweep her straight to his chamber.

So he contented himself instead with a rough, demanding kiss. This wasn't the kiss of a timid vicar, the succor of the poor and the rescuer of wounded animals. This was the action of a licentious rakehell, a man driven by lust, a man who took no prisoners. His mouth scorched across hers, a merciless barbarian with his wild-eyed queen, a man who invaded first, and asked questions afterward.

Still, he was a barbarian in control of himself. He didn't let his hands roam. Instead he told her with every stroke of his tongue just what he'd like to be doing to the tender under-curve of her breast, to that sweet spot at the inside of her elbow, to the curve of her hips.

It was an endless kiss, because Tom knew under it all, that when the kiss was over, he would go to his chamber by himself. So the barbarian fought with himself, keeping his hand on the Barbarian Queen's back, never allowing himself even to pull her luscious body against his.

Lina had twined her arms around his neck, and her fingers were compulsively clutching his curls. Through the hot waves of desire that kept breaking over him and threatening to make him buckle at the knees, he realized that her breathing was quick and rapid. Her hands began to wander down his back, a path that threatened to erase Tom's control.

"Lina," he said in a hoarse groan, tearing his mouth from hers.

She didn't open her eyes. He wanted to see languorous pleasure there, so he dropped kisses on her eyes, trying to calm the pounding of his heart, giving her space to recover.

"Reverend," she finally said, her voice just a wisp of sound.

His heart dropped into his boots. Reverend again. He was *Tom* no longer.

"My name is Tom!" he said, and the roughness in his voice would have been, again, unknown to his flock.

"If I call you Tom," she whispered, finally opening her eyes and looking at him, "will you kiss me all night?"

He froze, his hands on her back. He was pretty sure that the agony in his body was echoed on his face. "I can't sleep with you," he said harshly. "Never mind the fact that you belong to my brother—"

"Your brother hasn't entered my bedchamber in months," she said, tracing his cheek with her fingertips. Her very touch burned his skin. "And not very often even before that."

"That's not the crucial issue," he managed. "I couldn't sleep with you, because I don't"—he gathered strength because it was truly one of the hardest things he'd ever said— "I don't believe in engaging in intimacies outside of marriage."

Could Salome have ever been so beautiful?

159

"Are not kisses intimacies?" she asked, her eyes searching his.

"Not inadvisable ones," he managed. Now her small hands were wandering across his chest. "But you are touching me inappropriately, Lina."

Her hands flew away, although she didn't look chastised.

He nodded and put her away. She didn't hear him say "God help me," because he was already halfway down the corridor toward his bedchamber.

Chapter Nineteen

In Which the Household Gathers

Helene arrived at the house in a hackney. This time she didn't even bother having her maid knock on the door; she simply told Saunders to push it open. Saunders had been dumbstruck from the moment Helene informed her that she intended to return to her husband's house. Now she stared around the antechamber of the house as if she expected the devil himself to make his presence known by waving a forked tail around the corner.

"Where's the butler?" she finally asked in a hushed tone, for all the world as if they were visiting the Regent himself. Helene had taken off her pelisse and was looking around for somewhere to put it that didn't appear to be too dusty.

"Lord knows," she said. "His name is Leke, and he's not a bad sort. But I can't imagine how he manages to run this house with virtually no staff."

Saunders was beginning to see the dirt clinging to the corners of the entryway. Her lip curled. "Harries would keep the house clean, if he had to do it on his own hands and knees."

"No doubt we'll have to do a thorough cleaning of my room," Helene said grimly, heading up the stairs.

When they reached the next floor, Saunders paused, but Helene turned without a word of explanation and kept climbing. She hadn't told Saunders the unpleasant truth about

Rees's refusal to dislodge the strumpet. It caused enough commotion when she announced she was returning to her husband. The truth was demented. *She* was demented.

No one seemed to understand that she wanted a baby more than anything else, more than her dignity. If she had to trade a brief period of humiliation for a lifetime with a child, then so be it. Besides, she was hopeful that the presence of Rees's brother—a vicar, after all!—would anoint the household with some level of dignity.

The chamber next to the nursery wasn't terrible. It was large, with windows from which one could just glimpse the trees of St. James Park. "Look at this, Saunders!" Helene said, looking out, "I didn't have this view on the second floor."

"I don't like it," Saunders said, stumping around the room and looking with distaste at the furnishings. "I don't understand why you're not in the countess's bedchamber, my lady."

Leke had obviously made an effort to fit out the room as befits a countess; Helene recognized the beautiful Turkish rug that used to adorn the back sitting room. The bed had obviously belonged to the nanny, but he had found a dressing table and a rather motley collection of furniture and arranged them into a lady's boudoir. Helene sat down on a velvet sofa. "There's another lady in that chamber, Saunders."

"Another lady?" she said. "Is it the earl's mother, then?"

"No. She is a friend of Lord Godwin's," Helene replied.

Saunders generally offered any comments in a consciously genteel tone of voice. But shock brought out her Bankside origins directly. "He never has that singer here while you're in residence!" she gasped. And when Helene nodded, she pulled open the door so violently that it slammed against the wall. "I'll find a hackney on the corner, my lady!"

"I'm staying," Helene said quietly.

"Never! You're addled!" Saunders stared at her, eyes large. "Your mother doesn't know of your husband's depravity!"

"I trust you not to tell her." Helene took a deep breath. "Saunders, I need to be here, and Rees's mistress is really irrelevant. We will stay only until I find myself with child. Do you understand? Then we return to my mother's, and no one the wiser. Remember, no one except my closest friends knows I'm in this house. Callers will be informed that I am indisposed."

She looked directly at Saunders. "Obviously, the scandal that would ensue from people knowing of my presence here would be staggering."

"I can't even imagine," the maid said, gasping a bit.

"I trust you. There's no one else I could entrust with the truth."

Saunders blinked rapidly and straightened her shoulders. "Well, my lady, of course I should never wish to fail your confidence in me. You can trust me, naturally, but—"

"I am counting on you," Helene said earnestly.

"But it's impossible!" she protested. "How on earth are you to speak to each other? How will you take meals?"

"I shall take most of my meals in my room," Helene replied. "And since I have promised to help his lordship with his current opera, I doubt that I shall have much interaction with Miss McKenna at all."

Saunders slowly closed the door. "Thank goodness we packed all those gowns from Madame Rocque." Madame had delivered a season's worth of gowns in the past two weeks, all constructed with the same principles in mind: weightlessness and a vivid display of Helene's slender form.

"I hadn't thought to wear them here," Helene said, startled.

"That you will," Saunders stated. "I'm not having a light-heeled wench come out more elegantly dressed than the countess herself."

"I've met Rees's friend, Saunders. She's very young."

Saunders narrowed her eyes. "Face paints as well."

Helene sighed. "In that case, we should probably begin unpacking, because Rees generally eats the evening meal at an earlier hour than we're used to."

In truth, she was only barely ready when a dull gong downstairs signaled the dinner hour. Helene looked at herself in the slightly cracked glass of a dressing table that Leke had obviously found in the attic and slung into her bedchamber. She had chosen a simple gown of white muslin, embroidered at the hem and around the sleeves with gold thread. Its great secret was that the muslin was as light as thistledown and constructed in such a way that the hem rippled out around her ankles, and even fell to a small train in the back that floated behind her. The bodice wasn't low, nor were the sleeves uncomfortably small. It was comfortable, airy, dignified—and yet, ravishing, as the Earl of Mayne might say.

Helene smiled at herself. Thinking of the way Mayne had called her *enchanting*, and then touched her cheek, she found the courage to go downstairs.

If the truth be told, Helene had had very little contact with strumpets. She knew they wore garish colors on their cheeks, and gowns that barely hid their nipples. She knew that they pleasured men. She had met Rees's opera singer two years ago, when Rees brought her to the opera and to their box. Helene shuddered at the mere memory. She had made stilted conversation with Rees, while Major Kersting conversed with the singer.

As Leke opened the door to the sitting room, Helene had to pause to collect herself. Lina McKenna had changed. This was no untried green girl.

Sitting next to Rees's brother was one of the most beautiful women Helene had ever seen in her life. Her hair was swirled on top of her head in a gleaming mass of brown curls; Helene felt an instant stab of pain for the loss of her own hair. Her eyes were glowing with intelligence, curiosity and laughter. And her evening gown was neither outrageously revealing nor did it exhibit more décolletage than might any young woman in polite society. But she was obviously endowed with a bosom that rivaled Esme's.

Helene nearly turned and ran straight back to her room. How could she sit in the same room with this ravishing creature—she, a dried-up old stick? Why, if Miss McKenna were brought out as a debutante, she would have been judged a diamond of the first water.

But then Rees looked up and saw her. It was just a glance, but his eyes dropped from her hair to her toes. Helene couldn't read his reaction, but she didn't have to. He would be disdainful. Why should she care if she presented an unappetizing contrast to his mistress? After all, in comparison to the Earl of Mayne's sleek beauty, Rees's shaggy hair, great burly body, and all those heavy muscles were most unattractive.

She walked into the room and Rees's brother jumped to his feet and came toward her, holding out his hands. "Helene," Tom said, kissing her hand quickly, "you look exquisite."

She beamed at him. He had the same sweet brown eyes that she remembered from the first year of her and Rees's marriage. Truly, he was a very good-looking man: rather like Rees, except he was groomed and civilized. "It's lovely to see you again, Mr. Holland." And she really meant it.

"Please call me Tom," he said, squeezing her hands. "Are you quite certain that you wish to be here under these circumstances?"

She smiled again, but knew that this smile didn't reach her eyes. "Rees and I have an understanding," she said, turning to the couch.

Miss McKenna had risen as well. The better to show off her remarkable figure, Helene thought to herself sourly. "Lady Godwin," she said, dropping into a curtsy that would have sufficed when meeting the Queen, "may I say that it is a surprise to meet you?"

Helene nodded in reply. "I find myself in the grip of something like amazement as well." She could not curtsy to her husband's mistress; she simply could not. Instead she sat down and found that she was shaking. She gripped her hands tightly, in her lap.

"I'll bring you a brandy," her brother-in-law said in a low voice. "I'll be right back."

Helene never drank spirits, but she swallowed the whole glassful and concentrated on the burning liquid running down her throat. If she had had any idea that Miss McKenna was so beautiful, Rees would have had to drag her on the back of his horse before she agreed. When she met Rees's opera singer two years ago, Miss McKenna was a mere lass, a tongue-tied girl, whereas now she was formidable.

The brandy settled in her stomach, giving her Dutch courage. I can do this for one month, Helene told herself. One month, that's all. One month. She and Esme had decided that Rees had to be recruited to do his husbandly duty once a day. For a month.

Tom brought her another glass of brandy, and Helene drained it, sending another path of raw fire blazing down into her stomach. "Steady now," he said in a vicarish type of voice.

He truly was a sweet man. "What a shame that I didn't marry you," she said, with a little hiccup. "You have the same dark hair and eyes as my dissolute husband over there, and you would never—never—"

"Probably not," Tom said, patting her hand again. "But I don't know a thing about music either."

"Oh," Helene said. "That's a shame." She was beginning to feel altogether more cheerful. So what if her husband had a ladybird next to him on the couch? Why should it bother her? She could have had the Earl of Mayne or any number of others offering her compliments, if she so wished.

She got up with just the slightest stumble and walked back over toward the fireplace. "I forgot to say hello to you," she said to Rees.

"Helene," he said. Far from cuddling up to his mistress, he was scribbling on a piece of paper and looked utterly unaware of the tensions circling through the room.

Helene seated herself next to Lina, ignoring Tom's little gestures of anxiety. "We probably should discuss a few things," she said, trying very hard to remember what they were.

Lina's eyes were bubbling with amusement in a way that reminded Helene of Esme. *Not* that Esme was an improper woman. No. No indeed. She'd lost track of her thought again.

"I believe we should have supper now," Tom said, rather desperately. "Rees, why don't you summon Leke and tell him that we must eat?"

Rees shook his head without looking up. "Cook and Cook alone determines when the household sits to a meal. Leke will fetch us when the food is ready."

"That's a very nice gown you're wearing," Helene told Miss McKenna.

Miss McKenna blinked. I suppose, Helene thought to herself triumphantly, she expected me to be outraged, and now she doesn't know what to make of me.

"I think we should discuss Rees," Helene added, without waiting for a response. The brandy was giving her a lovely warm feeling of confidence. "If it is quite all right with you, I would like to borrow him once a day."

167

Tom was scolding his brother in an undertone. Helene heard him say, "Well, why didn't you tell me that she never drinks spirits?"

"From what I remember, I only need around five minutes of Rees's time," she told Miss McKenna. "That truly is a lovely gown, by the way." It was an odd color of orange that gave Lina's skin a tawny glow.

"Sometimes Rees is good for seven minutes," Miss McKenna said with just a hint of laughter in her voice. "I would give him the benefit of the doubt."

"Seven minutes!" Helene exclaimed. "How nice to know that one's husband has matured a whole two minutes in the past nine years."

"I like a man to have ambition, don't you?" Miss McKenna said, taking a sip of wine.

Suddenly Helene's eyes met those of her husband's mistress and they broke into laughter. Tom made a gulping noise. Rees looked up from his paper for a moment and shrugged.

"It shouldn't discompose your day at all," Helene said.

"I doubt that it will," Miss McKenna replied. "Your gown is also very lovely. Is it from Madame Rocque?"

"Indeed," Helene said. She decided not to nod again because it made her head feel quite dizzy. "I think I may have tried on your gown, but I looked a veritable scarecrow in it."

Miss McKenna's eyes had lost the sharp edge they had when Helene first entered the room. Helene found that now that she was used to Miss McKenna's startling beauty, she was taken aback by her composure. She was almost ladylike in her demeanor. If she hadn't known to the contrary, Helene would have assumed she was a rather formidable, if young, member of the *ton*. How very peculiar.

"How is your mother, Lady Godwin?" Tom said.

"Oh, she's very well," Helene said, with just the tiniest, ladylike hiccup. "But you might as well call me Helene. I am your sister-in-law, and after this, no one can say that we're not on intimate terms!"

Leke arrived at that moment. "Dinner is served," he said, in a voice of deep gloom. He had rather enjoyed the martyr-dom of remaining in Earl Godwin's employ when the rest of the servants fled a house of sin. But even he was wondering whether this situation was too much for his sense of propri-ety. It just didn't suit his nerves to find a mistress and a wife sitting next to each other and chatting, for all the world as if they were bosom friends.

Chapter Twenty

Inebriation Is Sometimes a Wise Choice

Helene sobered up slightly during the meal. But only slightly. At some point she realized that even another sip of red wine was going to leave her with a pounding headache in the morning, but she ignored the thought. Best to get through the evening, and let the morning worry about itself.

Rees sat at the top of the table, scowling at a score he had carried into the room. The conversation, such as it was, was carried by Lina, Tom, and Helene. After Leke had removed the pudding, even that chatter seemed to finally wilt. Helene took a deep breath and turned to Lina.

"If you will excuse us," she said politely, "I shall return him in five minutes."

"Please, take seven," Lina said with a twinkle.

A little smile wobbled on Helene's lips. Was it too, too odd to feel respect for her husband's mistress?

"Rees!" she said, standing up.

He stuffed the paper into his pocket. "Right," he replied. He showed no sign whatsoever of giving a damn about Lina's and Helene's remarks about the brevity of his bedroom activities.

But instead of heading up the stairs, he walked across the hall into the music room—well, the room that used to be their sitting room and was now occupied by three pianos.

"Rees," Helene said, trailing after him, "what on earth are you doing?"

"I need to show you this score," he said impatiently, running a hand through his hair. "We'll get to the rest of it in a few minutes."

"I would rather do the rest, as you put it, *now*," Helene insisted. She certainly didn't want to lose the little curtain of inebriation that was making the whole evening seem rather funny. And she particularly wanted to blunt the experience of bedding Rees, even if it was only a matter of seven minutes.

But Rees had strode to the piano and was leafing through sheets of paper. Helene walked cautiously into the room. Paper swirled around her feet with the same dancing motion as the hem of her skirt. She tried kicking a few in the air. "How do you live with all this mess?" she asked.

"It only appears messy," Rees said with an obvious disregard for the truth.

Helene laughed. "There's no method in this madness." She kicked a few more papers into the air.

"Don't do that!" he said sharply. "And it is organized. Drafts are on the floor. The various acts of the opera are arranged on the sofa."

"Sofa?" Helene wandered over and discovered that the hideous sofa given to them by her Aunt Margaret was actually still in the room, although buried under high stacks of paper. "You must have most of the opera here, Rees. I don't know why you can't be ready on time."

"Namby-pamby stuff," he said, hunching his shoulder. "I haven't written a decent line in the last year." He played a few bars. "What do you think of this?" he said.

Even tipsy, Helene retained full musical capability. "I can't say I like it overmuch," she said, wandering over and putting her elbows inelegantly on the top of the piano.

"That's because you're hearing it out of context," Rees

171

said. "Actually, it's one of the better pieces I have. Here, I'll play from the beginning."

He poised his hands over the keyboard and then let them fall. Helene allowed the music to pour through her and watched his hands. They were extraordinarily large and yet wondrously delicate in playing. Each finger tapered gracefully.

But when he stopped and looked up at her, Helene shook her head. "It sounds like a country ballad," she said frankly, "but not very interesting as pastoral music goes. Is it to be sung by a young girl?" Rees always wrote operas about young girls.

He nodded. "She's a princess who's run away and disguised herself as a Quaker girl."

Helene had long since learned to ignore the fragile plots that made up Rees's operas. "What's she supposed to be singing about at the moment?"

"She misses her lover, Captain Charteris. I'll play it again with the words, shall I? Fen did a good job on the libretto."

Rees had a dark, liquid singing voice as much at odds with his growling speaking voice as his elegant fingers were to his muscled body. "*While I'm waiting here in eager expectation, Always waiting for my lover to appear,*" he sang, "*In my fond and fanciful imagination, Every moment seems a year.*"

"Florid Fen," Helene said with some amusement. "Move over, Rees." She sat down, nudging him slightly with her hip. "What would happen if you used an ascending scale when she was *always waiting*, and then dropped when it *seems a year*?" She tried it out on the keyboard.

Rees was frowning. "That doesn't sound very wistful."

"She needs to sound as if she's yearning, not as if she's counting the linens. Try this," and Helene started singing as she played.

Rees moved over enough to allow her plenty of room for her elbows, but not so much that he wasn't touching her hip. He liked Helene's hips, he had discovered. In fact, he rather liked her new style of dressing for that very reason. Who would have thought that Helene had such a delicate yet sensual curve to her? He remembered her as angular and almost bony. But she wasn't, not at all. She made other women seem over-fleshy.

She had stopped singing. "Sorry," Rees said. "Could you sing it again?" She turned and looked at him. That was another interesting thing about Helene. She was tall enough to look right into his eye when they sat together. And her eyes were a very curious color, a kind of gray that shaded into green. Like a cat's.

"Pay attention, Rees," she said, looking rather amused.

She sang again. "It's better," Rees said, his attention now back to the music. "But I don't think the ascending scale works."

"You need to give her a sense of longing," Helene said again. "There has to be something to mark the fact she's desperate to see her captain."

"Perhaps she's not desperate," he growled, scribbling in the notes she had suggested.

"Then why bother writing about her?" Helene said with a shrug.

Rees's hand slowed. Why indeed? That was the problem with the whole opera. The piece was set to open the opera season next year, and he didn't have more than five measures of decent melody.

"Because she's my heroine," he said, crossing out his line so violently that the foolscap tore.

"I guessed that. You always write about princesses, young ones in love."

173

"I have two heroines, and one is a Quaker girl, not a princess. But princesses are in fashion," he said. "Damn it, Helene, do you always have to be so critical?"

She blinked at him. She did have lovely eyes. They were rather like the surface of a stream, deep with a gold-greeny quietness.

"I didn't mean to be disparaging," she said. "I'm sorry, Rees. You speak so lightly of your own work that I'm afraid I took license."

"If anyone's going to criticize, it might as well be you," he said gloomily. "I know this is paltry stuff."

"Shall we look at it again tomorrow?"

"I expect. But it's like trying to turn horse manure into gold."

"It's not that bad!" Helene exclaimed. "There's a very sweet bit of melody *here*," and she played the phrase.

"Don't you recognize it?" Rees asked. "That's from Mozart's *Apollo and Hyacinth*. Stolen. There's not a bit of music in here that's worth the paper it's written on," he said savagely, pointing to the stack on top of the piano. "It's all claptrap."

Helene put a hand on his arm. He looked down. She had the delicate, pink-tipped fingers of a real musician, not a charlatan like himself.

"I doubt that very much," she said.

"You might as well believe it, since it's true," he snapped, getting up. He walked one length of the room, but the papers swirling around his boots bothered him so much that he stopped. "I suppose we might as well get the tupping out of the way," he growled. "I'm going to have to be up all night rewriting that score."

Helene was biting her lip. She had a beautifully plump lower lip, he noticed, as if seeing it for the first time.

"Are you sure you want to?" she asked hesitantly. "We could wait a day."

Suddenly he was quite certain that he did want to. "It's best to start as we mean to go on," he growled, striding to the door. "My room?"

"Absolutely not!" Helene said, running after him. She wasn't going to engage in any such activities if there was even the slightest possibility that Lina could overhear. "We'll go to my room."

A moment later they were standing in her bedchamber staring at the bed. "It's no narrower than the sofa at Lady Hamilton's house," Helene said, rather uncertainly. It was one thing to make plans with Esme to bed her husband once a day. It was quite another when his large body was standing next to one. It gave her an odd zinging feeling in the pit of her stomach.

"It'll have to do," Rees growled, pulling off his cravat. A moment later he was down to a shirt. Helene watched with some fascination. His legs were just as muscled as she remembered from Lady Hamilton's music room. It was rather mesmerizing to see the powerful way his thighs flexed.

"How do you take exercise?" she asked.

"I walk between my pianos. Aren't you going to undress?"

"Well, you still have on your shirt," she retorted.

"I thought you'd prefer it."

"Why?" Helene asked, wondering whether there was something about shirts that she should know. Perhaps gentlemen always wore their shirt in the presence of ladies.

"You dislike the hair on my chest," Rees pointed out.

"Oh," Helene said weakly, "I'd forgotten." How extremely rude she had been, all those years ago. She was so hurt and desperate to injure him that she would have said anything. "I'm sorry if I made inappropriate comments," she added. "I believe I was quite rude."

175

He just stood in the middle of the room like some sort of big jungle cat, watching her intently. "It's quite all right. I'm not wedded to my chest hair. Aren't you going to undress, Helene?"

"I can't undo this gown by myself," she said, turning about and presenting him with an elegant row of pearl buttons.

Rees began unbuttoning. Helene's hair curled into little wisps just at the nape of her neck. She wasn't wearing a chemise. He would never have thought that Helene—his Helene—would wear a gown without a chemise and, underneath it, a sturdy corset. Every newly opened button revealed skin the color of snowflowers in the mountains, skin as clear and delicate as a baby's cheek.

His fingers, Rees noticed with a flash of objectivity, were trembling. It was absurd to be excited about the prospect of bedding one's wife. One's *estranged* wife, he corrected himself. And the bedding was merely for purposes of procreation. The gown parted far enough now so that he pushed it forward, making it fall forward off her shoulders.

"You have a beautiful back, Helene," he said, startled to hear the little rasp in his voice. He had obviously gone too long without visiting Lina, if he was getting excited over one slender back, albeit with an elegant curve that made a man long to run his hands down . . . down.

Helene didn't know what to think of Rees's compliment. Last week he had said she had beautiful legs, and now she had a beautiful back as well? She clutched the gown to her bosom. But she could hardly cover up her breasts forever.

So she turned around and let the gown drop to the floor. He might as well see it all, although surely he could remember for himself.

For a moment he didn't move at all, just drew in a breath. There was something about his eyes that made Helene feel a bit better. It was only Rees, after all. What was she so worried about? She walked over and sat down on the edge of the bed, crossing her legs. She felt rather wicked, sitting naked in the presence of a man. Back when they were first married, they had conducted all intimacies discreetly under the sheets, and here they were, estranged, and she naked in front of him.

"Do take off your shirt," she suggested. It hung past his hips. She didn't care about his chest either way, but she was very curious to see whether her memory of last week could possibly be accurate.

Her memory was absolutely accurate. Helene felt a stinging tingle between her legs; it was as if her body had its own memory.

He strode over and gestured at the bed. Helene lay back, trying to quell a heartbeat of anxiety. It hadn't hurt last time. She simply had to believe that it wouldn't hurt this time as well.

"I suppose," he said rather tentatively, and then seemed to make up his mind. His hand went straight down between her legs. Helene nearly jumped out of her skin.

"What are you doing?" she gasped, and then realized she sounded critical. Esme had told her that no matter what, she couldn't sound critical or she might cause him to be unable to perform. And since the only thing she wanted from Rees was performance, she was determined to be encouraging.

He seemed to be—well, whatever he was doing, Helene had to admit that it felt—well, it felt . . . He took his hand away.

"You're not ready," he said to her. His hand lay on her thigh. It felt as if it burned into her skin.

Helene bit her lip and her heart sunk. Trust her body to have got it wrong, somehow. "What do I need to do?" she asked.

177

"God," Rees said, "you really don't have any idea what happens between a man and a woman, do you?"

"Well, of course I do," Helene said with some indignation. She pulled herself into a sitting position and drew up her knees so that she felt less vulnerable. "I was married to you, if you remember. I mean, I am married to you. And I have perfectly accurate memories of that year we lived together. Not to mention the fact that we reenacted the process last week."

"Nine years ago," he said slowly, running one hand down her shoulder. It felt good. She shivered a little. "That's a very long time to be without bedding." So she didn't sleep with Fairfax-Lacy last spring, he thought to himself, with a distinct throb of pleasure.

Helene smiled at him ruefully. "Yes, but as you yourself said, Rees, I'm not made for this kind of activity. I can't pretend that I missed it."

"I said a lot of stupid things," Rees said. He wrapped a finger and thumb around her wrist. "You're much more delicate than I remember."

Helene caught herself, about to say, *and you're much bigger*. But perhaps he would construe that as a derogatory remark. It might remind him of how she used to complain of being flattened by his weight.

He was running his fingers up her arm now, almost as if she were a harp. "Do you mind if I touch your breasts?" he asked suddenly, not meeting her eyes.

"But—do you want to?" she asked in astonishment.

"Very much."

"Then of course you may," she said, feeling as if she were granting him permission to smoke a cigarillo in her presence, or something equally mundane. A moment later that thought flew from her head. He touched her with the same passion and strength with which he touched the piano keys. Helene felt herself begin to tremble. It felt—it felt—odd. His fingers were sun-dusted, dark against the cream of her skin, curling around her breast. A thumb wandered across her nipple and she almost jumped out of her skin.

A little smile crossed his lips. "Do you like that?"

She opened her mouth but didn't say anything. What was she supposed to say?

He did it again, and again. "Do you like it, Helene?"

"Well," she managed, "it's acceptable." There was a sense of tension between them that made her unable to meet his eyes. She was naked. Naked! And he was caressing her breasts, almost as if she had the same—

The thought of Lina brought a chilly moment of sanity. "Do you think we could progress now?" she asked. She certainly didn't want Lina to think that she was taking up Rees's time or even, horror of horrors, deliberately detaining him in her bedchamber in order to win him back.

"Mmmm," he said, and there was something in his voice that made her whole body thrum.

This time she relaxed her legs and let him feel there without protest.

"I don't think this is going to work tonight," he said, after a moment.

Helene felt a wash of disappointment. "Why not? Is there something wrong? Can't you just go ahead?" she asked, hating the fact that she was almost pleading with him.

"Not without hurting you," he said, shaking his head. "I believe that's why bedding was so painful between us years ago, Helene. I didn't know enough to wait for your body to be ready for me."

She could feel tears pricking the back of her eyes. It was all her fault, her body's fault. "I don't mind if it's painful," she said earnestly. "Please, Rees. Please. It wasn't painful the other night, I promise!"

"I'm sorry, Helene," he said, standing up. "I just don't know very much about bedding ladies." He stared down at her. His hair had fallen over his eyes before. "You were my first, you know."

"First lady?"

"That too," he said, with a wry grin.

"I had no idea! You certainly didn't act as if it was a new experience. I thought you had slept with hundreds of women."

"I wanted you to think that, of course. Back then, I was trying to cover up every imaginable shortcoming by pretending they didn't exist."

"What shortcoming?" Helene said. She was trying to avoid looking at him. Even a glimpse of his muscled buttocks seemed to do odd things to her stomach.

"That I was a virgin, among other things," he said. His smile was sardonic. "I bungled your first time, Helene, and I'm sorry about that."

"I don't see what you could have done differently," she pointed out, liking the apology though. "From what I've heard, every woman dislikes the first time."

"Whereas men are supposed to love it," he said and there was a distinct tone of self-derision in his voice now.

"But you didn't," she said, saddened. "I'm sorry if I bungled my part in it."

He stood up and pulled on his shirt. "I should get to work," he said, obviously dismissing the whole memory from his mind. "We'll try again tomorrow night, shall we?"

"What is going to be different tomorrow?" Helene insisted, watching him pull up his smalls.

He didn't answer, so she persisted. "What's going to be different tomorrow night, Rees? We have to do this every single day in order to ensure conception."

180

"Every day, hmm?" A flash of amusement crossed his face.

"Unless you have some serious objection. Esme says there's no way to know what particular day is the right one, so we can't miss even one day this month or we might have to continue into next month. And if I disappear for two months people will think I've come down with consumption!"

He pulled on his boots and went to the door, then paused. "I'll speak to Darby tomorrow and ask him about bedding ladies. I've never been the sort to engage in that sort of conversation at the club and my brother—" he shrugged. "Sometimes I feel as if Tom must have been born in that black frock of his. We certainly have never discussed women."

"Thank you," she said, watching him leave.

Chapter Twenty-One

Andante

Four hours later, Helene realized that she was not going to be able to sleep. She had been staring at the ceiling for hours, thinking. One sentence kept sticking in her mind: Rees said he was going to ask Darby about *bedding ladies*. So what was so special about bedding a lady? What was different between her and Lina, for example? Why did *she* need special treatment? She just wanted him to do it, and get it over with.

Far downstairs, in the depths of the house, she could occasionally hear pings from the piano. Apparently Rees meant it when he said he was going to work throughout the night on that lackluster score of his.

Finally Helene rose and pulled on her dressing gown. He could damn well do to her whatever it was he did to women who weren't ladies. She marched down the stairs, her bare toes curling against the smooth wood. The house was so old that each stair dipped a bit in the middle, presumably from the tramping feet of Jacobean Hollands, making their way up to their wives' chambers.

Outside the music room, she paused. He was still working on the same piece but it sounded a bit more adventurous now. Finally she pushed open the door. He threw up his head immediately and stared at her. The room was lit by two candelabra perched on top of the piano. His hair was standing on end, and there were black circles under his eyes. He looked desperately tired and, somehow, defeated.

Helene gave up the idea of bedding on the spot. "Can I help?" she said, tightening the cord of her dressing gown and walking into the room.

He shook his head as if to wake himself up. "I think it's improving." He played the bit that Helene had heard outside the door. "What do you think of this?"

"I like it." This time it felt natural to nudge him over and sit down. "What if you ended on D in alt? Can your soprano reach that high a note?" She played it again. "You could pause here on A-natural, and then either up or down to the D."

"Better the first time," Rees said. "It sounds a little florid with that triplet, but I like this minor chord." He pushed her hands off and played it himself. "Nice! You always were the better musician of the two of us, Helene."

"Not so," she said. "*You* write real music; I just play with notes. Real musicians don't spend months reworking Beethoven for four hands. They write original pieces, as you do."

He closed the top of the piano over the gleaming keys with a quiet click. "I write poppycock, Helene. You knew it, even back when we first married, before I'd had a single piece staged. You told me that I was doing nothing more than writing squeaky duets and that my harmonies were unremarkable."

"I didn't!" she said, startled. "I have never said such a thing, and I certainly don't think it either! Last year, for example, I didn't love everything in *The White Elephant*, but there were parts I thought were brilliantly conceived."

That lock of hair had flopped over his eyes again. He leaned against the closed piano keys and gave her a sardonic smile. She could see wrinkles at the corners of his eyes. "I can list precisely what you disliked in the *Elephant*. The tenor aria

183

in Act One, the oboe and clarinet duet in Act Three, and the minor scale that opened the Finale."

"True," Helene said. "As I told you last year. But I also thought your delineation of character was dazzling. The repeated pianissimo high F's in the Duke's aria were exquisite. The sense of pandemonium during the thunderstorm, when the elephant is running loose, was brilliantly executed. And the soprano mezzo duet, as everyone in London undoubtedly told you, was a glorious bit of inspiration."

He raised an eyebrow. There was a self-mocking smile lurking in the depths of his eyes. "*You* never told me."

"I didn't—" She stopped. "I should have. I didn't think you cared."

"Did you really like the pianissimo F's?"

She nodded. "It was daring—but it balanced the second half of the aria perfectly."

"I never thought of it in quite those terms. But did you read the review in the *Gazette*?"

"Written by Giddlesheard, and he's a fool," she said contemptuously.

A slow smile was growing in Rees's eyes. "He loathed that section."

"More fool he." And: "My opinion matters to you?" she asked, still confused. The answer was in his eyes. And this was no time to stand by her pride, not in the darkness of the music room, with the candles making his hair look like coal touched with edges of flame, his eyes like dark pools. No time for dishonesty. "I have always known that you were the true musician of the two of us," she said. "I never thought you'd want me to praise you." She looked at her hands. "I just wanted you to think that I was clever."

He still didn't say anything. She finally looked up to find his eyes fixed on her face. He had beautiful eyes, with the thickest black lashes she'd ever seen.

184

"You wanted *me* to think you were clever," he repeated.

Helene raised her chin: in for a penny, in for a pound. "I listen to your operas more carefully than any other piece of music," she confessed. "Obviously, I couldn't go more than once. It would seem odd. So I listen for something—anything—I can say to you that will demonstrate my own . . ." Her voice trailed off. "I have been wretchedly ill-bred and ill-mannered," she said quietly. "I'm ashamed of myself."

Rees reached out and pulled up her chin so his wife's eyes met his, those astounding honest, green eyes of hers. "Did you truly like parts of the *Elephant*?"

"I loved it," she said flatly. "Everyone did, Rees. You know that."

"The hell with everyone. Did *you*?"

"Of course."

He dropped his hand with a bark of laughter. "Do you know how I write these scores, Helene? Do you?"

She blinked at him. "No."

"I sit here and I try something, and then I think, *What would Helene think of that?* And then I hear your voice saying that it's underwritten, or tiresome, or—sometimes—clever. Never exquisite."

"Oh, Rees," Helene said aghast. "I had no idea. None!"

"I know you didn't," he said with that little half-smile again.

There was an odd silence between them. "I feel like such an idiot," she said miserably. "Here I've spent the last nine years picking your music apart, just to make myself feel clever." She couldn't even bear to look at him; a sense of humiliation was growing in her chest.

"You have never been an idiot," Rees said. He pushed open the piano lid with a snap that made the candles flicker and dance. "What if I wrote this section in B-minor, then moved into D-major from the *Cantabile*?"

"Why a major?" Helene said, distracted from her self-loathing for a moment. She tried it. "Moving it to G-minor would make it even darker, more interesting."

"But I want a witty resonance there, not gloom," Rees said, pushing her aside in his turn and demonstrating.

Helene looked down at his powerful hands, then at his black hair, gleaming in the candles, at his powerful shoulders. It's all changed, she thought.

"You're not paying attention," Rees said. "Listen to this."

"Try it slower this time," she said. "*Andante*."

Chapter Twenty-Two

The Vicar Falls in Love

Tom arrived in the breakfast room to find it empty. He was not a man given to self-delusion; he knew perfectly well that his step slowed at the door because he didn't see Lina, not because of the absence of his growling brother, nor Rees's incomprehensible wife.

"Would you like a dish of kippers, Mr. Holland?" Leke inquired.

"No, thank you, Leke. Merely a cup of coffee and some toast, please." He couldn't bring himself to ask about Lina. "Has my brother eaten yet?"

"Lord Godwin is still in bed," Leke responded. "He was working at the piano quite late at night." After fussing for a moment with the dishes on the side table, Leke left, closing the door behind him.

Tom sat down and found himself wondering what Lina looked like in the morning, all sleepy and rumpled. Before he realized it, he was struggling with the impulse to run up the stairs and knock on Lina's door. In the general run of things, Tom didn't find himself faced with much temptation of the ungodly sort. His parish was small and such nobility as there were in Beverley attended the much larger and more majestic Minster Church. That didn't mean he was ignored by the local gentry: the younger son of an earl, with a good private living, would never be ignored. But the temptations offered by local damsels had not, so far, been much of a struggle.

Lina was another story.

I want her, Tom thought to himself. I want her more than I've wanted any woman in my life. And it's not just lust (although he was uneasily unaware that he was possessed by a feverish variety of that emotion, such as he'd never experienced before). But I want all of her, he reassured himself: that silly chuckle, her odd knowledge of the Bible, even those horrible jokes she keeps offering to tell me.

Very precisely he cut his toast into small squares. He'd spent a great deal of his life respecting his instinct. An unmanly thing to do, perhaps, but it had worked for him. Instinct had led him to take the healthy inheritance his mother left him and more than triple it with shrewd investments. Instinct had told him to return to London and patch things together with his brother. Instinct told him . . .

Lina was the one for him. She was wildly unsuitable for a vicar's wife. Marrying her would likely ruin the possibility of his ever being transferred to a larger parish. Moreover, if his local bishop found out that he had married his brother's mistress, he'd be thrown out of his parish entirely. Marrying her would . . . marrying her was his only option, so why should he worry about the consequences? He finished his toast. If only he could just throw her over a horse and flee back to the North Country.

He didn't see Lina until afternoon. She didn't come to luncheon, and neither did Rees. And neither did Helene for that matter, although Tom could hardly blame her for taking meals in her room. He was surprised his brother's wife emerged at all. Finally, he was so tired of waiting around downstairs that he decided to visit Meggin in the nursery.

The moment he walked down the hallway, he heard laughter. Lina laughed with the clear, belly-rocking enjoyment of a child, not with the practiced thrills of a courtesan. Because she was not a courtesan, Tom thought to himself, pushing open the door. Her clear eyes could not lie to him. His brother—his own rotgut brother—had made her a kept woman, a mistress. Tom hated the truth of it. It made him feel as if a piece of steel was lodged in his chest.

Lina was sitting on a low stool next to the window and Meggin was standing behind her, drawing a brush through her long hair. Neither of them saw him for a moment. Meggin was utterly concentrated on watching the gleaming river of Lina's hair run by her brush, and Lina was saying, "so you see, Meggin, the miller didn't have any choice other than to send his three sons out to seek their fortune."

"Why couldn't they stay home with him?" Tom said, walking toward them. Lina looked up quickly, and there was a welcome in her eyes. "Good afternoon, Miss McKenna," he said, with a bow, and, "Hello, Miss Meggin." Meggin didn't even look up, just kept watching as if mesmerized, as her brush swirled through the silk of Lina's hair.

"Meggin, darling," Lina said, twisting about. "I think my hair is sufficiently groomed. May I ask you to brush my hair again later, please?"

A flash of real anger crossed the little girl's face and she reached out to grab Lina's hair and keep it in place.

"This afternoon," Lina said calmly, standing up and handing Meggin the swansdown muff.

Meggin blinked and began to brush the muff carefully.

"If you would ring that bell, Mr. Holland," Lina said, "Rosy will return to the nursery to take charge of Meggin."

Tom rang the bell. "Meggin," he said, turning back to the little girl, "would you like to go for a ride in the park this afternoon?"

189

She didn't look up or reply in any way.

"I thought perhaps you might like to see the lions in the Tower of London?" he tried again.

She still didn't look up, but she said something.

"What?" he asked.

"Izzat near the Pewter Inn?"

"No," he said.

Her mouth trembled for a moment and she went back to brushing the muff without a word.

At that moment, Rosy bounced into the room and so they left.

"Meggin is not happy," Lina said without preamble, after Tom closed the door behind them. "She speaks only in order to ask when she will see Mrs. Fishpole."

"I could take her back there, but only for a visit," Tom said rather helplessly. "Meggin was sleeping on a pile of rags in the corner, and Mrs. Fishpole's circumstances were not such that she could take Meggin in herself."

Lina walked down the hall. "So you rescued her? Just like that? Took her away without a second thought?"

"I had no choice," Tom said, feeling oddly defensive.

"Why not?"

"Because there I was, and Mrs. Fishpole said to take her, and so I—"

"But why were you there?"

"I saw Meggin in an inn yard, and I thought perhaps she was in an unenviable position."

"You meant to rescue her," Lina said flatly. "You meant to rescue her from the moment you saw her."

"It wasn't so simple," Tom replied, nettled.

"How many children *have* you rescued?"

Her hips were swaying before him in a way that made it hard for Tom to concentrate. "Not many."

"It must give you quite a glow of virtue." She walked into the library and tucked herself onto a couch, looking up at him.

Was her tone scornful? Tom felt a wave of irritation. "That has nothing to do with it," he said.

"Poppycock," she said flatly. "You vicar types are all the same. You enjoy wearing a halo, so you removed Meggin from the only mother she had ever known—Mrs. Fishpole. And that was a mistake."

Tom was conscious of a feeling of resentment. "Mrs. Fishpole couldn't keep her much longer. Meggin was sleeping on a pile of rags in the corner, and Mrs. Fishpole herself told me that she was worried for Meggin's safety. Do you understand what I mean?"

"Of course I do," Lina said impatiently. "So you galloped in like a knight in shining armor and took Meggin away, did you? It must have given you quite a pious glow, for an hour or two at least."

"It wasn't like that," he protested. "And why are you so scornful of an honest effort to help a child?"

"I'm not," she said. "But I am quite familiar with the godly sort rushing in to save people and doing it without forethought, and without the ability to admit that they may have been mistaken."

"So the mistake I made was to remove Meggin from Mrs. Fishpole, rather than Mrs. Fishpole from the inn," he said.

She nodded. "But surely you have thought of some pious justification for removing her so abruptly from her mother to counter my criticism?"

"Mrs. Fishpole is not her mother," Tom protested. But he'd never been one to deny a fair point. "You may be right. Although I do not agree that I did so merely for a sanctimonious bout of aggrandizement."

She wasn't looking at him anymore. Instead she was frowning and examining her fingernails. "We have to take her back."

Tom sat down next to her without asking for permission. "Meggin can't live in the kitchen forever."

"No, of course not," Lina said, throwing him an impatient look. "But she needs her mother. Mrs. Fishpole will have to find other circumstances. What a pity that Rees already has a cook."

"I suspect Rees wouldn't like a cook whose main facility seemed to lie in fish and sausage pie," Tom said. "Apparently he pays Cook one hundred guineas a year."

Lina gave up the idea of sacking Rees's Cook while he wasn't paying attention. "We have to do something. The poor little scrap: her eyes are like to make *me* start crying!" Lina never cried. That was a rule she set for herself the very first day she left home, when she got to London and discovered that her purse had been stolen and all her money was gone.

"I thought I would find her a family when I returned to East Riding," Tom said.

"Who would take in an orphan?" Lina asked. She had seen many so-called charitable people decline to give a farthing to a beggar.

"I could pay for her support."

"You? A vicar?" Lina laughed. "I can estimate how many pounds a year you earn, Mr. Holland. It's a wonder you had the money to come to London, let alone support an orphan!"

"How much do you think I earn?" he demanded.

"Of course, you may have money in rents, but your living is unlikely to pay more than two hundred pounds a year. An amount that would almost pay for this gown," she said, touching a fold of cloth.

Lina was wearing a crimson morning gown made in the Russian style, with white tassels on the shoulders. She looked adorable and utterly expensive. Tom had never had much use for the money his mother left him other than supporting charity, but now he sent up a fleeting prayer of thanks. Lina could be the best-dressed vicar's wife in the kingdom, if she wished. "The gown was a worthy purchase, in your mind?" he said, putting an arm on the back of the couch, but not touching her shoulder. "You certainly look lovely in it."

"Of course it was! I am particularly fond of the silk fringe, which is all the rage. One cannot step outdoors without a fringe this year."

"And would that gown cost more than I might give to a family to support Meggin for a year, in your estimation?"

She narrowed her eyes. "I despise that sort of trick, Reverend. Believe me, I'm an old hand at avoiding guilt. And I don't think much of you for trying it. I'm not one of your flock."

Tom grinned. "No more you are. A fact about which I am very sorry."

She shrugged. "You're a vicar. How else can you behave?" Suddenly she seemed utterly uninterested in him, as if he were no more than a tedious houseguest whom she was forced to entertain. "I shall ask Rees to support Mrs. Fishpole," she said. "He can more than afford it, and he never refuses any of my monetary requests." She said it flatly, without a gleam of triumph in her voice.

Tom looked at her until she finally looked away. This vicar with deep gray eyes was altogether disturbing. It's only his similarity to Rees, she had told herself the night before. For all Rees had never loved her, she had loved him. And here was the vicar, with all of Rees's unruly looks and burly body, but paired with eyes that felt as if they looked to her very soul. How annoying.

"Wouldn't you rather sell the gown?" he asked her.

"Given all your talk of my gown, I can only assume that you wish *me* out of the garment," she said; leaning back against the couch, she gave him her most enticing smile, the one she had practiced for hours.

He looked at her more intently than anyone ever had in her life; more intently than even her mama had looked when Mama knew full well that Lina had been stealing blackberries from Mrs. Girdle's garden. "That goes without saying," he said with a grin that made laughter lines appear around his eyes. "There's no man alive who wouldn't look at all those buttons and feel his fingers twitch."

Lina couldn't help but grin back, for all he was a vicar and she didn't like the species. "I thought a man of God was above such feelings," she said impudently. "Shouldn't you be upstairs praying for your soul?"

"Who told you vicars had no feeling?" he said, looking distinctly amused. "And my soul suffers nothing from loving you, Lina. You are as beautiful a creature of God as I've ever seen."

"Love?" she said, hooting. "Your tongue slipped there, Reverend!"

"No, it didn't," he said quietly. One touch of his hand on her cheek and she stopped her rather feverish laughter. He was looking at her that way again.

Lina felt a wash of nervous fear. "Did you hear the jest about the bishop who heard a noise in the night," she said, "but when he got up to see—"

"Hush," the vicar murmured, as he moved toward her, eyes intent on hers.

Lina knew why men had broad shoulders; it was so that one could clutch them when you couldn't see. And you couldn't see because the vicar—the vicar—had crushed his mouth against hers and he was kissing her in a way she'd never been kissed. Not by Hugh Sutherland, nor by Hervey Bittle, and never once by Rees Godwin.

"Are you"—she gasped some time later—"are you *sure* you're a vicar, Tom?"

He looked at her, and his eyes were glowing with something she couldn't quite recognize. "No question about it."

Well, she could have answered that herself. Look at the way he never touched her below her shoulders, although his hands had made havoc of Meggin's hairstyling. "You don't kiss like a vicar," she whispered. His lips were so beautifully shaped that she had to lean close again and taste him.

"And you don't kiss like another man's mistress. If I weren't a vicar," he said rather hoarsely, "you'd be in some danger, Lina."

Lina didn't see what *she* could possibly be in danger of. Sure, and she was a lost soul, they both knew that. The thought was a bit lowering. He seemed to read her thoughts.

A hand forced up her chin. "You're no strumpet, Lina McKenna," he told her.

"Just because you don't like the truth does not mean that you can command it not to be so," she said, managing a wry smile.

"I know it to be so," he said.

She had to marvel at the confidence in his voice. Men were like that. Her father was like that. Undoubtedly, he would welcome her back as a lost sheep . . . forgiveness is the Lord's, he would say.

"Doesn't it get tiring to be so good all the time?" she said, and the edge in her voice was half for him and half for her absent father.

He was running his hands through her hair, straightening out the tangles that he had put there. "Yes," he said frankly.

Her father never said such a thing. He was endlessly forgiving and loving, tiresomely understanding, tediously perfect. "Still, I suppose you have never broken one of your vows," she said sharply. "Not one of the Ten Commandments and their permutations."

Tom kept his hands sweeping through his Lina's glorious hair. He was learning something very interesting. "I haven't had much trouble with *Thou shalt not commit adultery*," he said mildly. "It's a good thing you're not married. I think I prefer, *Thou shalt love thy neighbor as thyself*." He paused and dropped a kiss on her head. "I favor adhering to *that* commandment, Lina. You are, after all, my neighbor."

She ignored his punning. "What about the question of fornication, Reverend? What of that?"

"Tom," he reminded her. "Fornication is not a sin I worry about."

"How can you say that?" she said sharply. "*You*, who wishes to unbutton my gown?"

He drew her close and said it in her ear. "Fornication is to couple with a woman whom one does not love. My temptation would be to make love before sanctifying our union. But it would be making love. Make no mistake about that, Lina."

She shook her head. "You're cracked, Reverend. It must go with the black frock."

"So who was the vicar in your life?" he asked.

"He still is a vicar," she corrected him. "My father. Reverend Gideon McKenna, County Dumfriesshire, Scotland."

She couldn't see him, so Tom let his grin spread across his face. She was a vicar's daughter, his rebellious little Lina. No wonder she talked so fluently of Salome. No wonder she hadn't succumbed to the greater sins of London, and fell only to the blandishments of his brother because she was in love

196

with him. "What is your father like?" he asked, hardly daring to breathe in case she got up and ran from the room.

"Perfect," she said flippantly. "Absolutely perfect in every way."

"An unusual trait," Tom said, rather taken aback. "Do you find the rest of humanity sadly flawed in comparison?"

"Oh no," she said, shaking her head rather violently. "There's nothing more wearing than perfection. I hate it."

"What do you mean?"

"No matter what I did as a child, no matter what the crime, he understood and forgave me."

Tom was silent. Her experience was so very far from his own that he hardly knew what to say.

"I know," she said crossly, "it sounds heavenly, to use the appropriate word."

He pulled her onto his lap. Surely this didn't count as over-intimate touching. A second later he changed his mind as he realized exactly where her sweetly rounded bottom was nestled.

"Those commandments . . . *He* never faltered in adhering to them," she said.

Tom tried to take his mind off his body. Outside the window was a fat squirrel, his little paws holding up a nut like a communion wafer, his plump cheeks moving briskly as he peered in at them.

"The only problem with living with a saint," Lina said, "is that he always loves God more than you."

Tom tightened his arms. Surely it wouldn't lead to sinful intimacies if he kissed her ear. It was so exquisitely delicate, peeping from her hair.

"One year I was chosen to sing the lead in the village Christmas pageant," she said. "I was so proud of it. I was singing the role of the Angel Gabriel, you see, and had all the best solos. I practiced for weeks."

"I expect you were marvelous," Tom said, and was alarmed to hear the husky note in his own voice. He quit kissing her ear. Any moment now she would notice what she was sitting on.

"I might have been," she said. "But the night before the pageant my father caught me kissing Hugh Sutherland behind the kitchen door. He was horrified, naturally." She looked up at him with the most beautiful hazel eyes that Tom had ever seen. "He prayed for two hours and then told me that he had to take away the thing that I most wanted, because God had strictly forbidden lechery. So no Angel Gabriel."

"I'm sorry," he whispered, kissing her nose, and the corner of her eye, and the sweet bend of her cheek.

"But that wasn't really the whole of it. He thought I took too much enjoyment in the song itself, you see, rather than in the content of the words. From the time I was a small girl, he tried to teach me not to love my own voice, but to love the words I spoke or sang."

"Make a joyful noise unto the Lord," Tom offered.

"Psalm sixty-six," Lina said wearily. "That night he told me I couldn't sing Gabriel, and that he didn't want me to sing at all for six months. Not at all."

Tom held her tight. It was as if someone had tried to silence a songbird.

"I was frantic. My mother begged him. I think in the end he regretted it. But he couldn't admit to having made an error, because it was undertaken for godly reasons. He had made a vow to that effect, you see—that he wouldn't allow me to sing for six months for the good of my soul—and he couldn't break the vow, no matter the consequences, or the foolishness of it." She hid her face against his shoulder.

"After midnight I sneaked out of the house and lost my virginity to Hugh in the cowshed."

"Lucky Hugh," Tom whispered.

"And the next day," Lina continued, "I caught the mail-coach to London at five in the morning. I was determined to find a place where people would ask, nay, *beg* me to sing."

"Oh, sweetheart," he said, holding her even tighter.

"Kiss me again, Tom?"

"I don't know," he said, nipping her ear with his teeth. "I have this odd feeling that I ought to go upstairs and start making a series of wild vows so that I can break them all tomorrow."

"Later," she said, turning her face up to his. "I *do* like the way you kiss."

"Am I more adroit than Hugh Sutherland?" he said, his lips hovering above hers.

"Kiss me again, and I'll tell you," she said, just before he stole her breath away.

Chapter Twenty-Three

Talk of Marriage

Lady Griselda Willoughby's residence
Number 14, Chandois Street
Cavendish Square

"The point is, darling, you must get married. It's your duty to
the name, etc., etc. Surely you can imagine the rest of the
lecture without my having to take the trouble to spell it out."
Lady Griselda Willoughby waved her hand languidly in the
air.

"You are a lazy creature, Gressie," the Earl of Mayne told
his sister, not without affection. "But you'll have no success
bringing me to that point, even if you exerted all your
energies."

"Well, I don't see why not. I quite enjoyed being married
to poor Willoughby."

"I doubt you can even remember what he looked like."

"Nonsense," Griselda said, quite stung by the sardonic look
in her brother's eyes. "It's only been ten years, you know, and
I do declare that the very mention of his name makes me feel
quite, quite *triste*." She caught sight of herself in the mirror
that hung over the mantelpiece and arranged her face into a
charmingly tragic expression. She was an enchantingly lovely
woman of thirty years, who prided herself on looking at least
eight years younger, and perhaps all of ten, by candlelight.

"You must have indigestion," her brother said rudely. "Willoughby was all right in his own way, but you were only married for a year or two before he popped off. And since you haven't shown any signs of fixing yourself in another marriage, I don't know why you'd wish the fate on me."

"*I* am not the question," Griselda said majestically. Then she rather ruined the effect by rummaging through her reticule and pulling out a screw of paper. "Although I might marry Cornelius. Do look at this, Garret! He has written me the most delicious poem."

"Cornelius Bamber is a fop," her brother said. "But if you can stomach the man's manner, I've got no objection to your marrying him."

"*My love is like to ice*," Griselda said dreamily.

"*And I to fire*," her brother put in.

"How did you know that?" Surprise actually brought Griselda to a sitting position, a rare event given as she thought her figure showed to its best advantage at a slight decline.

"On second thought, don't marry Bamber. A man paltry enough to borrow poetry from Spenser doesn't deserve your esteem."

"Piffle!" she said. "I never thought to marry Bamber. Is Spenser alive, a friend of Byron's, perhaps? It is the most delicious poem. I would like to meet him."

"Dead. Very dead. It's Edmund Spenser, and he was a contemporary of Shakespeare's."

Griselda pouted and threw the sheet of paper to the side. "To return to the point," she said, eyeing her brother. "You need to marry. You're getting doddering for the marriage market."

"I haven't seen any revulsion amongst my female acquaintances."

"That's because you don't know any marriage-minded mamas," she said.

He shrugged. "Why should I? A woman with a daughter to put on the market has no time for games."

"*You* need to think of something other than games as well," she said with asperity. "I'm the last to read you a lecture, Garret, but I haven't any children, and if you are uncivil enough to die and leave Papa's estate and the title to those rubbishing offspring of Cousin Hugo, I shall never forgive you."

"I don't mean to," Mayne said. The profusion of rosebuds sprinkled around his sister's drawing room was starting to make his teeth clench. "I'll marry in my own good time."

"And how old will you be by then?" she said, giving him a clear, direct look that he tolerated only from her. For all their teasing, neither of them had ever been as close to another person as they were to each other. "I'd like you to have a babe while you're still able to throw the lad up on a horse yourself."

"I'm not that old!" Mayne said.

"You're thirty-four. You're been caterwauling around town for years now. You're dangerously close to turning into a joke."

His customary sardonic gleam was replaced by a flare of real anger. "Careful. You're getting dangerously close to insulting."

She took out a fan and waved it before her face. "I mean to be. You need a shake-up, Garret. At this rate, there won't be a matron in London whom you haven't slept with."

He had turned toward the fireplace and was scowling down into the unlit logs. Griselda bit her lip and wondered whether to keep talking at him. But he straightened and turned around.

"I suppose I could consider matrimony," he drawled.

"Good," she said with some relief.

"But not at the moment. I've something in train, and I've a mind to finish it."

Griselda knew well enough when there was no moving him. "Countess Godwin?" she said, with a raised eyebrow.

"Precisely."

"I heard all about it, naturally. I'd keep an eye out for Godwin, though. The man's not fully tamed, you know."

"He was civil enough when he found us in the music room together," Mayne said indifferently. "The problem is that the lady has disappeared. No one has seen her in days."

"Perhaps she's retired to the country, worn out by chopping off all her hair," Griselda suggested, giving her own blond tresses a loving pat. She shivered with fear when her ringlets had to be trimmed.

"Her household claims that she is taking the waters. But I went to Bath and there's no sign of her. Nor in her country house either."

"Goodness, you *are* all het up over this one," Griselda said, rather entertained. "Traveling all the way to Bath. Well, I can tell you precisely where she is!"

He swung around. "Where?"

"Hiding until her hair grows back. I didn't see the effect myself, but I am told that she made a Statement. And you know, Garret, one does rather regret a Statement the next morning. I certainly did, after I wore that Prussian gown with the blue ostrich feathers to the Queen's Birthday."

"Hiding where?" Mayne demanded. "I don't want her to hide. I thought her hair was delightful."

"You'll find her," Griselda replied, giving him a narrow-eyed glance over the pocket mirror she had taken out of her reticule. "Just get the whole business out of your way before the end of the season, will you not? I'd like to see you tie the knot this summer, and you'll need at least two weeks to choose a bride and ask for her hand."

Mayne suppressed a shudder. "I can't imagine I'll find a woman whom I'd wish to see every morning for breakfast."

Griselda was painting her mouth with a small brush. "Don't bother," she suggested. "After I learned that Willoughby was fond of eating calves' head pie for his first meal, we never ate together again. And our marriage was perfectly amiable, I promise you."

"I'll let myself out," Mayne said, bending down and dropping a kiss on his sister's cheek. "Prettying yourself up for Bamber, *soi-disant* Edmund Spenser, are you?"

"Naturally," she said, patting her cherry-red lips delicately with a handkerchief. "I am most looking forward to exposing his little scheme. You are *such* a useful brother, dearest. And you have such unusual talents! There's not another man in London who could identify that Spenser poem, I warrant you."

But the Earl of Mayne paid her compliment little heed. He had no interest in his own ability to remember poetry (he'd always found a love poem or two to be the greatest help in fixing a reluctant matron's affections, although he scrupulously granted the poems their proper authorship). He just wished he were cleverer at finding errant countesses.

It was positively infuriating. He couldn't get her out of his mind: that slender, fawnlike grace, the tender curve of her slim shoulder, the way her eyes seemed to take up half her face, the way her eyebrows arched high at the corners of her eyes, the way her hair—damn, but he hoped she wasn't growing her hair. A woman that beautiful had no reason to doll up her hair with fussy little ringlets, the way his sister did. Helene's hair had felt as sleek and slippery as water, gliding through his fingers. He wanted more.

Outside his sister's townhouse, the earl paused and adjusted the shoulder capes on his greatcoat before springing into the seat of his high-perch phaeton. If Helene were indeed hiding until her hair grew back, he thought with a grin, there was no reason not to afford her some amusement while in retirement. His smile grew as he considered the possibility. He never believed that story of Helene taking the waters, for all her household and friends had insisted on it. She wasn't the type of woman to sit around docilely sipping cups of water that smelled of rotten eggs. No, his sister was likely right. She regretted her hair, and she'd gone to ground like a partridge during a hunt.

With a flip of the reins, the earl started off decisively down Chandois Street. He could guess who might tell him where Helene was.

And he was a master at the hunt.

Chapter Twenty-Four

Come, Come, Come to the Ball!

She and Rees had worked on the score until morning light started to creep into the music room; by then her headache was already in full force. At some point Saunders had crept into the bedroom and enquired whether she wished to rise, but Helene had waved her off with a groan. "Not until this evening," she'd said, wondering whether she would ever rise from the bed again without feeling the ground lurch under her feet.

When the door to her chamber opened at two o'clock, and brisk footsteps approached the bed, Helene wearily opened her eyes again. But it wasn't Saunders; it was Rees, standing next to her bed looking disgustingly healthy.

"Go away," she moaned, putting her hand to her brow like any self-respecting heroine in a melodrama.

"Time for you to get up," he said cheerfully. "I heard from Leke that you're not in the pink of health, so I've brought you Cook's remedy for a bad head."

Helene eyed the glass he held with great suspicion. "Thank you, but no. I never drink things that foam," she said with a shudder.

"Today you do," Rees announced, and without further ado, he grabbed her around the shoulders, hoisted her into a sitting position and stuck the glass to her lips.

"How dare you!" Helene protested, rather feebly as her head was reeling from the sudden movement. She tasted the drink. It was as vile as it looked.

"Drink every drop," Rees commanded.

"Why are you plaguing me?" she moaned.

"I've a new idea for the second act," he said.

Some women might think his excitement was adorable, the way his eyes were gleaming with exhilaration.

"It came from something you said last night, about the tenor aria in *The White Elephant*."

Helene had given up the battle and was struggling her way through the glass. At the end she pushed him away and flopped back onto her bed. She felt worse, if that was possible. "Go away," she said. "Please."

A footman staggered in carrying pails of steaming water, followed by a second with a tin hipbath. "Bit of a pity having to carry it all the way up here," Rees remarked. "I've had water piped into the water closet off my bedchamber, Helene. You'll have to take a look."

Helene covered her eyes and wondered whether she could have slipped into a long bad dream, without noticing. How could her husband think that she would overlook the presence of his mistress in *her* bedchamber and merrily investigate the plumbing arrangements? Maybe she was dreaming all of this, and she would wake up back in her own bed. But if it was a dream, why was her head hurting so?

Although . . . she had to admit . . . the pain seemed to be receding slightly.

"Do you need some help getting into the bath?" Rees said, looking perfectly prepared to jerk her from her covers and toss her into a steaming tub of water.

"No," she said wearily, managing to get her feet on the ground. "Get out of here, Rees."

"I'll wait for you downstairs," he said.

"I refuse to work on your score. I need fresh air."

"Where are you going to get that? You do remember that this house hasn't a garden to speak of, don't you?"

"I'll go to Hyde Park in a closed carriage," Helene said, abruptly remembering that all of London thought she was in Bath, taking the waters. "But I'm not sitting down at the piano, Rees, so you can just forget that idea."

"We'll go for a walk then," he said with unimpaired good humor. "Excellent notion. I can sing you the aria while we're strolling."

Helene put her head in her hands. "Out," she said hollowly. "Out, out, out!"

"I like your hair this morning," her husband said, giving her a wicked smile. "Especially the bit on top. The rooster crest is a nice effect."

"Out!" Helene said, lurching to her feet and glaring at him.

An hour later she trailed down the stairs, still feeling like a despairing heroine from one of Rees's operas, albeit one dressed in an exquisite blue walking costume that likely cost as much as a whole chorus's worth of Quaker costumes.

Rees was sitting at the harpsichord. He got up as soon as she entered. "The carriage is waiting and I've told Cook to pack a hamper, as you haven't yet eaten."

"I couldn't," Helene said faintly.

"Then I'll eat it," he said with a shrug.

"I had no idea that this part of Hyde Park existed," Helene said with fascination, a short time later. The grasses to either side of the little winding path had grown so tall that they touched the slouching limbs of the huge oaks. Daisies poked their heads above the seas of grasses like intrepid soldiers, fighting off nettles and thistles growing breast high.

"I've never met another soul here," Rees said. "All the polite sort prefer raked gravel paths."

Sometimes the oak trees bent down as if they'd been humbled, brushing their branches to the ground, and then suddenly they would fall back, leaving a patch of emerald grass, or a cascade of daisies. Twenty minutes later, Helene could no longer hear any din from the city at all, no sound of carriages, bells, or shouts. "It's like being in the country," she said, awed.

They rounded the bend and the trees trailed off again, forming another clearing. "How lovely," she said, walking into the middle of a lake of frothy white flowers shaped like stars and stooping to pick herself a flower or two.

When she glanced back, Rees was still standing on the path, his face unreadable. The sun fell relentlessly on his harsh face, on the lines around his eyes, the scowling eyebrows, the generous lower lip, those two dimples . . .

And Helene realized with a great thump of her heart that she'd never gotten over that first infatuation with him, that first blinding passion that had driven her out her bedchamber window and into his carriage, the better to make their way to Gretna Green.

She almost dropped the flowers she held, the realization was so blinding.

When Rees appeared at her side, hamper in hand and plopped himself onto the grass, squashing a hundred starflowers as he did so, Helene couldn't even bring herself to speak. She'd spent nine years telling herself that the brief infatuation that led to their elopement was a dream, a moment's blindness.

But it wasn't. Oh, it wasn't.

Numbly she helped Rees pull a tablecloth from the basket and load it with pieces of chicken, pie, fruit, and a bottle of wine.

She refused a glass of wine. "Hair of the dog," Rees said, "and very nice hair it is." He grinned at her. He had a chicken leg in his hand and was eating it like a savage. And he had that wicked look about him again, the one that made her think about the muscles hidden by his white shirt.

To her surprise, Helene found that she was hungry. She put a plate of chicken on her knee and began struggling to cut it properly.

"Don't bother," Rees said lazily. He was lying on his side, looking twice as comfortable in a bed of flowers as he did in a drawing room. "Just eat it, Helene."

She looked at him with disdain. "I don't eat with my fingers. I discarded that habit in the nursery."

"Who's to see? There's only you and I, and we're nothing more than an old married couple."

Old married couple implied comfort and ease, and she didn't feel any of that with Rees, particularly with the secret prickling awareness she had of his body. He had removed his jacket and rolled up his sleeves and one bronzed arm lay all too close to her. "It seems to me that you are always removing your clothing," she told him, eyeing him with distinct hostility. How dare he be so comfortable, while she was both overheated and hungry? Her beautiful little blue jacket felt altogether winterish with the sun shining on her back.

In answer, he sat up. Helene edged back. Rees was overpowering at close quarters. "Here," he said simply, holding the chicken leg to her lips.

"I couldn't!" But she hadn't eaten all day. Her stomach gave a little gurgle.

Rees laughed. "Go ahead. There's no one to see."

"You're here," she said mulishly.

"I don't count," he said, giving her an oddly intent look.

"That's one of the nicer things about being married, I always thought."

She took a bite. The chicken was delicious, faintly reminiscent of lemon. "It's exquisite," she admitted, taking another bite.

"I pay my cook extremely well," Rees said, ripping off a little strip of chicken and bringing it to her lips.

There was a dark, velvety something in his voice that made the little coil in Helene's stomach grow tighter.

But he drew back. "My idea is that I'll stage the second act not in the Puritan village, but in the court," he said. "You see, the Princess has left her beloved, Captain Charteris, behind. I'm thinking of adding a subplot in which the captain is being wooed by another lady."

"So the captain would be the focus of the act?"

Rees nodded. "I had an idea for a tenor solo. I took the words from the solo Fen wrote for the little Quaker girl who's in love with the Prince."

"I don't know how you keep all these lovers apart," Helene said, amused.

"See what you think," he said abruptly. And then he began to sing. "*Love, you're the brightest of bubbles, out of the gold of the wine. Love, you're the gleam of a wonderful dream, foolish and sweet and divine!*" Rees had a pure baritone that washed over her with as much potency as that brandy she had drunk the night before. And his music was wonderful: light, foolish, unutterably heartwarming.

Helene put the plate to the side and leaned back on her hands. Rees was watching her as he sang, which made her feel edgy, so she closed her eyes and tried to concentrate on the music. He was using too many long portamento phrases: it would sound mawkish in a tenor range, though it was lovely in Rees's warm baritone. Somehow, without the drive of the

211

last nine years to prove to Rees that she was intelligent, she couldn't think of another critique.

"*Come with me, come, come to the ball,*" Rees sang. The sunlight was warm on her eyelids. "*Flow'rs and romances fade with the day. Come in your beauty, fair as a rose . . . At the ball! At the ball!*" There was a finely tuned urgency in his voice, in the notes, a siren call that to miss the ball was to miss life, to miss love, to miss everything golden and beautiful.

Helene had to swallow a lump in her throat.

Now he'd reached the coda: his voice was deeper now, and slower, rather sleepy, but there was still that sense of deep urgency: "*Come, Come, Come to the ball . . . Romances fade with the opening of day . . . Come, Come, Come to the ball!*"

She didn't open her eyes when he finished, letting the emotion of it sweep through her, really enjoying Rees's music for the first time in years. Then the bright gold behind her eyelids darkened as his body blocked the sun. "Have I put you to sleep?"

At that, her eyes flew open, and she knew they were drenched and she didn't even care. "It was lovely."

He put a hand on her cheek. "Tears?"

She smiled, but the smile wobbled. "It was just so lovely. I've—I've missed your voice." She closed her eyes instinctively on seeing the look in his eyes and then his mouth was touching hers tentatively, just a brushing of lips.

How could she have forgotten how much she loved his kisses before they married? During her debutante year, they spent all the time they could retreating to the corners of ballrooms and talking of music, finding a piano and running through one of his compositions, and finally, when she knew him well enough, one of her compositions. And throughout it all, there was the thrilling matter of a kiss or two, stolen behind doors, taken in secret.

212

As to why they were so secret, who can tell? Her father was ecstatic that the heir to an earldom had formed an attachment to his gawky, plain daughter. "Why did we elope?" she asked now, weaving her fingers through his hair.

"I wanted you," Rees answered.

He was merely brushing his lips across hers. Helene hoped he wasn't thinking about how loudly she had proclaimed that kissing was disgusting, once it became associated with all the humiliation and pain of actual bedding.

Before those ugly times, before they eloped, her heart would become shallow and rapid at the mere sight of his mouth, and she dreamed of the moments he caught her behind a door and gave her a hard kiss. Those were the kisses of a boy, a boy without finesse and experience . . . at the time she thought he was the most potent and sophisticated lover who ever lived.

"Give me a real kiss, Rees," she said.

His hand was stroking her neck. It froze for a moment.

"Do you remember how you used to kiss me before we were married?" she asked.

"I must have been a beast, always pulling you into a corner."

"I loved it," Helene admitted.

"You never—"

"Ladies don't."

But Rees had clear memories of his wife refusing to kiss him with an open mouth, telling him he was disgusting to want such a thing. He hesitated. Their newfound friendship was so fragile and (although he didn't really want to think such a thing) important to him. Something about his wife made him feel, well, *whole*. He didn't want to frighten her off. To disgust her.

So she came to him. The wife who hated kissing opened her mouth and timidly, sweetly, begged for entrance.

Rees had always known he was no gentleman. And he'd known for years that he had no control around his wife either. Nothing seemed to have changed. He plunged into her mouth so violently that she toppled backwards into a bed of flowers and he came with her, his limbs tangling with hers, devouring her mouth.

All the while, some part of him was waiting for her to tear her mouth away, to push him away, to scream that he was depraved, disgusting . . .

But the only thing that happened was that slender arms wound around his neck and a slender body tucked itself into the hard curves of his body with such melting softness that he could barely stop himself from groaning with the pure delight of it.

Finally, he was the one who lifted his mouth from hers. "Helene," he said hoarsely. "You did say *every day*, didn't you?"

She opened her eyes, dazed. "Yes." Her voice was a whisper of sound. Perhaps he was crushing all the air from her lungs.

Of course he didn't move. Every inch of Rees's body was aware that he was cushioned between her thighs, his hardness pressing into her softness. But: "Am I too heavy for you?"

Her face was rosy, but her eyes had that clear honesty he loved. "I used to hate it when you lay on me," she said and stopped.

He propped himself on his elbows and dropped kisses on her high, arching eyebrows, on the edge of her eyes, on the delicate curve of her cheekbone. "Do you dislike it now?" he asked, carefully controlling his voice. His heart was pounding in his ribs, and it wasn't all a matter of desire either.

She had her eyes closed again. "No," she whispered, and to Rees's ears the little sound echoed around the glade with as much force as a shout.

Deliberately he thrust forward into the soft embrace of her thighs. A surge of blood went through his body so fiercely that he almost groaned out loud but caught himself. He didn't want to seem like an animal, grunting at his pleasure. "What about that, Helene?" he whispered, his lips slipping down to her slender neck. "How did that feel?"

Her hands were running feverishly through his hair and now one slipped to his shoulder. There was silence between them for a moment. Rees dimly heard the call of a bird in the distance.

She wasn't protesting. Cautiously he put a hand on her chest. She'd always hated his even looking at her breasts: he remembered that clearly enough. But last night she'd allowed him to caress them.

They gave in his hand with a movement that sent fire roaring through his blood. She had no corset on. Perhaps no chemise. His hands began to shake.

"Rees," Helene said, and there was an ache in her voice that startled them both. "Are you certain that you've seen no one in this forest?"

"Never, in five years of walking here," he said, looking down at her. Her face was flushed and her eyes were alive, glowing. "You can't be suggesting?"

Helene looked up at him and grinned. Esme had given her lots of instructions about little breathy moans, and cries of "Yes! Yes!" Esme had said nothing about smiles, or the laugh that seemed to be coming from deep in her stomach. "I don't feel like myself here," she admitted. "I feel—*wicked*."

His eyes were so dark that they sparkled like coal. "I like what you're doing," she said, tracing his eyebrow with one finger. "That—"

"Thrusting?" he said.

Her cheeks turned even pinker. "What a word!"

"Mmmm." Rees started unbuttoning the little porcelain buttons that ran up her jacket. He straightened, putting his weight on his knees. She lay under him like a slender nymph, the little twists of hair flying away from her forehead. "I like your hair," he said, to distract himself from unbuttoning.

"I thought you would hate it," she said, and there was an uncertainty in her voice that made him lean down and put a hard kiss on her lips.

"You look beautiful." Reverently he pulled the jacket open. She was wearing one of the muslin blouses that were so popular now, made of celestial blue muslin so thin that he could see the curve of her breast. He closed his eyes for a second, and then brought his hand to her breast.

She was watching him. "Do I look acceptable?" she whispered, holding herself perfectly still.

"Acceptable?" he said, and the word tore from his throat with a gutternal groan. "God, Helene, when have I . . ."

He seemed to lose track of the sentence, so Helene allowed him to help her out of the sleeves of her jacket. He didn't look at all as if he might laugh now. He was leaning over her almost as if—as if—and then his mouth closed over her nipple, covered by muslin as it was.

For a moment Helene was shocked into motionlessness. He was suckling her—actually suckling her, even though she was wearing a shirt. The shock of it sang through her veins like a trumpet.

"Rees!" she cried, and the sound floated away to the bird songs.

He jerked her shirt up, with such hunger that Helene swallowed another cry. Shutting her eyes against the sun, she felt as if liquid sunshine ran through her veins, as if her heart's blood thundered from the exquisite feeling of his mouth on her breast. She clutched his shoulders as hard as she could so that he couldn't move, couldn't leave, couldn't stop . . . But he left only to move his head to her left breast, and then his hand took up a tormenting rhythm, rubbing over her nipple hard and harder until she was twisting in his hands, her nails biting into his shoulders. Those hands could pick up any instrument, and coax an intoxicating melody from it, and it seemed she was no different.

So she didn't protest, not at all, not when he unbuttoned her skirt and there she was, naked in a forest glade. Not when his hand burned a trail down her stomach to her legs, and she—wanton that she felt—let him slip those fingers between her legs. The very touch of him made her shudder.

"Helene," he said. He'd taken his hand away, and the absence was almost painful.

She blinked at him. "Yes?" She had to clear her throat. "Yes?"

"I'd like to make love to you. Would that be all right?"

"Yes, yes of course," Helene whispered hurriedly, wishing that he hadn't asked her. "Did you speak to Darby?"

His eyes seemed oddly unfocused. "What? Why would I speak to Darby?"

Helene could feel waves of sobriety cooling her body. "You had a question about a lady's—" she stopped.

His face cleared. "No need," he told her, dropping a kiss on her lips. It felt so good that he lingered, hungrily, but his hands dropped between her legs. "See, Helene? See?" His fingers sank into her warmth.

She gasped. Instinctively her legs opened a bit and he slipped deeper. "You're ready," he whispered. "We didn't need any of those methods for ladies, whatever they are."

"Oh," Helene managed.

And then he was there instead of his fingers. Helene looked up at Rees. His face was dark with passion, jaw tight, and despite herself, despite the trembling pleasure she felt, she braced herself. There was no getting around the fact that bedding was something her body didn't do well.

Rees felt that rigidity as if her body was an extension of his own, and even though he hadn't entered her yet. "It will be all right," he said, swooping down for a kiss. But he wasn't sure, any more than she was. Would it be painful? By the end of the time they lived together, he was absolutely convinced that there was something about her body that prevented her from enjoying bedding. He'd heard of such things before.

She had her eyes closed tight. "It's been lovely so far," she said. "Go ahead, Rees. You enjoy this part."

He didn't move.

"Go ahead!" she commanded him, as fiercely as he told her to drink Cook's remedy, that very morning.

And so he did, cautiously, slowly, holding himself to an agonizingly slow pace.

Her eyes popped open. "It didn't hurt!" she said, obviously pleased.

"That's good," he said between clenched teeth. "Do you mind if I—"

"Oh, go ahead," she said, with a wiggle that nearly undid him. "It doesn't hurt a bit."

So Rees did. There was something missing though. He was flying, plunging into her tight warmth again and again, his vision black, not thinking of anything, except—

Except he wished that she found more pleasure from it. Helene lay under him with a little smile, and the very sight of her skin gleaming in the sun coming through the branches made him feel maddened, crazed. He slid hands under her hips and pulled her up.

Her eyes opened very wide and her mouth slightly parted. He searched her face, trying to see whether she found any satisfaction in what he was doing, but the roar of raw pleasure in his own ears racked his body, driving him forward. His vision went dim and he poured everything he had into her with a groan that burst from his lungs and echoed around the empty wood.

Two minutes later, Rees was lying on his back in the flowers, trying to force air into his gulping lungs, trying to stop shaking.

Helene was eating some chicken with her fingers, and chattering about how it *wasn't bad, not at all*, and *if it had been like this, years ago* . . .

Rees put his arm over his eyes. Foolish of him, to want anything else. To feel there was something wanting there. Stupid. Emotional. He had his release, and that was all that mattered. Wasn't it?

Chapter Twenty-Five
The Hunt Is On

Ambrogina Camden, the Duchess of Girton, was sitting in the garden of her townhouse, attempting to look regal. This wasn't an overly difficult proposition: Gina had a dignity and grace that made her a natural duchess. She was sitting bolt upright, her head carefully poised atop her spine, her pale red hair pulled back into a gleaming mass, the better to frame her beautiful facial bones. "How much longer?" she demanded of the man who had been scrawling sketch after sketch in black charcoal for the last two hours.

"Hush," the man said. And then, "Don't move, Gina, for God's sake!"

Gina quietly ground her teeth (duchesses do *not* show outside signs of irritation, even under extreme provocation) and straightened her spine again. If only Max's nursemaid would bring him down into the garden to play, he would certainly toddle over on seeing his mama and she could pick him up and end this tedious business of sitting for her own sculpture.

"One more moment," said the man, "this one is rather good. Lovely, in fact." There was a tone of ripe satisfaction in his voice. "I think I've got it, darling. What do you think?"

Gina hopped up and went around the man's shoulder to look. "No!" she said, on a rising shriek. "You promised, Cam! You promised!"

The Duke of Girton grinned at his wife. "What? You don't like the shell?"

"The shell?" Gina squealed. "Who cares about the shell? You've done me without a stitch of clothing!" She tried to snatch the piece of foolscap from him but he held it out of her reach.

"It will look lovely on the front lawn at Girton House," he said, his eyes sparkling. "I can't think of a better use for that pink marble that was delivered last week." With his free hand he caught his wife tightly to him.

"I won't let you," she promised, trying once more to grab the sheet of paper.

"It doesn't matter if you rip up this sketch," he said, lowering his other arm so she was trapped in the circle of his arms, and bending to kiss her neck. "I know your body, Gina . . . I could take a piece of clay from the riverbank and mold it in the dark, and people would call it exquisite." His mouth hovered at the corner of hers.

"You're naught but a rogue, to even think of sculpting your own wife without clothing." He smelled so lovely, and she *had* got up quite early to visit Max in the nursery, and her husband *did* have the most beautiful eyes, and his hands . . . "We're in public!" she scolded him.

"I could sculpt the curve of your bottom were I blinded," her husband said into her ear, sounding rather drunken. "Let's go upstairs."

"I couldn't," Gina said, enjoying herself immensely. "Max might come outside at any moment."

"He's in the nursery being bullied into eating far more rusks than he wishes for nuncheon." Cam had dropped the offending sketch to the ground and his hands were roaming freely. His mouth burned a trail across her cheek . . . Gina turned to meet his lips.

221

"Yes," she whispered, opening her mouth to him, to the charcoal and chalk, the wild man whom she married. His tongue slid slowly across her lips, came to her with a sudden passion that made Gina fold into his arms in helpless surrender.

"Your Grace," came a pompous voice.

Gina tried to tear her mouth from Cam's but he wouldn't let her, finishing his kiss, lingering there without regard for the liveried butler standing at a polite distance.

"Yes, Towse," Cam said finally, not looking up from her face. He was tracing the line of his wife's rosy mouth with a finger.

"Her Grace has a visitor," Towse said majestically, his eyes fixed on a nearby bush. "The Earl of Mayne."

"If Mayne thinks he's going to add you to the notches on his bedpost, he'd better think again," Cam said softly, and suddenly the urbane duke disappeared, replaced by a muscled wild man who had spent years in Greece and thought Greek husbands weren't overly savage when it came to protecting their women.

"Mayne is wooing Helene," Gina told him.

Cam thought about that for a second. "She could probably use his attentions," he said with a wicked grin. "I always thought she was a bit too sober for her own good."

"Cam!" Gina protested, an instant scowl appearing on her face. "I won't have my friends insulted by you or anyone else." She turned to Towse and called, "Please ask the earl to join me in the garden."

"I'll give you ten minutes with that seducer," her husband said, grabbing her slim waist again and pulling her back against his hard body. "Ten minutes only, Gina, and then you belong to *this* seducer."

Objections trembled on Gina's lips, and then she realized that there was no point to cutting off her nose to spite her face. She no more wished to deny her husband's provocative smile than she wanted to kiss the Earl of Mayne, be he the most seductive man in London or not.

"All right," she whispered. "Ten minutes." Even meeting his eyes, seeing that sweep of smoky eyelash, made her stomach curl.

"Don't be late," he said, and the urgency in his tone had nothing to do with ducal responsibilities.

The Earl of Mayne found the duchess clipping roses and looking rather flushed from her gardening endeavors.

"How delightful to see you," she said, smiling at him and holding out a delicate hand.

Mayne admired the lovely picture she made, pale red hair gleaming in almost the precise color of the blush roses she carried in a basket. "It's a shame that you're so happily married," he said, dropping a kiss onto her palm. "May I say that I would be very delighted should that circumstance ever change?"

She chuckled, and the low, happy sound of it jolted his loins. If he could find a woman like *her*, marriage wouldn't seem such an unenviable prospect.

"I suspect you have come to see me for reasons other than my supposed marital bliss," she said, but the smile curling on her lips left him in no doubt that *bliss* was likely the right word.

"In fact," he said, "I was hoping you could give me the direction of your lovely friend Helene."

"Are you and Helene on terms of such intimacy, then?" she said, eyeing him with obvious curiosity.

"She was kind enough to give me leave to use her Christian name."

The duchess obviously remembered the story she had been told to recite. "Helene has decided to take the waters," she said piously. "She finds herself exhausted by the season. I'm afraid that I'm not at liberty to give her address to anyone."

"Hmm," Mayne said. "I would have thought the countess was one to eschew ill-smelling medicines. And when I saw her last . . . she was in the very pink of health."

"Yes, well," Gina said, conscious that at least eight minutes had passed since Cam went upstairs, "I'm afraid that I can't give you her direction without betraying her confidence."

He sighed inwardly and took a billet from his breast pocket. "In that case, would you be so kind as to forward this to her?" he enquired.

She gave him a beaming smile and began walking rather quickly toward the house. "I shall give it to a footman immediately," she said, towing him along.

Two minutes later, Mayne found himself deposited, rather unceremoniously, outside the front door. He walked to the pavement and then paused, examining his watch fob until the Girton butler closed the door. The house, and indeed the whole street, were sleepily dozing in the unexpected heat that had struck London that morning.

The only sign of life was the servants' entrance to the left. As Mayne watched, a greengrocer dropped off an order of cabbages. He nodded to the footman standing beside his carriage. "We'll wait here a moment or two, Bantam." If he wasn't mistaken about the duchess's character, she would dispatch of business matters at once.

Indeed. A footman, smartly dressed in Girton livery, emerged from a side door. Mayne smiled to himself. The footman passed a note to a groomsman; Mayne smiled again. The groomsman trotted sedately down the street on a placid old horse, and never noticed that he was being followed at some distance by a coach with an insignia on the door. Mayne smiled and smiled. He only stopped smiling when he realized precisely where the note was delivered.

What in the devil's name was Helene Godwin doing at the Godwin residence? Why was she staying with her oh-so-estranged husband, to be blunt about it?

Chapter Twenty-Six

Darling Girl

Helene's stomach gave an odd lurch when she walked into the library before dinner and saw Lina sitting next to Rees on a small settee. Her shock was likely due to revisiting her youthful infatuation with her husband. All the better reason to forget she ever felt the emotion in the first place. It had only taken an hour after they returned from the picnic for Helene to remember that her husband had a beautiful young woman sleeping in the room next to his.

"Champagne, my lady?" Leke said now, bowing. Helene gave him a nod of assent.

"I should like to go to Vauxhall tomorrow night," she announced in a high voice that almost cracked like shattered glass. "It's the only place I can think of where I can go without being recognized, and I simply cannot stay in this house day and night."

Lina looked up, startled, and Helene was gratified to see her spring further from Rees's side. It was a sad thing indeed when one was grateful for the good manners of one's husband's mistress.

"Don't have the time," Rees growled.

"Make it," Helene said, with a tone of pure steel in her voice.

Rees looked up from his papers. "What do you think I should put at the end of Act Two, when Captain Charteris has discovered the Princess in the Quaker village? All Fen has noted is 'musical number.'"

"Some sort of dance, I expect," Helene said, sipping her champagne. It was deliciously cold and icy, and made her feel almost as if she would sneeze.

"I could do a polonaise," Rees muttered.

"I'd do a waltz," Helene said. She would have wandered over to look at his paper, but she wasn't going anywhere near the couch, even if Miss McKenna was a frigid distance from Rees's hip now.

"A waltz? I have never written a waltz. Weren't you working on one last summer?"

That was the odd thing about Rees. He never forgot a passing word said about music, although he had never remembered her birthday, not even during the first year of their marriage.

"Yes," Helene said, finishing her champagne.

"How do you think the audience would take it?" he said, frowning. "I have quite a prudish contingent going to the Theatre Royal."

"When did you ever worry about shocking someone?" Helene asked. Rees's brother was taking Lina away to look out the far windows. That was diplomatic.

"You know I'm conventional. When it comes to music," Rees replied with a lopsided smile. Helene's heart skipped and steadied again. "Will you play me your waltz?"

"There's no piano here," she pointed out. And what if he didn't like it?

But Rees was standing up. "We'll go in the music room. Tom and Lina can dance for us. Tom!" he called. "You know how to waltz, don't you?"

His brother turned around. "No, I haven't the faintest idea how to waltz. The sight of their vicar trotting around

227

the dance floor would likely give my parishioners apoplectic fits."

"My father used to dance once in a while with my mother," Lina said to him with a giggle. "Though not a *waltz*, of course!"

"Too fast for a vicar, isn't it?" Rees said with satisfaction. "I can't think why I didn't write a waltz before. Come on, Helene. Lina, you show Tom the steps. It's easy enough and there isn't a single member of your godly flock here to disapprove, Tom."

A moment later they entered the sitting room. Helene put her arm on Rees's sleeve. "Did you forget something?" she asked, nodding at the floor.

Rees stopped and stared at the ocean of papers as if he'd never seen them before. "We can't—" he stopped.

Helene picked up a sheet. It had three words scrawled on it: *night dances past*. She handed it to Rees and picked up another. It had three staves of cascading arpeggios.

"Unfortunately, we cannot dance on paper," Tom said, looking rather relieved. "It wouldn't be safe. Miss McKenna might slip and fall."

Lina rounded on Rees. "Why *are* you keeping all this garbage?" she asked. "Do you honestly think there's a good piece of music on the floor somewhere?"

He looked at her, his face unmoving. But Helene saw a spark of uncertainty in his eyes and cursed Lina inwardly. How dare she make him feel worse about his music than he already did?

"There might well be something marvelous here," she said quickly. "This piece is breathtaking and fresh, for example." She sang the little score she had picked up from the floor, adding a couple of minor aeolian triplets, for emphasis.

Rees snatched it out of her hands and then gave her a hard look. "Breathtaking after you got hold of it, perhaps," he said. But he didn't sound truly distressed.

"Supper is served, my lord," Leke said, appearing behind them.

Rees dropped both sheets back to the floor. "Right," he said briskly, standing back and allowing Helene, Rees, and Tom to pass before him. "You are spared the indignity of waltzing for the moment, Tom."

"Tell the footmen to clear up all this mess," Rees said to Leke, jerking his head at the floor.

Leke's jaw literally fell open for a second before he snapped it shut. "Yes, sir," he said hastily.

"I should like the room cleared by the end of our meal. And move that harpsichord to the side so that we have a dancing floor," Rees said, striding after his wife.

In point of fact, he was striding after Lina and Tom, but somehow he didn't think of it that way.

"I didn't know that waltzes had a song with them," Rees said with considerable curiosity. "Where did you get the words from?" He had picked up Helene's score and was looking it over. Her fingers itched to grab it back. In the middle of the sitting room, Lina was showing Tom the steps of the waltz with a certain hilarity.

Helene bit her lip. The part of her that was terrified of being exposed as a rank amateur was urging her to dash from the room. "I wrote the words as well," she said, watching his eyes move over the paper.

Once he looked up at her briefly, but he said nothing. Then he put the score back down in front of her. "I feel as if I have never understood you."

Helene's eyes dropped to her fingers, waiting on the

229

keyboard to begin playing. "There's not very much to understand," she said, embarrassed.

"Shove over," Rees said, sitting down.

"*I'm* playing the waltz," Helene protested. But her body traitorously welcomed that broad shoulder next to her, the heat of his body.

"I'm going to have to sing it with you, aren't I?" he asked.

"I can sing it myself," she said, the color rising even higher in her cheeks.

"I thought there were two voices!" he said, picking up the score again.

"Oh, no," Helene replied. "It's only one. I never marked a change of voice."

"Well, you should have done so," Rees said. "Look, here's your first verse, ending with *Let me, lovely girl, embrace you, As would a lover his lovable bride.* That line repeats, right? *As would a lover his lovable bride.*"

Rees never sang things with florid emphasis. Instead his deep baritone took Helene's rather simple lines and gave them a masculine flair that turned them incantatory. "It seems obvious to me that the next verse should be sung by the bride, not the groom: *So surrender ourselves to the delicious deception, Happily imagining what will never come to pass, Happily imagining what will never come to pass.* The male voice wouldn't want to emphasize the fact their embrace will never come to pass. The female voice might, though."

"I never thought of making it a duet," Helene said, staring at the words. "I would have to rewrite the fourth stanza."

"If it was a duet, they could sing the final stanza together," Rees said. "*What has wilted once, ne'er blooms again. Never will rosy youth bloom for us, again* . . . That's a bleak line, but it makes sense to have their voices intertwine."

230

"Let's try it," Helene said. Tom and Lina seemed to be ready. In fact, they were holding hands as if they were about to start a country dance, rather than a waltz. "Tom," Helene called. "Do you feel able to give this dance a try?"

"Of course," he said, turning to Lina so quickly that he almost tripped.

"Right!" Helene said, nodding at Rees. "There's a musical portion first. The song doesn't begin until I've repeated this section twice. I'll count to three," she told Lina and Tom.

Lina curtsied before the vicar and then his hand settled at her waist.

"This is dangerous," Tom said, almost under his breath.

"Ready," Helene called, dropping her hands to the keyboard. The music flowed around them sweetly, a languorous, swirling invitation to dance.

Lina knew exactly why Tom called waltzing dangerous, but she chose to ignore his meaning. "My feet are in little danger," she told him. "You dance very well, for a man who tries these steps for the first time."

"You may regret that confidence; I'm going to attempt a turn."

"Do," she said. "We ought to move right down the room."

He misstepped and narrowly avoiding trampling on her toes. "There, Lina," he said, laughing down at her. "Your feet *are* in danger!"

She giggled.

"I think if I hold you more tightly," he said to her, "we'll move better together. Would that be agreeable to you?"

"All right," she said, struck by an unexpected wave of shyness.

"I suspect our bodies are scandalously close," he murmured into her hair a moment later.

But she was too taken by the realization that she was—she truly was—in *danger* to answer.

231

Rees turned the page for Helene and gave her a nod, indicating he would begin the song. She nodded back and he launched into the first verse: "*Let me, lovely girl, embrace you, As would a lover his lovable bride.*"

Helene could feel her cheeks growing warmer. Could it have been she who wrote of a lover *embracing* his bride? What was she thinking? It was her turn to sing. Her voice caroled high. She didn't have tremendous range, but she liked what she had, as the saying went.

Rees's darker growl took over again: "*Face to face with burning cheeks.*" She could feel him watching her, so she kept her own eyes primly on her fingers.

It was time to sing together. "*What has wilted once, ne'er blooms again,*" she sang, high and clear, and Rees's voice twined into hers, in a sweet descant, lowered to his baritone range, "*Never will rosy youth bloom for us, again.*" And isn't that the truth, Helene thought, rather sadly.

Rees took the last verse, repeating: "*Let me, darling girl, enfold you, As would a lover his lovable bride, as would a lover his lovable bride.*"

"It's not *darling girl*," she objected, as she played the final coda to the waltz. "I wrote *lovely* girl."

"You want an expression of affection, not a point about her looks," Rees said. Then he lowered his voice. "Did you happen to notice how much my brother is enjoying your music?"

Helene raised an eyebrow as she played the final chord. "The vicar sheds his Roman collar," she said, rather absent-mindedly. She didn't want to think about Tom.

"Let's try it again," Rees said. "This time, every other line with the male and then the female voice."

"That won't work," she objected.

"The song could echo the waltz itself, bringing a male and female body together," he said patiently.

Helene felt she must be going purple. What kind of an old maid—even if married—was she, writing lascivious songs? "I didn't think of the waltz that way!" she said.

"That's why the waltz is so improper," he said with a smile that made her uneasy. "It simulates intimacy, Helene. Surely you recognize that."

"Well, of course," she hastened to say. "I mean, the man puts his arm around the woman. That in itself is terribly unseemly."

"That's not the point," Rees said, sounding rather amused. "You knew exactly what I'm talking about when you were writing that music. Lina!" he called.

"Yes?"

"Will you play the waltz this time? Helene needs to get a sense of it in her feet."

"Oh, I couldn't," Helene said, feeling as if the last thing she wanted to do was waltz with her husband. A moment later, she found herself curtsying to Rees's bow. "This is *too* odd," she whispered to him, taking his hand. His other hand went around her waist as snugly as if they danced together all the time.

Rees had only asked Lina to play, but she started to sing as well. Helene almost stumbled when she realized what a beautiful voice her husband's mistress had. It hung in the air like honey, making the words Helene had written sound infinitely better, wiser, more allusive.

Rees drew her closer to him and let the music move them across the room, his leg advancing, and hers falling back. And all the time his arm pulled her closer and closer until there was no air between their bodies at all.

"Rees!" Helene hissed.

But the glint of amusement in his eyes turned her silent. Her gown wrapped around his muscled thigh and then blew free as he turned her with just a touch, in circle after circle after circle across the floor. She felt dizzy. The music pounded in her blood and prickled between her thighs. It danced in her feet and made her press closer to his chest.

"Do you see what I mean?" he asked conversationally. "The waltz starts out with a bit of introduction, undressing, as it were. A bow here, a flourish there. Then when the preliminaries are out of the way, the two dancers begin, first rather slowly and then faster and faster—" He spun her as he spoke. "The man holds his partner more and more tightly. They are in a closed position, his arms around her body."

Helene frowned at him.

"You do know the instructions posted at Almack's regarding the waltz, don't you?" he asked her.

"No." Why would she notice such a thing?

"The man and woman must be dressed decently." His eyes had a wicked glint.

She couldn't help it: she giggled. He swept her in a great circle. "I *think* they may be referring to a doublet and coat."

"Undoubtedly!" Helene said severely.

"*As would a lover his lovable bride*," Lina sang slowly, and again: "*As would a lover his lovable bride*."

Rees glided Helene to a perfect halt on the last breath of the song.

"You dance very well," he said, blinking at her in an almost startled fashion. But he didn't wait for a reply. "There's one line that needs changing, Helene." He dragged her over to the piano and Lina hastily slid off the piano bench. "I don't think the line about *fires of our hearts burning out* is right. You should replace it with something more joyful."

"But that's what I meant," Helene insisted. "You may think the waltz is about bedroom matters, Rees." She said it in a sharp undertone so that Tom and Lina couldn't hear. "But I

234

wrote a song about youthful love that fades and dies at the end of the song. So it starts with a great deal of enthusiasm and musical flourishes, but towards the end—"

"No, no," Rees interrupted. "That's far too disheartening. How would it be if you changed that line to something simpler and more cheerful?" He hummed the bar. "*Love into air?* No, that's no good."

"I don't want to," Helene said stubbornly. "I wrote the words, after all. They move from the lover's exuberance to the loss of those feelings."

He paused for a moment, suddenly struck. Then he looked at her sideways. "You wouldn't have put any of your life into this waltz, would you, Helene?"

She colored. "Of course not!" she snapped.

He stared at her for a moment and then put down the score. Of course she'd written it about their marriage, about the fire she felt in the heart—burning out. Suddenly his own heart felt like a charred, blackened cinder. "You're right. It's much better as it is."

"Shall we plan on Vauxhall tomorrow then?" Tom said, popping up at Rees's shoulder.

"Yes," Helene agreed, moving toward the door. "I'll send a note to my friends, and see whether either of them might wish to make up a party with us."

"I should be working," Rees put in.

"Nonsense!" Lina said with a laugh. "You work entirely too much."

Because there's nothing in my life *but* work, Rees thought. It had never bothered him before.

Chapter Twenty-Seven

Morning Calls

Lady Esme Bonnington's Townhouse
Number 40, Berkeley Square

"Darling, tell all!"

Helene grinned. "I can't. I have to wait for Gina. You know she'll be outraged to miss anything."

"You can't wait," Esme moaned. "She's always late these days. It's the devoted mother in her."

"As if you aren't one," Helene pointed out.

"I am a perfectly respectable mother," Esme protested. "I see William at proscribed times, and I do not allow him to overtake my every waking moment."

Helene forbore to point out that a set of childish finger-prints, seemingly dabbed with blackberry jelly, had made an imprint on Esme's exquisite gown. Nor did she remind her friend that only last month Esme had left a dinner attended by the Regent himself, on receiving a message from William's nanny saying that he showed signs of a cold.

"Just tell me a few details," Esme urged, her eyes shining with curiosity. "I have not been able to sleep wondering what's happening to you."

Somewhat to Helene's relief, Gina burst into the room at that moment. "I'm so sorry to be late," she cried. "I simply could not get out the door." She fell into a chair. "Don't

236

pause for courtesies, Helene! What about the opera singer? What is it like, living in the house? Can you bear it?"

Her two friends were looking at her with expressions of identical curiosity, as if she were a calf with two heads or some other miracle of nature. "It's not so terrible," Helene said cautiously.

"I've done nothing but think about it, and I'm fairly sure that I would have to flay her," Esme said with frank blood-thirstiness. "Is she simply awful? What does she look like? Is she one of those brandy-faced women whom one sees around the Exchange, or the fancy articles who haunt Vauxhall?"

"Actually, Miss McKenna is not at all like a common light-skirt," Helene replied. "She's quite beautiful, and I have to admit that if I had the faintest particle of feeling for Rees—and of course I *don't*—I would be jealous of her looks."

"How can you bear it?" Gina asked wonderingly. "I know you're estranged from Rees, but he's still your husband. Even if I were separated from Cam for twenty years, I could not see him nuzzle up to some light woman in my presence without feeling murderous."

Helene shrugged. "They don't show any signs of intimacy in my presence."

"Well, that's quite considerate of her," Esme said, sounding rather surprised. "Frankly, I would think that she too would find this a difficult situation. After all, she's been living in that house for what, three years?"

"She knows which side of the bread is buttered," Gina said. "Why should she feel any distress, considering that she still lives in the house? Helene is obviously a mere visitor—*to her own house!*"

Esme nodded. "Have you found a moment to offer her a settlement, Helene?"

"No," Helene said slowly. "I'm not sure I would feel comfortable doing so, to be honest. She is oddly ladylike."

"Pooh!" Esme said. "She's no lady!"

Helene was silent. The awkward truth was that she was only beginning to feel pricks of jealousy now. And they didn't have anything to do with the fact Lina was sleeping in the vicinity of Rees, either. It was her voice. She had *music*.

"I told Sebastian about Rees keeping his mistress in your bedchamber regardless of your presence in the house," Esme was saying, "and he said that if you would like him to draw Rees's cork or worse, he'd be happy to do so."

Gina was nodding. "I haven't told Cam, because he hasn't the self-control. He would set off immediately to pummel Rees. But just let me know."

"No, no!" Helene said alarmed. "Rees is going to be the father of my child. Besides, that would lead to someone finding out where I am. Harries has been informing all callers that I am taking the waters in Bath." She turned a little pink. "Apparently the Earl of Mayne has called seven times."

"Didn't you get the note I forwarded to you?" Gina said, with an impish grin.

"Yes, and I brought it with me," Helene said, pulling a note from her reticule. "Listen to this: *I understand you are in seclusion, perhaps for as long as six weeks. Surely you are in need of diversion? I am entirely at your service.*"

"What a shame you can't meet Mayne," Gina said. "It must be utterly deflating to be in the same room with the opera singer, if she's all that exquisite. Mayne only stayed in the garden with me for a few minutes, while requesting your address, but I will admit that his compliments were quite amusing."

"The man has exquisite finesse in all areas, including the bedroom," Esme put in. "So Helene, have things improved at all on that front in the past nine years?"

238

Helene blinked. She had never gotten used to Esme's frank discussion of matters that she had been brought up to ignore. "I've told Rees, as per your instructions, that we have to do it every day, and he doesn't seem to find the prospect too insufferable." Then she remembered something. "His mistress made a joke out of his only needing seven minutes of time with me."

"You and she are joking together?" Esme said, clearly stupefied.

Helene felt a flash of embarrassment. "I was rather inebriated at the time."

Gina patted her knee. "If I were you, I would stay inebriated for the entire month," she said. "And if Rees's mistress is cracking jokes about his poor performance in bed, I think we can assume that his abilities are not going to improve in the next few weeks. It's a true shame you can't carry on a flirtation with Mayne. At least he would keep your spirits up."

"I don't see why I can't meet him if I wish to," Helene said.

"It's not worth the risk," Esme said. "You would be worse than ruined if anyone discovered the truth. I really can't imagine the scandal."

"I'll think about it," Helene said, unconvinced. She was not truly interested in a flirtation with Mayne, but whenever she thought about Lina's voice it gave her a queasy sensation . . . perhaps a few of Mayne's practiced compliments would restore her confidence. "Are you both free to make up a party to Vauxhall this evening?"

"Alas, no," Gina said with real regret. "Cam and I are dining with a delegation from Oxford. I'm certain it will be excruciatingly tedious, but Thomas Bradfellow from Christ Church is making my brother a professor, so we couldn't possibly miss it."

"I'll come!" Esme said. "I wouldn't miss a closer look at Rees's strumpet for the world. No one even knows what she looks like, you know. Naturally, we've all heard about her, but who has actually *seen* her? I do believe that her brief appearance at the opera with Rees—and that was some two years ago now—was the first and last time he paraded her before the *ton*."

"She will be wearing a loo mask and domino," Helene pointed out. "I'm not sure how much you'll observe. But thank you for coming, Esme. Somehow the idea of the four of us forming a party seemed uncomfortably intimate."

"How is Rees's brother holding up, then?" Gina said. "I find it hard to believe that a vicar countenances the presence of a fallen woman, let alone escorts her to Vauxhall."

"This is the oddest thing I have ever heard of," Esme said, sitting back with an utterly fascinated expression. "And it certainly will be the most scandalous evening in which I have participated—and that in a long and misspent life. Who would have thought that our docile Helene would be party to a dissipated revel of this nature?"

Chapter Twenty-Eight

Secret Flirtations Are by Far the Most Potent

Mayne turned over the little billet-doux with a feeling of potent satisfaction. It was a prim and proper white; it was not perfumed; it had no air at all of *assignation*. Why he should feel an overwhelming relief on receiving it, he didn't know. Probably had something to do with his sister lowering the boom on his head with her lecture about marriage.

Griselda was right, of course. He had to marry. But not until he had satisfied himself with the delicate body of Lady Godwin. He couldn't even imagine flirting with another woman until he sated himself with her.

The moment when an exquisitely dressed gentleman ambles from a closed, unmarked carriage to a hackney is so common in Hyde Park as to be unnoticeable. Mayne strolled over, knowing perfectly well that she was watching him from one of the little windows, likely savoring his strong legs. He was wearing pantaloons that were not quite in the newest fashion, as he found that ladies responded much better to the tight, knitted styles of last year. Not so out of date as to make him ridiculous . . . but enticing enough to make him appetizing.

To his surprise, when he paused in the door of the carriage, Helene was not peeking out the window. Instead, she was frowning down at what appeared to be a musical score. It wasn't until Mayne sat down opposite her and signaled the footman to close the door that she looked up.

241

Her reaction was all the more gratifying when she took in his elegance. Her eyes widened, just perceptibly. For his part, Mayne suddenly remembered that while he liked the look of stockinet pantaloons, they were damned uncomfortable when he encountered a beautiful woman. Helene was wearing a gown similar to what she had worn to Lady Hamilton's ball, even if it was designed for the daytime. And, significantly, she had taken off her pelisse. It lay beside her.

"It is indeed a pleasure to see you," he said. "I am particularly gratified, knowing that you are in seclusion from the rest of society."

Helene looked at him a little uncertainly. Seeing Mayne in the light of day, it seemed unlikely that such a man would wish to spend any time at all with her, let alone pay her compliments. "I do greatly desire to keep my presence in London undisclosed," she said.

The smile on his lips seemed to promise all sorts of things.

"I hope never to disappoint you in any way," he said softly, picking up her hand and putting a kiss on her palm.

Goodness! Helene had a sudden wish to fan herself with the musical score she held. Rees thought she had merely gone for an aimless carriage ride around London, and had thrown a score at her. Naturally, he could not countenance any time lost that could be spent working.

"Shall we drive into the country?" Mayne asked, his deep voice rolling over her like the finest chocolate sauce.

"I don't think we have time for that," she said rather nervously. "I must be back for supper, you see. I'm going to Vauxhall tonight."

"How interesting," he murmured. "With whom are you staying?" he said, turning her hand over and examining it closely, as if looking for guidance. She said nothing. "Your hands are exquisite," he continued. "I know I told you that before, but . . ." He started kissing the tips of every finger.

Helene rather liked it. She put the score to the side. Truly, Mayne was very delicate in his approach.

"I would very much like to pay you a call," he said silkily, "if circumstances allow."

"Unfortunately, they do not," she said firmly.

He was kissing her fingertips. "Because you are staying in your husband's house?"

Helene gasped. "How do you know that?"

"Are you reconciled?" Mayne asked. "You see, I ask only the questions that have relevance to . . . us." His French accent seemed more pronounced than normal.

"Oh, no," Helene said hastily. But she could hardly explain. "It's only for a month. I'm helping him with his opera."

"His *opera*," Mayne repeated, clearly stupefied. "I didn't know you collaborated on his operas."

"We don't," Helene insisted, feeling more and more embarrassed.

Mayne sat for a moment, still holding her hand. "All of London is under the impression that Earl Godwin lives with a young woman," he said, finally. "I gather they are mistaken?"

"Of course they are mistaken!" Helene said firmly. "My husband has ended the friendship to which you refer." But she had never been a good liar.

He didn't bother to ask again. "*Appalling!*" he said sharply.

"No!" she said. And then, "That is, I don't mean to tell you anything!"

Unless Helene was very wrong, there was an unusual expression in Mayne's eyes—at least, she had never heard tell that the Earl of Mayne was a sympathetic man. People said he was hard, driven, debauched as her own husband. She bit her lip. What if he decided to ruin her? But the look in his eyes . . .

She was wrong. That wasn't sympathy. "Whatever it is that your husband has done to you," Mayne said with precision, "that made you return to him under such humiliating circumstances, I'm going to kill him for it."

The stark chill in his voice froze Helene's marrow. "He hasn't done anything!" she said, with a little gasp.

Clearly he didn't believe her. Who would have thought that the man known for bedding most of London had such a principled streak to him? "Rees hasn't threatened me in any manner at all," she assured him. "I am staying in the house of my own free will."

Mayne spoke through clenched teeth. "You needn't explicate," he said. "I'll free you from the bastard if it's the last thing I do."

"No, no!" Helene said, anxiety coursing through her blood. "I don't want to be freed, truly I don't! I like being Countess Godwin." She clutched his hand. "Can't you understand, Mayne? Rees and I are *friends*."

"Friends?" His voice had a frozen edge to it. "A friend doesn't make his wife live in proximity to a whore!"

"I should think that you, of all men in London, would understand. You are known, after all, for consoling ladies whose marriages are something less than . . . ideal." Which was a nice way of saying he had slept with many married women, so who was he to cavil over married persons' behavior?

His eyes flashed. "There is no similarity whatsoever. I would never offer such an insult to any lady, let alone to my own wife."

"Rees and I are friends," she said again. "Don't you understand? We married years ago, and there's no feeling between us other than a mild friendship." She pushed away memories of very different feelings. She *had* to convince Mayne that she

244

was in the house of her own choice or he would kill Rees. She could see it in his eyes.

"*Mild* friendship," he repeated. "But every feeling of yours must revolt from proximity to a strumpet."

Helene let a teasing little smile cross her face. "There's no strumpet in the house," she said with deliberate falsehood, knowing he didn't believe her for a moment. "Yet I do believe that you may have overestimated the sanctimonious side of my character, Lord Mayne."

"I feel as if you are changing before my eyes," he said, staring at her.

She shrugged, knowing that her breasts moved with a delicious, unsteady wobble when she did so. "I am Countess Godwin, and I prefer to stay that way. I am helping my husband with his opera because he asked me to do so. I do not feel a particle of feeling for him beyond that fact." She let her hand slide to Mayne's knee. "Naturally, I would be most distressed if you felt moved to imprudent action. I could never be intimate with a man who had injured my husband."

Helene felt quite pleased with herself. For someone who had judged herself as having no subtlety whatsoever a mere year ago, she was developing a finely tuned dramatic sense. Perhaps *she* ought to audition to play the lead in one of Rees's operas.

Mayne obviously couldn't quite figure out what was going on. She let her fingers stay for a moment on his knee and then pulled them away. "I shall be at my husband's house for a month only," she said tranquilly. "Naturally, after that point I shall reenter society. You do see how much I honor you with this confidence, my lord?" She leaned back against the seat and sure enough, his eyes flew to her chest.

"I am nothing if not discreet," he said promptly. "But, Helene—"

Helene didn't want to talk about it anymore. In fact, the only thing she really wanted was to retreat to Rees's safe, messy music room and forget about this whole conversation, but she could hardly throw Mayne out of the carriage. Not when he might spread the tale to all of London and ruin her irrevocably, or—worse—do some injury to Rees.

"Garret," she said softly, interrupting him.

He was no idiot. He had her hand again and was pressing kisses in her palm, although for some reason Helene now found it irritating rather than enjoyable.

"Yes, darling?" he asked.

"I must allow you to return to your carriage in a mere five minutes," she told him.

The light burning in his eyes almost made her uneasy. He looked as if he wished to gobble her up, like an ogre in a fairy tale. "I've never met a lady who had your refreshing attitude towards marriage," he said, almost hoarsely. "I feel as if I never lived before this moment. I've never met a truly honest woman."

Helene suppressed a rather irritated sigh and let him press more passionate kisses on her hand. Thank goodness, Rees had taken up the challenge of fatherhood before she engaged herself further with Mayne. She would have never been comfortable with his passionate conversation. It made her feel embarrassed. Rees's brusque comments were more her style, in truth.

"You will be the making of me," Mayne was saying. "I never thought there was a woman so genuinely honest. So—so candid."

Feeling a pulse of guilt, Helene smiled at him. Why on earth was she bothering with this folly? Hopefully by the time she emerged from Rees's house, Mayne would have forgotten all about her. Everyone said he had the attention of a butterfly.

He was kissing his way up her wrist now. It is truly quite odd, Helene thought to herself, how little I appreciate these kisses after yesterday's encounter with Rees. The very memory made her turn rather pink, and then suddenly she realized that Mayne had slipped from his seat and was sitting beside her.

"You blush like the merest lass," he was saying in a throaty voice, "and yet you have the sophisticated wit and intelligence of a grown woman. I didn't think there was a woman like you alive, Helene!"

That's because there isn't such a woman, Helene thought uncharitably. Surely she could dismiss him to his carriage now?

"You truly have no feelings for your husband at all?" he said, his lips dancing across her cheekbone.

"No," Helene said, trying to make her tone even.

"In God's truth, a woman after my own heart," he said, and captured her mouth.

The Earl of Mayne's kisses would never be called objectionable. They were so sophisticated and sleek, persuasive and delicate, that Helene didn't even mind them—much. It was just that she really wanted to get back to Rees. She had a thought about the score he had given her.

"I must go," she said, pulling back. And then added, "alas."

His eyes had turned very dark. In fact, he looked half out of his mind. "But when can I see you again?"

"I'll send you a note once I leave Rees's house," she said cheerfully.

"A month? I can't wait a month! Not now that I've found you!"

"Well, I'm afraid that you'll have to. I am utterly incognita, naturally enough. It would be appalling if the news got out."

"But what has that to do with us? You cannot think to live like a nun in that house for a whole month, when you could be meeting me discreetly?"

Helene quelled a vivid image of Rees towering over her in the park yesterday. She could hardly be more indiscreet.

"You're blushing again," he said, seizing her hand. "Come to me, darling. I have a little house in Golden Square, close to Piccadilly—"

"Absolutely not," Helene said sharply. "I do not engage in surreptitious behavior."

He looked a little confused, as well he might, given that she was currently acting in a remarkably surreptitious fashion.

"I mean," she amended, "that our friendship will be conducted utterly in the open. I shall send you a note and request your company once I return to society." With luck, by then he would have found another married woman and forgotten all about her.

"Of course," he breathed. "Honesty such as yours is dazzling."

"Precisely," Helene said, rather uncomfortably. She rapped on the door and her footman promptly opened it. "I wish you good day, sir."

Mayne descended, but then he looked back, as if he couldn't bear to leave. "Helene . . ."

But she motioned the footman to close the door.

Wasn't she thinking of a glissando at the end of the seventh stave? Perhaps it would have more effect repeated as an echo at the end of the fifteenth.

Chapter Twenty-Nine

Vauxhall

They arrived by water. Tom sat in the rear of the boat, conscious of Lina quietly sitting beside him. She was always quiet when Helene was nearby, almost as if she were trying not to be noticed. He missed her throaty chuckle. But then— and the realization felt like a stab to the chest—perhaps her silence reflected pain, due to seeing Rees with his wife.

The waterman in the front pulled the boat through the waves with one mighty heave of his oars after another. The water was a lightless, lurid black, but rays from the lantern hanging at the prow caught drops sliding from the paddles, turning them silver, like black diamonds. There was a very un-vicarlike excitement in Tom's stomach. He had never been to Vauxhall; men of God didn't normally entertain themselves with such indecorous amusement.

As they neared the steps leading from the Thames he could hear a dim cacophany of noise, the sound of an orchestra in the distance, the humming sound of visitors, the calls of hucksters wandering the grounds. The boat docked before the entrance and they all traipsed through the door, emerging onto a broad walk. Dusk was drawing on quickly now, and the gardens that stretched as far as he could see were lit by gaslights strung through the trees. The lamps looked like small candles, burning uncertainly in a breeze, and certainly providing no proper illumination. No wonder Vauxhall had such a bad reputation, he thought. A young woman could easily get lost in the maze of paths, alone or with a companion.

There was a voluptuous smell in the air too, one that stirred all his senses. Helene's friend Lady Bonnington was exclaiming over the same scent.

"Evening primroses," her husband told her.

Lady Bonnington was wearing a cloak of deep green and a loo mask that emphasized her mouth. But Lina was an easy rival for her, less fleshy, less indecorous, far more beautiful, to Tom's mind. What was he doing, comparing two women's mouths? Had he lost himself, the securely proper self he had always been? Reverend Thomas Holland wasn't interested in comparing women's mouths!

His attention wandered again. Would he be Lina's companion? Would they lose themselves on a path, walking side by side?

"I've reserved a supper alcove," Rees said brusquely. "The fireworks are not until eleven o'clock, so I suggest that we visit the arcades." Then he grabbed his wife's arm and set off down one of the paths. Tom felt a bounding surge of happiness. Lina was his for the evening, at least. He put out his arm to her. Lady Bonnington and her husband had strolled directly after Rees, so they were suddenly alone.

Her large eyes looked almost frightened. "Are you all right?" he said with a sudden pulse of alarm.

"This isn't proper," Lina said in a low voice. "I don't feel right here, not with Lady Godwin. It was different before I met her. I thought this was all rather humorous, the wife who lived with her mother, and I in her bedroom. I must have been mad!"

"You're as much a lady as either of them," he told her.

"No, I'm not," Lina said, shaking her head. Her skin glowed alabaster clear in the light of the gas-lamp hanging from a tree above them.

"And yet, I think you are a lady by birth, are you not?" Tom said, deliberately ignoring the implication of her statement.

"That's hardly the point."

"You are a *lady*," he insisted.

She shrugged. "My father was well born enough. But I'm not any longer, and I don't feel comfortable with them. I don't."

"Your father?" he asked.

"Just as you said of your position," she said indifferently. "He is a vicar largely because he is the youngest son of a baron. The youngest of four, mind you. But that is beside the point, as the term *lady* has little to do with kinship, not really. I'm your brother's doxy, Tom, and I don't want to make up a party with his wife. It's not right. I'm ashamed that I ever agreed to Rees's scheme."

He pushed back the hood of her domino. Her hair caught sparks of light from the lamps and glowed a bronzed gold. Tom was conscious of deep happiness. He caught her hands and held them under his chin, kissing first one and then the other. "You're going to be my wife, Lina McKenna," he said.

She stared up at him. "You're mad," she said flatly. "As mad as your brother." She tried to turn and go, but he wouldn't let her. Then his arms slid around her and she stopped struggling.

"Where would you like to go, Lina mine?" he asked her, his lips skimming hers, tasting delight with restraint. "If you don't wish to join the others in the supper alcove, we shall explore the gardens on our own."

She blinked up at him, her eyes thickly fringed with lashes tipped with the same golden light as her hair. "How can we sit about and pretend to have genteel conversation in a supper alcove? I and your brother's wife? It's absurd!"

251

"You are a lady, as well as she," he said gently. "And even if that weren't the case, Vauxhall is notorious for being ripe with all sectors of society."

"I don't want to be one doxy among many," she said flatly.

"You're no doxy," he said, pulling her against him. He devoured her with that kiss, trying with every fiber of his body to tell her how he felt: about her, about the two of them, about their impending marriage.

She was cradled in his arms, breathing quickly, melting against him, joy in his arms. It wasn't until some five minutes later, when Tom looked up, breathless, his body on fire—

To meet the expressionless eyes of his brother. And behind Rees, the bright, inquisitive face of Lady Esme Bonnington, her mouth frozen in a silent "O."

For one long second, no one said anything. Then Rees said in an utterly normal voice, as if he'd seen nothing and cared for nothing, "Our supper alcove is to the left of the Pavilion, Tom." He turned and offered his arm to Lady Bonnington.

Lina was looking up at him with horror. "Was that who I think it was?" she asked. Her back was turned to the walk and she hadn't known of Rees's presence until he spoke.

"Yes," Tom said. His arms tightened around her. "Did you truly not wish to go to supper, Lina?"

She shook her head violently. Her lips were plump from his kiss; she looked young and utterly defenseless.

"Would you like me to take you home?"

She hesitated.

"I'll take you anywhere you wish to go," he said, tracing one of her eyebrows with a fingertip. "And my only payment is kisses. Would you like to go to the opera tonight? With me?"

Her eyes brightened, but then she shook her head. "I couldn't. What if someone saw us?"

"And what then?" he asked softly. "May I not accompany a beautiful young woman to the opera? I think I may."

"I'd like to go to the Pewter Inn," she said suddenly. "I'd like to meet Mrs. Fishpole."

"Mrs. Fishpole!"

"Yes." She smiled up at him. "Meggin is at home, Tom. I find it very hard to forget that she is alone in the nursery, albeit under Rosy's care."

Shame and wonder are infrequent companions, but Tom knew them both. "You'll be the better part of me, won't you?" he said, his mouth swooping down on hers again.

She pushed him away, but not very resolutely. It wasn't until some minutes later that a rather discomposed-looking young lady and her companion hailed a waterman and told him they wanted the Westminster Stairs, for a hackney to the Pewter Inn.

"Of course, I'm going to find her!" the gentleman said irritably to his companion.

"Yes, but what if you can't?" she replied, untangling a long curl from an emerald necklace that she was rather unwisely wearing, given the famed presence of pickpockets at Vauxhall. "Can't we simply enjoy ourselves, Garret? According to the playbill, there's a Spectacular Pyrotechnical Display tonight. I do love fireworks. I don't want to spend the whole evening traipsing around these dark gardens looking for Lady Godwin!"

"She must be here," Mayne told his sister. "Just hush, Griselda. Perhaps we can find her in the supper room."

"I don't want to go all the way over there!" Griselda said in some alarm. "My shoes aren't designed for walking miles and miles, you know. Why don't we sit in the Chinese pavilion? She's certain to turn up. Everyone visits the pavilion; you know that. And if she doesn't, I'm quite certain that some other flame of yours will wander by, and you can amuse yourself."

Mayne drew a reckless hand through his elaborately casual locks. At the moment he didn't give a damn for the effect his valet had achieved after some thirty-five minutes of devout labor. "You don't understand, Grissie," he said with frustration. "Helene is different from the rest."

"Poppycock," Griselda said, making her way toward the Chinese pavilion, whose delicate spires made patterns against the London sky. "You may feel that way now, but it will wear off. Contain yourself, please. And do remember that you're a man on the cusp of marriage. All these extremes of emotion are so tedious."

She waved to the attendant, who took one look at Mayne and his sister and escorted them to a prime table where they could both see and be seen.

"There, you see," Griselda said with satisfaction once she had arranged her reticule, fan, gloves and shawl just as she liked them, and checked her emeralds in a small mirror. "You can snap up your little countess as she passes, and I do promise not to giggle at her shorn locks. Though I must say, darling, that I begin to wonder at your taste. All this enthusiasm for Helene Godwin? I remember her in school as being just too, too tedious. All braids, restraint and pale skin. And no more interesting on further acquaintance, I assure you, unless you have a passionate interest in music."

"You're quite wrong," Mayne snapped at her. He was a fool to have brought his sister. He itched to be out strolling the paths. At this rate, he would miss Helene. She was probably walking down a shadowy path, and he could be next to

254

her, enticing her into meeting him at his little house in Golden Square.

"Here!" Griselda called, waving her reticule and hooting until Mayne longed to shake her. "It's Cornelius," she said. "Cornnneeelius!"

An exquisite sprig of fashion strolled in their direction, peering at them through his quizzing glass. His hair frothed above his forehead as if he'd been struck by curly lighting, but Griselda seemed to find nothing amiss.

"I thought you dropped that fop based on his poetic failures," Mayne remarked.

"Not yet," she said complacently. "I told him to write me another poem. Then I shall give the poem to you, darling, and we will discover who he stole it from. That is much more fun. What's to be gained from discarding the acquaintance?"

But Mayne had suddenly realized there was, indeed, something to be gained from the presence of Cornelius Bamber. "Good to see you, Bamber," he said rather shortly. "I would be most grateful if you would accompany my sister for a short time while I attempt to find an acquaintance."

"My pleasure," Bamber said languidly. "Who would not grasp at such a chance? She walks in beauty, like the night . . ."

"Didn't Spenser say that?" Mayne asked acidly. "Or wait, wasn't that Byron?"

Bamber ignored him, since he was in the midst of an elaborate bow that involved three or four hand flourishes, so Mayne strode off. He was conscious of a surge of desire at the very thought of Helene that felt like electricity going from his toes to his hair. He hadn't felt this way since he was a mere adolescent. With her clear, thoughtful eyes and her sophisticated, urbane view of men and women, Helene was his twin. A gloriously feminine, beautiful version of himself.

Behind him, his sister had been joined by Lady Petunia Gemmel. They were squealing at each other in a way that promised Lady Petunia had brought a luscious piece of gossip to the table. That should keep Griselda occupied for an hour at least; the two of them were positively savage when they began running down reputations, particularly if the people being discussed were near and dear acquaintances.

Helene walks in beauty, like the night, he thought to himself. Perhaps Byron wasn't such a bad poet after all.

Chapter Thirty

In Which a Songbird Develops Talons

The Pewter Inn was bustling with every kind of coach that trundled the streets of London: phaetons, barouches, landaus, and even a chariot. Postboys were shouting and running in all directions. Just as Tom and Lina walked through the gates (over which Pewter Inn was spelled out in flaking silver letters), the mail coach careened in, narrowly missing the left column, which would have brought the whole gate down on their heads.

"Meggin offered me an apple as I descended from the mail," Tom told Lina. "She was trying to sell apples to the passengers."

Shrieks reverberated around them as the boys began their game of throwing all the passengers' luggage to the ground, including a crate of chickens that promptly burst open and sent fowl fluttering in all directions.

"I see what you mean," Lina said, holding Tom's arm rather tightly. "She's very small to find herself amidst all this—"

She didn't finish because Tom abruptly dragged her to the right to avoid a landau being backed through the gates by a fine young gentleman who obviously felt that lowly persons should give way before his vehicle, and not vice versa.

"The kitchen is around the back," he said, taking Lina to safety under the covered walkway that ran around the yard.

Lina looked up and said something, but he couldn't hear it, due to the fracas (the owner of the chickens had taken in very bad part the fate of his chicken-coop, not to mention his fowl, who were comfortably roosting on the second-story balcony). So Tom shook his head at Lina and just brought her around the path that Meggin had taken, leading to the kitchens.

But when they walked through the door, Mrs. Fishpole had been replaced by a hatchet-faced individual wearing a dirty white apron. He had a bad-tempered look about him, as if he'd toss a pot of boiling water at the slightest provocation.

"No gentry coves in the kitchens," he growled, giving a ferocious stir to a pan of pale gray water, graced with a few bobbing vegetables. "Get around the front then, where your sort belongs." Without looking at them again, he grabbed a wine glass from the table and sucked a long draught of red down his throat.

"We're looking for Mrs. Fishpole," Tom said politely, removing his hat. "I wonder if you could tell me when she might be on duty again."

"Never, and that'll be too soon," the man growled, pouring himself another swig of wine. "Now be off with you. She weren't owed any wages, and if she's taken off without paying your tick, it's nothing to me."

"We merely wish to find her direction," Tom explained. "She owes us nothing."

But the man turned back to his pot as if he weren't even going to bother to answer. A potboy dashed in, calling, "Mr. Sigglet, Mr. Sigglet! Mr. Harper has arrived for his regular and wants the fish and sausage pie as always, what should I tell him?"

"Tell him that the harpy's gone this afternoon, and left me without a fish pie to my name," Mr. Sigglet snarled. "He'll eat vegetable soup and be glad with it, or he can take himself off somewhere else. I'll have another cook by tomorrow."

He swung around and waved the wooden spoon so that greasy drops flew, landing on his beard and hair. "You all can make your way out of here," he said. "That Fishpole has done a bunk on me, left her job without a word of warning, and all to go back to her family. Who would have thought the woman had a family? Family!" It was clear that Sigglet, at least, had no faith in the institution.

Without another word, Tom drew Lina backwards out of the kitchen; he was a little worried that Sigglet would lose his patience and launch vegetable soup in their direction.

"Where could she have gone?" Lina asked. "Oh, this is the worst of all situations!"

"No, it's not," Tom replied, hating the look of distress in her eyes. "It means you were right. You were absolutely right, and I was a blunderhead not to consider other options."

Lina shook her head. "No, *you* were right. That inn yard is no place for a little girl. And what sort of a mother could Mrs. Fishpole be, if she up and leaves her position without a word of warning? Meggin needs a reliable family."

He cupped her face in her hands. "Hush, you," he said, grinning down at her. "Mrs. Fishpole quit her position because she's gone to find Meggin. All she knows of me is that I'm the vicar of St. Mary's Church in Beverley. Her family lives a few counties over. And that's where she's gone; I'll bet my last shilling on it!"

She was so beautiful that he had to kiss her. And the kiss was so delicious that they likely would have kept kissing all night, bundled up in their loo cloaks and leaning against the back wall of an inn, except Lina had an idea.

"She only just left the inn this afternoon, Tom," she said,

rather breathlessly. "Perhaps Mrs. Fishpole hasn't set out for the North Country yet. Perhaps we could find her in London."

For a moment he didn't catch her meaning. His whole body was aching to make her his. "Will you marry me?" he asked rather thickly.

"No," she said. "Let's go find Mrs. Fishpole!"

"Not until you agree to marry me," he said, pulling her back against him.

"I could never marry a vicar!" The horror in her voice was genuine enough.

"Can we pretend that I'm not a vicar?" he asked.

"Ah, but you are."

"If I weren't a vicar, would you marry me?"

She hesitated.

"If I were the cook in this lovely establishment?"

"No!" she giggled and he had to kiss her for the impudence of it.

"If I were a mere country gentleman, living on an estate— because I do have an estate, Lina. And rather more than one maid, I promise you that."

"Estates have nothing to do with it," she said and there was a distinct chill in her voice. "I'm not interested in marriage."

"Not even to me?"

He looked down at her in the light of the one whale oil lamp that lit the back of the inn, and Lina's heart felt as if it turned over. Tom was so inexpressibly dear. And so beautiful too, with his dimples and deep-set eyes, and the masculine strength of him that made her feel—well, he wasn't at all like her ethereal, spiritual father. It was hard to believe that they were both vicars, to tell the truth.

"Perhaps if you weren't a vicar," she said reluctantly.

He dropped a kiss on her lips. "I love you."

Lina blushed, and she hadn't blushed in three years. "You're a fool, to be sure," she muttered, brushing away his hands. "Now, shall we find Mrs. Fishpole, or not?"

Without waiting for an answer she marched back through the dingy door into the kitchen. Tom strode after her. He entered the kitchen to find Lina with her hands on her hips and an air of command that he'd never witnessed on her face before. "You'll tell me Mrs. Fishpole's direction immediately," she was saying in a clear voice, "or it will be the worse for you."

"Pshaw!" Sigglet said, and spat on the ground for emphasis.

Lina opened her mouth and sang one high, ear-piercing note.

"God in heaven!" Sigglet gasped. The glass in his hand shattered. Splatters of red wine joined the grease clinging to his beard and hair.

"I wish to know Mrs. Fishpole's direction in London," Lina said conversationally, "or I shall stroll into your public room and give a free performance. Do I make myself absolutely clear, Mr. Sigglet?"

He was eyeing her with a kind of malice that made Tom step closer. Sigglet's eyes shifted to him, and Tom eased back his cloak, the better to give Sigglet an unadorned view of his muscled body.

"She lives in Whitechapel, on Halcrow Street," he gabbled. "I don't know the number, so you can break all the glasses in the house before I can tell you."

"No need," Lina said with a tranquil smile. "We shall find out the house ourselves, thank you very much, Mr. Sigglet."

She turned to leave, Tom protectively at her heels. Then she paused at the door. Sigglet had taken to swigging wine straight from the bottle.

"I did want to tell you," she said sweetly, "that I fear a little glass may have flown into your soup. Although"—she eyed the gray water with distaste—"it may add flavor."

Sigglet curled his lip. "Complaints! All I ever gets is complaints!"

Tom pulled Lina out the door.

Chapter Thirty-One
Lessons in Love . . . and Rage

They seemed to have lost the others. Rees wanted Helene to see Roubiliac's statue of Handel, so they had left Esme and her husband watching Indian jugglers. There was a stiffness in Lord Bonnington's behavior toward Rees that made Helene quite uncomfortable although Rees, characteristically, didn't appear to have noticed. To her relief, Tom had whisked Lina off to another area of Vauxhall.

"I simply can't get over the fact that your brother shows no disinclination to—" but Helene stopped, realizing that it was hardly polite to point out just why a vicar might not wish to wander Vauxhall with a fallen woman. Under the circumstances.

But Rees, naturally, waded directly into the subject. "My brother is showing a striking desire to shepherd Lina from place to place. All with the purest of motives, naturally."

"It seems odd for a vicar," Helene commented.

"Perhaps he's bent on reforming her. Actually, I'm not sure Tom ever really wanted to be a vicar. My father had him staked out for the church before he could walk, and he did seem suited to the task. But now he seems changed."

"Do you think that he might give up the profession?"

"Hard to tell. The whole piety and charity business comes naturally to him."

"He's a good man," Helene said with reproof in her voice.

"Exactly," Rees replied, unperturbed. "A far better man than I."

"You're a good man too," she said, slipping her hand under his arm. Then she looked up to find him grinning at her.

"Is this my shrewish wife speaking? Wife? Wife? Wherefore art thou? A changeling has taken your place!"

"All right," she said, with an answering smile. "You're a horrible person who occasionally has good moments. Most of which take place at the piano."

"I'm learning," he said. "I have a great deal to learn."

"What do you mean?" They were approaching a large hedge, from within which emerged the sounds of an orchestra tuning its instruments.

"Handel is inside," Rees said, steering Helene toward an arch cut in the shrubbery, "likely shuddering at the sounds around him. I'm afraid that the Vauxhall Orchestra is not going to achieve fame any time soon."

"But what did you mean by learning?" Helene persisted. "Are you thinking in a musical sense?"

"No," he said. And showed no inclination to continue.

Helene let him seat her on a marble bench before the statue, and then said, "Honest to goodness, Rees, you must be the most frustrating conversationalist alive! What on earth did you mean by that comment?"

"Something Tom said to me."

Rees sprawled out next to her on the bench, muscled thighs clearly outlined by snug pantaloons, his arms carelessly flung on the back of the bench. Helene quickly looked away from his legs. The very sight of them—and the memory of him standing over her in the pasture, quite unclothed—made her feel hot and prickly.

"Yes?" she said encouragingly. Unfortunately, her gaze had alit on his hands, and that made her think of the way his fingers curved around her breast, and the way he bent his head to the same place, kissing her almost—almost reverently. She shifted uneasily in her seat. It was mortifying to be looking forward to Rees's daily bedding. That couldn't be the case. She must be delusional.

"Well?" she snapped, suddenly irritated. "Either you're learning or you're not. Out with it!"

He turned to her, distinctly amused. The dimples in his cheeks had deepened and there was laughter in his eyes. Other people might have called his face expressionless, but she—

Helene took a deep breath. "Rees?" she said between clenched teeth.

"My father handily arranged his sons into two categories," he said, dropping his head back so that he could look up into the wilderness of black tree limbs curling into the night sky above them. "I was the sinner, and Tom the saint."

"Well, that seems fairly acute of him," Helene said a bit snappishly.

"Yes, but I begin to think I am less of a reprobate than he believed," Rees said. "I find it rather tedious, to tell the truth, Helene."

"Sinning?" she asked, disbelieving.

"Yes, sinning. And I begin to think that Tom is finding the saintly life just as tedious," Rees continued.

"Well, I certainly don't see any sign of your finding your life tedious!" Helene said, and then wished she could take the words back. He was watching her, so she carefully examined Handel's booted, marble toes.

"I don't find it tedious when I'm with you," he said suddenly.

Helene had to suppress a smile. "We hardly engage in *sinning*," she pointed out.

"That's just it," he said, and his hand began tangling in the little wisps of hair at the back of her neck.

Helene looked straight ahead, unable to turn her neck and see his expression.

He stood up, and his tone was utterly normal, as if he hadn't said something that turned her world upside down. "Shall we take a promenade?"

Helene rose and took his arm. They walked for a time in silence until he said, "I didn't mean to bring our conversation to a standstill with a disconcerting revelation. Lord knows, my father was probably right." There was something tired in his voice that made her stumble into speech.

"Do you think that—that you might, that some of your actions during our marriage might have been due . . ." her voice trailed off.

"No question," he replied. "I eloped with you rather than get married in a proper fashion, in order to irritate my father although I've only recently come to understand this. And Helene, sometimes I think your exit in a coach and the Russian dancers who then graced the dining room table were directed to the same man."

Helene bit her lip. "We were not happy together, and that had little to do with your father."

"I was a bastard about it, though," he said. "I had no idea how to talk without being insulting. No one in my family simply talked. We still don't."

There was something in his crooked smile that made her heart ache, so she tried to think of a light, clever thing to say. And came up empty. "Shall we turn here?" she finally asked, in desperation.

The walk into which they turned seemed much dimmer than the one they had traversed; the gaslights strung in the trees were few and far between now, and shadows stretched like sleeping beasts across the path.

"This is Lovers' Walk," Rees said.

"Oh," Helene said faintly. They walked on, until they hadn't met anyone for at least ten minutes. The din of the Gardens proper seemed very far away now, and the orchestra couldn't be heard at all. Suddenly there was a popping noise and great flowering bursts of color splayed over their head.

"We can watch the fireworks from here," Rees remarked, pulling her into a little recessed alcove graced with a marble bench.

He sat down next to her and bent his dark head back to watch lights burst and tumble in the sky. Helene watched him instead, until he turned and met her steady gaze.

"I haven't bedded you today," he said, in an absolutely conversational tone, as if they were discussing the weather.

Helene gasped and looked quickly down the path. "Don't say such a thing out loud!" she scolded. "What if someone heard you?"

"So what?" Rees grinned. "I'll bet I'm not the only man thinking hungrily about bedding his wife."

Helene's face was hot. He was *hungry* for her. That was an . . . interesting thought. No one had ever been hungry for her before.

Rees took off her loo mask and pushed back the hood of her cloak. The night air felt like a caress on her cheeks. Over his shoulder the London sky flew with sparks, as if the great fire of '66 had come again, as if a conflagration of huge proportions had seized the sky and was making kindling of the clouds.

Helene had made up her mind that pushing off her hood was the only intimacy Rees was allowed. It hadn't passed her notice that her husband took to marital intimacies in the outdoors like a duck to water. She certainly wasn't going to

267

add to the dismal reputation of Vauxhall Gardens by allowing herself to be intimately handled in Lovers' Walk.

At first he just kissed her. But could one call it *just*? Something about the way his tongue plunged into hers made her body burn to be near his. Yet when his hand strayed treacherously close to her bosom, Helene pushed him away. He kissed her so hard that at first she didn't notice his hand stealing up her leg, trailing a delicate, fiery caress toward her knees, and only belatedly squealed and pulled away. He followed her, and somehow she ended up half lying on the bench, with him laughing over her, pulling her cloak open and trapping her arms.

"It's only your cloak, Helene!"

"We're in public!" she said, struggling. "Anyone could see us."

"No one has come this way in a good ten minutes." His eyes were black against the sky and the feeble gaslight.

She licked her lips and the heavy droop of his eyelids suddenly became even more pronounced. "One could almost suppose you think that I haven't noticed what you're—you're doing," she managed. For one large thumb was rubbing over her nipple in a way that made her legs tremble.

"Do forgive me if I have disconcerted you," he said tranquilly, taking his hand away. Her nipple stood out against her light gown, and their eyes met as she glanced down. "I wouldn't like to do anything that you didn't enjoy, Helene." His voice was as low as a cello, and as seductive too.

She opened her mouth, but couldn't lie. His smile was pure wickedness. And the sigh that came from her lips when he put his hand back on her breast was pure delight. Yet Helene did not lose sight of her initial thoughts on the matter.

"This is all very well," she said—or rather, gasped—some time later. "But you are not going to bed me in Vauxhall Gardens, Rees, you are not!"

"I'm not bedding you," he said. He had rearranged herself and him so that she was lying across his lap, her body laid like a feast before him. One hand held her tightly against his chest, but the other—

The other wandered. From her breast, with an increasingly rough stroke that made the breath catch in her throat and her body arch toward him. To the sleek line of her leg, skimming under her gown, walking his fingers up her thigh so slowly that she started shaking all over and had to hide her face in his shoulder.

"What are you doing?" she moaned.

"Just playing," he said, and it seemed to her that his voice was more strained than it had been.

"With what?" she managed, with a fair degree of logic. For his hand had reached above her garter now, and he was swirling little circles on the skin of her thighs.

"With your body, Wife," he whispered into her neck.

"And what if someone comes by?" she demanded.

But he was bending over her and just as his lips captured hers, his fingers slipped into the sweetest space of all. He swallowed her cry with his mouth, and the next, and the next . . . Quieted her struggles with his body. For it didn't seem to him that she really knew what she wanted.

"No," she cried sharply, "you mustn't . . ." but her voice disappeared into a wave of pleasure that coursed through her body. He could see that well enough.

"If I hear anyone coming," he told her, "I'll simply drape your cloak over you."

"No!" she said tremblingly, but he tried a little flick of his finger, and was rewarded with a squeak of delight, and after that she stopped worrying about passersby, other revellers not enthralled by fireworks.

It took a bit of experimentation. Rees had never given

269

much thought to women's pleasure. They were there; he was a rakehell, a take-what-you-want-and-leave type of man. He'd known that since he was a youngster. And nowhere in the training of a rakehell did it say anything about touching women for their pleasure.

Nor did it say anything about allowing one's own body to burn with a fierce fire without respite, or feeling oneself shaking with passion—and all from touching a woman.

Not any woman. From touching Helene.

Her face was tipped back in the crook of his arm now, so that every time she came to herself enough to protest, he could swoop down and silence her with his mouth until she succumbed again.

In the first year of their marriage, he told her, with an edge created by his own sense of rage and failure over the whole business of bedding a wife, that her body must be unable to experience women's pleasure. And so warring in Rees's soul was a battle between passion and self-loathing. For Helene's cheeks were tipped rose and her eyes unfocused; her willowy body had turned to plush in his hands, and she was urging herself against his hand, murmuring incoherent things, her breath as ragged as his own.

But, as he said, he was learning.

It took a while, but finally he thought he had a rhythm, a pace, a cadence like a waltz that seemed to drive her farther and farther from logic, and more and more into an incoherent series of little breaths that were like the most beautiful music he ever heard in his life, a medley of "Rees! No! Yes!" and "Oh, oh—" and finally, "Rees!" And then she arched against him, her body shaking in his arms. Rees buried his face in her hair. Self-loathing stopped warring with passion, and was replaced by something infinitely more tender, and more terrifying.

For Helene, it was as if a crescendo—a whole fanfare of trumpets—took over the sweet, arching sounds of a concerto and blew free and clear in the air, the sound tearing to the utmost ends of her fingers, again and again, music crashing over her head so that she was utterly lost in its grip and Rees's warm steady body was her only fulcrum in a spinning world.

And for the Earl of Mayne, who rounded the turn in the path a split second before, recognizing immediately the moonlit gleam of Helene's hair, and then just as suddenly the silver gleam of said moonlight on a slender leg, and finally, with a bitter blow that he felt to his chest, realizing that his Helene, *his* countess as he had imperceptibly started thinking of her, was shaking in the arms of her husband.

That same husband for whom she felt only mild friendship.

He turned without a sound and walked away, the black sweep of his cape sending stray leaves on the path into a lacka-daisical spiral in the air.

Honesty is overrated.

Rage, on the other hand—rage has a good deal to be said for it. Rage coursed through his body with a black inevitabil-ity that left a bitter taste in his mouth. She was no more than a woman, like all the rest: faithless, dishonest. No more knowing in her understanding of men and women than any other woman.

Worse, actually. Taking her pleasure wherever she found it, apparently. Masquerading in society as a virtuous matron while she stole off to her husband's house to enjoy whatever attentions he had not given to his resident doxy.

With a faint objective edge, Mayne realized that he was literally shaking with rage. You're a bit out of hand, he thought to himself.

271

It's only a nuisance, that's all.

Another woman . . . just another woman. Nothing new there. And if she was rather more devious than many of the ladies he had bedded, that was hardly something for him to grieve over.

He was almost back to the Chinese Pavilion when he saw Lady Felicia Saville prancing toward him, waving her fan and chattering to one of her more foolish friends. Lady Felicia was notorious for two things: her unhappy marriage and her waggling tongue.

His pace slowed to that of a panther.

"Oh, Mayne," Felicia called, as they came into sound of each other. "Your sister awaits you at the Pavilion, sir." But he was moving toward her with a concentrated light in his eyes that she had only seen directed at other women. Felicia gulped. Could it be that Mayne—Mayne!—was finally going to approach her? She had quite despaired of the idea, and yet sometimes she felt as if his lovers were an exclusive gathering to which she had not been invited. And Felicia loathed that idea.

She turned to her friend Bella. "Darling," she said behind her fan, "do make an excuse to return to the Pavilion, will you? As a dear friend?"

Bella looked at her sharply and then at the earl, walking toward them with a little smile on his beautifully cut lips.

"Only if you visit me first thing in the morning!" she said, fluttering her fan as if a sudden tropical breeze had blown through London.

"Without question," Felicia said. She lowered her fan and smiled at Mayne. He didn't seem to notice Bella drifting away, slowly so that she could catch Mayne's greeting.

"I feel as if I never saw you before," he said, and his voice was dark and suggestive. "Do walk with me, Felicia."

"Into Lovers' Walk!" she said with a titter. "Dear me!"

But he tipped up her chin and brushed a kiss across her lips. "Only if you quite, quite wish to," he said, as his mouth came down to hers.

Mayne found it rather disappointing that when he strolled past the secluded little bench where the deceptive countess and her hell-born husband had been, they had disappeared, and so missed the sight of Lady Felicia Saville clinging to his arm, her cloak thrown off and her bodice slipping to the point of indiscretion.

There was a disappointing lack of revenge about it. He wanted to see Helene's eyes widen; he wanted her to know—absolutely *know*—that he had decided she wasn't worth waiting a month for.

He wanted her to know that he had never believed her in the first place. Never. He'd known immediately that it was all a Maygame, that talk about *mild friendship*. He had never believed her. He wasn't taken in.

Yet it wasn't until he was rather expertly, if with a dismaying lack of interest, sampling Lady Felicia's charms, that he realized just how to make Helene Godwin understand that he never, for a moment, believed her nor considered waiting for her to leave her husband's house.

"Felicia," he said, his voice as syrupy smooth as devil's broth.

"Yes?" she said, her voice quite steady and clear. Alas, Felicia was finding the famed Earl of Mayne rather less enthralling than she had been led to believe. But there you are. Reality, particularly when it pertained to men, was always rather disappointing.

"I heard the most dismaying piece of news today," he said into her ear, easing her bodice back over her breast.

"No, what?" Felicia asked, instantly revived.

So he told her. As her eyes grew bigger and bigger, he brought her to her feet and brushed a few spare leaves from the back of her cloak, and then they began their stroll back toward the lightened areas of the Gardens.

For Mayne understood as well as anyone that his duty, that evening, was to accompany Felicia wherever she wished to go, whispering intimately into her ear, and making it quite clear to all her acquaintances that she was one of his chosen lovers.

And Felicia didn't have to think twice to know what her duty was, since it came as naturally to her as breathing. She almost began trotting in her haste to return to her friends.

"I just can't believe it!" she kept saying, half to herself and half to Mayne. "I've never *heard* of such a thing!"

Garret Langham, Earl of Mayne, smiled down at her. Had she the perspicuity to notice it, she would have seen a murderous gleam in his eyes.

No one crossed Mayne.

No one.

Chapter Thirty-Two

Mother Is a Relative Term

"I'm just not certain that we should have brought Meggin," Lina said quietly, as she, Tom, and Meggin climbed out of the coach onto Halcrow Street the next morning. "What if this is a disappointment?"

"If Mrs. Fishpole is here, she'll wish to see her," Tom said again. "And look at Meggin!"

Meggin had been like a child transformed, ever since they told her after breakfast that they were going to find Mrs. Fishpole. She was dressed in an enchanting little pinafore and gown, with a pelisse to match. She was clutching Lina's fur tippet, even though it was far too warm for that sort of clothing. But it wasn't her external appearance that mattered; it was the way her eyes were glowing and her little body was rigid with excitement.

Halcrow Street must have been in the district of London devoted to the cloth-dying trade, because everywhere they looked there were huge tubs of bubbling reddish or bluish water and women dumping in armfuls of old clothing. Each load would send a choking cloud of colored smoke into the air, adding to the pungent stench of rotting vegetables and horse dung.

Mrs. Fishpole wasn't hard to find. An old man dozing in the sun nodded across the street. "Number Forty-Two, she's at," he said. "Though I do hear tell that she's leaving

Londontown and going back to somewhere else. I don't know but what she might have left already." And: "I thank you kindly, sir," as he tucked the coin that Tom gave him into an inner pocket.

They walked up three flights of stairs to the very top level. Meggin was clutching Lina's hand fiercely and Lina—for the first time in years—found herself praying. "Please let her be there," she said to that silent presence whom she used to know, but had put away with her childhood things. "Please, please, please, let Mrs. Fishpole still be here."

Tom knocked on the narrow door, while Lina and Meggin stood behind him on the stairs. There was no answer. Lina clenched her teeth and prayed harder. Tom knocked again, louder, and this time they heard the noise of feet approaching. Finally the door snapped open.

Mrs. Fishpole wasn't wearing a white apron anymore; she was dressed from head to foot in gray bombazine, and a shabby bonnet was jammed rather precariously on top of her hair. Her eyes widened and she opened her mouth, but at that moment a sturdy little body scrabbled past Tom and butted the gray bombazine skirt. And then it was just a flurry of tears and exclamations.

"My fiancée, Miss McKenna, told me the truth of it," Tom explained, a good five minutes later. They were all seated around Mrs. Fishpole's sister-in-law's table, there being no sitting room or extra room of that nature.

Mrs. Fishpole had Meggin on her lap and her arms around her as if she would never let her go. "I can't believe I did that," she kept repeating. "I must have been out of me mind. Clear out of me mind. Mr. Sigglet had been carrying on about the child, and then you appeared, and it seemed like Providence. But I knew within two minutes that I'd made a mistake. And then I was too late." Her arms tightened around Meggin until

276

it looked as if she might suffocate the child. Not that Meggin seemed to mind. Lina's fur tippet, which she had carried with her every minute of the day and even slept with, was forgotten on the floor.

"Too late," Mrs. Fishpole kept repeating. "I'll never get over it in my life, I won't. I ran out into that street like a demented woman, but no one could tell me where you'd gone. I'd given my Meggin away, and I didn't even remember your name for sure. Not even your name!"

"I'm truly sorry to have caused you distress," Tom said.

"Well, as to that, you shan't have her, of course," Mrs. Fishpole said, narrowing her eyes and looking as if she wished that she had her giant rolling pin at hand. "I've left my position, and I'll care for Meggin myself."

"Mr. Holland made a mistake," Lina said, smiling at Mrs. Fishpole. "But he meant no harm to you or Meggin."

"I can see that," Mrs. Fishpole said grudgingly, "but you shouldn't as taken her," she told Tom.

"I gather you were planning to travel to the North Country to find Meggin?" Tom asked. "May I enquire whether you wish to continue to East Riding now that you two are reunited, or will you find another position in London?"

"I'm going back," Mrs. Fishpole said decisively. "I've given it a lot of thought over the past few days. London is no place for us. I'm going back and I'm taking Meggin with me. She's to be Meggin Fishpole now, and anyone who says differently will have a taste of my tongue."

Lina was nodding encouragingly. "That's a marvelous plan," she said warmly. "Meggin is a very lucky little girl to have you as a mother, Mrs. Fishpole."

Mrs. Fishpole was blinking rather rapidly. "As to *mother*, well I never thought to be such a thing. But I suppose—"

"You are definitely Meggin's mother," Lina said cheerfully.

Meggin peeped out from the iron circle of Mrs. Fishpole's arms like a sparrow waiting for a plump worm.

"I believe that Father Rumwold in the Minster Church is in need of a housekeeper who can cook," Tom said, not thinking it necessary to add that Father Rumwold had never had a housekeeper and showed few signs of needing one. "You would be an excellent candidate. If you are interested, I could send a note, suggesting your services to the father. It's a small household, just himself and two clerics." And, he thought to himself, Rumwold is just the sort to enjoy a good fish and sausage pie.

"I'd be grateful," Mrs. Fishpole said with a sharp nod. "I've never done any housekeeping, but I wouldn't mind putting my hand in."

"Excellent," Tom said, scribbling a note for Reverend Rumwold and giving it to Mrs. Fishpole. "May I pay for Meggin's passage to the North Country, Mrs. Fishpole? I feel responsible for the distress that I caused both of you in the past few days."

"As to that, I won't say no," Mrs. Fishpole said. "Things are a bit tight, and I meant to borrow some from my brother-in-law, but he's not a ready man."

"It's my pleasure," Tom said. Lina was kneeling next to Mrs. Fishpole's chair and saying something in Meggin's ear without disturbing her snug place on Mrs. Fishpole's lap. The little girl was smiling and then Lina put something in Meggin's hand and closed her fingers around it. Mrs. Fishpole didn't notice; she was busy pushing back all the money Tom had given her except one guinea.

"This'll be enough to get us to East Riding, and I thank you for that. I'm not taking any charity, not if my name's Elsa Fishpole. Meggin and me will make our way with what we have, and a deal of hard work, and that'll be enough. Right, Meggin?"

Meggin looked up at her and then suddenly burst into tears.

"We'll be fine," Mrs. Fishpole told her roughly. But she was rocking her back and forth with a manner that belied her curt words. "No crying, now. We Fishpoles don't cry."

Lina and Tom finally tiptoed out of the room with whispered farewells, as Meggin seemed to be bent on proving that sometimes Fishpoles, especially the little ones, did cry. And cry.

"What did you give Meggin?" Tom asked curiously, when they reached the street and climbed into their hackney again.

"My ring," Lina said.

"Your ring? What ring?" Tom asked.

She shrugged. "A ring your brother gave me."

"He gave you a *ring*?" Tom hardly recognized his own voice. That was the voice of a man about to commit homicide against a member of his family.

Lina touched his arm. "Only when I dragged him into a shop and demanded it," she said, smiling up at him.

"Oh."

"It was a pretty little emerald, though," she said cheerfully, "and since Mrs. Fishpole does not know my name nor my direction in London, she will have no way to return it to me. Therefore, I would guess that she will swallow her pride, sell the ring, and be able to set herself up with some comfort in Beverley."

Tom felt a reluctant smile curl his mouth. "You've solved it all, haven't you?" he said. "You knew I'd done the wrong thing taking Meggin away; you forced Mr. Sigglet to give you the proper directions; you found a way to give some money to Mrs. Fishpole when I utterly failed in that respect. You are going to be a superb vicar's wife."

"Hmmm," Lina said. "Perhaps, if I chose to be." Then she stretched up and for the very first time, under her own initiative, gave him a kiss.

Chapter Thirty-Three

Because Rees Is a Very Good Student

Helene burst into the music room looking as vividly happy as Rees had ever seen her. He took one glance and went back to his score, pounding out a cello accompaniment to the Captain's aria he wrote yesterday. He didn't look up until she stuck something in front of his eyes.

"Do you know what these are?" she burst out.

"Flowers." He played the first few chords again. They sounded pedantic. Perhaps they would flatten the exuberance of *Come to the Ball!* Perhaps he should try oboes instead of a cello.

"Not just any flowers," Helene said, pushing him over on the piano stool. "I had them on my bedside table, ever since"—she seemed to be turning a little pink—"since we walked in the woods, day before yesterday."

"Yes?"

"And Saunders just told me that they are Star of Bethlehem flowers!"

Rees looked at the wilting starflowers. He vaguely recognized them, but the fact was hardly interesting. "Do you think that oboes are too windy to accompany the Captain's aria?" he asked her.

Helene paused and cocked her ear as if she were listening to silent oboes. "I'd try cellos," she said finally.

"That's what I thought," Rees said with some relief. He

played the first few chords again. A three-cello accompaniment would be right.

"Rees, you're not listening," Helene insisted.

"What?" he snapped. "I'm busy. I can't accompany you upstairs at the moment, if that's what you want."

"These are Star of Bethlehem flowers," she insisted. "Saunders just told me that if a woman lies on a bed of Star of Bethlehem, she'll have an easy childbirth."

"We're hardly at that stage yet," Rees said, trying to keep his mind on the sounds of invisible cellos.

"Not yet," Helene said, and the happy note in her voice made Rees want to smile. The sound of cellos died. He put a hand on her back, pulling her snugly against him.

"So would you like to do our daily bedding?" he asked, dropping a kiss into her hair. She smelled faintly of flowers herself.

"I've already asked Leke to have the coach brought around," she said.

"What?" He had started nuzzling her neck and wasn't paying much attention.

She jerked away. "Rees! There's no need for that sort of thing. We aren't in the right place."

He blinked. Yes, there is, he thought. But no. Their bedding was only for conception. Only for children. He reached up and pulled her back. "You're my wife, Helene," he said. "I'll kiss you whenever I want. And I want. We weren't in the right place last night either."

For such a practical woman, who eschewed caresses unless quickly followed by a practical bedding, for practical reasons, she melted into his arms with a gasp and a sigh. In less than a second, the blood was raging along his veins. It was as if the cellos had leapt from his script and began a fiery sarabande.

Rees was just starting to think about easing Helene over to the couch when a voice said from the doorway, "The coach is at the front door, Lady Godwin."

"Oh!" Helene gasped, jumping away from Rees so quickly that he toppled toward the piano bench and slammed his knuckles. "Yes, Leke, we're coming!" she called.

"Helene, it was raining this morning." Rees shook his hand, trying to get his wits together. How on earth could a mere touch of her lips turn him into a bumbling adolescent boy, all raging lust?

"Good thought," she said. "I'll instruct Leke to place a blanket in the carriage."

"That wasn't—" but she was gone, darting from the room.

Rees rubbed his chin. He had bathed, but not shaved in the morning; shaving seemed like too much work since he'd been up half the night working on the tenor aria. And he'd forgotten to send a note around to Darby, although he thought he was working out the problem on his own. What would he ask? *How does one tup a lady?* It sounded absurd.

Helene reappeared in the doorway. She looked like a graceful little linnet, her beautiful hair ruffled by his hand, her lips stained ruby by his kiss.

"Will we have to make our way to the wood every day?" he asked warily, receiving a glowing smile in return.

"Perhaps."

The woods were different this afternoon, soft and rain-soaked. They walked along, Rees inspecting the little spigots of water dripping off the oak leaves. The sky was distinctly gray. "It might rain," Rees said, thinking about just how uncomfortable cold rainwater would feel on his ass.

Helene ignored him. "Look at that fat redbreast!" she said. "He looks just like a plump squire scolding a recalcitrant stableboy."

Rees gave the bird a glance and it flew away instantly. The truth was he didn't want to return to Helene's narrow bed. He didn't want to wait that long. He was burning, from head to foot, with the desire to get Helene's clothes off and feast on that lovely body of hers. See her long pale legs spread under him again, hold a breast in his hand so that only a rosy nipple peeked between his fingers, slip another hand under her bottom ... He walked faster, blanket thrown over his shoulder.

The clearing looked very different today. All the starflowers were shut up, which turned the space to a muted green, very drowsy and wet-looking.

Helene paused. "Do you think that it counts if the flowers aren't open?" she asked.

"Of course," Rees said, plowing into the meadow with no regard whatsoever for the water stains that instantly blotched his pantaloons. She was hesitating on the edge of the path, so he said, "You do want to have an easy childbirth, don't you?"

"Well, yes, but it's just a superstition."

He threw the blanket on the ground and went back and picked her up. She put her arms around his neck and smiled at him. Rees almost shook his head. Could it be that he was in a dream? Was this his sharp-tongued, hateful wife, the one who called him an animal and made him feel ten times more clumsy and idiotic than anyone else? She had her arms linked around his neck and she was rubbing her lips against his and then she slipped her tongue—

He put her down quickly and started throwing off his clothes. "Be careful, Rees," Helene cried. "It's so wet here, and you just threw your coat onto the grass. It'll be soaked."

A moment later he stood before her, all that broad, muscular body hers for the taking. Helene had never felt more dainty and feminine in her life. Without speaking, and without taking her gaze from his body, she pulled her morning gown over her head. She had deliberately chosen not to wear a walking costume. Instead, she was wearing one of her light, floating pieces from Madame Rocque.

Rees made a hoarse sound in his throat and sank to his knees in front of her. Helene blinked. What a nice gesture. He had never gone on his knees, even when he asked her to—

The thought was lost in a squeak. "What are you—what—Rees!"

Helene's whole body contracted down to a small area between her legs. She could do nothing but stand there, weak-kneed, mind blurred. It was a sin, what he was doing. She was sure of that. Some sort of sin, if not a crime. And yet she couldn't hold onto any particular thought. They drifted into her head and then he would lick her again, sending a racking wave of fire down her legs, and the thought would disappear.

"This isn't—" she began. He put his hands on her bottom and pulled her closer. The sentence whirled away, lost in a moan.

"I don't think—" she began again, but his thumb had found its way there too, and now her knees finally did buckle and he lowered her to the ground, kneeling over her, his hand still moving.

"One doesn't do that to ladies, does one?" she gasped, even as her body writhed under his hand.

"No," he said briefly.

She closed her eyes and a delicious smile spread across her face, and then she opened her legs even wider. "Good," she said softly.

"Helene," Rees said hoarsely, a few moments later. She wasn't listening. He slid in slowly. He'd thought a lot in the middle of the night, about how to turn Helene-in-Vauxhall into Helene-in-his-bed.

He pushed in, a little way, and she clutched his shoulders.

He pulled out. Slow, that's what he'd decided to do. Very slow. She was, after all, a very delicate lady. If he just kept everything slow, perhaps she'd feel some pleasure.

So he did. Belying the jokes of his mistress, Rees had full control of his muscled body. He'd just never seen the point of prolonging the experience. But now he propped his elbows on the ground and slid in and out as if he had all day. At first she just lay there the way she had the last time they tried this.

But after a while, she opened her eyes and said, shakily, "Rees, are you almost done?"

"I'm afraid not," he managed between clenched teeth.

Her hand tentatively touched his back, slid down toward his buttocks and he involuntarily lunged toward her. And was answered by a moan. Her face was growing pink.

He waited, and waited. Her fingers were wandering over his back, caressing every ripple of muscle. She asked him again, gasping, if he were almost done, and he shook his head. And then, as if she didn't even realize what she was doing, she started moving a little. Tipping her hips up to greet him. Rees let himself go a little harder, thanked by a cry that broke from her lips.

He went a little faster, and even harder . . . Helene's breath was coming quickly and her eyes were dazed; she'd stopped caressing him and he could feel her fingernails biting into his shoulders. Then she started turning her head from side to side and straining against him.

"Come, Helene," he said hoarsely, praying for strength.

Finally, when he couldn't last any longer, he reared back and slid his hands under her sweetly curved bottom, pulled her toward him and thrust into her with all his strength, a broken groan coming from between his teeth.

And then Helene opened her eyes and looked at him and said, in a tone of the greatest surprise, "Rees?"

Rees knew perfectly well that he was an idiot where women were concerned. But on the other hand, he knew his wife. He'd never seen that particular look on her face, but he knew it.

He pulled her even higher, even harder, and she started shuddering and crying out. Rees closed his eyes in silent thanks, and relinquished his control utterly. They came together with desperate urgency, with rough tenderness, with one last fierce kiss.

Rees remembered, dimly, that his wife didn't like to be flopped on. So he withdrew, and then rolled over onto his back.

It was only then that he realized they had traveled off the blanket. A cradle of wet flowers felt delicious on his heated back.

"I did lie on a bed of Star of Bethlehems, didn't I?" Helene said dazedly.

Rees felt a drop of rain on his nose and then one on his cheek. Helene's slender leg lay next to his, milky white against the green leaves. She had the look of a child who had just experienced her first ice, an astonished, almost blinded look of pure joy. He knew instantly that he would spend the rest of his life trying to give her that particular pleasure.

He rolled toward her, one hand slipping to her leg. "Since childbirth is all taken care of," he told her, "perhaps we should ensure that the previous steps are successful, hmmm?"

In the end, quite a few drops of cold rain fell on Rees's ass, just as he had feared.

But he didn't really notice.

Chapter Thirty-Four

Disaster!

The elegant carriage that drew up before Number Fifteen, Rothsfeld Square had barely come to a halt when two ladies tumbled out, shawls flying behind them, hair all a whirl, a glove left on the floor of the carriage. Leke opened the door just in time to stop it being shoved in his face, only to find himself confronted by an army of two Amazons demanding to see the countess.

Helene was curled up in the library, trying very hard to concentrate on the score she held in her hand. Rees was thumping away on one of the pianos. More than anything she wanted to go into the room and bump him over with her hip and—and just sit there. Next to him.

I can't do that, she told herself. He must work. *I* must work. What if we added a French Horn to this section? she asked herself. What indeed?

The door burst open. "Oh, my goodness," Helene said, jumping to her feet. "Esme! And Gina! What on earth are you doing here?" It wasn't time for morning calls; they were over hours ago. And it wasn't yet time to ready oneself for supper, even if they had made plans to dine together, which they hadn't. To this point, the three friends had delicately avoided the fact that Helene couldn't receive callers, given Lina's presence in the house.

"Disaster!" Esme cried. "Helene, did you tell the Earl of Mayne that you were staying in this house?"

"No," she said. "But he knew—" She stopped, horrified. "I asked how he knew and he didn't tell me, and then I forgot to press the point."

"Do let me into the room!" Gina said, pushing Esme forward and shoving the door shut behind her, only narrowly missing Leke's nose. He had been on the verge of offering refreshments, but instead he retreated to the servants' quarters for a think. And then he ambled over to the Number Eighteen, Rothsfeld, because the butler in that establishment, by the name of Watts, knew everything worth knowing.

In the library, Helene sank into the armchair she had just vacated, feeling as if her legs had lost all strength. "He promised he wouldn't tell anyone," she said. And then, "Surely he didn't!"

"He did," Esme said grimly, sitting down opposite Helene. "Since you didn't tell him yourself, he must have bribed the footman who forwarded his note to Gina."

"It's all my fault," Gina said. She was stark white and looked anguished. "I'm so sorry that I ever, ever passed on Mayne's note to you. He's naught more than a cad!"

"Cad!" Esme cried. "That doesn't half cover it. The man's an utter bastard, and if anyone's to blame, it's myself. *I* put him on the list I gave to Helene; *I* sang his praises between the sheets!"

Helene's lips felt numb. "Blame is surely not the point," she said. "May I ask what the Earl of Mayne has done with his illicitly obtained information?"

There was a moment of silence. Helene faintly heard a plink-plinking coming from the music room; Rees must have switched to the harpsichord.

"He told everyone," Esme said, finally. "Last night, at Vauxhall."

"He was at Vauxhall?" Helene gasped. "I never saw him!"

"Neither did I. But he was there, because Felicia Saville is citing him as her source of information."

"Felicia Saville?" Helene asked numbly.

"I would guess that she's paid twenty morning calls today," Gina said quietly. "And all circling around two topics: the Earl of Mayne and his magnificent endowments, and your scandalous activities."

"Mayne and Felicia?" Helene was unable to conceive the breadth of the scandal that must be spreading about herself, so she fastened on the lesser matter.

"Felicia would appear to be his latest *inamorata*," Esme said with distaste, "though how he can put up with all that mindless gabbing, I don't know. Helene, do you think that you might have insulted Mayne in some way? I don't mean in the least to defend the man, but he's acting like someone bent on revenge. I'm told he put a bet in White's that—" She stopped.

Helene looked at her. "What did he bet in White's?"

"Sebastian was likely mis—"

"What did he bet in White's?"

"It had to do with the portion of the night that Rees granted to you as opposed to his mistress," Esme said.

"Obviously not a real bet," Helene said slowly. "He wrote in the betting book only in order to spread the scandal."

"I agree," Gina said. "But I don't think we have anything to gain by sorting through what insult he may or may not have suffered. We have to figure out what to do."

"What are people saying?" Helene asked. "Don't give me a watered-down version, Esme. We've been friends too long for that."

"You're ruined," Esme said, her eyes bleak. "I find it extremely unlikely that any woman of good reputation will receive you in her house ever again. Unless we do something."

"Do something? Do something? There's nothing to do." Helene leaned back in her chair. She could feel her pulse beating in her throat in a way that threatened to make her stomach flip over. But she wasn't hysterical. She, Helene, never became hysterical.

Gina was sitting bolt upright, lips pressed together. "There has to be some way out of this," she said fiercely. "There simply has to be. What if we make our own calls, and maintain that Mayne is a liar?"

Esme shook her head. "No one will believe us."

"What if Rees challenges Mayne to a duel?" Gina demanded.

"Duels are against the law," Esme began.

But Helene cut in, "And I don't want Rees fighting a duel. He'd never win against Mayne. I doubt he knows how to pick up a pistol."

Esme looked at her in disbelief. "I thought you cared nothing for Rees. If the truth be known, none of us are to blame for this situation except for that bloody husband of yours. Why *did* he force you to come here, with his mistress in residence? What on earth did he hope to gain from it?"

"I don't know," Helene whispered. "I should never have consented to do it."

No one wanted to agree with the obvious, so they just sat for a moment.

"Will you still receive me?" Helene asked, looking from one to the other. She was starting to feel a little shaky.

"Don't be a fool!" Esme snapped. "We're going to work this out, somehow. Maybe I'll send Sebastian to duel with Mayne."

"Or I'll send Cam to simply beat him senseless," Gina suggested. "Cam could tie him up and force him to recant.

And break his nose in the process," she added with a relish that belied her reputation for duchess-like behavior.

Helene managed a smile. "Rees can pummel Mayne just as well, if that's needed. But no one would believe Mayne if he recanted now. The damage is done. I'm ruined."

"Where *is* Rees?" Esme demanded.

Helene shook her head. "I want to know what I'm going to do, first."

"Rees's reputation was already in shreds," Gina said with stinging emphasis. "Yet it never stopped him from attending a *ton* party, should he so wish."

"There's no use crying over the unfairness of life," Esme said with equal sharpness. "We have to think of a way out of this. Think!"

Chapter Thirty-Five

A Sibling in a Righteous Fury
Is a Terrifying Sight

"I don't like it, Garret," Lady Griselda Willoughby said, her voice as sharp as the edge of a knife. She was standing in his study, looking the very picture of enraged femininity in a gown of pale blue sarsanet, trimmed with white lace.

Mayne looked up from his writing desk and scowled at his sister. "No one likes it, Griselda," he observed. "There's something remarkably distasteful about the whole affair."

She walked closer and then began pulling off her pale blue gloves, finger by finger. "That's beside the point," she said, slapping her first glove onto the table.

"I hardly think so," he said dryly.

"If there's anything distasteful here, it's you," his sister retorted. Her second glove slapped onto the polished mahogany of his writing desk.

Mayne's features set into forbidding lines. He may have been thinking something of that sort himself, but he wouldn't take the same from a younger sister. "I apologize if I offended you in any way," he said with an air of chilling *froideur*.

"You behaved like a shabby cad," Griselda cried, unconsciously echoing Gina's indictment. "I'm ashamed of you. And I'm even ashamed of *me*, for being your sister!"

Mayne stood up. "For God's sake, Grissie, don't you think—"

She pointed a finger at him. "Don't you dare call me Grissie, you—you—degenerate! I have no idea what happened between you and Helene Godwin last night, but I can only assume that she sent you packing. And for you to turn from practically panting at the mere mention of her name—because you were, Garret, you know you were—to spreading vile rumors about her is *low*! Low and unworthy of you!"

"She lied to me," Mayne forced out, walking to the mantelpiece.

"Wait!" his sister said contemptuously. "Do I hear the sound of violins wailing? So you've never lied, is that it? You—who've made a name for yourself by sleeping with half the married women in London? You dare reproach a woman for lying?"

Mayne turned around. The injustice of it had occurred to him in the middle of the night, but he hadn't known that his little sister would agree. "I didn't know you thought this of me," he said, lips stiff.

"I love you, Garret," she said, picking up her gloves in an ecstasy of irritation and slapping them down on the table again. "You know that. I love you more than any other person on this miserable planet. But that doesn't mean I'm blind to you. You have to marry because you're becoming more and more a fribble and less of a man of substance. It seems as if you spend all of your time wooing married women, and then when you've got them in the palm of your hand, you dance onto the next woman. Why, Garret? Why?"

He stared at her. "I don't know."

"Exactly! I think you're bored. And boredom is making you do shabby things."

"I—" But what defense did he have, exactly? He felt shabby. He wouldn't have put that word on it, but he'd had a smutty taste in his mouth ever since he woke up, and a leaden sense in his belly.

"All right, I'll marry," he said hollowly, walking over to the fire and sitting down, ignoring the fact that Griselda was still walking around the room like a demented vixen.

"Of course you'll marry!" she snapped.

"You can just chose someone and I'll marry her."

"Not until you've solved the mess you've made," she said sharply. "You know I love to gossip, Garret. I'm thought of as a gibble-gabbler, and I am one. But I'm not vicious. Helene Godwin would never have gone to that house of her husband's, not with a strumpet in residence, unless he forced her to do so. You should have seen that as clearly as I! I've no objection to jabbering about a woman—or a man, for that matter— who chooses to blacken his or her reputation by imprudent behavior. But I would never palaver about a woman forced by her husband into detestable action, *never*!"

Mayne felt really sick now. He'd forgotten his first reaction to hearing that Helene was staying in her husband's house. "She said—she said he didn't force her to stay there."

"You're a fool! I've known Helene for years, and if you didn't even see the monstrous puritanical streak in her, what did you see?"

"I don't know," Mayne said, pulling his hand through his hair.

"Godwin forced her into that house, and into the presence of his mistress—" Griselda shuddered. "I can't imagine how humiliating that must have been for her. And you—*you* break her confidence, and all because she doesn't choose to join the long line of women who've graced your bedsheets!"

Mayne's teeth were clenched. "You've made your point," he said, hearing a roaring sound in his ears. "You're right."

Griselda opened her mouth—and shut it again.

"The point is," she said after a moment or so, "what are we going to do to change things?"

"There's nothing that can be done," Mayne said through bloodless lips. "I've ruined her. I could let Godwin kill me in a duel, I suppose."

"Don't be a greater fool than you already are!" Griselda snapped. "I may be extremely annoyed with you, but you're still my brother and I won't have you shot by that degenerate. This is all *his* fault, at the base of it! We just need to *think*. Think!"

Chapter Thirty-Six

Great Minds, etc.

It is a fact long established about the human race that when a great many fine minds assert themselves to the same task, solutions are found with astonishing rapidity. At some point, a clever group of primitives came up with the wheel; a group of housewives bent on retail therapy discovered that metal disks work for bartering just as well as do chickens; a few fishermen managed to extract Napoleon from lazy exile on Elba.

And so it was.

When Lady Griselda Willoughby was announced at the Godwin residence, Helene looked confused, but Gina, who knew the precedence of every living member of English peerage, said instantly, "That's Mayne's sister. Show her in, Leke."

It was during Griselda's rather flurried and apologetic entrance that Esme suddenly said, "I've got it!"

Griselda instantly dropped her rattled explanation that Mayne was waiting penitently in her carriage, and said "What?"

"I think it will work," Esme said slowly. "We just need the cooperation of one person."

"Who?" Gina said breathlessly.

"Mayne will do it," Griselda said firmly. "My brother will do anything that needs to be done."

"Not Mayne." Esme looked at Helene. "It's your husband's . . . friend. We need her."

"For what?" Helene asked.

"She has to marry," Esme said decisively. "Become respectable."

"I don't know if Mayne will wish to go that far," Griselda said, feeling a sudden flash of panic. "He does mean to marry, but—"

"No, I don't mean she should actually marry someone," Esme said. "But she has to pretend to be married. Helene, would you mind very much if we asked the young lady to join us?"

"Join us?" Griselda squeaked. To tell the truth, she'd never been in the room with a kept woman. It was a good thing that she'd left Mayne in the coach. He had an uncompromising streak when it came to his little sister's acquaintances.

"I don't even know if she's in the house," Helene was explaining. "We don't exactly—I have no idea—" she foundered to a pause.

"I shall enquire," Gina said firmly. "What is her name?"

"McKenna," Helene said. "Miss Lina McKenna."

The three women sat in utter silence, listening to Gina sending Leke off to request that Miss McKenna kindly join them in the library.

Griselda found herself rather disappointed, to tell the truth. The young woman who was ushered through the door by Leke some ten minutes later was nothing like what *she* imagined a Bird of Paradise to look like. Miss McKenna had soft brown curls, and large eyes. She was beautiful, in a young sort of way. But she didn't look debauched, and she certainly didn't look as if she was—well—spicy. Naughty. Any of those rather exciting words that one associated with strumpets. Mostly, she just looked painfully nervous.

"Miss McKenna," Esme said, having made sure that the girl was seated. "I am afraid that the news of Lady Godwin's residence in the house, in tandem with your presence, has created rather a sensation amongst London society."

Miss McKenna gasped and looked to Helene. "They found out?"

"She's ruined," Esme confirmed. "No one in polite society will ever receive her again." Her voice was quiet but merciless.

Miss McKenna swallowed. "I'm sorry," she whispered. "In God's truth, I am so sorry."

Helene found a smile wobbling on her lips. "It's hardly your fault. I think we have universally come to the agreement that the fault lies directly at the door of my reprehensible husband."

Griselda was rather interested to note that Helene showed no sign of loathing her husband's mistress. Perhaps Mayne was more acute than she had given him credit for. Helene was, indeed, an unusual woman.

"I did not wish to remain in this house," Miss McKenna said, looking only at Helene, "and I'm ashamed that I ever agreed. I only did so because Lord Godwin offered me the lead in his next opera."

Griselda was feeling more and more confused. The supposed strumpet spoke like a lady, albeit a Scottish one. Griselda could hear a burr in her voice. And she wasn't even wearing rouge, for all Griselda could see. How could this woman be a self-respecting *élégante*? Helene didn't seem to have shed a single tear over the fact she was ruined, but Miss McKenna was obviously biting her lip to keep back a flood.

"You do not have the manner of a common woman," Esme commented.

"No," Miss McKenna admitted.

"How many of Lord Godwin's acquaintances have you met frequently, since becoming his mistress, enough so that they would recognize you instantly?"

Miss McKenna's face washed with color. "Almost none," she whispered. "Mr. Darby. Mr. Forbes-Shacklett. Oh, and Lord Pandross, but he hasn't been to the house in months."

"Simon Darby and Pandross won't present a problem; Rees can shut them up. Are the Forbes-Shackletts in town?" Esme asked Gina.

"I don't think so," Gina said slowly. "Lady Forbes-Shacklett was going to present her daughter this year, but then the family went into mourning, and I believe they remained in the country."

Esme drew a deep breath. "I think it's possible." She turned back to Lina. "I am sure you are aware how remorseless society will be to Lady Godwin. Her children will be shunned, should she have any. She will have to live in the country. She will lose her friends. How can we risk the reputations of our own children, by continuing to fraternize with a woman of her sort?"

Gina opened her mouth indignantly, but Esme silenced her with one glance.

Lina was trembling. "I am sorry," she said miserably. She had never felt so wretchedly ashamed in her entire life. "I'll leave the house immediately. I'll never—"

"I should like you to do something for Lady Godwin first," Esme interrupted. "There is only one way we can overcome this scandal. We must be so brazen that no one could possibly believe the truth." Esme turned to the others. "May I present to you Rees's third cousin, four times removed, recently widowed and come to London for peace and quiet?"

Gina's mouth fell open; Helene flinched; Griselda said, "Of course!"

"Third cousin?" Lina gasped. "Of Lord Godwin?"

Esme nodded. "From this moment on, you are a little-known relative from the country. No one has seen you as yourself, remember. No one is at all clear about what Rees's famed mistress actually looks like. We will announce that the mistress long ago departed. Rees had a distant connection staying here, and Helene joined the household temporarily, to act as a chaperone."

"Are you certain that everyone will believe us?" Helene asked, dawning hope in her voice.

"Obviously, we have to parade Miss McKenna before the *ton*. But I think that one occasion, if well handled, will suffice to silence the gossip. No one could possibly believe that the four of us"—she nodded to Lady Griselda—"would ever countenance being in the presence of Rees's mistress, let alone bring about the presentation of such a woman to the *ton*."

A little smile curled Griselda's lips. "And I know precisely who would best effect the presentation of this distant relative. My brother may have acted the fool last night, but now he can put his dramatic ability to work in our favor."

Chapter Thirty-Seven

Siblings Are Sometimes Quite Similar

Naturally, Rees was pounding away at one of his pianos when Tom found him. He seemed to be playing the same set of chords over and over again. Tom walked over to the piano and stood next to it until Rees looked up.

"Where's Helene?" Rees asked, by way of greeting. "I haven't seen her this morning."

"I have no idea," Tom said. "I shall be leaving for St. Mary's tomorrow, Rees."

His brother blinked up at him and his hands finally slowed on the keys. "I had gotten used to having you in the house."

Tom thought to sit on the couch, but it was stacked with paper. He pulled over a stool and sat on that instead. "I need to return to my parish. I intend to speak to the bishop about leaving the priesthood."

Rees was caressing the piano keys with long fingers, although he made no sound. "I would surmise that your change of profession is due to Lina?"

Tom lost his balance and almost toppled from the stool. "I—that is, yes."

"How does Lina feel about you?"

"She refuses to marry a vicar," Tom said, wondering if he should apologize for taking Rees's mistress and decided that he needn't. "Perhaps I will be able to change her mind. It will take me some time to extract myself from the church, but I would like to marry her immediately."

Rees raised an eyebrow. Tom had the unnerving sense that their father was sitting before him. He'd never realized before how much Rees took after the old earl.

"I had the impression," Rees said slowly, "that although you were enjoying a glimpse of life outside the parish, you would return to your church."

"I miss my congregation, and I miss being a priest," Tom said, feeling almost as if he were confessing to a weakness. "It's who I am, after all these years. But Lina doesn't wish to marry a man of the cloth." He tried not to sound as if he were defending a weakness. Rees was *not* their father, only an elder brother.

"What will you do if the Bishop grants your request and removes you from the parish?"

"Likely work with abandoned children," Tom said promptly.

"You're a better man than I am," Rees said. "You know, Father was proud of you, for all he didn't express that particular emotion."

"Expressing contempt came far more easily."

Rees was silent for a moment. Then he said: "I'm proud of you, Tom. You're a good man."

Tom watched him scowl down at his keyboard, and felt a rush of affection, although it would never do to express it. "So will you forgive me for stealing your mistress?" he asked.

"It was her voice, as I expect you've realized," Rees said, ignoring his frivolous question. "I heard her sing, and I couldn't think about anything except getting that voice into the house so that she could sing for me." He smiled in a crooked kind of way. "I was a right bastard. It only took me a month or two to realize it, but it was too late."

"I wouldn't have met Lina if you hadn't brought her here," Tom said, and the very idea chilled him. He did want to stay a vicar, but only if he had Lina to keep him laughing, and warm his bed, and stop him from turning into a sanctimonious ass.

Rees played one key. The sound hung on the air, melancholy and fading. "I suppose I can lure Madame Fodor from the Italian Opera House to play Lina's part. It will suit her voice very well." And then, looking at the keyboard: "I am going to ask Helene to remain in the house."

"To remain in the house—or to stay with you?" Tom asked gently.

The smile on Rees's mouth was rather grim. "She has a great deal to forgive me for."

"You're lucky she loves you so much, then," Tom said.

Rees's eyes flew to Tom's, and then he looked away without comment, standing up. "I need to find Helene and play this phrase for her."

Tom stood up as well and then, to his utter surprise, Rees pulled him into a rough hug. He didn't say anything; Rees was never one to use words when there was no need. Tom followed his brother from the room without another word between them.

He was free. Free to tell Lina that she had to marry him. Free to take her away.

As Rees stepped into the hallway, Leke came out of the library. "The countess has just asked for you," he said, holding open the door.

Tom stopped. "Where may I find Miss McKenna, Leke?"

"In the library," he replied.

They strode into the room looking, had there been a mirror appropriately placed, extremely like their father. Yet another glance would have revealed that they were far more like to each other, than to their father.

Chapter Thirty-Eight

Snippets of Conversation Overheard in London During the Week

"It's your penance," Lady Griselda Willoughby told her brother with some satisfaction. "If you have to endure a month or so of wretched bibble-babble, it will teach you to be more particular in your attentions. For goodness' sake, I may find Helene Godwin rather tedious, but I grow faint with ennui if I am unlucky enough to drift into the sound of Felicia Saville's voice. And believe me, you can hear her voice halfway across a ballroom!"

Her brother's answer was unintelligible; Griselda just smiled to herself. She had no need for an interpreter when it came to males and their childish dependence on profanity; after all, she had been married for all of a year, God rest his soul.

"You cannot leave the Church. I won't allow it!"

"For you. Only for you."

"I won't allow it!"

"But you said you didn't wish to marry a vicar." The said vicar's eyes burned down at his companion. "It never occurred to me that I could be anything other than what I am. But I could do so, for you. The only person I would ever give up my vows for is you, Lina."

"My name isn't Lina," she said, stumbling a little. "It's Alina. But my mother always called me Lina."

"You're my Lina now," he said into her ear. "And if what I do for a living would come between us, I'll do something else."

"I don't want you to relinquish your vows. You wouldn't be happy."

"The only thing that would make me unhappy is losing you."

"Then make me a vicar's wife, Tom."

There was nothing to overhear for a while and then, "You *will* keep me from becoming as perfect as your father, won't you, Lina?"

"I don't think that's a problem," she said with a giggle. "Take your hand away!"

He groaned. "Lord, I wish Rees would return with that Special License."

"Are you sure?" There was a hesitancy in her voice that wrung his heart.

"I've never been surer of anything in my life," he told her. "Never. Listen—I'll make a vow so that I can break it for you!"

"Don't be silly!" she scolded, laughing.

"I vow to God himself that I will never kiss your breast."

And she, whispering, with a rosy blush, "You won't?"

"God will forgive me for breaking my vow," he said, his lips tracing the very edge of her bodice. "He can see into my heart and knows that I love you with every bit of my soul. That's the most important vow."

"I love you the same," she said, and then his lips did slip below her bodice—but only for a moment or two.

Mr. Holland, vicar of St. Mary's, was a man of considerable self-control, and considerable patience.

The portly Bishop of Rochester viewed the young couple before him with keen interest. "I only have the slimmest

307

acquaintance with your father," he said to Miss McKenna. "I knew him at Cambridge, oh, many years ago, that was. He was quite the rapscallion, your father!"

That seemed to surprise Miss McKenna.

"Indeed," Bishop Lynsey assured her, with a belly laugh that made his vestments shake as if a tempest had struck the environs of Rochester Cathedral. "They do say that rascals make the best churchmen, you know! Well, mum's the word on that. He's an excellent man, your father, an excellent man. And you couldn't do better than marry Mr. Holland, my dear. I can see your father's influence in your choice. I'm only sorry that your family can't be with you. But I do understand the urgency of young love, even such an oldster as I."

He gave the bridegroom's elder brother a sapient look. It would be nice if that ne'er-do-well, Lord Godwin, were moved by the words of the marriage ceremony into conducting his own affairs with more propriety. It was surprising to see the earl and countess standing beside each other; Lynsey had heard gossip that suggested the two hadn't even spoken for years. But here they were, looking as married as can be. Well, the ways of God are mysterious indeed.

Still, he beckoned the married couple closer. It would do them good to hear the words of the ceremony since, if he remembered correctly, they had trotted off to Gretna Green in a harum-scarum fashion and married over the anvil. Likely two or three words in the whole ritual, if one could even call it that.

"Dearly beloved," he began with a fine flourish in his voice, "we are gathered together here in the sight of God, and in the face of this congregation"—he smiled encouragingly at Earl Godwin and his wife—"to join together this Man and

308

this Woman in holy matrimony, which is an honorable estate . . ."

"You're awfully quiet."

"That was a very sweet ceremony, didn't you think?"

"Mmmm."

"I believe I shall retire to my chamber."

His hands stopped. "Weren't we going to work on the étude before bed?"

"Rees!"—rather exasperated—"I'm exhausted. We can think of this in the morning." And then, "What are you *doing*?"

"Taking you upstairs," he said. "I'm going to carry you over the threshold."

"*What*?"

"I never carried you across the threshold of the house ten years ago, Helene, so the bedchamber door will have to do. I have a mind to pretend that I'm going to walk into an inn bedroom and find you there."

She had her arms around his neck, and he was climbing the stairs. "Are you going to laugh at my bosom then?"

He stopped. "What?"

So, in the way of wives, Helene reminded the earl that on seeing his wife's breasts for the very first time, he had suggested that she might have shrunk in the rain.

Repentance is an emotion that can be expressed in many different ways. Rees was not eloquent. He wasn't good at tossing off debonair little phrases or comparing his wife to roses or jewels.

So he did the very best he could. He took his wife into his bedchamber, pulled her gown over her head, revealing a pair of breasts whose pale pink perfection instantly fired his loins, and then fell backwards, flat on the floor.

"What's the matter with you?" the countess asked with some curiosity, walking over to peer down at him.

"I've fainted from the beauty of your breasts," he said, grinning up at her lasciviously.

And then, as she giggled, large hands circled her ankles and crept up her legs. "I'll make up for my stupidity, Helene," he said, kissing his way up a slender thigh. "I'll make it my daily chore to praise your breasts. Even before I touch the piano."

As one musician to another, Helene could tell when she'd received the greatest compliment of her life, although nary a rose nor a jewel was mentioned.

Chapter Thirty-Nine

The Plot Unveiled

Lady Felicia Saville gave one, and only one, ball each year. The night before the event she often couldn't sleep. There was so much to worry about: would Gunter's deliver half-melted ices, would the champagne punch be sufficient, would her husband appear reasonably sane or utterly cracked? The last question was the most pressing. The year after they married he informed a large and amused audience that he was actually the child of a black-tipped ewe, and then there was the occasion when he insisted that his horse was a blood relative. Over the years, she had realized that his particular form of mania was less disagreeable than it could have been, but it did require forethought to make certain that he did not regale the ballroom with tales to rival those of Aesop.

But this year was different. Last night she had slept like a baby. The ball would be easy, because Mayne would be by her side.

Contrary to his usual custom, and quite contrary to what she herself would have expected, he was still showing her marked attention. It was the most delightful and unexpected pleasure of her entire life. They had been *intimates*, as one might say, for exactly one week, and his ardor showed no signs of cooling. Felicia had to hug herself for the pure joy of it. Everyone wanted to know her secrets. How could *she*,

Felicia Saville, hold the attention of a man known to flit from woman to woman like the proverbial butterfly?

Felicia frowned over her morning hot chocolate. Frankly, she hadn't the faintest idea how she was keeping Mayne's attention. It wasn't as if they shared scintillating conversation. Nor were they terribly intimate with each other in private, if the truth were known. He certainly kissed her with a great deal of finesse, but then he muttered phrases about respecting her too much to overstep, and carried the business no further.

Which was rather disappointing. Felicia's marital partner, after all, was past hope in that area. After one night in which he shouted *tally-ho!* in an intimate moment, she banished him from the bedroom.

She was beginning to think that perhaps Mayne had never slept with any of the women he accompanied. Perhaps the women in question were so enchanted by his attentions—and their reputations so enhanced by his presence at their side—that they told no one their relationship was unexpectedly chaste. If that was the truth of it, Felicia was perfectly happy to continue the tradition. In fact, in the last week, when her friends kept noting that she was looking particularly becoming, she had given one and all a twinkling glance that put her renewed looks at Mayne's bedstead. The truth, after all, was hardly important in these situations.

With a shrug, she finished her hot chocolate and dismissed perplexing thoughts about Mayne's continued attentions. She was beautiful enough, wasn't she? Or at least, she would be, once she finished the four-hour dressing process that would ready her for the ball tonight.

She was three hours into the ritual, bathed, perfumed, painted and powdered, but only half-dressed, when a footman informed her maid that the Earl of Mayne wished a brief word, if she were available. A smile curled on Felicia's lips.

Oh, this was even better than she could have imagined! She cast a look at herself in her dressing room mirror. She hadn't yet put on her evening gown. She was wearing stockings of the palest rose silk, tied above the knee with a silver garter. Her chemise certainly covered her flesh adequately, and its edging of rose lace would entice any man alive.

"I'd like my corset," she ordered.

Felicia's lady's maid, Lucy, rushed forward with her corset and laced it tightly over her chemise. Yes! That was perfect. Now Felicia's breasts swelled enticingly and her waist looked to be the span of a man's hand. She had never done such a risqué thing as entertain a gentleman in her dressing room. Not even her husband. Mind you, Saville had never shown the slightest interest in joining her during the dressing process.

Her maid began tucking tiny rosebuds high into a coronet on her head, from which hung precisely four ringlets. Felicia reached out and applied more color to her lips. "He may come up," she said coolly, as if she entertained gentlemen every day of the week. "And Lucy, you may go. Return in a half hour, if you please, as I shall need to finish dressing with some dispatch."

Lucy could be counted on to gabble to all the maids in attendance at the ball tonight, Felicia thought happily. She tweaked one curl forward over her shoulder. She did have a long nose, but really, she was remarkably well preserved. It must be her beauty that tied Mayne so closely to her side.

There was a knock and the man himself strode into her bedchamber. Felicia almost gasped. Her chamber was all frothy lace and pink ribbons; in contrast, the earl looked like the very personification of sleek masculinity. Tonight he was dressed with supreme elegance, in a coat of smoky blue that outlined the breadth of his shoulders and gave his hair the sheen of a raven's wing. He looked utterly male and (had Felicia the wits to perceive it) rather dangerous, as if some subtle rage were driving him forward.

"Darling," he said, bending down and dropping a kiss on her cheek so that their eyes met in the mirror. "This is an honor that I didn't expect."

Felicia tilted her head back, the better to show her neck. Her mother had once called it a trifle long, but Felicia disagreed. A graceful neck was a never-fading virtue. "You are always welcome by my side, even in the most intimate of circumstances," she purred.

Somewhat to her relief, he didn't take up the obvious suggestion, but just smiled and brought over a chair for himself. Felicia could hardly contain herself at the sight of the two of them in the mirror: he so beautiful, so potent, so devastatingly powerful. And she, leader of the *ton*, exquisitely dressed . . . Their coloring was quite perfect together.

"I need your help," he said, bending close to her ear as if he couldn't resist kissing it.

Felicia shook with excitement. "Anything!" she said eagerly, and then contained herself, adding languidly, "Of course, darling, whatever you request."

"I seem to have made a small mistake," he said, "in the matter of Lady Godwin."

Felicia blinked. "You did?"

"You are the only woman powerful enough in the *ton* to salvage my disastrous follies," he continued, tracing her ear with his lips. And his hands . . . Perhaps Mayne *did* bed all those women. Perhaps he was just saving himself, building her anticipation for the moment when he would besiege her virtue. Felicia shivered a bit at the thought.

"If there's any way I can help," she said rather absentmindedly. It was hard not to gaze at the two of them in her mirror

314

as if she were at the theater, watching one of those Restoration comedies from the last century. But his actual comment had finally sunk in. "I doubt I can do much to salvage Lady Godwin's reputation, Mayne."

"Do call me Garret," Mayne said, trying not to breathe deeply. The woman had practically papered herself in rice powder! He was like to sneeze, if he didn't watch himself.

"My pleasure," she sighed.

"It appears that Lady Godwin had returned to her husband's house merely in order to chaperone Godwin's brother's fiancée," Mayne told her. "The girl is a tender little Scottish vicar's daughter, if you can believe it, and doubtless horrified to hear that she's been mistaken for a strumpet."

Felicia sat straight up in her chair with the air of a fox scenting a rabbit. "You don't mean it!"

Mayne nodded. "I've made an ass of myself," he said, pulling a face of laughing mock repentance. "Blotted my copybook."

"And what's your excuse?" she asked, fluttering her eyelashes at him.

"Something about Lady Godwin irritates me," he admitted. "I'm afraid that I didn't bother to corroborate my impression that Godwin was still living with an opera singer. Now I feel, naturally enough, culpable."

"I share your feelings about Lady Godwin," Felicia agreed. "And now that she looks for all the world like a shorn lamb, I positively shudder to look at her. Her hair *was* her only beauty, you know."

Mayne's lips tightened, but his companion simply trilled on. "Goodness me! Are you quite, quite sure about the Scottish fiancée, Garret darling? I mean, that she's the daughter of a *vicar*?"

315

"Alas."

"Well, I shall do my best," Felicia told him. "I shall inform everyone. But you know how it is!" she tittered. "Once a rumor starts, it's impossible to stamp out. It's not as if we *know* this Scottish girl, after all."

Mayne moved behind her. One hand slipped down her throat. "You blind me," he said softly. "Truly, you do." He bent over and kissed her cheek. This was the tricky bit; Felicia might well take offense at his presumptuousness.

"I invited them to your ball," he said softly.

Was that the tip of his tongue touching her throat? Felicia swallowed. "You did what?" she asked quaveringly.

"I took the enormous liberty of inviting the Scottish miss and her fiancé to your ball," Mayne murmured against her throat. His hand had wandered down and was tracing the shape of Felicia's breast. "They will be accompanied by the Godwins, naturally enough."

"Her fiancé," Felicia said, trying vainly to keep rational. "Godwin's brother."

"He is a vicar himself, if you can believe it," Mayne said, tasting her skin as if she were made of the finest cream. "The brother, I mean."

Felicia noticed that he had a white streak on his cheek from the rice powder she had shaken over her bosom. But he didn't seem to notice the taste on his lips.

"A vicar and a vicar's daughter," she said dreamily, winding her arms around his neck. "A match made in heaven."

"Just as are you and I," he said sleekly. "Will you forgive me, then, for the impertinence of inviting guests to your ball?"

She smiled at him, a smile that combined chastisement and permission. "After tonight, Lady Godwin will be received in every house in the land," she assured him. "And the Scottish

316

girl as well. I think we know each other well enough, Garret, that I might allow a few . . . *impertinences*?"

"Just what I longed to hear," he said. His smile, in the mirror, was meant both for her—and for his conscience.

Chapter Forty

Come to the Ball!

Elsewhere in London, others were preparing for the same occasion. Lady Griselda Willoughby was delicately applying a black patch to the right of her cherry-colored mouth; she had decided that her newest fashion would be to ape the ornaments of her Jacobean ancestors. She wore a gown with a small train, and the tiniest suggestion of a ruff. The Duchess of Girton was having a rather less peaceful time dressing, as her little boy kept wandering through her dressing room. He had just learned to climb down stairs backwards, and therefore he spent most of his time eluding his nursemaids and unerringly finding his way to his mama's chambers. Lady Esme Bonnington was even further behind in the process, as her husband Sebastian had appeared in her room with an urgent request, and what with one thing and other (some of which involved unbuttoning rather than buttoning), she hadn't even put on a stitch of clothing yet.

But the most assiduous preparations were taking place at Number Fifteen, Rothsfeld Square. Monsieur Olivier had been to the house and left again: Lina's glossy brown curls were now a shadow of their former self, thinned, curled and starched into rigid little ringlets that dangled about her ears.

"I'm so sorry!" Helene said again, staring at the glass. "He went too far! What will Tom say?"

But Lina couldn't stop smiling. She didn't give a fig for the demise of her hair. "It will grow back," she said.

"Do you think I ought to add more freckles, or am I overdoing the effect, Madam?" Saunders asked, stepping back.

Helene looked at the mirror and gave a faint shudder. Lina had sprouted a multitude of freckles. First Saunders painted them over the bridge of her nose, which was all very well. But then she went farther afield and now there were battalions of brown speckles marching along Lina's forehead, making her look far older than her years.

"I'm sorry!" Helene said again.

"Don't be," Lina replied. Their eyes met in the mirror and Lina knew that she didn't have to say the rest of it out loud. She would never stop being grateful for the gift of Tom.

Saunders was mixing a little red sandalwood with chalk. As she painted it onto Lina's lips they took on a slightly palsied air, as if the color had leached out of them.

"Well, that should do it," Lina said cheerfully. "No self-respecting opera singer would look like this."

"No, indeed," Helene said with some satisfaction. "You look—you look—"

"A proper fright," Lina finished.

"Not so terrible. Countrified, perhaps?"

"I *am* a country vicar's wife," Lina said, and there was a note of joy in her voice.

"Now for the gown," Saunders said. She returned from the wardrobe with a gown reverentially laid over her arms.

Two minutes later, Lina was swathed—positively swathed—in white lace.

"Perhaps it's overpoweringly innocent," Helene said dubiously. She had picked out the pattern and fabric herself, ordering it from a *modiste*, Madame Pantile, whom she'd long heard was liable to make ill-fitting and over-trimmed clothing. And Madame Pantile had certainly lived up to her reputation. Every inch of Lina's gown was trimmed with blonde lace, or point lace, or bunches of white ribbon.

"Are you certain that the wreath isn't too much?" Lina said, showing the first signs of uneasiness.

"Oh no!" Helene said. "I consider the wreath a stroke of genius! Who but Madame Pantile could have designed a wreath made of silver oak leaves ornamented with heron's feathers? At least . . . that's what she told me they were. Who would have thought that heron's feathers were quite so tall?"

"My head will topple to the side if I'm not very careful," Lina said, demonstrating her predicament.

"Excellent. You need to look awkward while dancing."

"That won't be a problem," Lina commented. "Wearing shoes that are too large makes it extremely difficult to be graceful."

Helene beamed. "That was a clever notion of Esme's, was it not?"

The night was going as well as Felicia could possibly have hoped. Mayne was at her side just enough so that her friends and her enemies couldn't help but notice his devotion, and yet he wasn't there so much that she felt constrained in recounting every detail of his physique and technique to her friends. Her husband was off in the card room, apparently acting in an appropriate manner. The ballroom was an utter crush. In all, the only thing missing to make her ball discussed throughout those boring fall months was a Sensation.

Something had to happen. An elopement, a betrayal, an argument. Something! She glanced around the room. What a pity it was that Esme Rawlings had married Lord Bonnington. Infamous Esme could always be relied upon to create some sort of a sensation, but now she had dwindled into positive

320

respectability. There she was, dancing with her husband and it must be for the third time, at least. That was a scandal, to Felicia's mind, a scandal of hideously boring proportions.

At that moment there was a bit of a flurry at the door, and Felicia turned with relief. Perhaps the Regent had decided to—no.

Who on earth could it be?

A grotesquely bedizened girl, with plumes so high they were likely to be set alight by the candelabra hanging from the ceiling, had appeared at the top of the short flight of stairs leading to the ballroom. Felicia didn't recognize her escort but there, behind her, was Earl Godwin so that must be—

There was a titter in her ear. "Famous, my dear! Your ball is going to be notorious!" The Honorable Gerard Bunge suddenly appeared, for all the world like a jack-in-the-box in amethyst stockings, if such a thing existed. "That must be the vicar's daughter, or rather, the strumpet as Mayne had it!" He reeled slightly from the force of his own giggles. "Could be Mayne's going blind if he mistook *that* one for a Bird of Paradise!"

"She's rather an eyesore, is she not?" Felicia said with amusement. "Come along, Bunge. I must greet her, you know."

At the tap of a hostess's fan on their shoulder, her guests fell away before her, leaving Felicia a full view of the uncultivated lass whom Mayne, *her* darling Mayne, had insulted. And what a mistake that was! Felicia had rarely seen such an ungainly, rustic girl as the one clumsily curtsying before Lady Bonnington.

"You'd better make haste," Bunge said in her ear, as they expertly made their way through the crowded room. "She just poked the Duke of Girton in the eye with those plumes. How could Mayne ever have thought this one was a fashionable impure? They wouldn't have let her in the door of the opera house!"

Felicia held out her hand languidly. The country miss bobbed an inept curtsy and gabbled something. Felicia backed away as quickly as she could, to avoid being struck in the face by her waving plumes.

"I must say, this is quite a surprise, to see you in the presence of Lord Godwin," she said aside to the countess. "I thought you two were quite, quite adverse to being in each other's company."

"Oh, we are," Helene Godwin said cheerfully. "But I couldn't allow Mrs. Holland to come to town without a chaperone."

"Mrs. Holland!" Felicia exclaimed.

Lady Godwin clapped a hand over her mouth. "Oh no, I let the truth out! Well, the fact is that Mr. Holland, my brother-in-law, married his fiancée this morning. But we didn't want to announce the news until the happy couple has informed her father, in Scotland. He is a vicar, you know, and I believe he hoped to marry them himself. So you *must* promise not to tell anyone, Lady Saville!"

Felicia nodded, already planning the three or four acquaintances who would be lucky enough to hear the news first.

Lady Godwin drew a little closer. "The dear girl was so *devastated* to hear of the rumors flying around London—you do know what I mean, don't you?"

"A crime!" Felicia whispered back, ignoring the fact that she herself had been instrumental in spreading most of those criminal rumors.

"Yes, I do agree," Lady Godwin said. "You know, Lady Saville, you or I may chat about a matter of interest that occurs in the *ton*, but we would never make something up out of whole cloth! And I'm afraid that is just what the Earl

322

of Mayne must have done. Why, everyone in London knows that my husband dismissed his mistress months ago."

Felicia nodded vigorously. "I had heard the same myself, from a number of people," she assured the countess. "Mayne has much to answer for!"

"Dear Mrs. Holland is happy now," Lady Godwin said. "All's well that ends well, after all. And who could possibly think her a woman of ill repute after seeing her endearing little face?"

"Who indeed?" Felicia murmured, suppressing a shudder as she watched the new Mrs. Holland stumble her way through a country dance.

"Marriage solves so many problems," Lady Godwin commented. "Now she and my dear brother-in-law can go back to the country, and she can simply forget this unpleasant little episode."

"And you, my dear?" Felicia said, returning to a more interesting topic. "Do you think to remain in your husband's house, or will you return to your mother?"

"Well . . . just for *your* ears only, Lady Saville—"

"*Do* call me Felicia!"

"Felicia," the countess repeated. "What a lovely name. The truth is, I haven't quite made up my mind! For some things, you know, husbands are a necessary evil."

Felicia nodded, although to be sure, she couldn't think of a single one of them.

Chapter Forty-One

The Seduction

Floating through the house, up the stairs, came fragments of melody. He was playing the same piece over and over, the madrigal from Act Two, she thought.

Finally Helene got up and put on her serviceable dressing gown, tying it tightly around her waist. It was a good thing there were so few servants, given the number of nights she had spent tiptoeing around the house inadequately dressed.

The candelabra on the piano were burning quite low. It cast a pool of light that made the polished surface of the piano look clover-yellow, and tipped Rees's eyelashes and curls with fire. She walked forward. Her robe made a gentle hushing noise as it dragged through the sheaves of paper that had again accumulated around the piano.

His head jerked up immediately. Without speaking, without taking his eyes from hers, he rose from the piano.

Helene was experiencing, for almost the first time in her life, the heady intoxication of being a siren, a *séductrice*. She pushed the ugly, white dressing gown from her shoulders as if it were made of flowing silk, let it catch on her elbows so the fabric framed her body. She'd left her night rail on her bed.

Rees took one step toward her and then Helene started to walk toward him. It was as if the candlelight drew her into its circle; as she came closer to him, her body turned to flame itself, heat racing up the back of her legs.

He seemed mesmerized. She slowly walked forward until she stood in the circle of light that made the rest of the room fade away into obscurity, as if there were only the two of them in the world.

Still without saying a word, he wrenched off his shirt. The swirl of air made the candles bend and dance. Golden tongues of fire swept over her body, over his chest. She couldn't remember why she thought chest hair was so revolting, years ago. Compared to Mr. Fairfax-Lacy's hairless chest, Rees looked ruggedly masculine, with a kind of burly strength that made her feel weak in the knees. His heavily muscled chest rippled when he moved, making her breasts tingle to be crushed against him.

She let a little smile play on her lips, and then she dropped the dressing gown entirely, allowing it fall to her feet.

The next second he was there, one arm under her neck and another under her knees, scooping her up and taking her over to the sofa. With a terrific swirl of paper, all the drafts and parts and pieces of the opera swooshed to the floor.

"I don't want to be treated like a lady," Helene said, but he was kissing her.

Kissing her. His tongue plunged into her mouth as if she were *terra incognita*, new land, and he an explorer. And she, rather than feeling any kind of revulsion, gasped and said, "Oh," and then said, "Rees," and then said . . . nothing. One of his hands was holding her head tight against his. But the other was sending trails of fire down her spine, roaming her body with hungry violence.

Helene had her arms wound around his neck, but she wasn't a lady. Not tonight. She tore her mouth away. "How did Lina make love to you?" she said, her voice oddly hoarse.

Rees pulled her back. "Who cares?" he said before crushing her against him again, capturing her mouth and pulling

325

them both into a whirlpool of desire and trembling sensation.

"I do," Helene gasped, when she got her breath back. "I do."

Rees let her pull back slightly. "It was nothing compared to you. Nothing." The rasp in his voice told her it was true.

"It's not that," Helene whispered back. "I want to know how to give *you* pleasure, Rees. Not—not like a lady. May I touch you?"

His eyes were pitch-dark in the candlelight. "Lina never touched me," he said, his mouth wandering hungrily over her skin.

"I want to," Helene said, her voice quivering as his mouth closed over her nipple. "I—" but she lost the thought as her body arched toward his, her hands clenched in his hair, a moan flying from her lips.

"Do you want this?" he growled, sucking harder, so that she shuddered under him, gasping, unable to speak. One of his hands curved under her body, jerking her up against the leg wedged between hers, making her cry out with pure pleasure.

But she still retained some small crumb of sanity, enough to twist suddenly in his arms and end up lying on his body. "I want to be just as wicked as you," she whispered, raw desire speaking in her voice like velvet. "I want to make love like one of those Russian dancers who performed on my dining room table."

He smiled at that, that sardonic crooked smile that she loved, so she had to kiss him. It was different, bending her head to him rather than the other way around, having that powerful body under hers. It made her feel even more sensual, if outrageously strumpet-like. Part of her simply couldn't believe that she was straddling him, naked, where anyone could see her.

"Do you see whether I turned the key in the door?" she asked shakily, when he let her mouth go.

He was lying back, his hands roaming over her breasts, a rough caress that made her compulsively shudder and bite her lip to stop a moan. He obviously didn't give a damn about the door. I'm starting to think in swear words, Helene thought with some wonder.

She started to get up to check the door, but his hands captured her.

"Didn't you say that you were going to touch me?" he asked, and the silky pleasure in his voice sent a wave of fire through her belly.

She bent down again, feeling an incantatory mix of possession and desire. It came out of her mouth like a vow, although she hadn't been thinking of it that way. "You are *mine*, Rees. If anyone is going to touch you, it's going to be me. From now on. So if you wish me to touch you the way Lina did, you'll have to teach me."

He stared at her and she couldn't tell what he was thinking, but all he said was, "Lina was a lady, Helene."

Helene could feel a smile of utter delight curl her lips. She shouldn't be so shallow. But she was.

She slid off his body and kneeled beside the couch. He turned slightly, and there he was, all of him, muscled, golden-skinned, dusted with hair that teased her skin into delirious heat. Just the sight of him made Helene want to pull him down to her so he would crush her with his weight, with his fierce, tender wildness.

Instead she licked his shoulder. His skin tasted like salt and faintly, like soap. Just as he had the night before, she whispered, "Do you like this?"

And as he had the night before, he said, rather hoarsely, "Yes. Yes, Helene, yes."

Tentatively she reached out and touched his nipple. It was flat and round, and looked like a copper penny. His muscles rippled at her mere touch. She did it again, a little more firmly, and then rubbed her thumb over him, the way he did to her. He made a hoarse noise that sent a surge of triumphant joy through her, so she bent her head and licked him. His hands clutched her shoulders. Slowly Helene wandered farther afield, discovering that she could make him tremble by gently dragging her teeth across his chest, that a ragged sound came from that chest whenever she suckled his nipple, that his entire body grew rigid as she made her way south.

"I'm not sure that you—" he said, and it sounded as if he were speaking between clenched teeth. Helene grinned to herself. She felt as if she were the most practiced courtesan in all London, and besides, it was too late for him to stop her.

The merest touch of her lips made him shudder convulsively. So she teased him, just as he had teased her. "Do you like this?" she said, laughter spilling into her voice.

"Yes," he gasped. "God, Helene!" He was clutching the sofa cushion beneath him. His body arched toward her.

"This?" she said. She had discovered that dragging her fingernails across his stomach seemed to drive him mad. She was really enjoying herself now. "And what about this?" she whispered, her voice a liquid thread of honey.

But it was too much. With one lunge, Rees pulled her up on top of him so she fell forward and down, onto him, her mouth an almost comical "O" that turned to a cry as she sank, all wet, sweet, warm, onto him. But it wasn't enough, it wasn't enough, so he flipped her over, and the last of the sheets of paper scooted onto the floor.

Then he drove into her in a way that replaced the last bits of laughter in those beautiful eyes of hers with a blurred desire, changed all that teasing to a panting, wanton cry that made him drive into her harder and harder, gritting his teeth against the glory of it. She was so beautiful, his Helene, delicate and supple in his arms, twisting up against him with little gasping moans.

The pleasure of it curled through Helene's body, streaks of heat pooling between her legs and then curling out toward her toes. Her hands sought purchase and found his muscled buttocks; she clutched him to her and he came to her harder in response, and it was building, she couldn't stop it, the curling was turning to streaks of fire.

She opened her mouth and nothing came out but a whimper, a scream, an echo of his name . . . He came to her hard and looked at her face, at the passion in her eyes, and the faint sheen of sweat on her forehead, at the way she was looking at him, and lost all control, plunging into her body as if he were a man possessed, until her cry was answered by his, his shudder answered by hers, finally . . . his caress met by hers, finally, his lips on her forehead.

And when his weight came to her, she didn't feel suffocated. But he remembered and rolled sideways, off the low couch straight onto a snowbank of paper, bringing her with him.

"Rees!" Helene protested with a weak giggle.

But he kissed her silent, and then said, "Quiet, love," and there was something aching in his voice that made her feel as if she might cry, so she had to bury her head in his shoulder and pretend to be sleepy instead.

He knew though. "I've been a fool, Helene," he said into her hair.

She bit her lip but said nothing.

"I never ever really wanted her, you know. I think Tom is right. I made an ass of myself because my father told me years ago that I would. I didn't even enjoy those Russian dancers."

329

"You didn't?" She pulled back her head and looked up at him.

He didn't smile. "I must have drunk two bottles of brandy a day for a month after I made you leave the house. It didn't help though. Nor did having a bunch of tarts cavorting on the table. I just couldn't figure out why I felt so sick all the time."

Helene held her breath.

"I was in love with you," he said slowly, his hands cupping her face. "But I couldn't admit it, not to you, not to myself. I just kept trying to get rid of you, and then feeling sick about it."

"I love you," Helene whispered. "I never stopped."

"How could you?"

She smiled at that. "I'm a fool, I suppose."

"You are," he agreed bluntly. And then, "Even when— even when I brought Lina into your chamber?"

"Oh, I didn't think I was. I kept telling myself that I was indifferent to you. But it hurt."

"I'm sorry."

"Were you—were you in love with her?"

He shook his head. "Never. She knew it too. I wanted her voice, you see. We stopped all sort of bedroom things a year ago, from pure lack of interest."

"I wish I hadn't said such cruel things to you," Helene said, dismissing Lina and the Russian dancers forever. "I do love your chest and every hair on it."

"I think I feel more than love for your chest," he said rather dreamily. "It's like an obsession. I shall have to compose a *canzonette*, To My Wife's Breasts."

"Silly," she said. And then, "I shouldn't have been cruel about your music, either."

"Nor I so dismissive of yours," he said.

330

She hesitated, and then, "I think . . . I think we may both write better with the other's help."

His arm tightened around her. "I know that is true for me, but I doubt there is anything I can add to your gift, Helene. Of the two of us, you are the brilliant musician."

"Not so!" she protested.

His lips traced a quarter note on her cheek. "I write at the peak of my ability when you are near; what more could a man want?"

"We have gifts of different kinds," Helene said slowly. "You are a genius at expressing emotion and creating a character, Rees. All I'm good for is doing a piece of music itself, with no story. *You* saw what my waltz was about, after all. I hadn't even noticed, though I wrote it."

Rees chuckled. "That was when I really started to wonder whether there was the faintest chance that I might be able to keep you in the house forever. When I saw that waltz."

"Scandalous, isn't it?" Helene actually felt proud of it.

"Worse than Russians on the table," he said. Then he sang: *Let me, dearest wife, embrace you, As would a lover his lovable bride . . .*" But he stopped singing to kiss her.

"*Face to face with burning cheeks,*" Helene whispered sometime later.

But her husband was kissing his way down her body, and she couldn't see his cheeks anyway, so she threw away the thought.

Much later, Helene lay against her husband's heart and listened to the steady beat of her life and her future.

She felt sleepy. Rees was already asleep. So the earl and his countess fell asleep, in a bed of opera scores, of discarded musical notes and florid lyrics, while the candles guttered on the piano.

It was morning when Leke opened the door and surveyed the room. By then, its occupants had vanished. Anyone less accustomed to Earl Godwin's organization methods might have noticed nothing amiss.

But Leke stood in thought for a moment or two, staring at the crushed papers piled high around the sofa, and then, even more intently, at a thick white dressing gown tossed to the floor next to the piano.

He left with his regular measured step, a garment neatly folded over his arm, and a smile curling the edges of his mouth.

Chapter Forty-Two

In Strictest Confidence . . .

18 January 1817

The Countess Pandross to Lady Patricia Hamilton

. . . I assure you, my dearest, that I am as startled as anyone. But it is quite true. Earl Godwin is positively lavish in his attentions, and you know that for a man like that to show any courtesy at all, particularly to his wife, is quite out of the way. The opera singer is definitely a thing of the past, and it's rumored that Countess Godwin is carrying a child, so perhaps all this attention he pays her has to do with the question of an heir. Men are so absurdly attached to the idea of reproducing themselves. Of course, it may also have to do with her part in that opera he's just put up, The Quaker Girl. The newspapers have all called it a triumph, although shamefully I haven't found time to see it yet. I told Pandross that if we don't attend this week I shan't be able to go anywhere in public, because darling, it is all that anyone is talking about. Almost, I envy you for your snug country life. You'll have to see it the moment you return for the season. The waltz scene is apparently scandalous, and yet I was told in the strictest confidence that Countess Godwin wrote the waltz herself, if you can believe it.

I do agree with you regarding your disappointment with Patricia's debut year. But have you noticed that this sort of thing happens more and more? I find that girls are not shot off until their second or even third year, so I would counsel you . . .

The London Times: Music on the Town

The Quaker Girl's popularity continues. On Wednesday last it was necessary to throw open disengaged boxes to the public, in order to accommodate the crowds demanding admission. This opera is widely regarded as the finest work of Earl Godwin, and the most exquisite example of opera buffo yet produced on the English stage. There are those who compare it more than favorably with works of Mozart. Lord Godwin's vocal music appears to us not only of a high rank, but of a different order from that of almost every other composer. We venture with some diffidence to characterize it, in order to record the impressions we receive from it, by saying that he expresses passion, and excites sympathy in his viewers, in a manner not seen by us for many years. The waltz scene, of course, continues to be a popular favorite; evidence of which can be seen in the fact that in recent weeks Lady Sally Jersey has allowed this waltz, and this waltz only, to be danced at Almack's.

22 January 1817

Rees Holland, Earl Godwin, to his brother St. Mary's Church, Beverley, in the North Country

Dear Tom,

Things are all right here. Yes, the opera appears to have been a success. Helene's waltz has created an enormous sensation and is being danced all over London. I'm glad to hear you both are well. I miss you, old sobersides that you are. Rees.

Miss Patricia Hamilton to Lady Prunella Scottish, née Forbes-Shacklett

Dear Prunes,

I'm so glad to hear that you are back from your wedding trip, and believe me, I want to hear about every moment. My mama is convinced that I shall end up an old maid, so I must needs hear of your exploits before I wither on the vine. On that front (although I tell you this, obviously, in the strictest confidence), I have received several billet-doux from Lord Guilpin! We danced several times during the season, but I didn't think he was in the least interested in me. But then we met quite by accident while riding in the Park and since then . . . I know I should not be accepting correspondence, but it is too, too delicious . . . At any rate, Prunes, I am not quite so distraught as my mama over the possibility of my withering on the vine, as you can imagine.

We just came up to London to see a performance of Earl Godwin's new opera, The Quaker Girl. My mother was positively galvanized with curiosity; everyone is talking of the piece. There is a waltz in Act Two that is the most romantic piece of music I've ever heard. I thought I might faint, and my mother turned quite pink! You must go to the opera the very first chance that you . . .

28 January 1817

Rees Holland, Earl Godwin, to Helene Holland, Countess Godwin, delivered by her maid

If you come to the music room, I have something I want to show you.

Rees

Helene Holland, Countess Godwin, to Rees Holland, Earl Godwin, delivered by a footman

I've had a visit from Doctor Ortolon. Do you think that Star of Bethlehem blooms in September?

Your wife

28 January 1817

The Butler's Daybook, as kept by Mr. Leke

That hamhanded footman James, the one I hired last week, was knocked over by Lord Godwin when his lordship exited rather rapidly from the music room and dashed up the stairs. James insists that his wrist is sprained.

Epilogue

Five Years Later . . .
A Small Hunting Lodge
Belonging to Earl Godwin

Rees was tired. He and Helene had stayed up half the night, playing around with a bagatelle for four hands, and now he was trying to compose a letter to Snuffle at the Royal Italian Opera House that would explain why he didn't plan to write an opera for next year's season. He and Helene were—he paused and cocked an ear. Far off down the sunny stretches of lawn, he heard a faint shriek of laughter. And then a call from his wife. "Rees! The river!"

Without a second's pause, Rees shoved back his chair and started running. Laughter that bright and that mischievous meant only one thing: little Viscount Beckford had managed to escape his nanny and his mama again, and was heading for the stream at the bottom of the garden. The river barely topped Rees's ankles; it was more of a rivulet than a river. But the danger was there.

Rees's long legs had him at the bottom of the garden in precisely three seconds, followed at some interval by his wife, waving a towel.

Sure enough, Wolfgang Amadeus Holland was standing fully dressed in the middle of the stream. Small blue butterflies were fluttering around his legs, startled from the grass and buttercups that lined the riverbank.

"Wolfie, out with you!" Rees bellowed, splashing in after him. "Haven't I told you a hundred times that you're *not* to go in the water unless Mama and Papa give you our express permission?"

Wolfie's eyes shone with pure joy. "Oh, let me go, Papa, let me go! Look what I found!"

He uncurled a singularly dirty little fist. He held a tiny, emerald-green frog. Rees stared for a moment, and let the fear and anger drain away. Then he bent down to examine the tiny prisoner.

When Helene made it to the riverbank, there were her two favorite men in the world, the smallest in water up to his thighs, and the other with river water washing about his boots, looking for all the world as if they were conducting a biology lesson. And, of course, neither of them had the faintest interest in the fact that their clothes were being ruined by river water.

"Wolfgang Amadeus!" she shrieked, sounding precisely like a fishwife down at the docks. "Get out of the water this very instant! Rees, how could you let him stand there in that brook!"

Husband and son spun about, their faces mirroring the same expression of guilt and surprise.

"I'm very sorry, dear," Rees said, scooping his son up onto his arm. "You see, Wolfie found a rather fascinating amphibian."

Helene narrowed her eyes at him. "You didn't let him pick something up from that filthy water!"

"Papa's holding it!" Wolfie piped up, as his father put him down on the bank. His mother started rapidly stripping off his wet clothing and drying him with a towel. "Look, Papa, water is coming out of the top of your boot."

338

Helene couldn't stay angry any longer. "So what did you find, love?"

"A frog, a tiny, tiny, tiny, frog. Papa has it in his hand so it can't hop away. I'm going to keep it in my bedroom."

Helene shook her head at her husband. "A frog in the bedroom?"

"Two frogs and a snake lived in my chambers for one entire summer. The crucial thing is to make it clear that the snake can't share his bed."

"You two are so much alike!" Helene groaned. "Look at you; your boots are ruined!"

He grinned down at her. "Your fate is to be surrounded by men who don't give a fig for fashion."

Wolfie wasn't paying attention. Still naked, with an unhappy frog clutched in his hand, he decided to make a dash for freedom, back up the lawn to where his baby sister was dozing in the shade of a huge elm tree. Naturally he wouldn't get far. He was unclothed, and his mother was always worried that he would take a chill, although he never even got the sniffles.

Boys didn't.

He trotted up the lawn naked as a peeled apple. But when he looked back to track his pursuers, his mother was locked in his father's arms, and neither of them was watching him.

He knew as well as the next person that once those two started kissing, there was no stopping them. The only thing worse was when they were sitting at the piano together. Or sitting at the piano *and* kissing.

So Wolfie pranced happily after a sky-blue butterfly. He was naked and meadow grass tickled his toes. He had a frog in his hand.

Could there be more joy in the world?

A Note on Waltzes, Operas
and Musical Exceptions

When I decided to create a heroine who was a musical composer, Clara Josephine Wieck Schumann, likely the foremost female composer of the nineteenth century, was the model I had in mind. Clara was born in Germany in 1819, and lived until 1896. One of her most extraordinary works was written very early in her life, a waltz for the piano: this is the piece that I have given to Helene. When she was still a teenager, Clara fell in love with a fellow musician, Robert Schumann. They married and had eight children. Yet hers was not the life of a conventional mother in the 1800s. She performed and wrote music throughout her life; she made nearly forty concert tours outside of Germany.

If Helene is unique for the Regency (she supposedly wrote her waltz just before Clara was born), Rees is equally ahead of his time. Rees's opera, *The Quaker Girl*, is, in fact, an Edwardian musical comedy, composed by Lionel Monckton. The lyrics were written by Adrian Moss and Percy Greenbank (including the lovely song, "Come to the Ball"). *The Quaker Girl* opened at the Adelphia Theater in 1910. In the early 1800s, when Rees was supposedly writing, comic opera was flourishing in England. The first so-called ballad opera was John Gay's *Beggar's Opera*, performed in 1728; its direct descendants were operettas by Gilbert and Sullivan.

Those of you who are actual musicians must forgive my inadequate attempt to describe lives bounded by and expressed in sound. Composers seem to hear language as a series of notes; I tried to give a sense of relationships defined by lyric. My failures are all my own, but I received tremendous help in learning about the lives of eighteenth-century musicians from my marvelous research assistant, Frances Drouin, and I learned of Clara's waltz from a brilliant lecture given by Professor Sevin H. Yaraman of the Fordham University Department of Art History and Music.

About the Author

Author of seven award-winning romances, Eloisa James is a professor of English literature who lives with her family in New Jersey. All her books must have been written in her sleep, because her days are taken up by caring for two children with advanced degrees in whining, a demanding guinea pig, a smelly frog, and a tumbledown house. Letters from readers provide a great escape! Write Eloisa at eloisa@eloisajames.com or visit her website at www.eloisajames.com.

Do you love historical fiction?

Want the chance to hear news about your favourite authors (and the chance to win free books)?

Mary Balogh
Charlotte Betts
Jessica Blair
Frances Brody
Gaelen Foley
Elizabeth Hoyt
Eloisa James
Lisa Kleypas
Stephanie Laurens
Claire Lorrimer
Amanda Quick
Julia Quinn

Then visit the Piatkus website and blog
www.piatkus.co.uk | www.piatkusbooks.net

And follow us on Facebook and Twitter
www.facebook.com/piatkusfiction | www.twitter.com/piatkusbooks

piatkus